REUNITED WITH HER SURGEON BOSS

AMY RUTTAN

A RING FOR HIS PREGNANT MIDWIFE

AMY RUTTAN

MILLS & BOON

First Published in Great Britain 2022
by Mills & Boon, an imprint of HarperCollins*Publishers* Ltd,
1 London Bridge Street, London, SE1 9GF

www.harpercollins.co.uk

HarperCollins*Publishers*
1st Floor, Watermarque Building,
Ringsend Road, Dublin 4, Ireland

Reunited with Her Surgeon Boss © 2022 by Amy Ruttan

A Ring for His Pregnant Midwife © 2022 by Amy Ruttan

ISBN: 978-0-263-30120-5

03/22

MIX
Paper from
responsible sources
FSC
www.fsc.org   FSC™ C007454

This book is produced from independently certified FSC™ paper
to ensure responsible forest management.
For more information visit www.harpercollins.co.uk/green.

Printed and Bound in Spain using 100% Renewable Electricity
at CPI Black Print, Barcelona

REUNITED WITH HER SURGEON BOSS

AMY RUTTAN

MILLS & BOON

For all those dreaming of a second chance
and a happily-ever-after.

CHAPTER ONE

YOU'RE OKAY. This is a minor setback. You've handled worse before. And who wouldn't want to work in paradise?

And that's what Dr. Victoria Jensen had to keep telling herself. This was a good thing. It was an opportunity.

Even though she felt alone again.

Scared, but she wasn't going to let anyone see that part of her. She'd kept that part hidden since her mother died. As she had no other biological family, she'd grown up in the foster system from the age of ten, bounding from home to home. No one had ever wanted to adopt her, so she'd locked her heart away.

She'd also learned she could either shy away and be a pushover or she could fight for her life.

She chose to fight.

And she chose to help by saving lives.

No one had been there for her growing up, and she didn't want anyone else to feel alone the way she had. Being a surgeon gave her the opportunity to help others while also giving her the perfect excuse to keep people at a distance. A career that would keep her too busy to even think about committing to a lifetime with just one person. It was better to be a lone wolf. Your heart never had to be on the line if it was just you.

Being a surgeon was what she'd always wanted. Even when she couldn't always control the outcome.

Which brought her back to why she was here.

She'd lost a patient.

A very important patient. A foreign ambassador to the US.

The hospital's board of directors had suggested she take a leave of absence until the autopsy findings were released and the media interest died down, and though she hadn't wanted to agree, she hadn't been given a choice.

The timing had been fortuitous, though, as her mentor, Dr. Paul Martin, had been asked to go to St. Thomas in the US Virgin Islands to assist with a domino kidney transplant surgery, and Paul had arranged for her to go in his place.

She'd lost patients before and it always stung, but this patient had the press hounding her.

Blaming her.

On assignment in the US Virgin Islands, she could lie low, do her work and wait for the attention to die down.

It was the perfect plan, in theory.

She straightened her white lab coat as she stared at her reflection in the mirror in the women's washroom and shook away the last tendrils of self-doubt that were swirling around in her brain. Her palms were sweaty, and she hadn't slept much the night before, but that didn't matter.

She could shake this off and prove to this hospital

that they were damn lucky to have one of the best transplant surgeons working for them. Even for a short time.

Inwardly she cringed at her pep talk. It was something her mentor, Paul, had taught her when she became his resident. Paul had taught her to be confident. To think for herself and exude confidence, which she knew often made her come across as cold-blooded and arrogant.

Be a shark, he'd say—*it's the only way to survive.*

He was cool, detached and only looked out for his career and those of the few students he deemed were worthy to be taught by him.

She had been one of them, and for the first time in her life, she had been chosen by someone. It was Dr. Paul Martin who had told her to not get bogged down by a family or love. She had understood that all too well living in the foster system.

Except there were parts of her that didn't like that. There were secret parts of her that wanted love, security and tenderness.

It was something she had wanted ever since she'd lost her mom.

But she only had herself.

She was the only person who had never let herself down…until she agreed to do the ambassador's surgery against her better judgment.

In the ten years she'd been a transplant surgeon, nothing had gone as catastrophically bad as the operation that had made her flee New York. And it wasn't even her fault. She hadn't wanted to do the transplant surgery. The ambassador wasn't in a fit state for the operation, and though she told her superiors that the surgery needed to wait, no one had listened.

A chain of events with an unstable patient had unfolded, and though she'd tried everything she could, he'd started to crash on her table. Just when she thought she'd managed to stabilize him and that the transplant might finally take, there'd been a blood clot from the suture line that she couldn't evacuate, which had ended it all.

The ambassador died.

So here she was in this island paradise, somewhere she could work in peace. Even though New York City was all that mattered and was where her life was, this would be a good change of pace.

The hospital here needed help running a complicated domino surgery for multiple patients who needed kidney transplants.

A domino was for those who needed a kidney and had someone willing to donate but wasn't compatible with their volunteer donor. So each pair—donor and recipient—were matched with someone else waiting for a kidney who was incompatible with their own willing donor. There were a lot of moving pieces, and it required coordination. Each participant was in a chain, much like a set of dominoes, and if one piece dropped out, the whole thing fell apart.

It could be a logistical nightmare for those unfamiliar with it, but thankfully she'd done domino surgeries before.

Before she got started, though, she needed to meet the new chief of surgery, which was the main thing currently causing her anxiety. The previous chief—the one who had agreed to her coming in Paul's place—was Paul's friend, but he'd had to take early retirement for personal reasons, and she didn't know who the new chief of surgery was. She'd been talking to Paul about it last night, but their call had dropped out and she'd missed the name.

There was a part of her that wondered if the new chief would be wary about her.

If they were a sensible surgeon they'd see that what happened wasn't your fault. They would know about the complication. They would get it.

Victoria might be a talented surgeon, but she wasn't God, and there was no way she could've stopped that blood clot from forming.

And if it wasn't for the press unfairly blaming her, she'd still be in New York.

Yeah, and miserable.

Victoria shook that sneaky little thought from her head.

You don't need anyone else.

Victoria adjusted her brown hair, which was tied back in a bun, except the humidity kept causing strands to escape. Once everything about her appearance was controlled, sterile and clean, she washed her hands and then nodded curtly to the reflection in the mirror and left the women's washroom.

The chief of surgery's office was at the end of the hall. Each step from her heels seemed to beat in time with her heart, and she tried to swallow the lump in her throat.

Come on. You can do this.

"Dr. Jensen?" the chief's assistant—Yvonne, according to her name tag—asked as she approached the office.

"Yes. I'm here to see the chief of surgery."

Yvonne nodded and smiled brightly. "Just a moment. I'll check with Dr. Olesen to see if he's ready for you."

Yvonne stood up and slipped in the office behind her desk.

Victoria frowned and worried her bottom lip. Dr. Olesen? Surely it was a different Dr. Olesen. There were a lot of Dr. Olesens out there. Fate wouldn't be that cruel as to put her in the hands of her old rival from her residency days.

Matthew Olesen had been the only man who had ever gotten under her skin. The only resident in their surgical program to be a threat. He drove her crazy, and she had been crazy attracted to him. He had made her blood sing with pleasure.

He had been her first. They had spent so many nights together, and she'd fallen for him.

Hard.

She'd fallen in love with him.

And even though she wanted more, she'd been scared by the intensity of their passion. She was scared of trusting him and putting her heart in someone's hands.

There had been only one position to work with Dr. Paul Martin in transplant surgery, and she'd wanted it.

Nothing was going to get in her way.

Not even a man she loved...

"You really want to end things like this?" Matt asked, his hands on her shoulders.

She tried to shrug out of his embrace but couldn't bring herself to pull away from him.

She really didn't want to end things, but this was better for her heart. She had plans, and Matt didn't fit in those plans. It was hard to walk away from him, to break the delicious connection when all she wanted was more of him, but she was too scared to risk her heart.

There was no way she could have both Matt and the career she'd worked so hard for.

Love was too complicated.

"Yes. I'm taking the job. There's one spot and it's mine."

Matt let go of her shoulders, and she suddenly felt cold.

"You're breaking my heart, Victoria. It's you I want."

She swallowed back the tears that were threatening to spill. She didn't cry in front of anyone.

"I don't want you, Matt. For me, this has always been about the job. That's all that matters. Nothing else."

Except it was a lie.

She did want him.

His gaze hardened, and his spine stiffened. "Fine. Then I won't bother you again."

It had hurt, but she'd gotten over it.

Have you?

She'd thought he would stay in New York, but he hadn't.

Matthew hadn't tried to fight for her, and she'd gotten the message. She was on her own. And that was fair. It was what she was used to. She was used to people leaving her, and she could deal.

She couldn't rely on anyone but herself.

Have you really gotten over it?

Dr. Matthew Olesen had disappeared from her radar, and she'd never bothered to look him up. It hurt too much, because as much as she wanted to tell herself she was over him, she wasn't. There was a part of her that still yearned for him and wanted him, but she'd ruined it, and so instead she'd focused solely on her career. She'd dated other men, but no one had ever held a candle to Matt.

No one made her heart beat faster. No one made her body tremble with pleasure with one simple look from his blue, blue eyes. Matthew still owned that small hidden part of her heart that she kept to herself.

You need to get control of yourself.

Yvonne came out of the office. "He's ready to see you now."

Victoria nodded and opened the door, holding her breath as she stepped into the room. Her hands were shaking and she was sweating like crazy, hoping that no one could see it.

It wasn't Matthew.

It couldn't be him.

His back was to her as he was typing on his computer. His hair was short, caramel colored, and she couldn't tell much from the back of his head. She stood there, the tension filling the room as she waited for him to turn around and look at her.

Fate wasn't this cruel.

Look at me, she silently screamed in her head. She wanted to be put out of her misery.

"You've come a long way, yes?"

The voice was a bit deeper than she remembered, but it slid down her spine with that tendril of familiarity that sent a shiver of dread and a zing of anticipation racing through her. Her stomach did a flip, knowing what it was like when that voice whispered sweet nothings in her ear as she melted for him.

Oh, God. Not him.

This was like some kind of sick joke.

She was in hell and being punished.

He turned, and her heart skipped a beat as she looked into the crystal-blue eyes of the only man who had ever made her swoon.

The man she'd let walk away. The only man she'd ever loved.

The man who still haunted her dreams, taunting her with something she could never have. Victoria didn't believe in happily-ever-afters, but a part of her always regretted and wondered if she could've had one with him.

And her body was still reacting to him. Even after all this time.

Traitor.

"Dr. Olesen," she said curtly, trying to swallow the hard lump that was threatening to choke off her air supply.

He smiled, but that smile didn't reach his eyes. It was cold, detached and hurt, and in trying to avoid his gaze, she noticed the wedding band on his finger. Not that she should be surprised, Matt had always wanted to get married and have a family, and she hadn't. Or at least she'd told him she didn't.

There was a part of her, deep down, that secretly longed for those things. But she knew they were just pipe dreams and were not meant to be hers.

Only because you're too scared to have those things.

"Dr. Jensen." He tented his fingers and looked at her, a look that chilled her to the bone. "I never expected or wanted to have to see your face again. But here we are."

CHAPTER TWO

IT WAS A LIE. He did want to see her again. For years he'd longed for her, even though she had made it clear she didn't want him when she ended things. She'd chosen a job over him, and he was still hurt over that.

There had been many years, many nights when she haunted him. Like some kind of ghost that had a hold on his soul. She'd possessed him for so long, it was a battle to put the memories of her to rest.

Then he'd met Kirsten two years after he left New York. She was a breath of fresh air. She'd made him feel like he could open his heart again. She'd taught him he could love, and he'd married her thinking they'd have a long and happy life together.

It wasn't meant to be, though, as cancer had reared its ugly head and Kirsten's life had been cut too short.

His heart had been shattered far too often. The only thing he cared about now was his job. Since Kirsten had died, he'd thrown his all into his work to try and drown out the pain. For the last five years, he'd been so focused, and it had finally paid off.

He was now chief of surgery at Ziese Memorial Hospital and just in time for a delicate and tricky domino surgery. Matthew had made plans to find only the best transplant surgeon he could to coordinate the surgery, but then he saw that his predecessor had already picked a surgeon just before he left for his early retirement.

And it was the one surgeon Matthew never wanted to see again.

His own personal demon.

Dr. Victoria Jensen.

And seeing her in person now, it was like time hadn't touched her. It was like he was staring at that same woman who had owned his heart and soul ten years ago. The same woman who took his heart and crushed it between her well-manicured fingers.

Her dark hair was pulled back in that severe bun now, but he could still recall how soft her hair was when she let it down. How it naturally curled around her heart-shaped face and how silky it felt when he ran his hands through it.

Her lips were still full and pink—they had been lips that were made for kissing, if there was such a thing as lips made just for kissing. And her eyes were large, brown and expressive. One moment they could be glazed over in passion and the next it was as though hellfire were burning in the depths of them.

He much preferred the pleasure in her eyes, especially when he was running his hands over her luscious curves, her body trembling from his touch.

Just thinking about all those memories that he had banished ten years ago fired his blood, and he was annoyed that he was letting himself think of her like that again.

There had been a part of him that wanted to put a stop to her coming and cancel the contract that had been signed for the next month, but he knew that Victoria was one of the best transplant surgeons in North America who would be an asset to the surgery.

And the surgery was in shambles, and he needed help.

There were patients and donors, but that was it. There was no coordination. Not many labs had been run, no prep. Nothing was organized.

It was chaos.

His predecessor had made the right choice in offering the position to her, but the only thing that Matthew couldn't figure out was why?

Why did she leave that amazing position and job in Manhattan to come to St. Thomas? He was pretty sure that it really had nothing to do with the domino surgery. Matthew had done part of his residency there—he knew that they often saw surgeries like this in New York.

So, why had she come?

Perhaps it was the death of the ambassador?

He knew better than most that no matter how hard you tried to save them, patients sometimes died during surgery. It happened.

He might have been harsh to her, but he needed to keep his distance from her. He needed to keep her at arm's length. And if she was the Victoria he remembered, he knew she could handle this domino on her own.

He had to be careful.

He had to be cold and detached.

He had to be harsh, so that he didn't fall into that same trap that he had before when he had been young and foolish.

"I'm sorry you feel that way," Victoria said stiffly,

breaking through his conflicted thoughts. "I don't want to be here working with you. So I don't like this situation, either."

"Don't you?" he asked under his breath.

Her cheeks bloomed in crimson, and he swore that he could see the flames of anger dancing in her eyes.

Maybe he had pushed her a bit too far.

"No. I don't. Look, I don't want to get into what happened between us. The past is the past and I'm here to work. That is, if you'll let me."

He grinned and leaned back in his swivel chair. "That is indeed an interesting prospect."

"What is?"

"Me letting you work here."

"Well, you are the chief," she stated, and he knew from her tone, the stiffness in her voice, that he was annoying her. Matthew was a professional and he didn't deal with other surgeons this way, but this was a unique situation.

And even though she was the best, he wasn't sure if it was the smartest thing letting her stay in St. Thomas and work with him.

This isn't like residency.

They weren't competitors. He was her boss.

It wasn't going to be like it was ten years ago. He had slept with a viper and been bitten by falling in love with her, and he wouldn't let that happen again.

Except she wasn't a snake. And it wasn't losing the job that hurt him.

Far from it. It was losing her. It was her choosing career over him when he would've chosen her over work every time.

She had been so soft in his arms. She'd melted,

and he had been consumed by her. He had loved her so much.

Get ahold of yourself.

"And why wouldn't I let you work here?"

"I don't have time to play these childish games, Matthew."

"It's Dr. Olesen," he said sternly. The familiarity with which she used his name was unnerving. It felt right and natural, and he didn't like it one bit.

"I'm sorry. Dr. Olesen, then."

"You're right. I am being childish, and the past is in the past. You were hired by my predecessor, and I am willing to honor the contract. I am thankful that you chose to come here at this time."

Her eyes narrowed, and she cocked her head to one side. "I didn't choose to come here. Do you not know why I had to come here? It's all over the news!"

"The ambassador dying? What of it? I mean, it's unfortunate, but that doesn't have anything to do with my domino."

She sighed and then pursed her lips together. "You're right. But I didn't choose to come here. I was forced to come here. I needed to lie low for a while."

She knew she was being melodramatic, but so was everyone else, and she was exasperated. She was so frustrated with the press and the rest of the world believing lies about her.

There was a snowball of things that had happened during that surgery that weren't her fault, but thinking about it made her stomach twist with anxiety and her palms were sweating as she clenched her hands together, trying not to wring them.

And now Matthew was her new boss.

Matthew.

"Tell me you don't love me," he demanded.

She looked away because she couldn't look him in the eye. Her heart was breaking, but she was terrified.

"I don't..."

"You can't even look at me, Victoria." He tipped her chin, and she melted under his touch. "Tell me you don't love me. Tell me you don't want me."

"I don't love you... I don't want you."

She had lied to Matthew then, because she had loved him, but the job was more important.

It was a lie to protect herself. She wasn't going to rely on anyone for her emotional or financial security. She'd worked so hard, to the point of exhaustion and starvation, to get herself through school. It had been stressful—there were days she couldn't eat because she had to pay for a book, and she'd sworn she would never go through that again.

Not even for love, because love could be lost.

A skill—surgical skill—was something that was always needed.

So she had had to lie to Matthew, even though their time together in New York had been one of the only happy times in her life, and there were moments when she was alone and she wondered if she had done the right thing.

The lie had done its damage. It was clear Matthew hated her, and she'd deal with it, though it stung.

"What happened, exactly?" Matthew asked calmly.

There was no censure in his voice, just professional curiosity.

She sighed in relief.

"It was a blood clot," she said.

"Walk me through it," he said gently.

Her heart skipped a beat. It was just like old times when they had been working on a case together and she would get overwhelmed. Talking it through with him had always helped. She missed this. It was calming.

"I was doing a liver and bowel transplant on the ambassador, and there was a string of complications. His blood pressure began to rise. His heart stopped. We'd get it stabilized, and then it would race. There was excessive bleeding and I got that under control, but one thing would lead to another. He went into multisystem organ failure, and a clot broke away at his suture line. I couldn't evacuate the clot in time. At that point, there was no way I could save him. I had misgivings about doing the surgery in the first place. He was too weak to handle such a major surgery."

"So why did you?"

"I was pressured by the patient. He insisted I had to do it. I shouldn't have done it."

He nodded. "Yes. I agree you shouldn't have taken on that surgery if your gut told you not to, but I don't understand something."

"What?" she asked.

"Why do you have to lie low?" There was a slight twinkle in his eyes, and she breathed another sigh of relief.

She smiled. "The press latched onto the story and were looking for a scapegoat. What they failed to realize was that the ambassador was already very ill and there were no guarantees with the surgery. If it had gone well, I could've been a hero, and because it didn't, I was handed over like a lamb to the slaughter by the press to the public. The board suggested I take the temporary position here until things die down, so I'm biding my time while we wait for the autopsy findings to be released."

Matthew's face relaxed, and she was relieved to see sympathy rather than censure or that cold detachment he'd exuded when she had first walked into his office. "I see, so that's why you left New York City."

She nodded. "For now. Out of sight, out of mind. The press will hopefully move on to something else soon."

A smile tugged on the corner of his lips, only this time it was friendly. "And you had no idea I had just been appointed as the new chief when you agreed to come here?"

Victoria let out a breath that she hadn't realized she'd been holding. "Right."

"Well, it seems we're both in a difficult situation. I'm sorry that the press has latched onto the idea that the ambassador's demise was your doing. Knowing how precarious transplant surgeries can be, I know you're not at fault. Our hospital needs you for this domino surgery. I know it's old hat for you, but here as Ziese Memorial, we don't get many surgeries that are this kind of complicated, and I would appreciate your expertise."

Victoria wasn't sure she was hearing him correctly. "You want me to stay?"

"I do," he said. "As you say, we can put the past in

the past and just work together as colleagues on this, can we not?"

"Yes. We can."

"Good."

Relief washed over her, and it felt like her knees were going to give out. All she wanted to do was collapse in a great big heap. She hadn't realized how on edge and stressed she had been.

For the first time in a couple of weeks, she was being listened to and accepted.

Maybe Paul was right and she could just disappear here in paradise. Maybe this was right where she needed to be before she could return to Manhattan and her normal life.

Your lonely and boring life.

Victoria shook that thought from her head. She wasn't going to let those kinds of thoughts in right now. That wasn't important. She'd chosen her life.

She would throw herself into her work and run this domino surgery. For the next month, she could hide away and do what she loved. The only catch: she had to work with Matthew Olesen.

Or rather, work under Matthew. He was her new boss.

They weren't equals in the hierarchy here.

Maybe the universe felt she needed some humble pie and atonement for choosing her career over him. This next month would undoubtedly be punishment enough.

She could keep her distance, though.

Ten years was enough time to get over someone. Wasn't it?

"Yes. I am grateful for you letting me work here,

and I look forward to getting to know all the patients and learning the case."

"Well, no time like the present." Matthew stood up. "Come on, I'll take you down to the boardroom where we have everything set up and information about the referring physicians."

"That sounds great, Dr. Olesen."

Matthew frowned. "No. That's not right."

"You told me to call you that," she stated. "Or do you prefer that I call you Chief?"

"No. I don't really like that, either."

"So what do you want me to call you? Jerk face? I used to call you that sometimes," she teased.

There was a hint of a smile at the corner of his mouth. "No, I mean, we're pretty informal here, and I'm sorry for acting like a pain and forcing you to address me as Dr. Olesen. If we're going to work together closely, then it would seem odd to the rest of the staff that you address me like that. They would ask questions, and I like to keep my personal life private."

"Same with me. I would prefer not to talk about why I'm here. I've been subjected to enough gossip to last a lifetime."

Matthew smiled and opened the door to his office, motioning for her to leave. "Good."

Victoria stepped out of his office as he shut the door and then fell into step beside him as he quickly walked away, instantly regretting her choice of heels but keeping up with him the best she could.

There were a few turns, and she was glad that he was showing her the way, because she knew that she could easily get completely lost. As they passed people in the hall, staff would greet him and he would smile brightly and wave, but the smile didn't reach his eyes the way it used to.

That was something that she had always liked about Matthew Olesen. He smiled with his whole being, which made you want to smile, too. He made you feel like he was your friend.

It was something that she'd also envied about him.

His bedside manner when they had been residents was something everyone in their program strived to mimic, but only Matthew could pull it off.

As they walked the halls of Ziese Memorial, she could tell that something had changed—there was something different about the man she'd once known so well.

And it was then she caught the glint of gold on his finger again.

He was married. He was off-limits.

And her heart sank when it had no right to.

Why wouldn't he be married?

Matthew was too good of a man to not sweep a woman off her feet. She, herself, had been almost swept away by him. Instead, she'd tossed him aside.

The lack of sparkle might be because he had a family waiting for him and he was spread too thin. Paul always said a family was a burden and bogged you down. Held you back as a surgeon.

The last thing Matthew probably wanted to do was spend time with her and show a new employee around the halls of Ziese Memorial. He probably wanted to go home and be with his family, and she couldn't help but wonder what his kids looked like.

She knew that kids had always been in Matthew's plans, but not in hers.

Liar.

That niggling little voice reared its head.

There was a part of her that wanted kids very badly, but she was so afraid. The pain of growing up in the foster system was still a deep cut that burned. She couldn't let that happen to her kids if something ever happened to her.

Victoria shook that unwelcome and uncomfortable thought away as he stopped and opened the door to a small boardroom, where all the files were laid out and there was a blank whiteboard.

The blank whiteboard made her heart sink. By now recipients should be tested. Donors and a plan should have already been discussed.

Instead she was staring at a blank board and a stack of files.

They really weren't far in their planning of this surgery, and she only had a month to figure all this out?

She had her work cut out for her.

No wonder they needed help.

Matthew could tell that Victoria was concerned when he opened the door of the boardroom. He had had the same thoughts when he took over as chief of surgery. This domino was far behind in its planning, and at this point he wasn't even sure if they could perform such a tricky and complicated procedure in the time frame they'd been given.

There were so many moving pieces to this, and nothing was going forward. It was all at a standstill, and he knew everyone involved was frustrated.

His own brother, who had referred one of his patients from the island of St. John to be a part of this surgery, had been on the phone with him constantly about the progress of the surgery, and it was starting to wear on Matthew.

He understood how frustrating it was for a doctor who had referred a patient to have to wait. It was also bothering him because it was his twin brother, Marcus, and they didn't exactly have the best relationship.

Marcus only called when he wanted something.

You don't call him, either.

Matthew shook that thought away.

They might be identical twins, but their looks were where their similarities ended.

Marcus was younger by twenty minutes, and he was the quintessential younger sibling. He had been babied. Growing up attending boarding schools since the age of eleven, Matthew had spent a lot of time parenting Marcus rather than being his brother. It was exhausting. Even when they were in medical school, Matthew had to help him study because Marcus preferred to socialize and party. It frustrated him. Even though Marcus was a doctor, he was too laid-back, too fly-by-the-seat-of-his-pants.

Matthew liked control and planning—that's why he was a surgeon. The operating room was his happy place. Everything in its place and everything in order.

That's why Matthew was now chief of surgery at Ziese Memorial Hospital and his twin brother was living on a boat off the shore of St. John. Even if there was a small part of him that envied his brother's lifestyle—how carefree Marcus was.

Marcus didn't get too involved with women. He dated casually. Matthew couldn't do that. That wasn't his style. It had never been his style.

Matthew missed the way their relationship had been, back before puberty had hit. Before both of them became hotheaded teenagers and fell for the same girl.

That girl had been the tip of the iceberg after years of friction. She hadn't been the cause of their strain, just the catalyst.

And even though neither of them got the girl, their strained relationship continued to worsen from there. So much so that they were now practically strangers who just so happened to be biologically related.

There was no trust on either side. Only censure, coldness and hurt.

This delay in the domino certainly wasn't helping their relationship, either. Matthew wanted to help Marcus's patient and all the others, but he needed assistance.

Which was where Victoria fit in.

He shook his head and then scrubbed a hand over his face. "I know it's pretty sparse. My predecessor wasn't the most organized."

That was the understatement of the year. All the people on this list were running out of time. The surgery had to start and soon.

Victoria had picked up one of the files. "I'll say. You know there is a lot of testing that needs to be done to make sure that antibodies match? It isn't as simple as saying, 'I'll give a kidney to you,' or there wouldn't be a need for a domino surgery."

Matthew narrowed his eyes. "I am very well aware of that. I am glad you're here, though. If I hadn't taken over the chief of surgery's duties, then I would be handling it all myself."

Victoria cocked one of her thinly arched brows. "And how many dominoes have you done?"

"What do you mean by that?" Matthew asked, bristling as he crossed his arms. "Are you implying that I'm an incompetent surgeon?"

"How did you get that from what I asked?"

"Well, I know Dr. Martin doesn't think much of our hospital. Since he was your mentor, I assumed that you thought the same," he groused.

Victoria rolled her eyes. "You assumed wrong. Besides, Dr. Martin recommended I come here in his place."

"Did he now? Would you have come here knowing I was chief?"

A blush tinged her cheeks. "I don't know."

"You must've known I came back home to the US Virgin Islands. You would've known I was here."

"That's presumptuous."

"Why?" he asked, needling her.

After the way she'd hurt him, there was a part of him that wanted to know why she'd chosen to come here now after all this time.

"I haven't followed your surgical career since you left Manhattan, so I don't know how many dominoes you've performed. I had my own career to think of."

It stung to hear her say that, but it confirmed his thoughts. She didn't really care about him the way he had cared about her.

"When I left New York, I came to work here, and I have participated in one domino since then." He rubbed the back of his neck nervously. "It's been a while, but I am aware of how they're done."

Victoria set down the file. "I want to get to work on

this right away and see if any of our patients have donors that are willing to be tested and bring them in."

"I'll help you," Matthew offered.

"I could be here until late," Victoria stated. "There's
a lot of information to go through."

"So?" he asked, confused.

And then her gaze landed on his hand, where he still
wore the ring. Kirsten had been gone for five years, but
he just couldn't bring himself to take the ring off. And
with her looking at it, it brought it all to the surface.

All those joyful memories of when he'd married
Kirsten that now just brought him grief because he
missed her so much. How they'd had only had a short
time together before she'd gotten sick with ovarian cancer. She was like a fleeting shooting star—in and out
of his life too quickly.

"You're married," she said gently. "Won't your wife
want you home for dinner?"

"No," he said stiffly. "No, I don't have a family, and
I don't have a wife."

Pink flushed her cheeks. "I'm sorry. I just assumed…"

"It's okay. I did have a wife, but she's dead. So in
answer to your question, no, she won't mind if I work
late tonight, Dr. Jensen. In fact, I would prefer to work
late and get this surgery up and running before these
patients run out of time."

Because he, of all people, knew how keenly time
passed before your eyes in a flash.

CHAPTER THREE

VICTORIA TRIED TO concentrate on her work as she went through the files, but it was hard when Matthew was sitting across the table from her and she was still processing his revelation that he was a widower.

She felt bad for him.

At first she had been jealous that he had moved on, but now she felt guilty and her heart hurt for the loss he'd suffered, because it was evident that he loved his late wife.

Victoria had learned from a very young age that there was only one person she could count on and that was herself, but Matthew was different. She'd known that from the first moment she met him, when they were residents and working toward the coveted spot she had ultimately won.

It had scared her how much she had wanted him. How he'd made her feel in that short time they were together. She had been so afraid of having her heart broken, and it was so much easier to push him away. It had been better that way.

Was it?

Her stomach knotted, and there was that part, that one she kept locked away, that couldn't help but wonder how different her life could've been if she had taken the chance on him rather than her career.

He was a stranger. Though they had been hot and heavy, neither talked too much about personal details. They were competitors, after all.

She shook that thought away.

Victoria glanced back at her work. She'd done the right thing. Love wasn't certain.

Look at Matthew—he was a widower. He'd had his heart broken when his wife died.

She didn't get attached to people for a reason.

There was a time in her life when she did. When she had this dream that the father or paternal grandparents she'd never known would come and get her, give her a home, give her security. But each year that ticked by, she grew more and more disappointed, so it was so much easier to disengage.

At least Matthew had had a family to support him. Parents and a wife.

Her heart ached for him to have lost someone he clearly loved.

As if sensing that she was watching him, he glanced up from the file he was working on and cocked an eyebrow.

"Is something wrong?" he asked.

Warmth crept up her neck, and she cleared her throat, tearing her gaze away. "Nothing, just a bit jet-lagged."

A quizzical smile spread across his face. "How? We're in the same time zone."

Drat.

"Hey, it's still tiring having to leave behind Manhattan and come to this…to this…"

"Tropical paradise?" he offered, that old glint of amusement in his eyes. The same sparkle that always made her weak in the knees. The one that made her heart skip a beat and her stomach flutter.

"I suppose." And she couldn't help but smile. She was in paradise. She could be hidden here and do what she loved the most.

Work.

"Look, I know it's a lot of work and probably way more disorganized than you're used to."

"Just a bit." She sighed and then straightened her spine. "I can handle this. I can help."

And she could. She was going to prove to all those naysayers that she wasn't a worthless surgeon.

She was still worth something.

This was what she was good at. She could control this portion of the procedures. All she had to do was do what she always did and throw herself into her work and ignore everything else.

Including all the emotions that Matthew was stirring up in her again.

She wasn't here for him.

She was here for herself. Except that realization made her stomach twist. When had she become so selfish? She was a surgeon, not only for job security, but because she wanted to help people. And as she stared at the large pile of patients' charts, she realized that there were so many people here that needed her.

She couldn't help but wonder how long they had been waiting, and she hoped they were all able to withstand the surgeries. Transplant surgery was grueling on the body, and all these patients would be on anti-rejection medication for the rest of their lives.

Even then, the kidneys wouldn't last forever. There was a lifespan to donated organs, but at least this was their best chance.

Matthew's phone went off, and he picked it up, frowning as he glanced at the screen. Victoria got a sinking feeling in her stomach.

"What is it?" she asked.

"It's one of the patients that we want to be part of the domino surgery. They're in the emergency room and the doctors want me to come. It's not looking good."

"Can I be of help?" She was worried that he would tell her to stay behind with the files.

"Of course. Follow me and we'll go check on Mrs. Van Luven." Matthew reached down and grabbed his coat off the back of his chair.

A sense of relief washed through her as she picked up the patient's chart out of the pile, and she smiled briefly as she followed Matthew out of the room. Matthew was giving her a chance. He didn't have to do that, but he was and she was very grateful. It was like no time had passed between them. Her heart skipped a beat, and tears stung her eyes.

It was nice to have someone who trusted her again. *Don't get attached. You're not staying here.*

And she had to keep reminding herself of that, because once the whole thing in Manhattan blew over, once the press forgot her, she could go back to New York. She could go back to her job and her position.

The one that she won and Matthew didn't.

Right now, she didn't feel like such a winner, but she was grateful for him giving her a chance and letting her be hands-on. She was a good surgeon. She wasn't going to let a rare complication and the press tell her otherwise.

Victoria kept up with Matthew as they made their way back through the twisting hallways of Ziese Memorial down to the emergency room. He waved to the emergency room doctors as he entered and made his way over to a trauma pod that was isolated from the other curtained beds.

Because she was vulnerable and on the donor list, they had isolated the patient to keep her from being exposed to whatever else might be in the air. As Victoria walked through the emergency room, she was impressed with the facilities the hospital had, which were comparable to her hospital in Manhattan.

Ziese Memorial was new and surrounded by the paradise of the city of Charlotte Amalie.

She was a bit jealous of Matthew's good fortune. She had been so focused on New York City, and now, surrounded by this beautiful hospital in the Caribbean, she couldn't remember why.

Matthew put on a mask and Victoria grabbed one, too, from the box before they stepped into the isolation pod.

"Mrs. Van Luven, I thought I told you I didn't want to see you anytime soon," Matthew joked.

The middle-aged woman laughed, her sunken eyes twinkling slightly despite her waxy and jaundiced complexion. "I'm sorry, Dr. Olesen, I really just can't help myself."

Victoria could tell Matthew was smiling by the way his eyes crinkled over the top of his mask.

"I've brought you a world-renowned specialist."

Mrs. Van Luven's gaze rested on Victoria, and she smiled. "Have you?"

"This is the Dr. Jensen from New York City. She's a transplant surgeon. One of the best."

A blush heated her cheeks, and she was glad that the mask was hiding her reaction to Matthew's compliment.

"It's a pleasure to meet you, Mrs. Van Luven," Victoria said.

"Are you going to help get this domino up and off the ground?" Mrs. Van Luven asked hopefully. "I've been waiting for some time, and I'm too sick to leave the island."

"I plan to," Victoria said, nodding.

"Oh, good." Mrs. Van Luven closed her eyes and relaxed against the pillow, obviously tired.

"What brought her in here today?" Matthew asked the emergency room doctor.

"She was having her regular dialysis, and the dialysis department sent her here, as she's not eliminating enough waste and her numbers are up." The ER doctor handed Matthew a tablet that displayed all the tests they had run, both at the hospital's dialysis center and in the emergency room.

Victoria leaned over Matthew's shoulder to glance at the information.

She frowned, seeing the numbers from the patient's blood work. The dialysis wasn't working, and Mrs. Van Luven was heading toward kidney failure.

This was a difficult case.

"How does it look?" Mrs. Van Luven asked weakly, not opening her eyes.

Matthew and Victoria shared a glance, one that she

knew well, and even though she'd done this countless times with other patients, it still felt like there was a rock in the pit of her stomach.

"I think we're going to admit you, Mrs. Van Luven," Matthew said, handing the tablet back to the emergency room doctor.

"Is that necessary?" Mrs. Van Luven asked sadly.

"I'm afraid so. You'll have to stay here while you wait for your transplant," Matthew said gently.

"You mean until I get a transplant…or die," Mrs. Van Luven said softly.

"It's so we can monitor you and provide you the medicines you need," Victoria stated. "That way, I don't have to keep calling you in here all the time to get the cross-match tests I need while I set up the surgery."

It wasn't a lie, but Mrs. Van Luven didn't need to be told that her kidneys were failing, that she was dying. Victoria was a firm believer in the power of the patient's will to live. It wasn't always a sure thing, but it couldn't hurt. Patients needed to know they had a chance.

And as she said that, there was a spark in Mrs. Van Luven's eyes. As if she understood. It gave the patient a glimmer of what Victoria found was sometimes the most potent medicine in the world—hope.

Matthew couldn't help but smile as Victoria gave Mrs. Van Luven that dose of hope, because the numbers that he saw from her tests weren't very encouraging, and he was worried.

Mrs. Van Luven was a forty-three-year-old woman in acute kidney failure.

Matthew knew she had two teenage children and a loving husband at home.

She was too young to die, but then again, so had his wife, Kirsten, been.

And it was the part of the job that he hated the most, losing someone.

Death.

It made him feel like a failure.

Matthew shook that niggling voice away. Victoria had come in and given the patient hope by not promising anything more than stellar hospital care, which was what they provided at Ziese Memorial, but he couldn't form the words, and it hit him hard.

When was the last time he had felt hope?

When had he become so jaded and maudlin?

He wasn't sure, but what Victoria had said to their patient had worked—there was a little twinkle back in her eyes as Victoria gave instructions to the emergency room doctor about admitting Mrs. Van Luven. He smiled as he watched Victoria. He'd forgotten how smart she was. How good she was with patients. She had never thought she was, but she was wrong.

Victoria always tried to come off as cold and detached, like she didn't need anyone. Except he knew the real her. The compassionate, caring surgeon she tried so hard to hide.

That was the woman he had fallen for.

It's also the woman who'd broken his heart.

"Dr. Tremblay will admit you and I will check on you later. Where is your husband, Rick?" Matthew asked.

"At work," Mrs. Van Luven said. "He wasn't going

to leave me, but I thought I'd be okay today. He'll be devastated to know I'm here alone."

Matthew knew that feeling all too well. He sympathized with Rick. "I'll personally call Rick and let him know what's going on."

Mrs. Van Luven nodded. "Thank you, Dr. Olesen and Dr. Jensen."

"You're welcome. I'll be running some labs on your cross matches soon. Try to rest," Victoria added as they left the emergency room pod and closed the glass sliding door behind them. Victoria pulled off her mask, disposed of it and sanitized her hands.

Matthew did the same. "You were great in there."

"How so? I just did my job."

"Yeah, but when you were a resident, I remember you saying you didn't have the best bedside manner. Only you did and you still do."

Victoria snorted, and he knew she didn't believe him. She could never take a compliment. "I still don't. It's one of the chief complaints I seem to get in New York."

"You were great in there. You gave her hope."

Pink tinged her cheeks, and she cleared her throat. "You have the better bedside manner."

"Hardly," he groused.

"You do. I always envied it."

He didn't know what she was talking about. His twin was far more charming than he was.

Matthew rolled his eyes. "Oh, come on, can't you accept a compliment? I mean, I know that you like to be all aloof and cold and detached from patients, but you're anything but."

Her eyes narrowed, and she crossed her arms.

"When have I ever said that I like to be detached from my patients?"

"Ten years ago, when I met you," Matthew stated.

And he remembered that day clearly. The first time he'd laid eyes on her, he was immediately attracted to her, but then she'd opened her mouth and he was kind of annoyed at her for a long time.

She always tried to come off as cool and matter-of-fact, but he could see through her facade and knew she actually did care. It was grating on his nerves a bit that she was still denying her gentler side. Like she was afraid of it.

There was nothing wrong with having a gentler side.

A vulnerable side.

And he was keenly aware of that side of her.

"Well," she said, clearing her throat again. "Perhaps, but I don't think I'm much of an ace at it."

"At least you're admitting that you do care about your patients. When I first met you, you didn't even want to admit that."

"It's complicated," Victoria said. "I do care... I mean... Never mind."

"Never mind?" he asked.

What was she hiding? Why did she always have to be so closed off? She hadn't changed.

Did you expect her to?

She rolled her eyes and then blushed again. "Do we really have to do this right now?"

"Why not?"

"Uh, because we're standing in a busy emergency room."

"So, you're willing to talk with me. Just not here?" he asked.

Victoria's eyes darkened into that flinty, menacing, "I'm going to kill you" look. She hadn't changed a bit and he knew that he was pushing her buttons, but he couldn't help himself. Even though he shouldn't, he automatically fell into the old habit, even ten years later.

"Fine," she said stiffly between pursed lips.

"So you're willing to talk?"

"Just not here."

"Okay, then how about we have some dinner tonight and talk? You know, like the good old days. A working dinner while we plan the surgery."

It shocked him that he'd asked her out to dinner. That hadn't been his intention, but it had just slipped out, and to be honest, it wouldn't be bad to have dinner with someone. Usually his dinners were lonely and sad. He hated them, but it was his reality. He'd loved and lost, twice, and he had no plans to risk his heart again.

A working dinner would be a nice distraction.

Her eyes widened. "What?"

"Dinner. We can have a working dinner." He reiterated it was a working dinner, because that's what it was. It couldn't be anything else.

He wouldn't let it.

Who are you fooling?

He ignored that niggling thought in his head.

"Okay," she said, almost numbly. "Where? I'm not completely familiar with the island…"

"I know a place. I'll take you there. It's not far from the hospital."

"Okay." She nodded again. "Sure."

What am I doing?

Matthew wasn't sure what was coming over him. He didn't want to wallow, and he didn't want her to feel sympathy for him. He didn't want any of that. He was tired of everyone thinking of him as poor wid-owed Matthew. Even his twin brother, who usually held barely contained annoyance for him on the best of days, sometimes gave him that empathetic doe-eyed look that drove him crazy.

It had been five years since Kirsten had died. It still hurt, but he didn't want sympathy. He wanted to be known for more than being a widower. He wanted to be Matthew again, even if he wasn't sure how to be that person.

So he didn't want that from her.

Not Victoria.

Not the woman who broke his heart.

Then why are you going out to dinner with her?

All he could think was that he was taking her out to dinner because he felt sorry for her. Her career was on hold. His wasn't. She was in hiding, and he wasn't hiding from anything.

Aren't you?

"So, shall we meet in the lobby, then?" Victoria asked, breaking the awkward silence that had fallen between them.

"Yes."

"Okay. I should get back to running labs and the patient profiles."

"Do you need me to take you back the conference room?"

Victoria looked away, tucking a strand of chestnut hair that had come loose from her bun behind her ear. The bun he'd always hated. He much preferred her hair down, but he also liked to see the slender curve of her neck. And he recalled vividly the way she responded when he kissed her there.

What're you doing?

"No. It's fine. I'll meet you in the lobby at seven."

He rubbed the back of his neck awkwardly, trying to shake the memory of kissing her from his mind.

"Okay. Sounds good."

Victoria nodded and left. Matthew watched her walk away. He couldn't tear his gaze from her and her curves. He cursed under his breath as he ran his hand through his hair, completely frustrated with himself. Even after all this time, he was still drawn to her.

Still wanted her.

Dinner with her was a bad idea.

He turned to walk away and ran smack dab into someone, because he wasn't paying attention and was just trying to get away.

"Sorry," he mumbled, trying to right himself.

"You never usually apologize to me. Though you should on a regular basis," the person quipped.

Matthew groaned.

His twin brother was not the person he wanted to see right now. Hadn't he been tortured enough today?

"I thought you didn't like coming to my island?" Matthew asked dryly.

"I don't. I much prefer St. John, but since you won't answer my calls…"

Matthew sighed. "I'm not ignoring you. I've been busy."

Marcus crossed his arms and cocked an eyebrow. "Really? That's not your usual modus operandi."

"What're you talking about?" Matthew asked.

"You usually ignore me, but my patient—"

"You don't call me socially, either," Matthew said.

"I get busy," Marcus said. "I go out and meet with friends. You just work."

"Work is important."

"So is having a life."

"We were waiting on the organizing surgeon to arrive," Matthew stated. "Give me a break, Marcus. I'm trying my best."

Marcus's eyes narrowed. "My patient is dying, Matthew."

Matthew felt that pang of empathy. He could hear the pain in his brother's voice, and he was very familiar with that tone of desperation.

"I know, and we have a surgeon who is very familiar with dominoes. She just came in from New York."

Marcus raised his eyebrows, impressed. "From New York? How did you manage that? You know what, it doesn't matter. That's great news!"

"Now, will you get off my case?"

Marcus grinned. "We'll see."

Marcus pushed past him, and Matthew shook his head. "Where are you going now?"

"To plead my case with your new surgeon."

Matthew rolled his eyes and watched Marcus leave. He missed his brother sometimes, but today he was stretched to his limit, and Matthew was glad Marcus was out of his hair.

He headed back to this office and sat down in his chair. Bone tired, he leaned back, closing his eyes, before it hit him that Victoria didn't know he had a twin brother. When he and Victoria had been together, they were either in bed or talking work.

Nothing more.

Except that the nothing more had led to love.

He'd lost his heart to Victoria.

And the last thing he wanted was Marcus to know anything about his love life.

You were friends once.

When they had been young, they had been inseparable. Matthew would get so frustrated that Marcus just didn't seem to care about anything and their parents catered to his every whim.

He missed the friendship that they'd had before hormones and teen angst had taken over.

And even if they were close, Matthew wouldn't want anyone to know about his past with Victoria or how she'd broken his heart. He got up. He had to try to stop them from meeting before something bad happened.

Victoria was still stunned she'd agreed to go to dinner with Matthew. That was not what she was here for.

You've got to eat, though, right?

She did, but she was more than capable of eating alone.

In fact, she preferred it.

Who are you kidding?

So maybe she didn't really like eating alone, but was having dinner with Matthew a bad idea? It probably would be fine. Except it hadn't been fine that first time ten years ago, when she'd thought it would be okay to get together with a competitor and had ended up falling into bed with him. She'd gotten lost in his blue eyes, and just thinking back to that moment made her blood heat. And all she wanted to do was kiss him again.

She craved his touch.

Over the years she'd longed to melt in his arms again. So this dinner was a bad idea. It wouldn't be fine. Far from it.

But how would it look if she backed out now? She would look like a big old chicken if she did that. What she had to focus on was that it was a working dinner.

Nothing more.

Just two colleagues discussing business. They'd done it hundreds of times in the past. Of course, those talks had almost always ended with them in bed... Heat rushed through her, and she touched her cheeks, suddenly feeling quite flustered. She had to get control of herself.

There was a knock at the door, and she tried to regain her composure.

"Yes?" she called out, her voice shaking slightly.

She turned and saw Matthew standing in the door— or rather, leaning against the doorjamb and gazing at her appreciatively.

Speak of the devil.

"Dr. Olesen, how can I help you?" she asked. Keeping it formal would help her keep her distance.

There was a small moment of surprise, but then his gaze roved over her hungrily, and it sent a shiver of anticipation down her spine. She recalled vividly the last time he'd looked at her like that and what had happened.

The many heated nights they had spent together, wrapped up in each other's arms. The only times in her life she didn't want a romantic moment with someone to end. The only time she had felt safe in someone's arms and hadn't wanted him to leave.

It had scared her. It was hard to breathe when he looked at her like that.

Her stomach did a flip and her skin broke out in gooseflesh, her blood heating. She hated that her body, after all this time, still reacted this way.

"I came to talk to you about the surgery," he said.

"Right. Well, I'm still figuring out the plan. Perhaps we can talk more at dinner?"

He smiled at her. A sly smile, his blue eyes twinkling with a dark promise, one she had seen many times before. "That sounds great."

Now she was confused, because he sounded like he'd forgotten about the dinner he'd just suggested less than half an hour ago. Something seemed a bit off.

"You're the one who suggested it," she said.

"I don't recall doing that," he said, coming toward her.

"What're you talking about?" she asked, annoyed.

"Dinner." And he took a step closer. "What time?"

"Seven." She crossed her arms as he moved closer, as if her arms could be some kind of protective barrier.

"That sounds divine. Where were you thinking?" he asked.

"I don't understand. You said you had a place in mind."

"Actually, I don't."

"Are you being purposefully annoying?" she asked.

"He is." A terse voice came from the door. Her eyes widened as she stared at Matthew standing in the door…while also standing in front of her.

"Matthew," the Matthew who was standing in front of her acknowledged.

"Marcus," the Matthew from the door responded.

"What is going on?" Victoria asked, annoyed.

"Dr. Jensen, meet my identical twin brother, Dr. Marcus Olesen. Marcus, Dr. Jensen is our transplant surgeon, and she's off-limits."

CHAPTER FOUR

"YOU HAVE A TWIN?" Victoria asked after Marcus had left and she got over her embarrassment at thinking that Matthew had been coming on to her and how she'd reacted. Now, as she thought about it, she could see the difference between Matthew and his twin.

They were fairly identical, but she felt foolish for not seeing the differences right away.

It was in the eyes. Although they both had blue eyes, Matthew's made her heart beat faster. When he gazed at her, she went weak in the knees. Marcus didn't have that same spark that gave her a secret thrill.

"Yes." Matthew sighed in exasperation.

"You never told me you had a brother, let alone an identical twin."

Matthew shrugged. "Why would I? You were never really interested in learning anything about me. It was just sex and work with you, wasn't it?"

It was like a sucker punch. Their relationship hadn't had a lot of talk for a reason. She didn't want him to get close so she could protect herself from being hurt. When she was with Matthew, she kept it strictly about work. Although, in hindsight, she had longed for more. She just hadn't known how to get it.

She couldn't connect.

It was easier that way. She wouldn't get hurt when it ended and they parted ways. Even if she didn't want to.

You're so afraid that no one will ever be able to love you.

Victoria shook that thought away. That secret fear she tried to keep buried deep down inside her.

"It's not like you tried to get to know me, either," she replied.

A small smile tugged at the corner of his mouth. "Touché."

"Well, I can see the difference now," she mumbled.

Matthew cocked an eyebrow. "Oh, really? How?"

"Well, his hair is slightly longer, and he's more charming. Less rigid," she teased.

Matthew crossed his arms. "What?"

"I'm joking. Well, I guess I'll have to be more careful in my interactions around here. Don't want to confuse the two of you."

"Marcus doesn't work here. He's a general practitioner and works on the island of St. John."

"So you two live on separate islands?" she asked.

"Yes. It's better that way," Matthew said firmly.

Victoria cocked an eyebrow. "Really? I would think as twins you two would be really close."

"A common misconception."

"It's not a misconception. Twins are close."

"Usually," Matthew stated gruffly. "Not me and my brother, though. I wish at times we were, but it's always been a competition with him. We're like night and day. Although there are admirable things about him. Such as his bedside manner. His patients like him more."

"I've told you, you have a great bedside manner," Victoria said.

Matthew snorted. "As you have said, he's less rigid."

"Maybe, but you're just as good as him."

"Sure."

"Have you ever told him you want a relationship?" she asked.

Matthew rolled his eyes, clearly annoyed with her. "You're a surgeon, not a therapist. I don't wish to discuss Marcus further."

Victoria understood. There were things she didn't discuss with anyone, either, like her past.

Her lonely, sad, traumatic childhood. Her mother dying when she was ten and her time in foster care.

A shudder traveled down her spine, and for one brief second, she felt that sad pain from when she was a little girl, sleeping on a threadbare mattress, alone in the dark. And all she'd craved was comfort.

Touch.

Victoria wouldn't let herself think about that. She cleared her throat to collect herself. "As a transplant surgeon, I have to make sure my patients are mentally ready for their surgery. There can't be any doubt," she said. "So I guess there's a bit of therapy involved in ascertaining that."

"I'm aware."

She could tell from his serious tone that the discussion was closed.

"So your brother has a patient that needs this surgery?" Victoria asked. "They're on the list, I assume?"

Matthew nodded. "And he's been hounding me since I became chief of surgery to deal with the domino procedure. Not that I blame him."

Victoria sat back down. "And that's what I'm doing. It'll get done."

He smiled, relieved. "I know you will."

Her heart fluttered again at his belief in her. It meant a lot. Especially after what had happened in New York.

There was a knock at the door as a young doctor appeared in the doorway.

"Dr. Jensen?" the young man asked her.

"Yes."

"I'm Dr. Gainsbourg, and I have Mrs. Van Luven's new numbers."

Victoria took the report and went through it. It didn't look good. Her heart sank. "And what kind of dialysis is Mrs. Van Luven currently on?"

"Hemodialysis," Dr. Gainsbourg answered.

Hemodialysis cleaned the blood, but it was clearly no longer working for Mrs. Van Luven. She needed to have abdominal dialysis, which meant surgery.

"We need to get her into surgery so I can place the tube and she has time to heal before we start peritoneal dialysis. Ready Mrs. Van Luven for a surgical procedure once she's done her hemodialysis."

Dr. Gainsbourg nodded. "Of course, Dr. Jensen."

Dr. Gainsbourg left, and she noticed Matthew was staring at her.

"What?" she asked.

"You don't have surgical privileges yet," Matthew stated.

"You had me examine her in your emergency room."

"I know, but I'm more than capable of prepping her for surgery."

"Okay then. By all means, do that. I just want to help, Matthew. I want to do my job."

Matthew's lips pursed together in a thin line. "Fine. You have privileges, obviously, but try to defer to me next time when dealing with my residents."

"Do all your surgeons defer to you? Seems inefficient."

"No," Matthew admitted.

"Then why do I have to?"

"I know my other surgeons. I don't know you. And I'm in charge of the surgical education program here."

For one moment she'd thought he was trusting her. She'd thought she could do her job effectively here.

Apparently, she'd been wrong.

Victoria clenched her fists and tried to calm her annoyance. "You do know me."

"No. I don't, Victoria. Not really." And with that last comment, he left.

She sat back down, frustrated.

He was right, of course. They didn't know each other. Not anymore. And not really ever. Ten years ago they had had hot, steamy sex and worked well together. She'd fallen in love with him and he with her, but they didn't really know each other. She hadn't known he had a twin and he didn't know about her childhood. They were a force to be reckoned with in the hospital, but that was it.

In every other way, they were strangers.

Strangers who once upon a time had seen each other naked.

Nothing more.

She was here to work, and she was grateful for the opportunity.

Matthew was her boss, and she had to tread carefully.

Matthew knew he'd been a bit of an ass there, but he didn't trust Victoria. When she'd shown up, he'd planned to keep his distance from her. Only that wasn't working very well. He was falling into the same old routines. He couldn't stop thinking about her, and he hated how panicked and vulnerable he'd felt when he'd realized Marcus had gone up to see her. And when he saw how Marcus looked at her, he'd lost his mind.

He was glad that Marcus hadn't stuck around and found out about his past with Victoria. That was something he didn't want to explain to his nosy brother.

And then it flashed in his mind again—the way his brother had looked at Victoria, like she was some kind of tasty morsel.

Hungrily.

And all he felt was possessive.

And angry.

Don't think about it.

It was done and over with. It was clear that Victoria was not interested in Marcus. Hopefully those two would not run into each other again. Marcus was placated that the domino was on the move again. Patients and potential donors had been notified about testing, which would start in a couple of days, and Matthew was about to go into surgery with Victoria on a simple procedure to keep Mrs. Van Luven stable.

Matthew took a deep, calming breath and headed into the scrub room, where Victoria stood washing her hands. She barely glanced at him, but he could tell she was annoyed. He might say they were strangers, but he did know when he'd ticked her off.

"Dr. Olesen," she grudgingly acknowledged.

"Dr. Jensen."

"Are you going to grill me on my surgical technique?"

"No."

"Oh, really? I figured you would, since you don't know me and all."

Matthew sighed. "I'm sorry for what I said."

"You're so freaking hot and cold you're driving me crazy!" she stated. "I don't remember you being this annoying when we were residents."

At first he thought she was mad, but then he saw the twinkle in her eyes.

She was teasing him.

He chuckled softly, leaned over and whispered, "I was, but you were blinded by my sexual prowess."

Then he froze, not sure what had come over him. He had teased her the way he used to. For one moment he'd forgotten ten years had passed, and he hoped he hadn't offended her or made her feel uncomfortable.

Victoria snorted. "Right."

He breathed a sigh of relief.

Just like old times.

"I'm sorry," he said, scrubbing under the water. "There's been a lot going on."

"You're preaching to the choir," she ruminated. "Can we just work together and be professional? Now I know you have a doppelgänger on the other island, I'll avoid St. John and him."

"Thank you. It's a shame, though, as St. John is a beautiful island, too."

"If only it didn't have your brother?" she teased.

He smiled. "Precisely."

"Well, I don't understand sibling relationships, as I don't have any, but consider it noted."

There was a bit of sadness in her voice, and he couldn't picture being sad about being an only child. There were many times he'd wished he was an only child himself.

No, you don't.

An image of Marcus and him in their goofy tree house on St. Croix flitted through his mind. They had been ten at the time. Before they had been shipped off to boarding school.

Before Matthew had taken on the role of parenting Marcus.

When they'd still been friends.

He smiled to himself as he remembered it clearly. The joy, the happiness and the fun. It had been some time since he'd thought of that ramshackle tree house.

Victoria finished scrubbing and headed into the operating room, where they were finishing the prep on Mrs. Van Luven.

Matthew finished and followed her as the nurses helped him put on a surgical gown.

Mrs. Van Luven was visibly shaking. The operating room was usually colder than the rest of the hospital, but that wasn't why his patient was shaking.

She was terrified.

And he couldn't blame her.

Matthew made his way over to her.

"How are you?" he asked, gently.

"Nervous," Mrs. Van Luven said, her voice quivering.

"Don't be. Dr. Jensen knows what she's doing, and this is a standard, straightforward procedure." Though Victoria was just assisting him, he wanted to ensure his patient had complete trust in Victoria's skills, because he did.

Mrs. Van Luven smiled, but it was still wobbly. "Okay."

Matthew headed back over to Victoria, who was waiting as the anesthesiologist worked to put the patient asleep.

"The patient is under," the anesthesiologist said a few moments later.

"Why don't you take the lead, Dr. Jensen?" Matthew offered.

Victoria's eyebrows raised. "Are you sure?"

"Positive. Let's see what you can do after all this time."

Victoria nodded and began the procedure. Matthew didn't know why he was here. Victoria didn't need him. She was so talented. The press was crazy for questioning her, and the hospital in New York was crazy for forcing her to take a break.

Although he was thankful they had, as it meant she was here and he could watch her work. He'd forgotten how much he enjoyed working with her.

How much he admired her.

"You okay?" Victoria asked, looking up from her work.

"Fine. Why?" he asked.

"I thought you were going to assist, since you handed me the lead."

"Do you need me to?"

"Not really."

"I'm here to observe and assist if needed." As he stood back to watch her work, an alarm went off, and a sense of dread traveled down his spine.

"Dammit," Victoria cursed under her breath.

"What's wrong?"

"I'm pretty sure there's a clot," Victoria murmured, panic lacing in her voice.

"Okay," Matthew said calmly. "We can deal with that."

He stepped forward and helped her as he glanced at the patient's vitals.

"Sats are dropping," the anesthesiologist announced.

Victoria was frozen, her eyes wide, as if she didn't know what to do. He'd been teaching residents for a year or so, and he knew that look of fear.

"Hey," he said gently.

Victoria looked at him, terror in her eyes, which was so unlike the Victoria he knew.

"We can deal with this, Victoria. What do we do?"

"Evacuate the clot."

"Right. You know what to do next," he said.

Victoria nodded and got back to work, as if that blip hadn't happened. It was only a moment that she'd frozen, unsure of herself.

It was a side of her he'd never seen before. Not that he could blame her for feeling this way after New York. And in that moment he wanted to hold her. She was capable, but her confidence had been shaken.

"Push some epinephrine," Victoria barked over her shoulder, pulling out the laparoscopic instruments and opening the incision wider.

Matthew tuned out all the flurry of activity and focused on the patient. Now was not the time to get panicked.

The only time he'd let the wearing sound of the

monitor get to him was when Kirsten had been slipping away and he'd had to watch her leave him.

And then there it was. The bleeding and the clot.

"Do you see it?" he asked.

Victoria glanced up. "Yes. Suction."

Matthew nodded as Victoria cleaned up the source of the problem. The moment the clot was evacuated, Mrs. Van Luven's vitals returned to normal. Victoria breathed a sigh of relief and continued with the procedure.

Matthew stepped away. "I'll let you finish up, Dr. Jensen. Excellent work."

"Thanks." Her voice shook as she spoke. "And thank you for your help. I don't know what came over me."

He smiled behind his mask. "You're welcome."

He turned and left the operating room, disposing of his gown, gloves and mask.

As he scrubbed out, he took another deep breath. For one moment he'd thought he was back there with Kirsten as she died, and he hated that that thought had crept in.

There were times he had become almost paralyzed with fear just after Kirsten first died, but there had been no one to talk him out of his trance.

He'd had to work it out himself.

He didn't like sharing that with anyone, but he was glad that he'd been able to help Victoria at that moment. He was glad to be there for her, and that thought scared him.

He needed to keep a firm grasp on his emotions, and he was annoyed at how fast he'd lost control around Victoria.

CHAPTER FIVE

SOMETHING STRANGE HAD come over Matthew during that surgery, and Victoria wasn't sure what it was.

Then the clot had struck, and she'd frozen.

All she could hear was the flat-line monitor from New York in her head. Then she'd seen Matthew, and she'd remembered what to do. He'd gotten through to her, and it scared her that he had. She'd been vulnerable and exposed, and he'd talked her down. He calmed her and she was glad he was there, but it scared her how she had relied on him in that moment.

Victoria was certainly questioning her sanity as she made her way down to the main lobby of Ziese Memorial Hospital for her dinner date with Matthew. There was part of her that hoped he wouldn't be there waiting for her so she could head back to the small apartment she'd rented for the month and have an easy night instead.

Yeah, that's what you need. Time alone with your thoughts.

Victoria shook that thought away as she entered the main lobby and spotted Matthew standing by the doors. He looked so different out of his scrubs and white jacket. He was dressed in jeans, a blue button-down shirt that brought out his blue eyes and a brown suit jacket. It was business casual, and her heart skipped a beat.

When they had been residents, he had never dressed as tailored or professional, but then, they had been still learning and really didn't have time to worry about their images. Most of their time was spent at the hospital.

Her stomach did that flip again, and she recalled the way he used to look at her with those blue eyes that always held a promise of something more. Something that made her weak in the knees. He didn't look at her the same way anymore, and that was her fault.

Still, she couldn't help but feel nervous as she walked toward him.

At least she hoped it was him. She wouldn't know until she looked into his eyes.

"Matthew?" she asked cautiously.

He turned, and a small smile tugged at the corner of his mouth. "Yes, it's me. I thought you could tell us apart?"

She smiled, relieved. "I just wanted to make sure. Your brother might've gotten his hair cut or something."

He chuckled at that. "He's gone back to St. John, or at least I think he has. He tends to come and go as he pleases."

"Does he have a plane? Because I was led to believe that the ferry schedules are set."

"He lives on a boat," Matthew mumbled.

"He really does rub you the wrong way, doesn't he?" she asked.

"Just a bit." He glanced at his watch. "Are you ready to go?"

"Sure. I'm looking forward to this working dinner."

He looked at her strangely. "Such an emphasis on the *working* part. What do you think is going to happen?"

"Nothing, and that's why I emphasized it," she snapped and then instantly regretted her outburst. Matthew was complaining that Marcus pushed his buttons, but she'd forgotten about all the times that Matthew and she had gotten on each other's nerves when they were residents.

They were either driving each other crazy at work or in each other's arms.

It had been one of the best times of her life. She could have loved him, but she was so scared to reach out and take it. So scared of what love would do to her life, so she'd let it go.

Even though she'd regretted it ever since.

She quickly shook that thought away as she followed Matthew out of the hospital and into the warm, breezy dusk of Charlotte Amalie.

Ziese Memorial was located farther up from the main turquoise waters of the harbor. Charlotte Amalie, the capital of St. Thomas, with its distinctive red rooftops, was built against the lush green volcanic hillside of the island, and as the sun set, the lights of the city were coming on, and she could see the lights of the large cruise ships that were docked in the port.

It was like something out of a travel guide.

She liked the lights sparkling against the darkness, letting her know that there were lives out there.

She wasn't alone.

She wasn't afraid with that comfort.

Matthew stopped in front of a luxury car and opened the door for her.

"This is your car?" she asked, shocked.

"It is. The restaurant is down by the water, and your heels aren't really made for walking."

"I'm a New Yorker—we're used to walking. Even in heels."

"If I'm not mistaken, by my memory, New York City is fairly flat. Charlotte Amalie is hilly. Get in," he urged gently. "You'll thank me."

She slid into the leather passenger seat, and he shut the door. She watched him walk around the front of his car and climb into the driver's side.

"I hope you like seafood. There is a little bistro down in French Town by Cay Bay that I like to frequent."

"That sounds good." She really didn't care where they went, as long as she could get a glass of wine. "Honestly, I thought you'd take me to Bluebeard's castle and have me beheaded like the rest of his women."

Matthew chuckled. "Hardly—well, at least not until you get your work done."

Victoria laughed. "I will get it done."

It was nice to laugh and tease with him like they had when they were residents.

She had missed this.

They drove in silence through Charlotte Amalie to French Town. The bistro was located almost on the water's edge in sight of all the luxury yachts that were moored in the harbor. Matthew parked, got out and opened the door for her.

As he locked his car, he muttered under his breath.

"What?" she asked.

"My brother is still here. His boat is moored out there in the Cay."

Victoria's eyes widened as she looked at all the luxury boats that were anchored in the turquoise waters. They weren't the kind of boats that she had been picturing when Matthew had mentioned that his twin lived on a boat.

"I didn't think general practitioners made money like that!"

Matthew shrugged. "They don't. Our parents bought him that boat. Well, technically, it was my father's first boat, but he has something bigger and faster now, and Marcus got the old one."

"Your parents live nearby?"

"They live on St. Croix, where I grew up. It's about a ninety-minute ferry ride from here."

They walked down the cobbled street toward the bistro, which was lively and full of tourists. She was worried they wouldn't be able to get a table, but as soon as Matthew approached the maître d', he was shown right in.

All Victoria could do was follow as they wound their way through the crowded lower restaurant and up some narrow stairs to a beautiful rooftop patio, which was much quieter and cooler.

"Is this suitable, Dr. Olesen?" the maître d' asked.

"Yes. Thank you."

The maître d' smiled and held out Victoria's chair for her. "Your waiter will be with you shortly. In the meantime, would you like some of our house wine?"

"Yes!" Victoria said, a bit too eagerly, which made Matthew chuckle.

The maître d' smiled and nodded. "I'll be back momentarily."

Matthew nodded as the maître d' left them, and then it was just the two of them, under string lights overlooking the water of Charlotte Amalie. In the distance she could hear music playing, and there was a murmur of chatting and laughing below.

"So, if your parents gave your brother a luxury yacht, is the car a gift from them, too?"

"Yes. I've had it for a while. Another one of my father's castoffs. Not that I mind this particular castoff."

"I had no idea your parents were megarich, which they are by the sounds of it."

Matthew shrugged. "Things were not always handed to us. My father reminds us all the time he worked to amass his fortune and made it clear we had to work to live. He doesn't pay our way."

"Fair enough. I wanted to thank you for your help in the surgery today."

A strange expression crossed his face, his lips pursed together. "Why? I didn't do much."

"You calmed the patient down, and you were my second set of eyes when we were looking for that clot. I'm glad you were there."

"No, you're not."

Victoria rolled her eyes. "Are you going to argue with everything Io say?"

"No," he said softly. "I'm sorry. I guess I'm really not used to you complimenting anyone, because you certainly didn't when we were residents. You were sort of a force to be reckoned with."

"Were?"

They smiled, and that twinkle in his eyes, the one that she was so familiar with, was back, and it made her heart skip a beat.

The maître d' returned with the wine and poured them both a glass.

"Here's to a successful domino?" Matthew asked, raising his glass.

She raised her glass to meet his. "There is no question. This will go off well."

They both took a sip, and it was exactly what she needed after such a trying day. Victoria was completely wrung out.

"I know it will," he stated, setting his glass down. "And I know you'll quickly get a handle on it. I'm annoyed that my predecessor let it sit for as long as he did, and I'm glad you were able to come and help."

"I didn't really have a choice, if you remember," she said, clearing her throat and trying not to think of the nightmare that had brought her to this tropical paradise. She missed Manhattan and her life there.

Or, at the very least, she missed her work life there.

She really didn't have much of a social life.

There was no time, given that she devoted every ounce of herself to her work.

Her gaze roved over the yachts that were gently bobbing in the water below them. "So which one is Marcus's?"

"Why? Are you interested in my twin?"

She shot him a withering glance. "One of you is enough, but you have me curious. You said your father gave it to Marcus because he upgraded, and I'm having a hard time picturing what he upgraded to."

Matthew chuckled softly. "The one closest to the shore. It's slightly smaller. It's called *Tryphine*."

She cocked her eyebrow. "That's an unusual name."

"Well, it's related to the Bluebeard myth."

"I don't know much about that. I was only remarking on it because of the Bluebeard's castle historic site. So, tell me about Tryphine."

"St. Tryphine," Matthew corrected. "She is the patron saint of sick children and overdue mothers. She is thought to be the basis for the Bluebeard fable. She was from Breton and married an awful man named Conomor to stop him from invading her father's lands. When he was away, she found the bodies of his deceased wives, and as she prayed over them, they warned her that Conomor would kill her if she became pregnant."

"And she was pregnant?"

Matthew nodded. "It had been speculated that his child would kill him, so he would kill his wives when they were pregnant so that none of his children survived. The deceased wives tried to help Tryphine escape, and she did. She gave birth to their son, but soon Conomor found her and cut off her head."

Victoria winced. "A lovely thing to name a boat after."

"It has a happy ending. St. Gildas found her and restored her life. Meanwhile, there's debate about whether it was Tryphine's son that actually ended up killing his father, or the castle itself, as some say after he beheaded Tryphine, he went back to his castle and the castle crumbled on top of him. The moral is that Tryphine protects pregnant mothers and sick children, and my brother deals a lot with pregnant women and sick children. It's his passion, so when he got the boat, he changed the name from *Freja*—our mother's name—to *Tryphine*. It's one thing I actually think he got right. My late wife thought so, too."

And then she saw his spine stiffen.

She wanted to ask him what his wife had been like, but suddenly the waiter appeared with their menus and was rattling off the specials. Victoria couldn't focus. All she could think about was how much it clearly pained Matthew to talk about his late wife, and she wondered how long it had been since his wife had passed. The waiter left to give them time to decide what they wanted.

She tried to figure out what she wanted to eat but couldn't make up her mind. "Any suggestions?"

Matthew glanced up. "To eat?"

"Yes. How about you order for the both of us? I'm not picky. You do it and get me something that St. Thomas is well-known for."

"You're putting a lot of trust in me," he remarked.

"Shouldn't I?" she asked.

He grinned and winked. "Okay, then I think we should have conch and fungi."

"Conch and what?" she asked.

"Fungi. It's like a polenta—it's lovely and I think you'll enjoy it."

"Okay. I like the sound of that."

The waiter came back, and she let Matthew order for them.

"So, when do the people come in for the cross-match tests?" he asked.

"They start coming in tomorrow. The sooner we get

this done and I can refer them to counseling, the better. We have six potential recipients, and I need six donors."

"And if we don't have enough donors?"

"That's what I'm worried about. Mrs. Van Luven is incredibly unstable. She needs peritoneal dialysis, and it should've been done long before this. Hemodialysis has been failing her for some time."

Matthew nodded. "I know. Her physician was the former chief."

"Well, the tubing is in now, at least, but she needs to heal. So we're going to have to keep her hooked up for hemodialysis and keep trying to keep her stable. I need her stronger for the transplant."

"She's young and a mother..." He trailed off.

"How long ago did your wife die?" she asked gently.

The question caught him off guard, but as he thought of Mrs. Van Luven dying, knowing that she had children, he couldn't help but think of Kirsten and the cancer that took her life. They had wanted kids, but when she couldn't get pregnant and had irregular bleeding, she'd gone to see her doctor.

It was then they had found the unimaginable—cervical and ovarian cancer that had spread.

Marcus had named the boat *Tryphine* because Kirsten wanted him to name it that. Marcus adored Kirsten, and it was something small that took her mind off the cancer treatments.

Marcus and Kirsten's friendship gave her pleasure, and for a brief period of time Matthew was glad to have Marcus there, and Marcus actually wanted to be around him. A time when they had pulled together to support Kirsten...

* * *

"What shall I call it? I really don't want a boat named after my mother," Marcus stated.

Matthew rolled his eyes. "There's nothing wrong with Freja."

Kirsten scolded him. "Don't be so mean to your brother. He's absolutely right that this is his vessel now and he needs to choose a name he likes."

"Don't you like my mother?" he teased.

"You know that I do," Kirsten said sweetly. "Still, a single man shouldn't have a boat named after his mother."

Marcus stuck his tongue out at Matthew and then laughed.

"Don't be childish, Marcus," Matthew groused, trying not to laugh as well.

"Don't be such a stick in the mud, Matthew," Marcus snapped back. "Kirsten, since you're always kind and sweet to me, I want you to name her."

Kirsten smiled. "How about Tryphine?"

"What?" Matthew asked, confused.

"The patron saint of sick children, I believe," Marcus said.

"And of overdue mothers," Kirsten said sadly. "Mothers who never got to be mothers..."

Marcus and Matthew shared a look. Marcus knew how much Kirsten wanted a child, and with the cancer that just wasn't possible at the moment.

"Tryphine it is, then!" Marcus announced. "She'll be the only one in the Caribbean, I'm sure."

Matthew shook the memory away.

He had no problem with his brother's boat, but the

memories it brought… He missed those times when Kirsten brought peace between him and Marcus. She was a beautiful light, and he missed her.

Kirsten was always present in the back of his mind since she'd died five years ago, but since Victoria had landed back in his life, his late wife was suddenly front and center in his thoughts again.

When he was with Kirsten, he was haunted by memories of Victoria, and apparently when he was with Victoria, he was haunted by memories of Kirsten. The two times he'd loved, he'd lost, and it still hurt. He never wanted to feel that way again.

Yet Victoria was already getting under his skin. Just like she used to do.

He couldn't let himself fall for her again.

It would hurt too much.

Except it was so hard to keep away from her.

"She died five years ago." he said stiffly, answering the question. He didn't like talking about Kirsten with anyone. Yet here he was talking about her with Victoria. The only other woman who had broken his heart, though in a very different way.

"I'm so sorry," she whispered.

"Thank you, but I'd rather not open up a pity party. She's gone, and when I talk about her, people change around me. Their sympathy…it makes me feel like I'm drowning, trapping me in a never-ending cycle of grief. And though I do grieve for her—I always will—I don't want to wallow in it."

"I understand that."

"Do you?" he asked, because she'd never mentioned her family. The only thing he knew about her was that she was from New York and she didn't have any siblings. When they were together ten years ago, she'd never shared that part of herself.

And he'd never shared his life with her. They had been so wrapped up in each other, they didn't want to let anyone else in to upset the balance.

He reached across the table to touch her but drew his hand back when the waiter brought their food.

"Let me know what you think of it," Matthew said, trying to change the subject after the waiter had gone, hoping she hadn't noticed how he'd tried to reach out and touch her, like the weak fool that he was when he was with her.

"It smells great. I've never had conch before. I've had polenta…"

"Fungi is better, trust me, and for dessert we'll have some johnnycakes."

Victoria took a bite, and he could tell that she approved of his choice. They had come a long way from eating hot dogs from the cart outside the hospital. Thinking about all those times they'd dashed outside on a quick break to get one made him smile.

"What're you smiling about?" she asked.

"I was thinking about how we'd huddle around Jacob's cart. Remembering the steam and the biting cold wind, but those dogs were great."

"Yeah. I miss him."

"Is he no longer there?" Matthew asked.

"He passed on, sadly. A year after you left."

"I'm sorry to hear that."

"Yeah, now I mostly go to that deli—the one we went to when we were tired of hot dogs. That's still there."

"Oh, the delicatessen is still there? That's good to

know. I do miss those pastrami sandwiches. You can't really get good pastrami here."

"This is much nicer scenery, though," she said. "And probably a bit better for overall cholesterol levels."

They shared a laugh again.

"So, is your family worried about you being so far away?" Matthew asked.

"Family?" she asked, confused. "I'm not married."

"No, I mean your parents. You mentioned you don't have siblings…"

"No," she said quickly, looking down at her plate. "No. I don't have any family missing me."

"Oh, I'm sorry."

She shrugged indifferently. "It is what it is. I'm just glad that I was offered a chance to escape here and help."

"Is this an escape?" he asked gently.

"Yes," she stated. "I freely admit that I ran here because it was the only place I could come."

"If you'd known that I was here, would you still have come?"

A pink blush crept up her slender neck and bloomed in her cheeks. He was expecting her to say no. He wanted a reaction from her, something to let him know that she was struggling just as much as he was with being back in his life, but instead of Matthew getting her answer, the waiter came back and refilled their wine and took away their plates, letting them know their dessert would be delayed as he discreetly left.

Matthew didn't care about the wine or the dessert, he just wanted an answer. He was so focused on it.

Gentle music played in the background as they sat there in uneasy silence.

It made him agitated and anxious. He couldn't just sit here. He had to do something.

"Come on," he said, standing up and holding out his hand. He didn't know what he was doing. Maybe it was the wine, or this night, or this day in general, but he just couldn't sit here.

"What?" she asked, confused.

"We're going to dance."

She looked at him like he was crazy, but she didn't argue as she slipped her hand in his and stood. He took her in his arms but didn't hold her too close. Matthew was experimenting, and he wanted to see how close he could get to her, but even though he tried to keep her at bay, his body still reacted.

He could remember what it was like to hold her in his arms, to run his hands over her curves and kiss her.

The way her body quivered under his touch.

His blood heated, and his mouth went dry.

She was so close.

"You're an idiot," she murmured, not looking at him.

He laughed. "What do you mean?"

"What possessed you to dance on the rooftop?"

He shrugged. "It's a good song, and it seemed like a perfect night. I felt like dancing. Haven't you ever felt like dancing before?"

She gazed at him, her eyes twinkling. "No. I can't say that I have."

"That's a shame." He spun her around, making her laugh as he spun her back toward him. Only this time, she came closer.

"You asked if I would still have come here knowing that you were chief, and the answer is yes. I would've."

"You would?"

"If you'd asked me to," she whispered, the pink blooming in her cheeks again.

He stared at her lips. Drank in her intoxicating scent and felt her tremble in his arms. Before he knew what he was doing, he stopped the dance and leaned in to kiss her.

To drink in those soft lips.

Her body went limp, and he wrapped his arms around her, pulling her in for a deeper kiss. Drowning himself in her softness. It had been so long since he'd been burned by her kisses and he welcomed the fire.

What're you doing?

Victoria pushed him away, stepping back. "We can't."

"I know," he said. "I'm sorry. I don't know what came over me."

"It's okay, but I think we'd better skip dessert and I'll just go back to my place and you go back to yours. We need to keep this professional."

He nodded. "I'll go pay the bill, and then I'll take you home."

Victoria sat back down, and he headed downstairs.

What had come over him?

He was acting foolishly.

They had to keep this strictly professional. He couldn't get lost in Victoria's kisses again.

He just couldn't.

CHAPTER SIX

MATTHEW HAD BEEN avoiding her for the last week, which was fine by Victoria. After that kiss, she couldn't sleep. It had been wonderful, but also so bad.

So very bad.

There was also a part of her that had missed him this week, even though she knew it was better they keep their distance, because her time here was temporary.

She'd gotten over him once—she could get over him again.

She'd done it before, even though there was a part of her that didn't want to do it again.

It was better this way, though.

Matthew was the most infuriating man she'd ever known, but she'd forgotten what it was like to be with him and how she forgot herself and all the protective barriers she'd set up to protect her heart. Even ten years later, he could get through them. And she didn't know why he'd been the only man to do so.

She'd learned as a child not to trust anyone, that you could only rely on yourself. That's why she kept people at a distance.

But then she'd met Matthew, and she couldn't keep him away. She was lost to him.

She was weak when it came to him, and she didn't like being that powerless.

Not to anyone.

What're you so afraid of?

She ignored that niggling thought, just like she tried to forget about that dance and that kiss they'd shared a week ago.

The only solution was work. That's how she had gotten over him before.

She threw herself into her work and getting the domino surgery up and running. Dr. Gainsbourg had been assigned to her, and she had the young student run all her labs while she vetted potential donors and waited for cross matches to come in.

Each recipient had an incompatible donor or donors, and the only way a recipient who wasn't eligible to donate to the person they cared for would donate was if their person got a kidney in return.

So it took a lot of prep work. It took a lot of labs.

There were a lot of moving pieces to this surgery, and since she didn't have any other regular surgeries planned, she took it on with gusto.

Plus, it kept her distracted and away from Matthew, who was busy with his own surgical practice as well as running the hospital.

It was better this way. No one would get hurt again this way.

Once this domino procedure was over and done with, she was hoping that she would be able to head back to Manhattan, but so far, she hadn't heard a word from Paul or the hospital there. She had to wait until the autopsy cleared her, but she was still disappointed a week had gone by and the press attention hadn't blown over.

Victoria sighed and went back to reading the lab reports, but it was no good. Thinking about New York also reminded her how she had frozen when Mrs. Van Luven threw a clot.

She loathed the uncertainly and the terror she had felt in that moment. She was so sure of her work. Clots had never fazed her before.

If it hadn't been for Matthew… Well, she didn't want to think about it.

It was just better to keep her head down and out of people's way.

In particular, out of Matthew's way.

She had thought it was absolutely absurd when he took her hand and pulled her up to dance—it was like he was trying to tempt fate—but she couldn't deny she'd been thrilled to be in his arms again. The memory of his kiss flashed through her mind, and her cheeks heated. She touched her lips and smiled.

She'd lost herself.

And she didn't know when it had happened.

Victoria set down the report she was reading and got up to stretch her back.

She was antsy and full of nervous energy, so she paced around the room and stared out of the window of Ziese Memorial at all the red-roofed buildings that wound their way over hillsides and down to the turquoise water. There were palm trees blowing in the breeze. She couldn't remember the last time she had seen trees blowing in the wind like this, or when she'd taken the time to just watch them. It was relaxing. There was another large cruise ship making its way into the port, and for one brief moment she wished she could escape.

Just climb aboard the ship and go off somewhere new.

No responsibilities.

Not a care in the world.

Except she loved her job. She was living out her dream, and she wasn't going to stop because of a temporary setback.

There was a knock at the door, and she turned to see Matthew's lookalike, making her heart skip a beat, just for a fraction of a second. At least she could tell them apart now. She felt foolish for not noticing the differences before.

"Dr. Olesen… Marcus. How can I help you?"

Marcus grinned. "So you've figured out how to tell us apart, then?"

"I have." She left the window and motioned for him to come in, which he did, shutting the door behind him. "What brings you here today? Matthew told me you went back to St. John, but then he was grumbling when we saw your boat in the port on the way to dinner."

Marcus paused and raised his eyebrows, in a quirk so much like his brother. "You were with him at night?"

"Yes, we had a working dinner the day I got you two confused and accidentally suggested you and I were going to dinner."

"Yeah, but I didn't think you'd choose my brother over me. I'm much better dinner company than him. He's too uptight." There was a wide grin that she was positive probably charmed people, but it did nothing for her.

It wasn't the same as Matthew. Matthew's smile made her pulse race.

Marcus might think Matthew was uptight, but Victoria didn't think so. She smiled as she thought about him, about his arms around her as they danced.

Then she remembered Marcus was waiting for her response.

Quick. Think of something to say.

"We were discussing the surgery. A work dinner, as I said. Then he saw your boat."

"Well, I did eventually go back to St. John, but I had some other business I had to attend to, and as it pertains to the surgery, I came back to discuss it with you."

"Oh? And what's there to discuss?"

Marcus handed her the sheet. "It's a lab result, and it solves your problem. I know that the surgery is being delayed because you're having a hard time finding a cross match for Mrs. Van Luven, as no donors in the other incompatible pairs match with her."

It was true.

Mrs. Van Luven was the only one in the domino who didn't yet have a donor, even though she was the one who needed it the most. Victoria was aware that Mrs. Van Luven was also far down the deceased donor list. If she became any more ill, she would move up the list, but there were no guarantees she would still survive the surgery at that point. She glanced at the report and saw the antibodies were a match.

It was almost absolutely perfect.

She smiled. "This is fantastic!"

"Yep, it's a donor who has a mild interest in the operation, as someone they care for is having the surgery."

"Who? What patient?"

"The patient happens to be a fifteen-year-old boy, and that boy happens to be my best friend's kid and my godson."

A sinking feeling knotted her stomach. "Oh, no, Marcus, please don't tell me it's you!"

"And if it is?" Marcus asked.

Victoria sighed. "We can't take you."

"Why not?"

"It's a conflict of interest."

"How? I'm not a surgeon on this file, and I'm not Mrs. Van Luven's physician. Jonas is my godson, and his father is like the brother I never had."

"You have a brother, Marcus. He's my boss."

Marcus snorted. "Biologically, but we haven't been close since we were teens. Everything is a competition with him."

"Funny. He said the same about you."

Marcus's eyes narrowed, and a strange expression crossed his face before he shook his head in frustration. "Look, Jonas means the world to me, and I want to donate my kidney to Mrs. Van Luven so this surgery can take place and Jonas can get his kidney in the domino."

Victoria glanced at the report. She couldn't recall if there were any specific rules against this. He was donating it of his own free will, just like all the other donors were. Would it be that much of a problem if he was in the domino? She could do the retrieval herself and have Matthew start on Mrs. Van Luven until she got there.

It was a solution.

Except he was the chief's brother.

She wouldn't want to put Matthew's identical twin

in any kind of danger. Marcus sat down backward on a chair across from her, grinning.

"You're thinking about it, aren't you?" Marcus asked.

"Perhaps." She glanced at the report again. "I don't know about this, Marcus. You're Jonas's physician."

"Only because there was no other physician on the island at the time to take care of him, but I'm his god-father first. I always have been. I want to do this. He'll die if this surgery doesn't happen, just like the others."

"I'll have to talk to your brother about this."

"Why?" Marcus asked.

"He's the chief of surgery and your brother."

Marcus rolled his eyes. "I get it, I suppose. Look, I'm not a surgeon, and I don't have hospital privileges here. Here, I'm just someone who wants to do something for the greater good."

She smiled at him, moved by his selflessness. "Fine. I will run it by Matthew, and if he approves, you still need to go through the counseling sessions I've set up."

"Counseling?" he asked.

"Yes. It's mandatory for all donors and recipients." She stood up. "So you're really, really, really sure about this?"

Marcus nodded. "I am."

"Thank you. This might solve our problem."

He grinned a sideways grin that was sort of like Matthew's, only his mouth curled to the opposite side of his twin brother's. "I'm glad I can be a problem solver."

"Stick around. I'm going to go see your brother right now."

"I will."

Victoria left the room, her stomach was twisting in a knot as she walked toward Matthew's office. She knew that he was going to have a problem with it, but that wasn't what was bothering her. She was nervous. Her stomach was doing flip-flops. She hadn't seen him since their kiss, and she couldn't stop thinking about it. She just hoped it wouldn't be weird when they saw each other. Victoria knew Matthew was avoiding her, too.

He'd sent her emails, but that was it.

He hadn't come to personally check on the progress of the domino.

Maybe he has faith in you?

Victoria snorted to herself. She highly doubted that.

She wondered if he regretted the kiss just as much as she did. Except she wasn't really regretting the kiss. Not at all. It shouldn't have happened, but there was a part of her—the one that she had long thought she'd buried deep down inside her—that actually wanted it to continue.

The part of her that wanted to stay with him because she loved him—the only man she had ever loved.

The part of her that wanted to say to hell with the job and take a chance on love, but that had lost out to the rational side of her.

The survivor side of her.

Even if she'd regretted that moment for the last ten years.

And she knew that kiss was a mistake. She wanted to be friends and colleagues with Matthew, but that was all. They couldn't go backward. There was no way to turn back time.

Why not?

Victoria shook that thought away and knocked on Matthew's door.

"Come in."

She opened the door, and he glanced up, his eyes widening, and he opened his mouth, probably to tell her he was busy or something.

"Yeah, I know you're not busy, and you don't have to fake a phone call or a meeting. This won't take long." She shut the door.

Matthew frowned. "Fine. I've been avoiding you."

"Oh? Have you? I thought I was the one avoiding you," she teased.

He smiled. "What do you need, Victoria?"

"A donor has come forward. One that is an excellent match for Mrs. Van Luven."

"Really?" Matthew asked, and he held out his hand for the report.

"There's a catch," she said, her stomach twisting.

"What's that?" He was scanning over the numbers.

"It's Marcus."

"What?" He set the report down like it was on fire.

"Marcus did a cross match, or had someone do it. Apparently his godson, Jonas, is one of the recipients, and though he wasn't a match for Jonas, he's a match for Mrs. Van Luven. I don't have to explain to you that we're running out of time to find a living donor match for Mrs. Van Luven or even a nonliving organ donor. There are others ahead of her on the list. Ones not compatible for the domino and from other islands. If we wait for her to get sicker to move up the list, I'm worried she won't survive the surgery. She needs to be a part of this domino. It's her only chance."

Matthew leaned back in his chair and scrubbed a hand over his face. "I know."

"I thought it could potentially be a conflict of interest, but he doesn't know Mrs. Van Luven, and he's not a surgeon or a physician here. He's just someone who wants to be a living donor."

"He knows a lot of the surgeons here, though. Who is going to do his surgery?" Matthew asked. He sounded tired or possibly annoyed.

"I will. You can start on Mrs. Van Luven while I retrieve Marcus's kidney, and then I can continue with Mrs. Van Luven's procedure."

"While also overseeing the others?" Matthew asked in disbelief.

"I have done this before," she reminded him.

"Dammit, Marcus," Matthew cursed under his breath.

"I get the feeling you think of him as the evil twin and you think of yourself as the good twin. I also think he thinks the opposite."

"Of course he does," he mumbled. "Because he's the evil twin. Besides, that's cliché of you."

"Well, what am I to think? You hate him so much."

"I don't hate him," Matthew said tiredly. "I just hate how he always tries to one-up me."

"I think this has more to do with his godson."

Matthew's expression softened. "Of course. I guess I can't fault him for that."

"If you do, you're clearly the evil twin," she teased.

Matthew chuckled. "Fine."

Victoria smiled. "Are we good to go with this surgery?"

"Did he agree to getting the counseling?"

Victoria nodded. "Yes. I told him I wouldn't accept him unless he did the therapy."

"Well, that's something. I guess I have no choice but to agree. I'm worried about him, though."

"Of course," she said softly.

Matthew ran his hand through his hair. "Well, I'm glad he stepped up. This is good, right?"

"Yes. This is good news for everyone. I've been driving myself crazy working on this for a week and not doing anything else. I'm used to being in and out of the operating room, and I'm eager to get started on the surgeries."

Matthew cocked an eyebrow. "Well, I do have something else you can do. Something I was going to do myself, but since you've managed to finish with this, I think I can hand it over to you if you're interested."

"I'm intrigued."

Matthew handed her the file. "There's a living donor surgery this afternoon. It's a liver donation."

"Yes, that's great. I can help."

Matthew nodded. "I thought you might like that. It's a foster child and parent. The foster parent is planning to adopt the child after this procedure, but the little girl needs a liver donation due to extrahepatic cholestasis. She had a tumor, which damaged the biliary duct."

Victoria had tuned him out, because as soon as he'd said, "foster child and parent," she'd been triggered, and her hands began to shake as she went through the file. Every foster parent she had had was awful to her.

And she just couldn't imagine someone doing this for an orphan.

Just because you had an awful experience doesn't mean it's awful for everyone. Remember that.

She had to repeat that mantra in her head one more time.

Tears stung her eyes.

She was glad there was some positivity in this world.

"Are you okay?" Matthew asked.

"Why wouldn't I be?" she asked quietly.

"You seemed to freeze up, like you did in Mrs. Van Luven's surgery. You're trembling."

"Am I?" She glanced at her hands.

Matthew reached out and took her hands in hers. His hands were warm and strong. It calmed her.

She wanted him to hold her.

What're you doing?

She pulled her hands from his.

Victoria cleared her throat. "I'm fine. I would love to help with this, and I'll get right onto prepping them."

Matthew nodded. "Okay. I'll see you in a bit. The surgery is set for five. Only this time, I lead."

Victoria nodded. "You're going to break the news to your brother about his donation?"

Matthew groaned. "I suppose so. Thank you for doing this."

She nodded again and left the office. Her heart was pounding, and she clutched the file for support.

You can do this.

All she had to do was bury all those emotions away. They wouldn't serve her in this situation. There were decent people in the foster system, and she often wondered what her life would've been like had she encountered some of them.

If she had had someone who cared about her.

She was envious of the start in life this little girl had, the support she was getting, but it was fleeting. Victoria had worked hard to get here, and she was going to do her job.

Like she always did.

CHAPTER SEVEN

MATTHEW WAS SO angry with Marcus as he stared at the report Victoria had brought to him. Volunteering for and becoming a living donor and complicating his domino surgery by inserting himself into the mix was ticking him off. And organ donation was a major surgery.

It was bad enough his brother had been harassing him about the surgery and when it would be organized, but now this? Now Marcus was becoming one of the donors? He could die. And the thought of losing someone else he loved was too much.

Matthew leaned back in his chair and scrubbed his hand over his face.

When had his life become so complicated?

It had been complicated when Kirsten got sick and had her short battle with cancer.

For a year he'd wandered around numb.

Lost.

He just existed. Work was his only escape. It was normal and steady.

But it wasn't normalcy. It was routine.

Either way, it was easy to do. It was easy to follow.

About a year ago, he'd tried to date again, but it was

all wrong. He didn't go through with it, and he'd just accepted that he was going to be alone.

Which was fine.

He was used to it. He didn't want to experience that heartbreak again.

Since he'd taken his promotion to chief, his life had become increasingly more stressful. He didn't think it was the promotion or the domino that was making him anxious, so much as the appearance of Victoria back in his life. Something he hadn't been expecting. It was bad enough that he had been avoiding Victoria all week because he was angry at himself for allowing himself to be weak or having a moment of weakness when he took her in his arms and kissed her.

That moment—the one he'd thought about constantly for the last week, especially as he dodged her in the halls of Ziese Memorial Hospital—when he'd held her again had burned his soul. He'd dreamed of holding her since they'd parted ways, and in that moment that they were dancing and smiling on that rooftop patio, it was like no time had passed.

It had felt right.

And he didn't want it to feel that right.

Now Marcus had to go and interfere and play the hero in the surgery that Victoria was organizing.

Marcus is being unselfish and you're being a jerk!

He had to admit he was scared about his brother going through this life-changing surgery. In fact, truth be told, he kind of respected Marcus for offering up his kidney so that this surgery could happen, and Matthew felt like a fool for not realizing why.

Since he became chief, he hadn't had much time and

so hadn't really looked closely at the domino patient profiles. He hadn't noticed that Jonas Fredrick was one of the recipients, and he was angry at himself for not catching that detail earlier.

Chase Fredrick was more Marcus's friend, but the Fredricks were friends of the Olesen family, and he'd known Jonas for a long time.

When Matthew had taken over as chief, he'd had a lot of fires to put out. Now, realizing it was Jonas, it made perfect sense why Marcus had been harping on at him and why his brother was stepping up to the plate to be a living donor.

He was going to have to apologize to Chase for not reaching out sooner.

Everything was just a mess, and this wasn't like him.

He usually had better control, and he hated that he was losing it.

There was another knock at the door, and he groaned inwardly.

Now what?

"Come."

Marcus poked his head in. "Vic's told you, then?"

"Vic?" Matthew asked. He didn't like the way Marcus called her Vic—Marcus's familiarity made his possessiveness prick.

"Victoria," Marcus responded, clearly noticing it irked him to hear Victoria called by the short form of her name.

"She doesn't like nicknames," he groused.

Which was true.

He'd tried it once—called her Vicky and received

a bit of a tongue lashing from her in front of all the other residents.

"How do you know? Or did she tell you that over dinner?"

His stomach dropped to the soles of his feet. "What're you talking about?"

"She told me you had dinner last week and saw *Tryphine* in the Cay. So, naturally, I assumed she'd told you then."

"Yes," he said tightly, but then he sighed. "I've known Victoria for some time. We were residents together in New York."

Marcus quirked an eyebrow and came into his office and sat down. "You've slept with her, haven't you?"

Matthew clenched his jaw and his fists, which were resting on his lap under the desk. "I don't have time to talk to you about this, Marcus. I have a hospital to run."

Marcus smirked. "You so did."

"Grow up. That's not your business!"

Marcus smiled smugly. "Yep. You definitely have."

"What does it matter?" Matthew asked tersely.

"Well, you actually are a bit of a hot-blooded male after all. I thought you'd never move on from Kirsten."

Just the mention of his late wife's name made his blood run cold. "And why should I move on from Kirsten?"

"Matthew, you deserve to be happy."

Matthew stood up. He was done with the direction this conversation was taking. He didn't want to be happy. He was perfectly fine.

No. You're not.

"I have to prep for surgery. We're done with this discussion."

Marcus stood in front of him, blocking his exit.

"Fine. You don't want to talk about your feelings. What else is new? But you haven't even told me if you've cleared me for surgery. It's for Chase's boy. Victoria had no problem with it. Do you?"

Matthew wanted to tell Marcus that he was worried for him. That he was scared, even, but he couldn't, and he hated himself for it. For so long he'd looked out for Marcus. Taken care of him when his parents were off traveling or working.

And he was worried about this.

"Have you talked to Mom and Dad?"

"Yep, and they support me completely," Marcus said.

"So they're coming back home?" Matthew asked.

"No, I told them not to worry about it. I trust Victoria to do a great job, so there's no reason for them to worry or disrupt their cruise."

Matthew frowned. "They should be here."

"I'm fine. I don't need them here," Marcus said. "I can handle it. I know what I'm doing. They are worried, but it's okay. I reassured them."

Matthew cocked his eyebrow. "You reassured them? You know this surgery will change your life."

"I know. I understand what's involved," Marcus replied firmly. "Stop trying to parent me."

Matthew's heart softened a bit, but he didn't let his brother see that. "I'm not your keeper. You can do whatever you want with your kidneys. I'm clearing you for surgery."

"Thank you."

Matthew nodded as Marcus stepped away and left his office. He was angry that Marcus had brought up Victoria and Kirsten. That was none of his business. It shouldn't matter to his brother what his love life entailed.

Marcus had gone on about Matthew moving on before, and he knew Kirsten wouldn't want him to be alone. But the mention of Victoria...

The familiarity Marcus had with her and calling her Vic, making light of the love they'd shared when he didn't know the history...that rubbed Matthew the wrong way.

He shared that with no one.

That was his and his alone.

Matthew made his way down to the preoperative floor. Victoria was already there, speaking with the liver donor and recipient. He could see her through the glass windows. Although the recipient looked a bit bored, he didn't blame her—she was only a child and probably didn't understand many of the technical words Victoria was saying.

Matthew watched her, and his heart melted. Why hadn't he stayed away from her like he said he would? He shouldn't have kissed her, but he couldn't help himself. That night had been magical. She had felt so good in his arms, and her lips had tasted as sweet as he remembered.

He couldn't distance himself from her professionally and didn't really want to. She was an excellent surgeon. He liked working with her. He'd missed working with her.

Their dinner last week had been a mistake, but that was a momentary lapse, and he wasn't going to make that mistake again.

Yeah. Right.

She got under his skin. He'd thought he was over

Victoria, but he wasn't sure that he ever had gotten over her. Victoria left the room then, and he approached her. She immediately took a step back from him and made a face.

"What?" he asked.

"You have a face like thunder."

"Does thunder have a face?" he asked.

She tilted her head to the side. "Honestly, I don't know. I heard my… I heard that expression a lot when I was a kid but never really understood it."

She had clearly caught herself, and he wondered what she was going to say.

"I just had a discussion with Marcus, that's all. I'm fine with him being a living donor, but he likes to push my buttons, so I suppose that's why my face looks a bit annoyed."

"Well, the patients understand the procedure. They're ready. The residents should be back with the latest labs, but from reading their charts, I think they're both fit for surgery."

"Have you worked on a lot of pediatric patients before?" he asked.

"Not often, as we had a pediatric transplant surgeon in Manhattan, but I'm not unfamiliar with them," she said.

"Good. I'll work on prepping the recipient while you harvest the piece of liver from the donor."

Victoria nodded. "I'm fine with that."

"And when it's all done, it sounds like the little girl will have a loving home to be welcomed into."

"Yes." There was something off about her voice. As if something was bothering her. He noticed it when he gave her the file.

"Are you okay?"

"I'm fine. No face like thunder for me." She smiled, but the smile didn't reach her eyes. He could tell it was forced and he wasn't sure that he completely believed her, but it was none of his business.

As long as she did her job, it didn't matter.

And he knew she was going to do excellent work. She was one of the best.

Now they were just standing there. Awkwardly.

"Look, we're okay, right?" Victoria asked frantically.

"How do you mean?"

She worried her bottom lip. "About last week…"

"We're okay."

"Good."

"It won't happen again."

"You promise?" she asked.

"Yes." Although part of him didn't want to promise that. A part of him wanted more, but this wasn't the place to talk about it.

He glanced over his shoulder and motioned for her to follow him into a small room so that no one could overhear them. It was bad enough that Marcus knew they'd had dinner together; he didn't need the rest of the staff knowing his business. Once they were in the room, he shut the door.

"You don't seem okay," she said. "I'm sensing something is off."

"I'm fine. I thought we worked this out? We both agreed that what happened was a mistake."

"Yes, but I don't want us to be estranged, either. I like working with you."

"We're not. We can be professionals."

"You avoided me this week," she stated.

Which was true. He had. "And you weren't avoiding me?"

"Maybe."

"So why worry?" he asked.

"When I was in Manhattan after the incident, I was ostracized, and it sucked. I don't want that to happen here."

He crossed his arms. "I thought you didn't care about what other surgeons thought?"

"I don't usually, but it doesn't feel so good when you're being purposefully avoided by others."

"I'm sorry."

"Good," she said. "And I'm sorry, too. I'm here to do my job, and I want to be able to do it well. I take pride in my work. It's the most important thing to me."

It was like a slap across the face from his past. Matthew was keenly aware how she felt about her job. He knew that she put her career first, because the last time she did that, his heart had suffered.

It had shattered.

And he was sure that it had never fully healed right.

Kirsten had helped, but he wasn't sure that he ever gave himself fully to her, as there was always a piece of himself that he had been holding back because he was so afraid of getting hurt. Well, he wasn't going to put himself in that kind of situation again.

"I know how much your job means to you," he said icily. "And I take my job as chief of surgery quite seriously, too."

"I know."

"Then we agree. Colleagues and friends. Nothing more."

She nodded. "Right."

He could see the pulse in her slender neck and noted that it was beating quite quickly. And suddenly he recalled that many of their most heated, passionate moments had started with a fight.

He might be hardening his heart, but there was nothing wrong with meaningless, detached sex, was there?

What is coming over you?

Matthew opened the door, desperate for an escape. "I'll see you in the scrub room?"

Victoria nodded quickly. "Yes. I look forward to working with you today, Dr. Olesen."

"Same, Dr. Jensen."

He left the room quickly. His body was reacting to her presence, and he had to make a mental note to not allow himself to be alone in a room with her again.

He refocused on the task at hand. It had been more than a week since he had done a surgery, which was unusual for him. He'd been so busy since he took over as chief, with paperwork to do, people to meet, balances and budgets to oversee, and he hadn't had a chance to step into the operating room.

Today's procedure was the kind of surgery he most liked to do. A live liver transplant was a win-win in his books. The donor's liver would grow back in time, and the recipient had a second chance at a healthy, happy life.

And since it was a young girl—a child—it was even better.

This was the best part of his job—saving a life.

Victoria was at the operating table, along with the rest of his staff.

An energy of hope passed through the room, and he

took a deep, calming breath. This was what he liked to do just before he took hold of the scalpel.

Victoria watched him, her dark brown eyes keen and bright. He liked being here with her in an operating room. The first surgery they'd ever performed together hadn't been nearly as calm. He'd been in competition mode with a feisty, fiercely independent, beautiful surgical resident named Victoria back then.

As they'd worked side by side, he'd been aware of her talent and worried about his own position in the program. Just as he was worried about his attraction to her. How much he wanted her.

Now there was no fight for a spot. He was in charge. Although that undercurrent of sexual attraction was still there. He was hoping it wasn't, but it was. What was it about her that ensnared him so?

"You ready, Dr. Olesen?" she asked, standing next to him.

"I am, Dr. Jensen."

The scrub nurse handed him the scalpel, and he went to work to harvest a healthy piece of liver. Victoria stepped up as an assist, and for the first time in a long time, he didn't have to explain anything to the other surgeon.

She anticipated his moves, and they worked together seamlessly.

She was flawless.

It had been a long time since he'd worked with a surgeon of Victoria's caliber. He had missed this.

It was comfortable.

It was familiar.

It was like coming home.

"This is a healthy liver," Victoria murmured as she worked.

"It is."

"The girl is lucky to have such amazing foster parents." There was a bit of censure in her voice, and her hands trembled ever so slightly.

"Are you okay, Dr. Jensen?" he asked, worried she'd freeze up again.

He knew how much her experience in New York City must have traumatized her. He could tell from Mrs. Van Luven's surgery it was still affecting her.

And he understood trauma. It had been hard for him to walk in the oncology ward for a couple years with the memory of Kirsten haunting those halls.

"I'm fine," she said quickly. "I'm okay to do this."

"Well, it's a pleasure to work with you again."

She cocked an eyebrow. "And it was a pleasure to work together when we were residents and fighting for position in that program."

"Of course, the others weren't a threat. You were because of your talent. I appreciate talent."

"Why, thank you, Dr. Olesen."

"You sound surprised."

"You've never said that to me before. Ever."

He smiled. "Well, it's deserved. And you're welcome."

She snorted in response, and he chuckled.

What're you doing? a little voice in Matthew's head asked. He kept telling himself he had to keep his distance from her. The problem was, he couldn't.

He missed her camaraderie.

Her friendship.

Her body.

All this time and the rift between them hadn't changed a thing.

He missed her.

Victoria was exhausted. Her body ached, and she felt like her feet were cement blocks. She sat down on the floor of the surgeons' changing room and rested her head against her knees. The surgery had gone well, but she was emotionally wrung out.

When had her life become so complicated?

She was so glad the little girl had pulled through. That little girl had a new liver, and she would have a mom and dad who cared for her.

She had a chance.

Something Victoria had never had.

She was envious of that little girl's good fortune.

She'd wake up from her surgery and she'd have a family.

Victoria had never had a family, but it was something she always secretly wanted.

Whereas Matthew had a brother and parents, yet he seemed to have no desire to be around them.

She didn't get it.

It was obvious he was cared for and loved. And she wondered what that was like.

You could've known if you hadn't pushed Matthew away.

Matthew walked into the changing room and paused.

"You okay?" he asked.

No.

Except she didn't say that. "Just tired. It was a long surgery."

"Yeah, but it went well."

She nodded. "I was a foster child."

He seemed shocked. "You were?"

And she couldn't quite believe the words were coming out. "You asked me before why I seemed off, and it's because I grew up in the system."

Matthew's expression softened, and he came to sit beside her on the floor. "What happened to your parents?"

"My mother died when I was ten. I have very small, fragmented memories of her. You know those kinds of memories that are orange-hued and faded?"

He smiled. "Yeah. What about your father?"

"I never knew him, so I was put in the foster system when my mother died."

"I'm sorry. That's horrible."

She shrugged. Numb. She never cried and she wasn't going to start now, but she felt relief sharing this with him. Like it was a huge weight off her chest.

"Not all foster parents are bad. Most aren't," he said softly.

"I know. I've met wonderful people since then, but that wasn't my experience growing up." She sighed. "I'm exhausted."

And she was. There had been a lot going on since she'd come here to St. Thomas, and she felt like she was crashing from it all.

Like she was free falling.

"You need to go home and get some rest."

"Right." She stood, and Matthew got up, too. "I better call a cab. I usually just walk, but it's midnight."

"I'll drive you."

"I thought we weren't going to get involved with each other."

"We're not. A friend can drive a friend home."

She should say no and just take a cab, but she wanted to be friends with Matthew. She'd missed her friend.

"Okay. I'll grab my stuff and meet you in the lobby."

"Sounds good," he said as he left the room.

Victoria quickly got out of her surgical scrubs and back into her street clothes. She grabbed her stuff from the boardroom where she worked and made her way to the lobby, where Matthew was waiting for her. They walked out to his car, and she climbed in, her body relaxing against the supple leather of the interior.

"Where do you live again?" he asked. "I somewhat remember, but I'm not exactly sure."

"In the condos at the end of A Street."

"Right. That sounds familiar. I know those places."

It wasn't a long drive, but she was appreciative of his offer when he pulled up in front of the building where she was staying.

"Thanks for the lift."

"It's no problem." He smiled. "What're your plans for tomorrow? I know it's your day off."

"I don't know. I haven't had a day off yet. I don't usually take time off."

"I remember. I think you need to see St. Thomas."

"What?"

"You took me on that tour of New York City when I first arrived. This is payback! If you recall, I didn't really want to go on that tour."

Victoria groaned and then smiled as she thought of that tour of Manhattan she'd taken him on and how he grumbled through it all, though she'd known he was just teasing her. She knew they'd both had had a lot of fun. It had been one of those halcyon memories she cherished. They had seen the Statue of Liberty and Rockefeller Center and gone to the Top of the Rock. They had been to Central Park and Times Square. They had done all the real touristy stuff.

She usually didn't do things like that, and that day with Matthew had been one of the best, goofiest days of her life.

She hadn't thought about it in so long.

You shouldn't go.

But the part of her that wanted to go was stronger.

She was lonely and stressed out, and she just wanted some fun so that she could try to forget everything that had happened to her in Manhattan.

"Fine," she said grudgingly, but with a smile so he didn't think she was a total grump. "If it's payback, then I guess I have no choice but to accompany you."

Matthew nodded. "Right. I'll pick you up at nine?"

"Sure. That sounds good." She climbed out of the car and shut the door.

Matthew waved and drove off.

Her stomach started to do that flip-flop it always did whenever she was around him.

She should stay home.

She should've turned him down, but for the first time, she wondered if maybe she didn't have to be alone.

And it scared her.

CHAPTER EIGHT

VICTORIA HADN'T SLEPT a wink.

Between telling Matthew about her childhood, which no one knew about, their kiss and this domino surgery, her mind was racing a hundred miles a minute.

She was tossing and turning all night as she imagined about what today would bring. There were times she thought this was a bad idea and then other times she was excited about spending a day with Matthew.

Even though she didn't deserve to feel excited about being with him again. Not when she had hurt him all those years ago.

Spending her day off with him was not keeping her distance from him. Only she couldn't help herself. She was lonely. She usually always had her work to distract her, but here, other than planning the domino, she had nothing else, and so it was just her and her loneliness.

What else have you got to do?

Victoria eventually gave up with her waffling back and forth, put on a light, airy sundress and made her way outside when it was time for him to pick her up. She didn't know what today was going to bring, but she was going to go with the flow, which wasn't her usual tactic. She was hoping she'd be able to relax and calm her mind. The sun was bright and warm, but there was a gentle breeze blowing, and it helped break the heat.

It was a perfect day in paradise. A day in paradise with Matthew. Her stomach did a flip.

It was just a day out with a friend.

She could spend a day with an old friend.

Nothing had to happen.

Nothing would happen!

Matthew pulled up in his Audi, and as she climbed into the passenger seat, it felt like butterflies had taken over her entire abdomen. She was so nervous being around him, which was a first, and she knew it was because of what she'd shared with him. He knew about her past.

He knew too much about her. It made her wary, even if there was a part of her that liked him knowing that about her. It was like a huge weight off her shoulders.

"Good morning! You look nice," he complimented.

"Thanks." Her cheeks bloomed with heat. "You look great, too."

And he did. He was wearing khaki pants and a light blue cotton shirt. She loved that color of blue on him. It brought out the color of his eyes.

Eyes she had gotten lost in time and time again.

"How do you feel about boat rides?" he asked.

"Did you convince your brother to lend you the *Tryphine*?" she asked, confused.

Matthew snorted. "No. I was thinking more of a ferry ride."

She didn't like boats at the best of times. "I've ridden the ferries in New York. Are you taking me to St. John, since your brother is here?" she teased. She wouldn't mind doing some island hopping. Work in

New York kept her busy, and she didn't take much time off. She wanted to travel around the islands a bit before she went back to her lonesome life in Manhattan.

"No, I thought you might like to go to St. Croix. See where I grew up."

Her stomach knotted and then dropped like a rock to the soles of her feet. "You're taking me to see your parents?"

"No." He laughed. "They're not home. They're on a round-the-world cruise, but I have been tasked with checking on their place from time to time, and I thought it was a good time to show you the island."

"How long is this ferry ride?"

"About ninety minutes or so."

"What?" she choked.

"You'll have plenty of time to visit St. Thomas, as it's pretty easy to see most of the island. St. John and Water Island aren't far from Charlotte Amalie, but to get the full Virgin Islands experience, you'll have to go to St. Croix."

"So we're island hopping today?" she asked cautiously.

He grinned, his eyes twinkling. "Yes. We are. And you can experience the luxury car my dad leaves parked at the Gallows Bay Dock."

"Oh, so it's not a car ferry?"

"No. Just a passenger ferry," Matthew said as he pulled up to the ferry terminal at French Town.

Victoria could see the little bistro where he'd taken her out to dinner, in particular that rooftop where he had pulled her into a dance that ended with a kiss. One that she still couldn't stop thinking about, even though she knew she had to.

They had already decided that the kiss was a mistake.

But there was a part of her that felt like it hadn't been.

It had felt *right*.

It had felt like something that had been missing. And this line of thinking wasn't going to help her keep her distance from him. It just made her want him more.

Matthew parked the car and then came around to open her door for her. She followed him as he walked up to the ticket booth and bought two round-trip tickets from Charlotte Amalie to Christiansted on St. Croix.

The ferry didn't look like the big ferries that she was used to seeing in New York City. This one reminded her of a tourist sightseeing boat, and she paused. It seemed a bit small for open water. Matthew turned around.

"Nervous?"

"I'm okay with larger vessels. Not sure how I'll feel about this." Her voice shook slightly.

Matthew smiled and held out his hand. "It'll be fine. I promise you."

Victoria slipped her hand in his as they boarded.

"Do you want to sit up on deck?" he asked.

"Yes. I think that might be better. That way if I feel ill, I can just run to the side of the boat."

He chuckled. "I swear, you'll be fine, and the sea air will do you good."

Victoria wasn't sure, but she didn't let go of his hand as she followed him to the upper deck, where there were bench seats. Her hand in his felt right. His hand was strong and reassuring, and she didn't want to let it go.

And as they sat there, she still held on to him, like

it was the most natural thing in the world. Like he was her security. Just like when she had frozen in the operating room and he'd talked her through and when he'd held her hand before she told him about her past. It calmed her nerves.

She was safe with him.

She'd only ever felt that safety with her mother.

So long ago.

They found a bench to themselves near the back and settled in as the ferry continued to load. Matthew didn't try to pull away, either. Neither of them said anything as they sat there together. The only sound was the water lapping against the hull and buzzing talk of boarding passengers.

It wasn't long before the moorings were pulled up and the green-and-white vessel made its way out into the Cay and toward St. Croix.

The turquoise waters gave way to the darker blue of the deep Virgin Islands trough of the Caribbean Sea. Victoria didn't say much, because she wasn't sure if she could speak over the sound of the wind and the water.

Or if her churning stomach would let her.

Matthew didn't seem to mind as he stared out over the water, his arm draped along the back of the bench. Even though his arm wasn't around her, she found it reassuring that he was there, and she slid a bit closer, enjoying the sight of St. Thomas slipping away and keeping her eyes fixed on the horizon line, waiting for that first glimpse of St. Croix.

The sun felt good.

It had been a long time since she'd sat out in the sun and just drunk in the vitamin D.

Usually, she was too busy at the hospital, but there

were rare times when a nice spring day would hit the city and she would sneak off to Central Park to sit out and listen to the city and enjoy the outside.

It was a peaceful voyage, and the ninety minutes it took seemed to slip by. Soon she could see the sliver of the island of St. Croix looming in the distance—the lush greenery and vibrantly colored roofs as they approached Gallows Bay.

"See," Matthew said. "That wasn't so bad, was it?"

"No. You're right. When is the next ferry back?"

"Already trying to escape me?" he teased.

"No. I just want to make sure we don't miss it. We have a lot of work tomorrow."

He cocked his eyebrow. "We? The domino surgery is yours."

"Fine, me, then. Are you happy?"

"I am." He smiled smugly, and she laughed.

She didn't mind that the domino was hers to coordinate. It had been a long time since she had organized one. Since becoming a full-fledged attending, she'd had her own residents to do much of the grunt work.

Matthew glanced at his watch as he stood. "Four. It's ten now, so we have a couple hours to kill. Better make the most of it."

Victoria nodded, and they disembarked.

She followed him as they headed to a parking garage that wasn't far from the Gallows Bay terminal, and he pulled out a fob to a Lamborghini that was hiding in the shadows, but it wasn't like a usual one. It was an open-topped speed car. It looked kind of monstrous.

It was like nothing she'd ever seen before.

"Your father drives that?" Victoria asked, shocked.

Matthew nodded. "I know. Wait until you see the modest homestead."

"Is it far from here?" She was worried about the trip back to St. Thomas.

"About twenty minutes."

She nodded and climbed into the car. What else was she going to do—hang around the docks worrying about getting back to Charlotte Amalie and Ziese Memorial Hospital?

She had to trust Matthew.

Matthew started the engine and the car revved to life, making her body quiver with a bit of excitement as he grinned at her.

"You ready?" he asked.

"I think so."

He slipped on his shades and drove out of the parking garage and out onto the streets of Christiansted. He made his way slowly through traffic and then headed east, where he allowed the speed to creep up.

She started to laugh as the wind whipped at her face as he sped along winding roads, the urban center dropping away to be replaced by country homes and farms. The sea disappeared as they tracked south through lush greenery and fields, and they passed through towns like Sally's Fancy and Madame Carty before the road turned and they were climbing up a hill, the water below them. It gave her a thrill, feeling as though they were racing along the edge.

Every so often she'd catch a glimpse of a serene-looking white beach, she wished she could walk through the soft sand and swim in the turquoise waters.

Matthew pulled off the main road and took another long, windy road up a mountain until the trees gave way and she spied what looked almost like a Spanish castle sitting on top of the hill. Her mouth dropped open at the sight of the white-domed structure.

"You lived in a castle as a child?"

Matthew chuckled. "Yes. I told you, my father likes things big."

"I thought you were teasing," she mumbled. "I don't know why I thought you were teasing."

He laughed as he slowed to a stop at the gate and punched in the security code. The gate slowly opened, and he crept along the long drive until they were in front of the house.

He parked the car. "Welcome to the Olesen homestead."

Victoria got out of the car and stared. The view from where the home was seated was spectacular—there was a vista every direction you looked, and she felt like it would be the perfect place to watch for pirates.

"Wow" was all she could say.

"Yeah, again, my father is not a subtle man. He grew up in Denmark, in a very small apartment in Copenhagen. He had to be crammed in there with his siblings, so this is his compensation for that. At least, that's what he's always told us."

She chuckled. "I can see that."

"Come. I'll show you around." He held out his hand again, and she took it naturally, without thinking. It felt right to hold his hand.

They walked into the house, and there were marble and gilded ceilings, with a large winding staircase that led up to the dome.

It was open, and her voice echoed as she stared up at it.

"Come on, I'll show you the patio, because it's my favorite place."

"The patio is your favorite place?" she teased. "All of this and the patio is what you like?"

"I'm a simple man. My father, not so much." He grinned. "Come on."

She followed him out under the staircase to a pair of French doors. He let go of her hand to open them, and she gasped at the white stone and the complete, unobstructed view of the Caribbean Sea.

An infinity pool clung to the edge and seemed to mix in with sea and sky. The edge of the pool had a translucent side, so it felt like you were swimming over a cliff. It was stunning. At the far end of the pool was a hot tub and a waterfall.

It was like something from a resort.

The entrance to the large pool sloped like you were walking into the ocean, and there was even sand.

"Would you like a swim?" he asked. "It is quite something swimming on the edge of a cliff under a castle."

"Okay, this definitely tops the Statue of Liberty," she murmured in awe.

He grinned. "No, you can't compare the two. That was impressive, too. The tall buildings of New York making you feel so small. It was the edge of America, or that's how I felt standing there."

"Sure, but this is like something out of that show that showed how the überrich always lived. One of my foster mothers was obsessed with how the far wealthier lived."

"Our house was on that show. Of course, it wasn't as impressive as it is now."

She looked at him in disbelief. "You're not serious?"

He grinned, his blue eyes twinkling. "No. I'm not serious. My father likes his showpieces, but he's also very private, too. He's a bit of a paradox."

Victoria laughed. "I find that hard to believe."

"Do you want to have a swim or not?" he asked, crossing his arms.

"I would, but I don't have a bathing suit."

"My mother has tons of them. She even has guest ones in the pool house. Grab a suit and change in there, and I'll grab us some drinks and snacks."

"Fine," she said. She wouldn't mind having a swim in that luxurious pool. When would she have the chance to experience a pool like this again? Probably never. Matthew opened the door to the pool house, which was a white stucco building that looked more like a small cottage than a pool house. She shut the door behind her and saw it was indeed set out like a cottage with a cozy living room and gleaming teak floors.

There was a modern kitchenette and a small, luxurious bathroom. She eventually found the master bedroom, which had one of those beds that she always pictured in the Caribbean, with the beautiful netting, and when she opened the French doors there was a tiny little balcony that overlooked the sea.

She took a deep breath, breathing in the fresh sea air.

She could definitely get used to this.

Not the massive home, but a small house like this next to the sea. The little dream caught her off guard, because she'd never really thought about something like that.

She never really dared to dream of something other than her career and New York.

There were times in her life when she'd allowed herself to dream, and those dreams were always crushed.

She'd always dreamed of having a loving home.

Security.

Safety.

But as each year went by and no one adopted her, Victoria eventually stopped dreaming.

With a sigh she headed back into the room, shutting the doors and finding the wardrobe full of bathing suits.

Nothing in black, which was her usual color.

It was all white.

And all two-pieces.

Victoria swallowed the lump in her throat.

He's seen you naked before.

She swallowed her fear and picked up a two-piece and changed. All they were doing was going for a swim.

Two friends swimming.

That was all.

Matthew changed into a pair of swimming trunks and set out the lemonade and the fruit salad he'd found in the kitchen. He'd called the house staff yesterday and told them he was coming with a friend when he got this brilliant idea to bring Victoria out here on his biweekly check on his parents' estate.

His parents had staff, but they still insisted Matthew or Marcus come every once in a while.

Although Marcus never did.

Matthew was the responsible one. His parents always

expected it, so he couldn't let them down. Although it would be nice if Marcus stepped up occasionally.

Don't think about Marcus now.

Marcus would bug him about how bringing a woman out here was a recipe for seduction. Well, that might be his twin brother's usual operation, but it wasn't his. He didn't bring women here.

And when he was with Kirsten, they had been too busy working to come here as often as they'd liked. Then she had been too sick to travel.

He could see why Marcus brought women here.

And he understood why his dad had built something like this—it was opulent, and his parents both liked showing off.

He didn't particularly like showing off. He preferred his modest-size home just outside Charlotte Amalie with a private beach.

That's not really much different. You have your own beach.

He set down the tray, and the pool house door opened.

"Would you like a…" His voice trailed off as Victoria came out in a white bikini. Suddenly he couldn't breathe. It was like he'd been punched and all the air had been forced out of his body.

"Would I like a what?" she asked, tying back her long, silky brown hair.

Say something.

Except all he could hear was the pounding of his pulse between his ears.

"Iced tea?" he asked, finally finding his voice.

"Yes. Thank you." She made her way over to the table, and he poured her a glass. He was hoping his hand wasn't shaking and tried not to look at her. Suddenly, he felt like a dorky young man again. All awkward and uncomfortable around his crush.

She took a seat, and he sat on the other side of the table, staring out over the blue water.

"This is beautiful, but you know, when you told me that we were going to do touristy stuff I thought you were going schlep me around a bunch of old forts and tourist traps."

He cocked an eyebrow. "Is that what you want to do?"

She laughed softly. "No. This is better. I didn't realize how stressed I actually was until now."

"Agreed. It's been some time since I came out here and enjoyed the sun."

"You okay?" she asked.

"I was just thinking about my late wife. She loved it here."

"I can see why," Victoria said. "Do you mind me asking how she died?"

"No." He wasn't sure he wanted to talk about it, but also there was a part of him that did because he was tired of holding it all in. There was no point in hiding it—Victoria knew he was a widower. "It was cervical and ovarian cancer. By the time they discovered it, it was too late. She was gone six months later. She was only thirty-two."

"I'm sorry. She was so young."

He nodded. "She was."

"We were only married for a couple of years, but after she died, I threw myself into my work. I took every surgery I could, filled my roster up, and I guess that's why the board of directors offered me the position to become chief of surgery."

"I can see that. That's kind of how I rose to the top. Work and only work. It's easier to work than deal with…other things."

"I remember," he said dryly. "You were very focused on work."

"Well, work provided security. Work meant that I had a roof on my head and I wouldn't starve."

A pang of guilt washed over him. It all made perfect sense.

She had no one, and he'd grown up like this.

His parents had been absent a lot, but his parents loved him and made sure that he was provided for. He didn't have debt when he came out of school. There was never a night that he had to go hungry or worry about a roof over his head. Still, his parents left him and Marcus a lot. Which was why Matthew often felt more like a parent than a brother. He hadn't really had a childhood, either. Suddenly, he understood Victoria just a little bit better.

He felt closer to her.

"Okay, enough of this," he stated, setting his glass down. "I'm going swimming."

He made his way over to the pool and wandered in. The water was cool and refreshing. It had been a long time since he'd gone swimming, and he paddled to the edge of the infinity pool, glancing down at the ocean below him.

He turned around, expecting Victoria to follow him. "Are you coming?"

"Yeah, I like wading, but I don't know how to swim."

"What?"

"I grew up in the system. Swimming lessons weren't part of my upbringing." She got up and gingerly made her way into the water. He swam over to her.

"Do you want me to show you?" Matthew asked.

"I don't know," she said nervously.

"Come on." He held out his hand. She slipped her hand in his, and he gently guided her into the water until she was up to her waist. She was trembling. "It's okay."

"Are you sure?" she asked.

"Positive. This is also a saltwater pool—it's more buoyant." He pulled her into the deeper water, closer to the edge.

Victoria threw her arms around his neck.

His pulse began to race having her so close, and he held her as she freaked out slightly.

"This is crazy," she said, her voice on edge.

"It's not. Everyone swims."

"Not me."

"It'll be fine, look." And he swam over to the edge and disengaged her limbs from around him and had her hold on to the side of the pool. Her eyes were closed. "Kick your legs and you'll stay up."

She nodded and opened one eye. "Oh, wow."

"See. It's worth it."

She nodded, gripping the edge. "Okay, maybe I can get used to this swimming thing."

He chuckled and they floated there, on the edge of the pool, watching the ocean. It was so peaceful. Why was it so right with Victoria? Why did he keep getting sucked into something with her? Why couldn't he stay away from her?

It didn't have to be anything. It could just be this. It could just be this moment as friends.

He could be her friend, but he wanted to be more with her. A year after Kirsten died, his brother and his parents had tried to get him to move on, but he had never been interested in anyone else.

He'd tried to go on a date, but it was just never right, and that was the end of it.

He really didn't have any desire to continue anything.

No one ever really sparked any interest in him.

The only two women in his life who had done that were Kirsten and Victoria. And for so long he'd thought both women were gone, out of his life for good.

"Why would your parents want to leave this to see the world?" Victoria teased. "This is paradise."

Matthew laughed. "I know. They don't stay put too much. Even when I was a kid."

"Who looked after you and Marcus?" she asked.

"Nannies," Matthew responded. "Or boarding school, or me, but when they were here, it was home."

She smiled, but he could see the sadness in her eyes. He could see the pain and longing. It was a different side to her, and it made him want to reach out and take her in his arms.

To protect her.

He didn't want her to feel that pain of loneliness anymore.

"Thanks for bringing me here. I actually think this really isn't fair."

He cocked an eyebrow. "How do you mean?"

"Well, you said the tour would be payback, and you were implying that my tour was terrible. This is lovely."

He grinned. "I'm glad you're enjoying some downtime. I can still take you to the fort if you'd like?"

"Pass." She laughed. "I wouldn't mind some lunch somewhere, though. The fruit salad was nice, but I'm still hungry."

"Want to take another ride?" he asked.

"I hope you mean in the car."

A zing of anticipation ran through him, and he moved closer to her. "Of course."

"Well, help me get out of this pool."

Matthew took her in his arms, his body reacting to holding her body so close to his as he helped her swim until her feet could touch the bottom of the pool again. He didn't want to let go of her, but it was for the best.

He needed to put some distance between them.

Although, as she waded out of the pool, he couldn't help but notice her curves, and he recalled being able to touch every inch of her, making her quiver with pleasure.

That was a long time ago.

And he had to keep reminding himself of that, because he couldn't stand getting close to her and losing her again.

He couldn't take another loss, even though he was so tempted to have just one more night with her. To have her in his arms again.

The rest of the day passed in a blur.

After their swim in the pool, something had changed between them. Victoria wasn't sure what, but it was probably for the best. When they had been in the pool and his arms had been around her, she'd felt something.

Terror, but also something else.

Similar to that heat, that electric pull, she'd felt when they had been dancing on the rooftop and they'd kissed. It was probably best that they got out of the pool and left his parents' opulent castle on top of the hill.

He drove them down the mountain to a small bistro just outside Christiansted, and their entire conversation had been about work.

Which was so much safer.

Now they were back on the ferry, headed back to St. Thomas.

Except this time, Matthew wasn't sitting next to her. He was leaning on the railing and staring out over the water.

Her purse began to vibrate, and she pulled out her phone.

"Hello?" she answered, confused.

"Dr. Jensen? It's Dr. Gainsbourg from Ziese Memorial Hospital."

"Yes, Dr. Gainsbourg?" As soon as she said his name, Matthew glanced over his shoulder at her.

"It's about the domino."

Her stomach sank like a rock. She'd done this enough times to know that there were a few different things that could go wrong at this stage. Donors could pull out or a recipient could pass away. "We lost a donor, didn't we?"

Matthew spun around, his brow furrowed, his arms crossed.

"We've lost two. The domino surgery is collapsing," Dr. Gainsbourg stated. "It's a mess right now."

"Thank you. We'll be back as soon as we can, and I'll deal with it." She ended the call and worried her bottom lip.

"It's the surgery, isn't it?" Matthew asked. She could hear the edge in his voice. "It's falling apart, right?"

"It is. Two donors have pulled out. We need to fix this."

CHAPTER NINE

Victoria poured herself another cup of coffee and stared at her whiteboard. Seven days—a whole week ago—her domino had fallen apart, and she still hadn't been able to set it right yet. As soon as the ferry docked at Charlotte Amalie, she'd headed straight for the hospital and tried to get more testing done, to find other matches out of the willing pool of incompatible donors.

She had found one replacement donor, but she was having a hard time finding a second. Mrs. Van Luven was rapidly deteriorating and the young boy Marcus was worried about, the reason he'd stepped up to become a living donor, was also in rough shape—Jonas had been transferred to Ziese Memorial Hospital from St. John because he needed to be monitored and his dialysis was no longer working.

It worried Victoria that two of the recipients were now hospitalized and both were receiving peritoneal dialysis over hemodialysis.

She just needed one more donor, just one more match to step up, and then she could get the domino up and running. She had her team of surgeons waiting. There were so many people in the wings ready for this to be a go.

Matthew wandered into the boardroom, and she noted that he had bags under his eyes as well. She knew that he had been just as stressed as she was since the domino surgery had fallen apart.

"Any luck?" he asked, a hopeful tone to his voice.

"No. I still need another donor, and I'm running out of time." She sighed. "I'm hoping someone steps up, but I get it. It's a surgery, and it's a big deal."

"Jonas is stable, and he's taking to the peritoneal dialysis well," Matthew stated, sitting down in a chair across from her.

"That's at least something. Mrs. Van Luven is somewhat stable, but she needs the surgery soon."

"I've contacted UNOS. I know it's a long shot, but if we can get a kidney from a deceased donor, then we can do a five-way live donor domino."

"It's worth a shot."

She didn't have high hopes. There were still people ahead on the list, but they had to try something.

Anything.

"How is Marcus doing? Did he pass his counseling?" Matthew asked.

"He did. He's been cleared."

Matthew frowned.

"I thought you'd be happy," Victoria said. "You wanted him to have a clear conscience before he made the decision to have the surgery, and he does."

"He's grown man, but…he's my twin brother." He gave her a half smile. "I can't help but worry."

"As you say, he's a grown man. You don't need to parent him."

"I don't parent him. He's just… He drives me crazy."

"Maybe you do have feelings for your brother?" she teased.

"You're exhausted and saying foolish things," he groused.

"How do you know that? I said I was stressed, not tired."

"You look tired," he murmured, purposely changing the subject.

"So do you."

"I have a hospital to run, and I want this surgery to be a success, too." He scrubbed a hand over his face. "Explain to me again why those two donors pulled out of it in the first place?"

"One was too scared, and the other is moving overseas. They got a big promotion and have to move soon."

Matthew raised his eyebrows. "We could write a doctor's note for the donor who has to move for a job, or maybe we can convince one of the donors to come back?" he asked. "One of the original ones who dropped out when we had our matches."

"That's against every procedure under UNOS and would jeopardize this surgery. We can't try to persuade a donor and you know it. Even if I want to so badly."

"I know. It's frustrating, but I understand."

Dr. Gainsbourg came into the room just then, his face grim. "Dr. Jensen?"

"It's Mrs. Van Luven. Her numbers are deteriorating, aren't they?" she asked, her heart sinking.

Dr. Gainsbourg nodded. "I managed to get her stable, but I thought you'd like to see the report."

Victoria nodded and took the report from the younger doctor.

The numbers confirmed her fears, and suddenly this felt like what had happened with the ambassador…

"I don't think I can operate on the ambassador. Not with numbers like this."

"The board of directors would like you to. The ambassador knows you are the best, and this would be an absolute coup for this hospital if you did. This would completely advance your career. Isn't that what you want?" Paul asked earnestly.

Victoria stared at the report.

"I'll try," she said, even though her every instinct was telling her this wasn't safe.

Victoria shook that memory from her mind. What she should've said was that she didn't feel comfortable and she should've walked away from that surgery.

Why didn't she listen to herself? Why was she so desperate to please Dr. Martin and the board of directors?

She hated herself for that, but she'd learned something, too. She was going to always go with her instincts. Numbers on lab reports didn't lie. Sure, miracles happened, but she was never, ever going to put a patient at risk ever again.

Medicine wasn't a business to her.

It was life.

And it was clear from the lab report that it wouldn't be much longer until she couldn't do a surgery on Mrs. Van Luven. Her body would be too weak and wouldn't be able to handle the transplant.

"Thanks, Dr. Gainsbourg. Keep me posted on her condition."

Dr. Gainsbourg nodded.

"What're we going to do?" Victoria asked.

Matthew shook his head. "I don't know. The only way this surgery works is if everyone is involved. If Mrs. Van Luven doesn't get a kidney, her donor won't give to the next person. You know how it goes."

"Except that Marcus is Mrs. Van Luven's donor. The question is, would your brother still donate the kidney even if this whole thing falls apart?"

"I don't know. And we can't ask that of him," Matthew responded quietly.

"I hope UNOS calls. I hope we can find an answer soon." She sighed and stared out the window. "What I wouldn't give to go for a swim in your parents' pool right about now and maybe have some rum punch, too."

He chuckled. "I have been thinking about that myself. Although drinking and swimming isn't that wise."

"I never did thank you for that day," she said softly. "We got back to Charlotte Amalie, and this whole surgery fell apart and I've been scrambling since."

"I know. So have I." He stood up and wandered over to stand beside her. "Has the situation in New York blown over yet?"

The question caught her off guard. It suddenly felt like he was trying to get rid of her.

Her spine stiffened, and she worried her bottom lip. "Not exactly. I got an email from the board of directors saying that the autopsy findings have been published and my name has officially been cleared."

Matthew's brow furrowed. "So you're leaving?"

"No. I'm going to finish the domino and see it through. I don't leave jobs unfinished, so I'll stay here until it's done."

Relief washed over his expression. "I'm glad to

hear it, but won't New York want you back as soon as possible?"

"There's no rush. The press is still circling, and the board did add that they were thrilled with the domino surgery I'm undertaking here in this little hospital. Though it's hardly little."

"St. Thomas is part of the United States. We even have some their big box stores here," he said jokingly.

"I know, but if it's not Manhattan, then it's 'little' to them." She smiled. "Eventually this surgery will be over and I'll be able to return to my practice."

A strange expression crossed his face. "You'll return to New York?"

"You just asked me about my job. Why wouldn't I go back?

"You could go somewhere else," he hinted.

"Where?" she asked, amused.

Matthew shrugged. "Anywhere."

He was right. What would happen if she didn't return to New York? She could go anywhere, except there was a niggling thought at the back of her mind.

Even though she knew the autopsy results had cleared her of all fault, the bad press wouldn't exactly gain her new patients for a while, and if she wasn't earning money, what board of directors would take her on?

Probably not many.

Matthew might.

She was lucky to be here, but this wasn't where she was supposed to be. She wouldn't risk her heart or his. It was better to be alone. Alone was safer than risking it on something foolish like love, so she'd return to New York. Ultimately, she knew she was too scared to leave the security of the city of her birth—the city she'd shared with her mom before she'd died.

She cleared her throat, trying to break the tension. "No, I'll go back to New York."

Matthew seemed disappointed with her answer, but he didn't say anything further. "Well, I need to check on my other patients. If I hear anything from UNOS, I'll let you know."

"Thanks."

Matthew nodded and left.

She sighed, frustrated. New York City was the only home she knew. Yet there was a part of her that didn't want to go back.

You could stay?

Only it was obvious from Matthew's suggestion that she could go anywhere. After this domino and her time in St. Thomas were over, she wouldn't be able to stay here. He hadn't exactly asked her to.

Do you blame him?

She'd hurt him so badly ten years ago.

The thing was, it had hurt her, too, when she pushed him away. It had been ten years, and she still wanted him.

It scared her how he made her feel safe again. It had been a long time since she'd felt that security. Not since she was a child and her mother had been alive. Not that she remembered much, but there were those small, happy memories. And then those memories of her time with Matthew. She had ruined their love.

It was her fault, and though she wanted that back, she was so afraid it could be taken away from her again.

That she'd lose him because she loved him too much.

Even though she had been completely stressed about

this surgery falling apart, she couldn't stop thinking about their time on St. Croix. How safe he had made her feel on the ferry and when they were in the pool together. His touch grounded her, and when she was with him she felt like she could do anything.

She had been so self-conscious when she walked out of the pool house in that bikini, but then when she saw him, all of that melted away, and when he held her in the water in his strong arms, her body melted.

It had taken all her willpower not to kiss him.

And when she was relaxing at the edge of that pool, all she could think about was how wonderful it would be to take him into that lovely small room in the pool house and fall into that big, beautiful bed.

Heat bloomed in her cheeks.

She was obviously tired, because she usually had better control over her emotions than this. Except she was losing control. She loved being here in Charlotte Amalie and working with Matthew. She didn't feel so alone.

She had her best friend back.

She had her lover back.

Heat rushed through her as she thought of their first time together. She would give anything to experience that heady, pleasure-filled night again.

Even if it was a bad idea.

"Victoria?"

She turned as Matthew came back in the room. Her heart skipped a beat, her body trembling as she gazed at him.

What could it hurt to indulge in one night again?

When he had kissed her on that rooftop, she'd pushed him away, but she knew that he was feeling it, too. She knew that Matthew wanted her just as much as she wanted him.

They weren't strangers. They were both adults.

She closed the gap between them.

"Don't say anything," she whispered.

He looked surprised as she pulled him tight against her and then paused as she looked deep into his eyes.

The moment she looked into those blue eyes, she knew she had made a huge mistake, and it was probably because she was completely exhausted and really hadn't thought it through. All she had been thinking about was Matthew and their first night together ten years ago.

She hadn't looked at him closely enough, and she felt foolish.

She let go of him and took a step back.

"You're not Matthew." She sighed, annoyed with herself for her mistake.

Again.

Marcus grinned, his eyes twinkling. "No, but I could be if you'd like!"

Why hadn't Victoria said she wanted to stay here?

He was offering her a chance to remain in St. Thomas. He couldn't actually offer her a job unless it was okayed by the board of directors, but he didn't want her to go. It hurt him that New York City came first. It always did.

He wanted her to think beyond Manhattan.

Even though he'd vowed he wouldn't put his heart at risk with her again, he still wanted her, even after all this time. And he wanted her here.

With him.

Only she wanted New York, it was clear. Why had he thought she would change after all this time?

Ever since their trip to his parents' place on St. Croix, when she had come out of the pool house in that white bikini, he hadn't been able to stop thinking about her. And then when they were swimming up to the edge, it had taken all his willpower not to kiss her.

And for the past week, even though they had been completely stressed and focused on getting this domino back up and running, all he could think about was her in that bikini.

Which then drifted to his memories of her naked and in his arms...

"Why are you looking at me like that?" she whispered huskily.

He was propped up on one elbow and running his fingers through her brown hair as they were lying in an on-call room, crammed into one small bed.

"How am I looking at you?"

She grinned. "I don't know."

"You're beautiful."

"You're crazy," she said.

"I know."

And he wanted to tell her that he was crazy for her, but he didn't want to scare her off.

"Hey, do you have a minute?"

Matthew turned to see Marcus in the doorway to his office and groaned inwardly. Of course Marcus had to intrude on his thoughts now. Memories that he wanted to savor but now were melting away in the presence of his twin.

"Now is not a good time, Marcus. I'm trying to find another donor."

"I'm not here to bug you." Marcus shut the door behind him. "I have good news."

"Oh? You have three kidneys, so you're giving up two?" Matthew teased.

Marcus grinned. "You know if I did, I would."

"I know," Matthew admitted.

Marcus raised his eyebrow. "Wow."

"What?" Matthew asked.

"You've never admitted that I've been right before."

"Marcus, I don't have the patience for this today." He rubbed his temples. "What is your news?"

"I've found a donor, and they are getting cross matched and ready to go through counseling."

"Who?"

"A friend of Jonas's is donating in the surgery. By the way, I would've still given my kidney to Mrs. Van Luven. I thought I would put that out there. I wouldn't have left your patient in the lurch."

Matthew sighed. "Well, that is good news. I hope that the cross match works for Jonas."

"Me, too. There's also something else."

"What?" Matthew asked.

"What're your intentions with Victoria?"

Matthew's spine straightened. He didn't like where this was heading. Marcus was a lothario. Had never had a serious relationship. He was a playboy through and through, and the thought of Marcus setting his sights on Victoria made his blood boil. "What do you mean?"

"She pulled me into her arms and was going to kiss me…and then she realized I wasn't you."

Matthew's pulse thundered between his ears. "She what?"

"She almost kissed me." Marcus grinned. "I was kind of hopeful, but she pulled away pretty quickly once she realized that I wasn't you. She's into you, so my question is, what're you going to do about it?"

"Nothing." Even though his heart was racing and he couldn't help but smile.

Victoria wanted to kiss him, but he wasn't going to admit to his brother that he wanted Victoria, too. His brother didn't even know the details of their shared past. No one knew about that. It was his alone.

He didn't like Marcus questioning him about it. It was too intrusive.

"What do you mean, you're not going to do anything?" Marcus asked in shock. "She's obviously into you."

"So?" He acted like he didn't care even though it gave him a secret thrill.

"So? Kirsten has been gone for five years, Matthew. She wouldn't want you to be alone."

"Don't talk to me about Kirsten," Matthew snarled.

"Why?" Marcus asked. "You're unbelievable. If I were you—"

"But you're not me."

"Thank goodness for that! You're too uptight. Though heck knows Mom and Dad always wanted me to be more like you. You act more like a parent than a brother. I'd rather have a brother!"

Matthew crossed his arms. "What are we doing,

Marcus? Why are you suddenly so concerned with my love life?"

Marcus shrugged. "I honestly don't know, but I thought you'd want to know this. And I know that you two knew each other in the past, but I think more happened than you're letting on."

Matthew didn't say anything, so Marcus left his office, slamming the door behind him. He felt bad, but he didn't want Marcus to know about his past with Victoria.

Why?

He couldn't answer that niggling little voice inside his head.

Marcus wanted a brother.

He wanted that, too.

And he wanted Victoria.

What was holding him back?

She wanted him.

That gave him a secret thrill.

Why was he fighting that old attraction?

It was his fault just as much as hers when things crashed and burned ten years ago. He'd left her and New York, after all. He could've stayed. They had both grown and moved on.

Why couldn't they just have one more night?

Does she even want one more night?

He wasn't sure, but he would take one more night with her, if he could. He was scared of being hurt again. He didn't have much luck when it came to love.

There were no happily-ever-afters for him.

Of course there won't be if you don't try.

He left his office and made his way back to the

boardroom. Victoria was pacing back and forth. She was mumbling to herself, and she looked annoyed.

He knocked on the door.

She paused, her cheeks turning red, and she took a step back. "Matthew?"

"Yes."

"Do you know how frustrating it is that you're an identical twin! Did Marcus tell you what happened?"

Matthew chuckled softly. "He did."

"He promised me he'd grow a beard," Victoria groused. "So I could tell you two apart faster."

"So why did you pull him into that embrace?"

The red deepened to crimson. "I wasn't thinking straight."

"Obviously. I'm much more dashing than my brother." He grinned.

"Stubborn is more like it," she said, smiling.

"He says uptight." Matthew laughed. "It's okay that you mistook him for me. I get it. Twin thing."

"Well, okay. Thank you. Again, I'm sorry, but Marcus did have good news. Did he tell you about it?"

Matthew nodded. "Yes. Now we just have to wait to make sure that the cross match is good."

"My fingers are crossed." And she held them up.

"Well, there's nothing more we can do here today. Do you want to get dinner?"

She froze. "Do you think that's wise?"

"Why wouldn't it be?" he asked, confused.

"Because of what happened that first time we had dinner."

He took a step closer to her and touched her face. "I'm okay with what happened last time. Victoria, I like being with you, and I think it's safe for us to have dinner together while we wait for the news. How about I cook you dinner?"

"You can cook?" she asked, surprised.

"I can. So what do you think?"

She worried at her bottom lip and then nodded. "That sounds like a plan."

"I'll send you my address. I'm going to leave a bit early today."

"Why?" she asked.

"I have to buy some groceries to actually make you dinner. Unless you have affinity for warm beer and a half bag of crackers."

She chuckled. "Send me your address and the time you want me there."

"I will. Try not to stress about the domino. Have faith."

"No promises."

Matthew nodded and left the room.

He wasn't sure what he was doing, but he was going to take a chance.

It didn't have to mean anything other than two friends getting together.

That was it.

His heart didn't have to get involved—even though he was pretty sure that his heart was already in serious danger.

CHAPTER TEN

THE CAB DROPPED her off at the bottom of Matthew's hilly driveway. Thankfully it wasn't long, and she walked up the hill to a white stucco-walled house with a red roof. It was cute and modest. It was completely different than the house he'd grown up in.

As in, it wasn't a castle. It wasn't a showpiece.

It blended in with Charlotte Amalie like it belonged, and you wouldn't even really notice it was there unless you looked for it.

It really suited him. He might have called himself uptight, but she didn't see that side of Matthew. Or maybe it was that she was the one who was the most rigid and he seemed mellow in comparison.

That thought made her smile.

Matthew's home kind of reminded her of the pool house on St. Croix. It was red and white against the lush green that grew up the volcanically formed island. The roof was a bright cherry red that stuck out from the green that climbed and grew around it.

After Matthew had suggested they have dinner, she'd gone straight back to her place and changed out of her work clothes and into a flowing black dress that she had bought in the local marketplace.

The air was so humid, and she needed something breezy tonight. Something she could feel comfortable in. And she needed to feel comfortable. Something was in the air, and she was a bundle of nerves.

She wasn't sure what or if anything would happen, but at least she wouldn't be dying of heat in her work clothes.

She knocked on the door, and Matthew answered it.

"Hi," he greeted her. "Come on in."

She stepped inside and was shocked at the inside of his home. From the outside it looked like a small house built onto the side of the hill, like all the other homes in the neighborhood.

It was like an optical illusion. Tiny on the outside, large and spacious on the inside.

"This is beautiful and so deceptive."

"Deceptive? That's a word I've never heard to describe my house before."

She chuckled. "What I mean was I wasn't expecting it to be so big!"

He waggled his eyebrows. "Well…"

Victoria groaned and then laughed at his joke. "Ugh, you know what I mean."

"I do, but I can have some fun, can't I?" His eyes were twinkling, and she had butterflies in her stomach. This was the Matthew she remembered from the first time she'd met him.

"You sound like your brother when you say stuff like that."

Matthew winced. "Like a dagger to my heart."

"Oh, stop. Really, though, this is gorgeous and not what I expected."

Matthew smiled. "It's built up the hillside. It was

a wreck when I bought it, but it helped with my grief. Work at the hospital during the day, renovating at night."

"You bought this place after your wife died?"

He nodded. "We had a small condo and it reminded me of her pain and her suffering. I couldn't stay there."

"I get that."

"We're really getting into a depressing subject, aren't we?"

She laughed nervously. "Yes. It's been stressful enough recently, and I really don't want to add to it while we wait to see if the new donor is viable."

"Agreed. Let's have dinner al fresco tonight," Matthew suggested.

"That sounds great."

Even though it was humid, there was a nice breeze as the sun was setting. Matthew's house was modern and open. It was a blend of contemporary and that old Caribbean vibe.

Dark wood and white.

She followed him through an open set of French doors out onto a secluded patio surrounded by green fronds, flowers and vines, intermixed with twinkle lights. Almost like a secret garden that was tucked away.

"Not as stunning as a sea view on a mountain, but it's a quiet retreat in the city."

As if he had to explain. If she had to choose in this moment, she would pick his home, tucked away in the city, over the castle on the hill on St. Croix.

"It's beautiful," she murmured. There was a trickling, bubbling sound of water from a fountain. It was perfect.

"I do have a sea-slash-city view from my room,

but sometimes you just need a quiet place to think. If you follow those stairs down, I also have a small private beach."

"A private beach sounds wonderful."

"It's really peaceful."

"Yes," she sighed. "I could do with that tonight."

Matthew pulled out her chair and she sat down.

"Would you like some wine? Nonalcoholic, of course, just in case we get a call!"

"Yes, please."

He poured her a glass of sparkling white and sat down across from her.

"Do you have your phone on?" he asked.

"I do. Not that I can rush into surgery tonight if it was a match, no matter how much I want to. Everyone needs to be present and ready to make it work, but as soon as we have a kidney, I'll start calling everyone in to get it started."

"Marcus is more than ready," Matthew mumbled.

"I know. He's made a lot of this possible."

A strange look crossed his face. "Marcus likes you, you know."

"What?" she asked, laughing nervously.

"He told me," he stated firmly.

Heat unfurled in her belly. Was he jealous?

"I like Marcus, too, but not in that way. As soon as I knew he wasn't you, I stepped away from him."

"Really?" he asked. "Why? Most women like him."

"He's not the brother I cared for." Her pulse was pounding between her ears, and she was trembling.

Had she really just said that?

Even when they were together in New York, she

had never really told him how she felt about him. She'd never told Mathew that she cared for him.

That she loved him.

That she thought she still might.

It killed her that she did, because nothing could come from it. She could put her heart on the line, but she wouldn't risk his.

Her life was in New York. It was not here in St. Thomas.

Why can't it be?

She shook that thought away. She wasn't going to follow a man or put her heart on the line, no matter how much she wanted to.

And she did want to.

He gazed at her, his eyes mesmerizing her, and she was frozen, unable to move—not that she wanted to.

She yearned for him.

Even after all this time, she wanted him. Nothing had changed.

"He said you're interested in me and I should go for it," he whispered.

"Should you?" she asked, breathlessly.

"Should I?"

Her breath quickened, and she laughed nervously. "So I suppose he knows about our past, then?"

"No."

"No?"

"What we had, what we shared, isn't anyone else's business. It's my memories, and he doesn't deserve to know. I don't want to share that with him."

It was getting harder to breathe. "So what did you tell him?"

A smile tugged at the corner of his lips. "Nothing."

"I see."

"Why did you want to kiss me?" he asked softly, his voice husky and full of a promise she wanted desperately to indulge in.

She wanted to be with him.

He stood and knelt in front of her. "I've wanted to kiss you every day since you first arrived back here."

"Have you?" Her voice caught in her throat.

He nodded. "You broke me when you ended things."

Her heart shattered, knowing that she had hurt him. She had known he was angry, but she hadn't realized he was actually hurt by it. She'd beens hurt, too, when he left and didn't fight for her, but it was her choice to stay and take that job, so she didn't feel like she had the right to be angry.

"I never wanted to hurt you. I thought you were mad and I thought it was about the position in New York."

"It was never about that," he said.

"You know that's all that mattered to me. I told you that right from the beginning."

"I know, but I couldn't help it. I fell for you. For so long after it ended, I was mad. I didn't understand why you chose the job over me, but I understand why now."

Tears stung her eyes. "I never wanted to make you feel that way. Against my better judgment, I cared for you. I don't think I've ever stopped."

"You've haunted my soul for ten years."

She swallowed the lump in her throat. She reached out and touched his face. "I've never stopped thinking about you, either, Matthew. And I think you know why I wanted to kiss you. I have missed you, but I need you to know that I'm going back to New York when this is all over. That hasn't changed. My life is there, and I don't want to hurt you again."

He nodded. "I know, and I don't want anything more. I just want one more night with you. One more night to lay the ghost of us to rest."

She bent over and kissed him. A light kiss as she trembled with anticipation.

She didn't know what she was doing. All she knew was she wanted him.

Even if was it was just temporary. Maybe he was right and this last time would be closure.

As he said, it was laying the ghost of them to rest.

She wanted tonight.

She wanted to be with him again.

His hands slipped into her hair as the kiss deepened, and she melted into the hot desire that had been bubbling under the surface for years. Matthew was all she'd ever wanted, and she had always been too scared to reach out and take him.

She'd ruined it, but she could have this with him. One more moment of absolute pleasure.

His hands moved down her back, and he broke the kiss only for a moment to effortlessly scoop her up into his arms and carry her into his house. It was a few stairs up to the loft bedroom, and a zing of excitement went through her as she spied the large four-poster mahogany bed. The kind she'd pictured making love to him in.

He set her down, and she ran her hands over him, slipping her fingers under his shirt to touch him and reveling in the feel of goose bumps on his skin as she traced her fingers over his flat stomach.

"Are you sure you truly want this, Victoria?" he

asked, leaning his forehead against hers, his arms around her.

"Yes. As long as you have protection, then yes, I want this, Matthew."

I've missed you.

Yet she couldn't bring herself to say those words out loud. She kept them locked away inside. She was still too afraid to tell him, to risk her heart.

But she could have this.

"Yes. I have protection."

"And you want me, too?" she asked, kissing his neck.

He chuckled. "I do."

He cupped her face, kissing her again as she unbuttoned his shirt.

She wanted nothing between them. She just wanted them together. Skin to skin.

For one night she'd feel safe again, with his arms around her.

His hands trailed over her body, touching her, and she responded, even though the light silk of her dress separated them. Her nipples puckered as he cupped her breast. Her body was quivering with desire.

He undid her dress, pushing it over her shoulders. It pooled at her feet. She was naked save her black lace underwear.

"Victoria," he murmured as he brushed her hair to the side and kissed her neck, running his hands over her exposed skin.

She shivered in delight.

There was no turning back now. Not that she wanted to.

This was what she had dreamed about in her darkest hours for the last ten years when she was alone, missing him.

She pulled off his shirt, baring his sun-bronzed chest, and then worked on his belt. He sucked in his breath and gripped her wrists, pushing her against the mattress.

She cried out in delight, and he grinned as he moved over her and kissed her.

His kisses trailed from her mouth then down over her body to her breasts, his tongue igniting her blood as he captured one of her nipples with a kiss.

She cried out.

"Protection," she murmured, reminding him again.

He grinned lazily. "Right."

He moved and pulled a condom out of the nightstand drawer.

She sat up. "Let me."

Matthew moaned as she rolled the condom over him. She liked touching him, teasing him the same way he'd teased her.

"You're torturing me," he murmured.

She laughed. "I know."

He pushed her back down, slipping off her underwear, and this time his kisses trailed lower and she cried out when his tongue touched her between her legs. Her body burned for him to fill her.

To take her.

She arched against his mouth.

"Please," she whispered.

"As you wish." Matthew settled between her thighs, and their gazes locked as he entered her. She moaned as he filled her, her legs locking around his hips, not wanting to let him go. He moved so slowly, gently, taking his time when all she wanted was fast.

Hard.

She wanted him to take her.

It had been so long and she was hungry for him. He quickened his pace in response to her hips urging him to take her like she wanted. Pleasure began to unfurl in the pit of her stomach, and she tightened her hold on his back, her nails digging into his skin.

She cried out as heady pleasure washed through her.

Even though she wanted it this way, she wanted it to last forever.

She didn't want this to end.

Matthew came soon after her, resting against her as he caught his breath. He rolled away, but he pulled her with him, not letting her go as he held her.

Victoria clung to him, not wanting this to end as she listened to the comforting sound of his heart.

Her eyes were stinging, full of tears that she wouldn't shed. She couldn't let them come.

She couldn't risk her heart or his.

So she swallowed the tears down.

Instead, she just reveled in this moment with the man she now knew she had always loved.

The man she wouldn't—couldn't—ever let herself have.

CHAPTER ELEVEN

MATTHEW COULDN'T QUITE believe that had happened. He'd dreamed about this happening again for so long, but he was never sure that it would.

He'd thought Victoria was his past, never his future.

She still isn't. Don't get attached.

He'd dreamed about it happening so many times over the years, because he missed her, but he hadn't thought that he would ever see her again.

He'd made his peace with that and moved on.

Then he'd lost his wife.

And he was left alone, with just the memories of the two women he'd loved more than anything haunting him.

It was like some kind of dream when she told him that she still wanted him. And it was a dream that he didn't want to end, even though he knew it was going to.

She had told him that it would.

She was going back to New York.

At least this time he would be prepared for it. He wouldn't be blindsided, and he wouldn't be hurt when she left.

Liar.

His heart wanted more, even though he couldn't have more. He was angry with himself for falling for her again. For setting himself up for more pain.

She rested her chin on her fists and stared at him. Those deep brown eyes were so mesmerizing, and all his anger at himself melted away. All that mattered was being with her in this moment.

"What?" he asked, still touching her back as they lay there in the dark.

"Did you actually cook dinner or was it all a ruse to get me into bed?" she teased.

Her little joke broke the tension, the anxiety he was feeling in those fleeting moments.

He laughed. "I did plan a light dinner, but I hadn't started cooking it yet. Maybe a part of me was subconsciously hoping this would happen."

Victoria grinned. "I'm glad that it did."

"Me, too. Shall we try and make something of dinner?" he asked, even though he didn't want to get out of bed. He wanted to stay here forever with her.

"That sounds good." She got up and he watched her, his body stirring with desire as she padded across the room and pulled on her clothing. She tied back her long, soft hair.

He got up and sneaked up behind her, wrapping his arms around her to kiss her slender neck.

"I thought you were hungry?" she asked.

"I am, but not for food." And he kissed her neck again.

"Stop." She laughed, pushing him away, but he wasn't so easily put off.

He wanted her again.

They had said only one night, and the night was not over.

He pulled off her dress and pushed her against the wall, kissing her, touching her.

The phone rang then, like a shrill harpy, and he groaned, annoyed by whoever was disrupting him.

"It could be about the surgery," she reminded him, but there was disappointment in her voice.

"Why are they calling me, then?" he grumbled.

She pulled her phone out of her purse. "My phone's dead."

"Fine. I'll answer," he groused.

"You really have no choice."

He nodded and let her go. He pulled on his trousers and made his way downstairs to answer the phone.

"Dr. Olesen speaking."

"Hi, Dr. Olesen, it's Dr. Gainsbourg. I was trying to call Dr. Jensen, but she's not answering."

"It's okay. Her phone is dead. What do you need, Dr. Gainsbourg?"

"The new donor has been approved and cleared."

"Great." Matthew gave Victoria thumbs-up, and she mouthed a silent thank-you to the ceiling.

"Mrs. Van Luven and Jonas Fredrick have both taken a turn for the worse, so we need to prep them for surgery. The domino needs to happen now."

Matthew's heart sank. "I see."

"Do you want me to call the others in? We have two donors and three recipients here already in Charlotte Amalie."

"I'll pass you over to Dr. Jensen. It's her surgery." Matthew handed her the phone.

"What's going on?" Victoria asked, and he watched her face, but it was unreadable.

Calm.

Collected.

A true surgeon.

And he couldn't help but admire her. He loved her. He always had. He just couldn't have her.

His life was here, and hers was in New York. She would leave him again.

Maybe they won't want her back?

That idea thrilled him, but it was hard to believe. She was an excellent surgeon. It was why she'd earned that coveted position ten years ago. The autopsy findings had cleared her of any fault, so the press would soon move on from what had happened and no one would care anymore.

Her life could go back to normal.

"Get them all in and schedule the operating rooms as early as you can." Victoria hung up and worried her bottom lip.

"So we're doing the domino?" he asked.

She nodded. "First we eat. We need food."

He grinned. "And then straight to the hospital to start prepping."

Victoria smiled. "Marcus has already admitted himself."

Matthew rolled his eyes at the impertinence of his brother, but something else struck him. The stark reality that his brother could die.

That his twin was putting his life on the line for another.

He shook that thought away. "Eager, isn't he?"

"Are you ready?" Victoria asked.

"As long as you handle Marcus's harvest, I can work on Mrs. Van Luven."

She nodded. "This will work. Your staff are ready."

"I know." He took her in his arms, even though he knew he should keep his distance. Her month was almost up. She'd soon be gone from his life. "Thank you for helping me. Thank you for coming here and organizing this."

"I didn't have a choice. Remember?" she murmured.

"I know, but I'm glad it's you here." He let her go, even though he didn't want to.

It felt like she was already slipping away. Like his dream was melting with the dawn.

"Go have a shower. I'll get dinner ready," he said.

She nodded and headed to the bathroom.

Matthew sighed and started the coffee machine, because he had a feeling they were going to need it.

After a quick bite to eat where they talked of nothing but the procedure, they headed to the hospital and were there in time to get the first arrivals admitted. All the other elective surgeries had been postponed and the surgical floor was mobilized, primed and ready for the procedure.

They arrived at the hospital at three in the morning, and the first surgery was slated for six.

There was a buzz of anxiety and excitement in the air. A few of the local newspapers had started sending reporters as news got out the domino was about to take place.

Ziese Memorial Hospital was a new hospital in Charlotte Amalie, and this surgery was a first for the hospital. There was also the fact that Dr. Victoria Jensen was the lead surgeon.

Matthew had been expecting it. He was worried it would affect Victoria, but the attention didn't seem to faze her.

A whiteboard in the unit laid out the procedure so that all staff could see where each patient was going and which surgeon was involved. Six donors and six recipients. Matthew's stomach did a flip-flop to see Marcus's name up there on the board.

He was up first.

He's a grown man.

But he couldn't help but be worried about his twin as he stared at Marcus's picture.

What would he do if he lost him? He'd never really thought about it before, and it was an unwelcome thought that made him sick to his stomach.

When Marcus had said he wanted a brother, Matthew realized he wanted a brother, too. Only he hadn't said that, and if Marcus died, he would lose the chance to tell him.

He would lose someone else he cared about.

"It'll be okay," Victoria said from where she was standing beside him, as if sensing his apprehension.

Only a few hours ago, they had been wrapped up in each other's arms. Now they were standing on the precipice of a historical surgery. A complicated surgery that relied on so many moving parts.

"I'm glad you're handling Marcus and Jonas," he said. And he was. There was no one else he would trust more.

"And I'm glad you've got Mrs. Van Luven. I wouldn't

trust anyone else but you with her," she said. "You're my right-hand surgeon."

"Thanks."

"Have you gone to see Marcus?" she asked.

"No." He swallowed the lump in his throat.

"You should. He'll need support after this is done. You're his family."

"Hardly. He's never really needed me."

And when have you needed him?

Matthew was keenly aware of how many times he'd pushed Marcus away...

"I can help," Marcus said. "We can talk. I'm here."

"Talk about what?" Matthew snapped.

"You're grieving."

"Don't. You know nothing about my pain. You know nothing about heartache. You bounce from woman to woman. What do you know of love?"

Marcus frowned. "Fine. You don't need me. I get it. I don't need you, either, but you're wrong about me."

"Am I?" Matthew asked.

"Yes. I've known heartache. I've known grief. But it's obvious you don't care, because you notice nothing around you. Just yourself."

After that Marcus had pushed him away for good, made it clear he didn't need Matthew.

Just like Victoria didn't really need him.

Go, a little voice told him. Only he couldn't. He was too ashamed of his stubbornness.

Victoria looked at him, unsure. "Are you sure you don't want to go see him? I'm about to wheel him into surgery."

"I'm sure. He's a grown man, and he won't want to see me before he goes under the knife."

There was a part of him worried for his twin.

This was major surgery.

Marcus was doing something very unselfish for what, Matthew felt, was the first time in his life. Matthew had spent so many years trying to look out for Marcus, thinking his brother couldn't take care of himself.

Clearly he'd been wrong.

No wonder Marcus didn't want to be around him.

He wasn't a very good brother or a very good friend.

Right now, though, he had to focus on saving a life. Marcus was in good hands. He had to focus on Mrs. Van Luven.

Victoria wanted to do the laparoscopic approach, which was a longer surgery than the open procedure but would be better for recovery. Although open surgery was always an option if things went bad.

Matthew's heart sank.

He hoped things didn't go bad.

Marcus was wheeled into the operating room just as Victoria was getting her gown on and the scrub nurses prepped the surgical field.

She knew Matthew was in the next operating room prepping Mrs. Van Luven to receive Marcus's kidney, and he was putting all his trust in her to take care of his twin brother. She was shocked he hadn't wanted to see Marcus first, but Matthew was stubborn.

Victoria hoped Marcus had that same stubborn streak. It would help him during recovery.

Once she had Marcus's kidney out, it would go to

Mrs. Van Luven, and then the next donor would be wheeled in.

Each step was precise in its movement.

It would be a long, grueling day as this multistep surgery was performed.

As she stepped into the operating room, she did what she knew Matthew always did—something she never did—and that was to take in a deep breath and breathe in the energy.

The life that swirled through these hallowed halls. The life on the table that was in her hands.

"Vic, are you here yet?" There was a hint of nervousness in Marcus's voice.

"I'm here," Victoria responded. As she approached the surgical table, she saw there was fear in his eyes, those eyes that were so similar to Matthew's, but also different. She smiled at him, even though he couldn't see it behind her surgical mask. "I thought Matthew told you I didn't like being called Vic."

He grinned. "I'm sorry. I'm nervous. Doctors can be anxious, too."

"It's okay. I don't care if you call me Vic. Actually, I like it from you."

"You do?" he asked.

"Yes, because it's you. And I like you, Marcus."

He smiled. "I knew I'd like you, too, Vic. Just make sure my pigheaded brother knows it's okay I can call you that. I don't need him on my case."

"I promise. He does care about you. He doesn't mean to always be on your case."

Marcus snorted—just like Matthew did, she noticed—then he frowned. "There's a lot of press out there."

"I know," she said dryly.

"I know why. I read your story."

Her heart skipped a beat, her blood running cold. "You shouldn't worry about that."

"I'm not," Marcus said. "I know that was beyond your control. I know you're an excellent surgeon. It's why my brother loves you."

She swallowed a lump in her throat, trying not to react to what he was saying. "They start painkillers early here, I see."

She was trying to deflect from the truth.

He grinned. "I trust you, Vic. I'm in good hands."

"Thanks."

The anesthesiologist took over then, and Marcus was put under.

Victoria took a deep, calming breath as she stared at the surgical field.

You've got this. You've done this before.

She was a good surgeon.

The ambassador's surgery might have had a sad outcome, but she had never once doubted her surgical abilities.

She knew who she was and what she was capable of.

This was Matthew's twin, and she was going to keep him safe and make sure this gift he was giving was put to good use in saving a life.

"Scalpel."

The scrub nurse handed her what she needed as Victoria drowned out everything else.

She knew this surgery well.

She'd done it numerous times before. That was why she was the best transplant surgeon in New York. That was why the ambassador had come to her hospital and wanted her, and as she worked she thought about all the lives that would be saved because this domino was taking place.

All the happy families that wouldn't lose a loved one.

Not that she knew anything about that, but she got a high from saving lives. This was why she'd wanted to be a surgeon. It wasn't the money.

It wasn't the business.

It was helping people.

Marcus's kidney was beautiful and healthy. She removed it and placed it on ice, dousing it with preservation solution as she closed up the artery.

It was then that history came to bite her in the butt one more time as fate decided that this was the moment to test her. The monitors tracking Marcus's vitals sounded the alarm.

"His sats are dropping. Blood pressure is low," the anesthesiologist stated.

Her pulse thundered between her ears as the artery began to bulge and bleed. There was a clot.

"Come on, Marcus. A clot. Really?"

The urgent beeping of the monitors echoed in her head, but this time she refused to freeze up. This was Matthew's twin. She wasn't going to let him die.

The flat-line echo dissipated, and she continued her work, finding the clot and evacuating it. The bleeding slowed, and monitor's alarms ceased.

"Blood pressure is rising to normal. The patient is stable."

"Good." Her voice shook as she finished the repair. Her whole body apart from her hands shook, but she didn't have time to give in to that anxious energy.

Marcus was stable, and she had a kidney to deliver.

"Dr. Gainsbourg, please finish up here," she said, hoping her voice didn't shake.

"Yes, Dr. Jensen."

Marcus was doing well now, and she had to prep for the next surgery. She wanted to bring Mrs. Van Luven's new kidney to Matthew and let him know that Marcus was okay. She might not understand their sibling dynamic, but she wanted him to know that everything was fine. His brother would recover.

She carried the kidney into the next operating room, where Matthew was working over Mrs. Van Luven.

Matthew looked up as she came in.

"I was expecting you sooner," he said.

"There was a complication."

Matthew's eyes widened. "What?"

"A clot at the suture line. It's fine now, though."

"He's okay then?" he asked, and she could hear the fear in his voice.

"He's excellent. Is Mrs. Van Luven ready for her new kidney?"

"More than ready," Matthew responded.

Victoria handed the kidney off to the resident assisting Matthew. She then stayed to watch, as she had some time before the next procedure because Jonas's donor had only just been taken into the theater.

She watched as Matthew gently lifted his brother's kidney and grafted it into Mrs. Van Luven's body. She leaned over, watching with trepidation as they waited for the pink color to return to the kidney as Matthew finished suturing it into place and removed the clamp.

Victoria held her breath as Matthew nudged the kidney with his finger. Pink flooded the organ as blood began to flow, and there was a small spout of urine, which was a good sign.

"Excellent work, Dr. Olesen."

"Thank you, Dr. Jensen." Matthew smiled, and she felt relief.

Victoria left the operating room.

Her day of surgery had only just begun, but this was a great start to a long day.

An excellent start in her books.

And things were looking brighter than she'd thought they would.

When Matthew finished with Mrs. Van Luven, he went on to the next procedure, even though all he'd wanted to do since Victoria had told him about the clot was to rush to the intensive care unit and check on Marcus. His life with his brother flashed before his eyes, and he regretted all those years they'd wasted fighting.

Marcus was stable, and Matthew knew his brother would kill him if he didn't stay and finish the domino.

And he couldn't let his team down.

He wouldn't let Victoria down.

It was a long day, and he was out of the practice of doing back-to-back surgeries, but he wouldn't be anywhere else. This was where he belonged, working alongside Victoria.

Except she doesn't want to stay.

The world would know soon this domino had been a success, and she'd leave. She'd made it quite clear that when New York called, she'd be gone.

The donors were stable in the postoperative care unit, and he had heard that Marcus had been taken to his own room.

Matthew stretched his back and wandered the halls looking for Victoria, but he couldn't find her, and he had to go speak to the press about the surgery soon.

Eventually he found her in the doctors' lounge. She was leaning against a wall with her eyes closed, and she looked exhausted.

"There you are," he said, his heart melting. She'd done so well today. So many lives saved. He wished she would stay for their hospital. He wished she would stay for him.

Only he couldn't ask her to do that.

She opened one eye and looked at him. "If you're looking for your usual celebratory sex session, keep moving. I need sleep."

He chuckled. "The thought had crossed my mind."

She smiled weakly. "How is everyone?"

"Stable. Doing well. Including Marcus."

"Have you gone to see him?" she asked wearily.

"No. I will soon, though."

"Good."

"The press wants to speak with us."

Victoria groaned. "Of course they do."

"I could speak to them alone so that you can go and sleep?"

"Would you mind?" she asked.

He shook his head. "No. Not at all. I'm the chief of surgery—this is my usual job."

"I would, but I just don't want questions about the ambassador. I told them what happened, but that doesn't seem to matter to the press. I don't want anything to do with them."

"Go. Sleep. I've got this."

She nodded. "I'm headed to an on-call room, so

AMY RUTTAN 165

that's where you can find me if needed. I'm not leaving here until everyone is out of the intensive care unit."

Victoria shuffled off to an on-call room, and Matthew made his way to the hospital media room.

The press would be disappointed. He knew it was her they wanted to speak to, and only because of what had happened in New York, but he didn't want the world to focus on what she had done in the past. He wanted them to focus on the good she'd done today.

Maybe you need to let go of the past, too?

He shook that niggling thought away as he straightened his white lab coat and headed into a room of reporters.

CHAPTER TWELVE

VICTORIA TRIED TO SLEEP, but her phone kept pinging, and finally she was forced to give up and opened her email instead. There were messages from Paul and the board of directors at the hospital saying she'd been cleared to come back and take up her practice again. Which annoyed her. Was it only because she'd "redeemed" herself with the domino that they wanted her back?

They weren't begging her to return when the autopsy had first cleared her.

Not that she would've abandoned the domino.

It was almost like the board had been waiting to see how this surgery played out.

It felt like they weren't really on her side.

It made her angry.

Going back to New York City was everything she'd wanted since she first came to St. Thomas.

So why was Matthew the only thing she could think about now?

Maybe because he had faith in you all along.

Matthew was the type of guy who wanted forever, and she wasn't sure she could ever give anyone that.

You could if you weren't so afraid.

And she was.

She was terrified of relying on someone else or having someone rely on her. She didn't want to let him down. She wouldn't hurt anyone if it was only her. She would only have to worry about herself, and if she died she wouldn't leave anyone behind. No one would have to mourn her.

Miss her.

There would be no children who could be lost in the foster system the way she'd been. Even if part of her wanted that family.

A home.

She wanted it all, but she was terrified of losing it if she took the chance. She was terrified Matthew would leave her.

He'd left her once before.

She set her phone down and curled up on her side, trying to sleep. She couldn't, even though she was bone weary.

In the dark of the small on-call room, she felt like she was that frightened kid again.

Alone.

No one to love her and yearning for a family.

She'd broken Matthew's heart ten years ago. If he did love her, she'd ruined it then, but she was glad they were still friends.

She didn't need any more than that.

Liar.

Except she did.

There was a knock at the door, and Matthew peeked his head in the room.

"You awake?" he asked.

"Yeah. I couldn't sleep," she said.

Which wasn't a lie. She couldn't. All she could think about was having to leave Matthew, how she'd ruined things ten years ago, and there was a part of her that was wondering how her life would've been different had she chosen another path. If she'd chosen love over her career. How much had been wasted because of her fear of the unknown?

"Press conference is over. The world knows you are a success again."

"Thanks." And she meant it.

Matthew always seemed to come to her rescue.

She didn't deserve a guy like him.

He came in and shut the door. "I checked on Mrs. Van Luven."

"Oh?"

"She's putting out yellow urine and her creatinine is the best I've seen it since she was admitted."

A thrill surged through her. "That's wonderful."

"I thought that would please you. Her family is ecstatic."

A lump formed in her throat. Mrs. Van Luven had a family waiting for her. Every single one of her recipients and donors had someone that cared for them, because even though Matthew didn't want to admit it, he cared for his brother, Marcus.

If it was her, she would have no one to lean on.

She never had anyone to lean on.

You have Matthew.

Except she didn't. She couldn't stay here and risk her heart.

She had to go back to New York City.

She was glad for her patients, though. Their lives

were saved, their families made whole, and that's why she was a surgeon.

She might be alone, but she saved lives.

"I'm glad they're happy." She patted the spot on the bed next to her. She wanted him to join her. Though she shouldn't tempt fate, she wanted him again. To forget her loneliness, the sadness that her time here was almost over.

She wanted to make love with Matthew one last time before she headed back to New York City and her empty, lonely life.

Before the phone had rung, before the surgery, they had been headed back to bed, and just thinking about his hands on her, his mouth kissing her everywhere, fired her senses.

Tonight, she wanted him one more time.

Matthew sat down next to her, and she leaned against him. He stroked her back.

"Thank you for all your help," she whispered.

"You were amazing. You're such a talented surgeon. I'm in awe of you." He touched her face, and her body trembled under his gentle caress.

"I still couldn't have done it without you."

You're my everything.

Only she couldn't say that out loud. So instead she kissed him, putting all the things she couldn't say into that kiss.

"Victoria," he murmured against her lips.

"I need you, Matthew."

And she did. Not just for this night. She wanted him always, but she was too scared to take a chance and grab forever.

Matthew stood and locked the door, peeling off his

white lab coat as she pulled off her scrubs. She wanted hot and heavy tonight.

Her body trembled with need, her pulse racing with anticipation, knowing what was to come.

She was ready for him.

Her body craved him, and even though she shouldn't do this, she tried to tell herself this would be the perfect goodbye. As he'd said before, a way to lay the ghost of them to rest.

Or wake the beast.

It didn't take long to get out of their scrubs, and soon she was in his arms, his lips on hers as he pressed her against the wall.

"Dammit," he cursed.

"What?"

"I don't have protection."

"It's okay. I'm on birth control." She was, and she didn't want to him to stop. She preferred to have both the pill and a condom, but this time she'd just take him.

She wanted to feel all of him.

She needed him.

"Are you sure?" he asked.

"Positive."

His hand slipped between them as he pressed her against the wall. He was touching her, causing zings of heady pleasure to zip through her body. She reached down to touch him. He was hard and ready for her.

Matthew hefted her up, and she wrapped her legs around his waist as he thrust into her.

"Why do I want you?" he moaned against her neck. "You consume my every thought."

"I want you, too," she murmured against his lips as he thrust into her again.

She wanted to tell him how she felt. She wanted Matthew to know that she loved him and that she had always loved him.

She couldn't form the words, so she reveled in the feeling of him taking her the way she'd always wanted.

"Victoria, you feel so good," he moaned.

"Don't stop," she cried, holding on to him.

She was weak when it came to him. She always had been. Victoria though she was strong, but she wasn't. The tears stung her eyes again, and she didn't want to cry.

Not now.

Not with him buried inside her.

She came quickly, and he followed her. Her body felt boneless.

The tears started flowing then. She couldn't hold them back anymore. She was lost to him, and it scared her. She hated this and loved it at the same time.

"Victoria?" he whispered. "Are you okay?"

"No." She brushed the tears away. "I'm tired, Matthew."

What she didn't say was she was tired of being alone. She was tired of fighting her feelings for him.

Matthew kissed her lips softly as he carried her to the bed.

They curled up side by side, and he ran his hands over her, stroking her.

"Why don't you sleep?" he asked.

"I don't want to sleep."

If she slept, then she'd wake up and the dream would end. It would all be over, and she didn't want that. She never wanted to wake up, so she kissed him again. Slow and lingering, igniting her desire, her need again. Matthew was the only one she wanted.

The only one.

She was ruined.

"Victoria, I can't get enough of you."

"Do you want me to stop?" she asked as she stroked him.

"God, no."

The rational part of her told her to end it, but she couldn't. She never wanted this to end. She wanted forever, but she was terrified by what that would mean. She was terrified of what might happen.

Matthew dozed off with Victoria in his arms. It felt so right holding her and being with her.

What're you doing?

He was setting himself up for heartache. The whole world now knew she had successfully done the domino surgery. It was only a matter of time before she headed back to New York. She'd made it clear that that was where her life was. And he didn't want his heart to be broken again.

He also wasn't sure he could ever take a chance on love again. Losing Victoria and Kirsten in one lifetime was enough heartache.

"You awake?" she asked.

"I am."

She sat up. "We have to talk."

"I know."

She raised her eyebrows. "Do you?"

"New York got ahold of you, didn't they?" A shiver of dread ran down his spine.

This was it.

He was expecting it, but he was angry it was here and happening again. She was choosing New York over him.

"Yes. They want me to come back as soon as possible. Apparently they have a domino they need me to organize."

"Right." He got out of bed and started pulling on his clothes. His stomach felt like a rock, and he cursed himself for getting wrapped up with her again.

He was a fool.

"Well, we both said this was temporary."

Victoria looked disappointed. "Right."

"When do they want you back?"

"There's a flight out in the morning."

"And what about the patients in the intensive care unit?" he asked coldly.

"What about them? They're stable and in a good hospital," she replied. "I told you I'd stay for the surgery. I did."

"Okay." He finished getting dressed.

"Okay?" she asked, sounding a bit confused. "Don't you want me to stay until the patients are more stable?"

"You don't need to. We can handle it."

"I think I should stay."

"Why? It's okay to go, Victoria. I'm giving you an out. I mean, that's what you want. You want an out."

Although he didn't want her to take it, he couldn't ask her to stay, not when he knew she didn't want it. He could see that. New York came first; her career came first.

"An out? I see," she said quietly.

"Don't you want to go back to New York? That's

what you've always wanted. That's why you ended things ten years ago."

"You know why I took that job! You grew up privileged with a family who loved you. I had nothing."

"I didn't know that then."

"You know it now. Nothing has changed, Matthew."

"Hasn't it, Victoria?"

"No. I have no one. I had no one."

"You had me."

"That wasn't enough." Her voice shook. "I needed that job."

"More than me."

"Yes," she admitted. "Love isn't a sure thing. Besides, you didn't stay for me. You left me, too."

"Well, then you need to go back. New York is important to you. You don't need to worry about me. I moved on from you once before and I can do it again."

She pulled on her clothes. "That's it?"

"What more do you want?"

"I don't know. I didn't realize how much I had hurt you. I'm sorry."

"I'm okay," he said. "I'll be okay. I knew what I was getting into."

"I don't think you are. You've been hurt, and you lost Kirsten."

"Don't," he warned. "I'm fine. We didn't make any promises, Victoria. You're free to go."

She nodded, but her lips wobbled. "Well then, if I'm free to go… I will."

Victoria pushed past him and out of the on-call room.

His heart ached watching her leave. He didn't want

her to go, but he couldn't let her stay here. This was not what she wanted.

New York City was all that mattered, and when she'd come here, back into his life, she hadn't hidden the fact that she wanted to go back as soon as she could.

He was giving her an out.

He was letting her go before he lost her.

Who says you'll lose her?

He shook that thought away. It was too scary to think about anything else. He was cursed when it came to love. He couldn't risk having his heart broken again.

Except that it was.

He still loved her. No matter how much he wanted to deny it, he'd always loved her, and he'd lost her again because he was scared.

Matthew wandered around the hospital for a long time—until the sun came up—thinking about everything, and finally made his way over to the floor where the domino patients were recovering from surgery.

He found his brother's room.

Marcus was sitting up, flicking through the television stations. Matthew walked into his room, and Marcus glanced over at him.

"Hey," Marcus said weakly. He looked pale, and as Matthew picked up his brother's chart, he could see Marcus had lost a lot of blood during the surgery.

His twin had almost died.

Someone else he had been pushing away for far too long.

"How are you feeling?"

"Great. Only because of the painkillers." He winced. "Vic did a great job."

"She did."

"What's wrong?" Marcus asked.

They used to be so close. He was tired of hiding from his twin. He'd missed too much trying to be his brother's keeper instead of being his brother's friend.

"Victoria and I had a fling ten years ago."

Marcus eyes widened. "What?"

"We were residents in Manhattan together. Both of us competing for the same position. She was offered it. She took it and ended our romance. I was broken."

"You loved her?" Marcus asked.

"I did."

Marcus tiled this head and studied him. "You still do."

"I do, but she doesn't love me."

"How do you know? Did you ask her?"

"No, but I know."

"I didn't realize you were omnipotent." Marcus smirked and then winced.

"I know. Trust me. Her career is the most important thing to her. She's going back to New York."

Marcus shook his head. "You're a chicken."

"Excuse me?" Matthew asked.

"Chicken. You're just making an assumption. Why did you leave her the first time? You could've stayed."

"You don't know what you're talking about."

"New York City is a big place. Why didn't you stay there? Get another job? Fight for her then? Instead you left and came home."

"Home is where I met Kirsten."

"And she was wonderful," Marcus said. "But she's gone, and she wouldn't want you to spend the rest of your life miserable. Of course, I've tried to tell you this time and time again, but you think I don't know anything."

"What do you know about love and loss? You bounce from woman to woman."

Marcus's eyes narrowed. "I've loved and lost before. Of course, you wouldn't know because you never talk to me. I've said it before and I'll say it again, you've tried to be my parent rather than my brother."

"I know," Matthew said gently.

Marcus winced, and Matthew checked his chart. He was due for some morphine in his intravenous line. He prepped the vial.

"Oh, great, now you're going to murder me," Marcus said dryly.

"They can detect morphine in an autopsy," Matthew teased, and they shared a smile as he injected the pain-killer into his brother's line.

"Matthew, you love Vic. I think you always have."

It was a simple statement and something else he had been ignoring for so long. He'd thought if he ignored it, he could let go of that pain. It just didn't work that way, though. He'd met Kirsten and was glad for her—he'd loved her deeply—but he'd also never stopped loving Victoria.

His heart had never let her go, no matter how hard he'd tried.

He hated when Marcus was right.

"You're wiser than you let on, Marcus," Matthew teased.

"I know." He grinned, the morphine kicking in.

"I'm sorry I've ignored you and been so distant. You're right, I'm not your father. I will do better. We've missed too much time. I want to be your friend again. When I heard about your complication, I was scared."

"I want to be your friend, too. I don't want you to look out for me. I can take care of myself. I get on your nerves, but I care for you, Matthew. You've been miserable for five years. Just like you were miserable before Kirsten came into your life. I just want you to be happy."

"And if Victoria doesn't want me?"

"Then you'll know," Marcus said groggily.

"Thanks, bud. I'm proud of you, you know."

"Sure, tell me that when you know I won't remember," he mumbled.

Matthew chuckled. "Precisely."

Marcus drifted off to sleep, and Matthew stayed with him awhile before slipping out of his brother's room. He was terrified, but what Marcus had said made sense.

He loved Victoria.

He always had.

He could've stayed in New York, but he'd felt rejected and so he'd left. He was just as stubborn as she was. He didn't know what to do, but he knew one thing was for certain.

He loved Victoria.

Even after all these years, he loved her, and he was willing to get hurt if it meant a chance of having her again.

CHAPTER THIRTEEN

VICTORIA WAS WATCHING the rain out the window. She'd been back in Manhattan for the last three days, and it hadn't stopped.

Just absolutely poured down. It was miserable.

She never used to mind the drizzly weather when she was in New York, but now she missed the sun and sea of St. Thomas, wishing for the green and vibrant colors over the concrete jungle that was currently her view.

Of course, she'd never really paid much attention to the weather when she was in New York—she was always too busy with work.

That's what you wanted.

She'd wasted so much time.

There was a knock at the door, and she turned to see Paul step into the meeting room where she was waiting.

"You looked tanned and rested!" he said brightly.

"Three days ago I did a grueling domino surgery. I'm hardly that rested."

"Well, you looked better than you did when you left," Paul stated.

"I was worried about my career when you suggested I leave and take your place in St. Thomas," she corrected him. "I'm sure I looked a little bit more stressed then."

"That may be, but what you pulled off in a third-world hospital was impressive."

Victoria frowned. "It's not a third-world country. It's part of the United States. You need to educate yourself, Paul. You sound ignorant."

Paul waved his hand. "Whatever, the point was the hospital doesn't have the same kind of facilities that we have here."

Victoria rolled her eyes. She used to listen to Paul so eagerly, but right now she couldn't believe the nonsense that he was spouting. Had she also sounded like that before? All stuck-up and full of herself?

"Ziese Memorial Hospital is state-of-the-art," she said, feeling the need to defend the hospital...and to defend Matthew. She needed to get back to work. If she threw herself into her work, then she could hopefully get her mind off Matthew.

She should've just stayed away from him.

Then she wouldn't have realized how much she still loved him.

Even after all these years.

Why did you leave him again?

Victoria shook that thought away. It didn't matter. What was done was done. She'd walked away from him again, but this time it was him that had pushed her away. She'd tried to reach out and offer to stay longer, but he'd told her to go.

He'd let her know that he didn't want her. Just like what had happened with all her foster parents.

"When can I get back to work, Paul?" she asked.

"Well, we called you back to do a domino, but the

board would like it if you could arrange an even bigger domino surgery!"

She was shocked. "An even bigger one?"

"More than six."

"I'm not sure that's possible. You can't always put those kind of transplant surgeries together. Sometimes the stars just align."

Paul frowned at her. "We're one of the best hospitals on the Eastern seaboard. Everyone comes here for transplant surgery."

"Only the people who can afford it," she said quickly.

"That's why we're opening up spaces for pro bono cases. We want to widen our pool and have you build a domino surgical team that surpasses all other hospitals. Then everyone will forget what happened with the ambassador."

It was like a slap across the face. "You know that it wasn't my fault. You know the complications I encountered, and you know I didn't even want to do that surgery in the first place."

She had been pressured into it by Paul and the board. She could see it now.

And here they were bullying her into something again. Something she didn't want to do because it was for all the wrong reasons.

They didn't care about the patients.

Victoria crossed her arms. "I'm not sure I'm comfortable seeking people to put in a domino, as you suggest. UNOS might have a problem with that."

"Victoria, this is your chance to get back in the good graces of the hospital. The one that started your career. I showed you everything," Paul said, as if she was a naughty child. Well, she was done trying to make him proud of her.

She was done trying please him or impress him.

She was done trying to prove her worth to unworthy people.

She was done trying to hold on to this position she'd won, because she didn't feel like much of a winner right now.

"And I appreciate that, but I can't in good conscience do this."

"What are you saying?" he asked.

Her heart began to race. She wasn't sure what she was saying. This job was everything she'd ever wanted. This was what she'd worked so hard for since she got that first scholarship for medical school. This had been her sole purpose when she was an intern and had fallen in love with transplant surgery.

Victoria hadn't realized that during her years here she'd lost her passion and her love for the surgery and it had become something of a business.

And she hated that.

When did she get like this?

Even though it terrified her, she knew what she had to do. She had to take the risk.

"I can't do it, Paul."

"What do you mean?" he asked, still confused.

"I need the place I work at to support me. If the hospital is only going to support me if I do something specific, something I can't control and something I don't feel comfortable doing, then I have to ask myself, what am I doing here?"

And it was true. She didn't know what she was doing here. Something she never thought she'd say.

"Are you telling me you want to resign?"

"Yes." Her voice shook a little bit. She really couldn't believe she was doing this. Her whole life had been centered around keeping her job, because it was security. She only wanted to rely on herself, because then she would only have herself to disappoint.

Except she was realizing that was no way to live a life.

"Victoria, don't be hasty. Think this through."

"I have thought it through."

She just wished she had figured this out sooner.

"Victoria, see sense," Paul said.

"I have. I quit, and since I can't work out my notice because the board doesn't feel comfortable having me practice, except for doing what they want me to do, I guess I can leave now."

Her hand shook as she took off her identification card and set it down on the table.

Victoria held her head up high and marched out of the office. Her stomach was doing flip-flops, but she knew she was doing the right thing.

Matthew might not want her anymore, but she had to tell him how she felt. She had been a fool, but she was going to put some things right again.

She was going to fly back down to St. Thomas, march into Ziese Memorial Hospital and tell him exactly how she'd felt all these years.

If she wanted any chance at any kind of happily-ever-after, she had to stop being so scared of what might happen. Life was passing her by.

She'd been frozen for so long. She just hadn't realized it.

Victoria collected the rest of her belongings and

walked out of the hospital. She hopped in the first cab she found, which dropped her off in front of her Central Park West apartment.

When she got out of the cab, her heart skipped a beat to see Matthew leaning against the side of the building, his gaze focused on her.

"Matthew?" she asked in disbelief.

"Hi."

"How long have you been standing there?"

He glanced down at his watch. "A couple of hours. Well, I did wander around a bit. I kept coming back and checking with your doorman to see if you'd come back."

Her heart skipped a beat. "You were planning to wait here all day?"

"If I had to." He smiled at her. "Would you like to go for a walk? The rain has stopped."

"Sure." She went up to her doorman, who gladly took the box of her belongings to hold in his office until she got back.

She and Matthew walked silently side by side down the busy sidewalk toward Central Park. The sun was peeking from behind the gloomy clouds.

"Why are you here?" she finally asked.

"Are you upset to see me?"

"No," she said. "Just...surprised."

"Well, I came to offer you a job. Seems my board was pretty mad at me for letting you go back to New York without at least making you an offer."

"You could've emailed your offer to me. You didn't have to come here."

"I know." He grinned. "Marcus also wanted me to

pass on his appreciation for the minimal scarring you left on him. He's quite impressed with your work."

Victoria laughed. "That's a great compliment. I guess."

"From Marcus, yes. It really is."

"Have you two made amends?" she asked.

"Sort of. We have a long way to go, but I think we're on the right track."

"Did you really fly hundreds of miles just to offer me a job and tell me that you and Marcus made up?" she teased.

"And if I did, what would you say?"

"You're crazy!"

He smiled that half smile that she loved so much. "So are you."

"So why did you really come here?"

"I want my transplant surgeon back."

Her heart skipped a beat again. "Just your surgeon?"

"No," he whispered. "I want you back."

She swallowed a lump in her throat. Tears were stinging her eyes. "You want me back?"

Matthew took a step toward her and took her hand in his. "You're trembling."

"A lot has happened today," she whispered.

"I love you, Victoria. I have for a long time, and I shouldn't have left you ten years ago."

"You didn't leave me. I chose a job over you."

Matthew smiled at her, touching her face softly. "I could've stayed in New York. It's a big city. I could've gotten a job at another hospital to stay with you, but I left you. I abandoned you."

"You didn't. I pushed you away. I didn't want a relationship. I just cared about my job. If you had, do you think we would've stayed together? Our relationship started off as sex and competition. Hardly a strong foundation."

"It doesn't matter. I should've stayed. I loved you, and I didn't fight for you. I'm sorry."

A tear slipped down her cheek. "I'm sorry that I chose something superficial over you, because I love you. I've missed you, and I want to start a family with you. I want to be a family with you."

Matthew pulled her into his arms and kissed her.

She sank into him, her heart melting.

"I love you, too, Victoria," he said. "I'll go anywhere to be with you. Even here."

She shook her head. "I want to go back to St. Thomas and work with the best chief of surgery on the island."

He grinned. "Deal, but I have one condition before I can offer you the job."

"Oh?" she asked, curious. "And what's this one condition?"

"Marry me."

"Well, I think that I can take the job with that condition."

Matthew kissed her again. "I love you, Victoria."

"I love you, Matthew."

She took his hand, and they walked back to her place. She was ready to leave New York behind and start her life anew in paradise.

EPILOGUE

One month later, St. Croix

MATTHEW STOOD WAITING for his bride-to-be. His pulse was racing, not because he was nervous, but because this was all he'd ever wanted.

Just him and Victoria.

His parents were watching the wedding from their cruise ship. They'd offered to fly back, but he'd told them there was no need. His parents were loving and supportive, but it was better just him, Victoria, Marcus as their witness and the officiant. No fuss. Just a few people and a gorgeous view, as his parents had given their blessing to use their castle on top of the mountain for their very simple wedding. Not that having it at their castle was simple...

Marcus escorted Victoria out of the house, and Matthew's breath caught in his throat.

She wore a simple white sheath gown, but she was breathtaking because she was his. Marcus nodded, smiling behind his new beard that he'd grown during his recovery so Victoria wouldn't mistakenly try to kiss him again.

He looked like he was still having a bit of pain while

he was walking Victoria down the aisle. It wasn't surprising, as he'd just had surgery a month ago, but Matthew knew Marcus's gift had given a family back a wife and a mother.

And that, to Marcus, was worth every ounce of pain.

Marcus handed Victoria off to him with a wink and sat down.

Matthew took her hand in his and found she was trembling.

"Are you okay?" he whispered.

"Never better." She beamed at him, her dark eyes twinkling as the sun set over the turquoise sea, filling the sky with pink and gold. It was the perfect night, and not because of the sunset, but because Victoria was finally his.

The officiant stepped forward and started speaking, but Matthew couldn't focus on the words coming out of the man's mouth. All he saw was Victoria.

"Do you, Matthew Frederick Olesen, take Victoria Elizabeth Jensen to be your lawfully wedded wife?"

"I do." And he slipped the wedding ring on her finger.

"And do you, Victoria Elizabeth Jensen, take Matthew Frederick Olesen to be your lawfully wedded husband?"

"I do." And she slipped a ring on his finger.

"By the powers vested in me by the United States Virgin Islands, I now pronounce you husband and wife. You may kiss your bride."

Matthew pulled her in his arms and kissed her as Marcus escorted the officiant out.

Matthew wanted his brother to go, too. He had plans

for his wife, and they involved just the two of them, the hot tub and then the bed.

Marcus came back. "The officiant is gone."

"Thank you," Matthew said. "Are you heading back to your boat now?"

Victoria nudged him. "Be nice."

"I am!" Matthew said.

Marcus rolled his eyes. "I'm so happy for you both. You'd better take care of Vic, or I'll kick your ass."

Matthew snorted. "As if!"

"Hey, I may be minus one kidney, but I can still take you," Marcus said.

"There will be no ass kicking today," Victoria stated.

"Why? Because it's your wedding day?" Marcus teased.

"No, because you're still recovering from surgery and I don't want you to mess up my work," she said.

Marcus and Matthew laughed.

"Well, congratulations, guys. I'll come visit in a month or two." Marcus winked and left.

It was just the two of them now. Matthew pulled her close, and they started dancing without any music, just like they did on their first date after she'd come back into his life.

This time he didn't have to fight any of these feelings.

They were together.

Finally.

"Do you want to dance all night?" she asked, teasing him.

"No." And then he kissed her. "I thought we could take this to the hot tub."

She made a face. "That's probably not the best idea."

"Why?" he asked.

"Remember a couple of days ago when I was feeling sick?"

"Yeah."

She looked at him pointedly, expecting him to come to a conclusion, but he couldn't figure out what she was hinting at.

"Matthew, you're a doctor. Think about it."

"I know I…" He trailed off as everything clicked into place. "Are you serious?"

Victoria nodded and kissed him. "Yes. I'm about six weeks."

"Six weeks. That puts us at…"

"I think it happened in the on-call room after the domino surgery. If you recall, you didn't have protection, and the pill is not exactly one hundred percent reliable. We were in a bit of a celebratory, albeit sleep-deprived, mood that night."

"That was a night to celebrate," he said huskily.

"Are you happy? I know kids weren't in our plans right away."

"Ecstatic. I know my parents will be, too." He pulled her into a kiss.

"So since the hot tub is out, do you have any other plans for tonight?" she teased.

"Oh, yes. The hot tub was just plan number one." Matthew scooped her up in his arms, and she laughed.

"So what are your other plans, then?" she asked, wrapping her arms around his neck.

"Just forever." And he kissed her, carrying her off

to the pool house, where he planned to show her just what forever with him looked like.

They were finally a family.

Finally together.

Forever.

* * * * *

A RING FOR HIS PREGNANT MIDWIFE

AMY RUTTAN

MILLS & BOON

For my editor, Julia.

I'll miss working with you.

Thank you for putting up with me these last
couple of months and helping breathe life
into Marcus and Matthew.

CHAPTER ONE

MARCUS WINCED AS he tried to climb out of the narrow bed on his sailboat. He was eight weeks past his transplant surgery, but the incision was still healing.

His new sister-in-law, Dr. Victoria Jensen-Olesen, had given him a clean bill of health, but his body was not bouncing back quite as fast as he would have liked. His brother, Matthew, would say it was because he was getting older, but Matthew was twenty minutes older than he was, so the joke was on him. Marcus was the younger and fitter twin.

In theory.

He winced again and grabbed a pillow to brace his side.

Ugh. Maybe Matthew is right. Maybe I'm getting too old.

He laughed as he stood up.

Truth be told, he was bored out of his mind. He'd had to take a sabbatical from his work as a physician while he healed, and Victoria had warned him that he couldn't get back to his regular practice until he was twelve weeks postoperative. It felt like an eternity.

Only a month to go.

All he wanted to do was get back to work.

Work kept him sane.

That and women, but since his godson, Jonas, had gotten sick, and Marcus had volunteered to be part of the domino surgery in St. Thomas that would provide Jonas with the kidney he so desperately needed, he hadn't paid much attention to dating.

Not that he ever dated seriously.

He'd made that mistake once before, and once was more than enough for him to learn his lesson.

In his early twenties, Marcus had fallen in love with Dawna, the smartest and most beautiful woman in med school.

He'd lost his heart to her.

When his brother went off to New York to do a residency in surgery, Marcus had followed Dawna to California and taken a post in the emergency department at a hospital in San Diego. He had learned triage and was one of the best emergency physicians on staff.

Marcus had thought he'd had the future all planned.

He was going to have an extensive practice in San Diego, and then he was going to ask Dawna to be his wife. He had carved out this whole life for them. Unfortunately, Dawna had other plans, and he was left devastated when she left him for an uptight surgeon that sort of reminded him of his twin brother.

It had crushed Marcus to lose the woman of his dreams to a man who was so like Matthew, because he'd spent so much of his youth being told by his parents that he should try to be more like his brother.

Instead of sticking around in California and working with Dawna and her new surgeon husband, Marcus headed back home to the US Virgin Islands to lick his wounds, vowing to never, ever put his heart on the line again.

Famous last words. Look at Matthew.

Marcus ignored that thought and slowly got dressed for another day of sitting around and healing.

"Yo! You up, Marcus?" a voice called from the dock.

Marcus made his way out into the galley of his boat, the *Tryphine*, and saw his best friend, Jonas's father, Chase Fredrick, looking down at him from above deck. His friend smiled, but Marcus could instantly tell that there was something wrong with him.

"Chase, it's not Jonas, is it? I thought he was still in Charlotte Amalie?"

Chase nodded and walked down the stairs into the galley. "Jonas is stable, thanks to that amazing surgery your brother and sister-in-law performed. He's taken well to his anti-rejection medicines, and he's due to be released soon,"

Marcus smiled. "Good. I'm glad to hear it. What can I help you with then?"

"You're not back to work yet, are you?"

Marcus shook his head. "Nope. I haven't been cleared to practice yet. What's wrong? Is something wrong with Pepper?"

Pepper was Chase's wife and Jonas's mother, and she was currently pregnant with their second child. Pepper had had problems when delivering Jonas, so the couple was understandably nervous about this new pregnancy.

"Actually, there is something wrong. You know that St. John is having a shortage of midwives, especially midwives that can handle the kind of issues Pepper had previously?"

"Right."

Chase rubbed the back of his neck nervously. "Our midwife, who is from England and who is so phenomenal, is about to get deported."

Marcus's eyes widened. "Deported?"

"Her visa's up," Chase said. "She's helped women like Pepper before and successfully dealt with pre-eclampsia and sickle cell disease. She's so knowledgeable and Pepper adores this midwife. Completely trusts her and no one else."

"Well, I'm sorry to say that she might not have a choice if her midwife is going to be deported."

"Well, that's where you come in." There was a nervous tone to Chase's voice, and Marcus had a sinking feeling in the pit of his stomach.

"What do you mean?" he asked carefully.

"Well… I don't know how to ask you this since you've done so much for our family already, but I'm desperate. I don't have any other single friends."

Marcus suddenly felt like he was going to be sick and he sat down, bracing himself. "Chase…what exactly are you asking me?"

"Would you ever consider a marriage of convenience?"

Marcus started to laugh at the absurdity of the question. "Be serious."

"I am being serious."

Marcus stopped laughing and cocked an eyebrow at his best friend. "You've been so stressed going back and forth between Ziese Memorial Hospital and home, plus dealing with a pregnant wife. You're obviously overtired and talking nonsense."

"I'm not!"

"So you're serious?" Marcus asked in disbelief.

"Deadly. I have a clearer head than you, not to mention the fact that I'm younger and better looking."

"That's what I tell my brother."

"And that's what I'm telling you," Chase teased.

Marcus rolled his eyes. "Uh-huh. I would believe what you were saying if you weren't proposing such an insane idea. You can't be serious."

Chase nodded. "I'm being serious. Look, it's the only way I can think of keeping her in the country. You know that Pepper has sickle cell anemia, and this midwife is the best we've seen. I don't trust Pepper in anyone else's hands."

Marcus sighed.

It was a big ask, but he could tell that Chase was desperate, and he knew his friend had undoubtedly thought of everything else before proposing this idea. Chase knew about his past with Dawna, and he also knew that Chase wouldn't have made this big ask if it wasn't his last resort option.

"The doctors in Charlotte Amalie could take care of Pepper, Chase."

"I know, but Pepper is really comfortable with Alexis, and Pepper isn't her only patient. There are others, and everyone loves Alexis on the north side of the island. We can't lose her."

Marcus sighed again. "I don't know. How long would this take? How long would I have to be married to this person?"

"Two years, give or take."

"Two years?" Marcus shook his head. "I can't do that."

"I know it's a long time."

"It's more than just a long time—it's years. Not days or months, but *years*! Can you imagine me married for that long? I have no desire to have a wife or be a husband. Real or imagined."

"Not even a fake husband?" Chase asked, with hope.

"Not even that. Imagined means fake. Not real. No. It's not happening."

"I know you swore off marriage and relationships a long time ago…much to Pepper's chagrin." Chase smiled and Marcus chuckled.

Pepper had been trying for years to set him up with the right woman, and Marcus had managed to rebuff her at every turn. Matthew's late wife, Kirsten, and Pepper had also teamed up for a while, but Marcus just couldn't let go of how much Dawna had hurt him.

You're afraid. That's why.

Marcus shook that thought away. "What does this fake marriage entail?"

Chase grinned. "Just a quick trip down the aisle so that Alexis can apply for her green card. Any immigrant with a pending green card application is allowed to remain in the US until the application has been decided on, which means not only will Alexis be able to stay and see Pepper through a safe delivery, she can also help countless other mothers-to-be while she waits for her green card to be approved. Once she has it, you can get a quickie divorce."

"You know this is fraud, don't you?" Marcus asked dryly.

"Yes, but I'm desperate. Alexis is an asset both to Pepper and to the medical profession. She *deserves* to stay, and I know her application will be approved, so all we're really doing is helping the process along so that she can keep helping women like Pepper."

"Pepper needs to stop reading so many romance novels. I'm sure that's where she came up with this crackpot idea."

Chase laughed. "She's hooked on Mills & Boon, what can I say?"

Marcus stood and sighed. "Does this Alexis person know of this plan?"

"She does, but she's not convinced. Yet. I'm confident we can talk her around to it. Together."

Marcus groaned. "Now, I suppose?"

"You have something better to do? You're on medical leave."

"You're being awfully pushy today, Chase," Marcus groused.

Chase grinned. "No more than usual."

Marcus shook his head and grudgingly finished getting dressed. "You owe me big-time, Chase. Big!"

"I know." Chase climbed up the stairs and stepped out onto the deck to let Marcus get ready in private, but turned back at the last second, and Marcus could see he was worrying his bottom lip.

"What now?" Marcus asked with trepidation.

"The thing is, she's also pregnant."

"Pepper? I know Pepper is pregnant."

"No, our midwife."

All the blood drained from Marcus's head, and there was a strange ringing in his ears.

Surely he hadn't heard Chase correctly. It sounded like the most absurd thing ever.

"She's pregnant?"

Chase nodded. "Yeah, the father of the child left her and doesn't want anything to do with the baby."

"I can't get involved with a pregnant woman. I'm not involving a child in this kind of…of ruse. It's two years or more before she'd get her green card. It's somewhat acceptable when it's just two consenting adults involved, but she's pregnant and that child will be born into a union that isn't genuine. This isn't right."

"It's not a ruse. She'll get her green card. She just needs a husband on paper for the time being. You don't have to be a father, and the child never has to know."

He was surprised to find that that stung.

Marcus had always wanted to be a father. One day. He shook his head.

Of course Marcus was worried about Pepper, and he knew that if this midwife was as good as Chase believed, it would be an asset to keep her in St. John. But was this truly the only way?

Aren't you a little too old to take part in a scheme like this?

Marcus shook that thought away, and he couldn't help but wonder what Matthew would think if he knew what was happening. He could only imagine that he would disapprove. Matthew was always the responsible one, but he wasn't sure about that now. Victoria had certainly relaxed his uptight brother.

Maybe he would think this was smart, a straightforward way to help multiple people.

Doubtful. It's fraud.

A quick search on Google told Marcus that he would essentially be tricking the government so that this midwife could stay in the country. If they got caught, she'd be deported and he would be fined, jailed and would probably lose his medical license.

All reasons to say no.

The thing was, he wanted to help Pepper and because he wasn't allowed to return to work for another four weeks, he had time on his hands to at least meet this woman and talk about the possibility. He wasn't planning to ever get married for real, so maybe there was no harm in a convenient marriage for the time being.

Of course, he wouldn't completely know if it would work until he met Alexis. He hoped he liked her so they could pull this off.

You're doing this for Pepper and Chase.

They had always been there for him. Especially in the years after he had came back from California, when his heart was in tatters after Dawna, when his brother wasn't part of his life and his parents were too busy traveling around the world to recognize that their son was hurting.

Chase and Pepper had been his family.

He could do this for his family.

Couldn't he?

Alexis winced.

Great.

She had to use the bathroom.

Again.

Pregnancy was the miracle of life and Alexis had always envied her patients secretly, but this having to go to the bathroom every few minutes was getting old quickly.

Not that she really minded, of course. For most of

her adult life, she'd been told by her own OB/GYN in London that she had unexplained infertility and so the fact that she was pregnant at all was a miracle.

She and her ex-husband had tried everything over the years, desperate to have a child, a family.

At least that's what she'd thought they both wanted.

The moment she finally became pregnant was the exact moment that her husband, Bruce, the man she'd loved for the last five years, told her that he actually didn't want a family. He thought that she would eventually give up trying to get pregnant when all the avenues had failed, and then they could enjoy their life together.

He'd been so angry six months ago when he found out she was pregnant.

And then he'd left her and filed for divorce. His reason? That she deceived him. He claimed he had married her specifically because he believed she couldn't have children, and so the pregnancy voided their agreement.

If that wasn't the complete kicker, he also quickly began a new relationship with someone else.

It was then that Alexis knew that it wasn't the pregnancy that had made him end their marriage. Bruce had moved on from her long before that, and had been making plans to leave. It crushed her completely, but it also gave her the push she needed to close that chapter of her life. There was no point in trying to hold on to something that toxic.

She'd been blinded by love, and she wasn't going to let that happen ever again.

Alexis gladly signed the decree of divorce and made sure that Bruce signed over all claims to their unborn child so that she would have sole custody and parental control once the baby was born. She wasn't going to have him swoop in later and try to disrupt her child's life. She'd had a father like that—an absentee father who cared more about his work than his family—and she wouldn't put her own child through that.

She'd seen the toll it had taken on her mother.

It was still a burden on her to this day.

There were times when Alexis had wanted to tell her mother to run, but she knew her mother would never listen to her. So instead of having her baby go through that, Alexis sold her flat in London for a tidy sum, quit her practice and headed to the US Virgin Islands on a short-term contract.

An escape to paradise had sounded like the perfect next step.

The problem was that now that her four-month work visa was up, she found that she didn't want to leave St. John. She was in love with the island, the people and all of her patients.

Alexis had never felt more at home than she did here.

This was where she wanted to raise her child.

The problem was, she couldn't stay.

It was breaking her heart. As if in response to her worried thoughts, there was a tiny kick, almost like a nudge or a poke. Alexis smiled and rubbed the small swell in her lower belly.

"I know you want to stay, too."

"Are you talking to yourself again?"

Alexis looked up from her desk in the clinic to see Chase Fredrick standing in the doorway. Her stomach sank.

"Is it Pepper? Is she having a flare-up?" Alexis asked nervously.

Pepper Fredrick was one of the patients that Alexis didn't want to leave.

The woman had a lot going on—her son had recently had a kidney transplant in a major domino surgery, and she was eight months pregnant and high risk. She had sickle cell anemia, and Alexis had been surprised to find that none of the other midwives she worked with on St. John had dealt with it before. Alexis had seen it many times and Pepper was in her care, but beyond that, Pepper and Chase had been like a surrogate family to her since she'd arrived.

And she didn't want to leave them.

She wanted her baby and Pepper's baby to be best friends.

Alexis had never experienced the support and the community that she got here and couldn't imagine finding it again anywhere else. Even though she had biological family in England, she was mostly alone there.

Plus England reminded her of Bruce and his betrayal. It held too much sadness, too many memories she wanted to leave behind for good.

St. John made her happy and this is where she wanted to stay, but she had to go back to England. She had been so busy with work she'd left things too late. By the time she returned to England and applied for another visa, she'd be too pregnant to travel back safely and she'd be stuck, unable to be here to help Pepper through what would be a tricky final few weeks of her pregnancy.

"No, it's not Pepper. Pepper is fine. I've come here to tell you that I have a solution to your problem!"

Alexis cocked an eyebrow. She was intrigued.

"You have a solution to indigestion and my need to use the bathroom every five minutes?" she teased.

Chase grinned. "No, but wouldn't that solve a lot of problems? I have a solution to your visa problem. I have a way to keep you in the country."

Alexis smiled. A miracle solution at this late stage seemed too good to be true. She'd already spent ages racking her brain, trying to think of something—anything—that would keep her here legally, but she hadn't come up with anything.

"What is it?" she asked, trying not to appear too eager or to get her hopes up.

"Well, it was Pepper's idea actually."

As soon as he said that, Alexis knew exactly what Chase was going to say, because Pepper had already suggested it to her. She had come up with some inventive ideas in the short time she had known her, but her latest had taken the cake. It was straight out of one of those novels that Pepper was devouring regularly.

And that was the problem with it.

It was fiction.

It wasn't real life. People did not have marriage of conveniences. It was too far-fetched.

"No. Absolutely not. I'm not getting married," Alexis said quickly.

That was a hard pass for her. There was no way that she was putting herself through that again. Bruce had hurt her, shattered her trust. She would have to be an absolute raving lunatic to try and attempt another marriage.

Even if it was fake.

"How did you…? Oh. Pepper already told you, didn't she?"

Alexis nodded and stood up. "She did and it's a wild notion. Stuff like that doesn't happen in real life."

"Of course it does," Chase said. "People pretend to be married all the time. This is your only option, Alexis. It's not a real marriage. You just have to pretend for a while so you can stay in the country."

"A green card takes a long time, Chase. You do realize that?" she asked.

Chase nodded. "Of course."

"Who is going to be fake married to me for two-plus years without some kind of compensation? I can't afford that."

"The man in question doesn't want compensation."

"So he's doing it out of the goodness of his heart?" she asked in disbelief.

"Yes." Chase grinned.

"Seems too good to be true."

"Some would say that about him. Not me, mind you. What do you say, Alexis?"

Alexis worried her bottom lip.

She really did want to stay in the country. She wanted to be able to take care of her patients, and she wanted her and her baby to start a new life here.

She'd never really been happy in England, but here in St. John she'd discovered her happy place. She loved everything about this island. The warm breezes, the greenery, the people, the food, the white sand beaches and the turquoise sea.

There were so many mornings where she would just sit at the window in her small room, staring out over the water and watching the big cruise ships slowly sail by on their way to Charlotte Amalie on St. Thomas.

It made her want to explore even more, to see all

the different corners of St. Croix and then maybe even leave the US Virgin Islands and head out to other countries like Jamaica, Haiti, or Cuba. Maybe even farther south.

She always had a secret dream of getting a boat and sailing around the world.

Bruce hadn't been into that idea.

She should've taken it as a warning sign, but she'd been young and in love.

Alexis shook her head, clearing her dreams out of her mind so that she could focus on what Chase was saying.

"If I do decide to attempt this idea of Pepper's, who is going to agree to marry me?"

Chase grinned, his brown eyes twinkling. "I have just the man for you. A stand-up citizen and native son to the islands. Alexis Martin, may I introduce you to your future husband and my best friend, Dr. Marcus Olesen."

Alexis's eyes widened when she realized Chase had brought the man with him, and the moment that this Marcus Olesen walked into her office her breath was nearly taken away. Her pulse quickened as she gazed into the bluest eyes she'd ever seen. He had sandy blond hair that was a little longer than she usually liked, but somehow it suited him. He had a neatly trimmed beard, and the way his eyes twinkled at her made her knees shake.

A little voice inside Alexis told her that this man was a bit of a rogue—that he could be dangerous to her heart—and she was annoyed the way her body responded to him.

The way he took her breath away.

It took her a minute to find her voice as she was forced to swallow the lump that had suddenly formed in her throat.

"It's a pleasure to meet you," she finally squeaked out.

He smiled, but that smile didn't extend to his eyes, which made her suspect that he wasn't exactly a willing participant in this either.

"Pleasure," he said stiffly. His gaze roved over her body in a way that made her blood heat and yet made her feel vulnerable.

Naked.

Exposed.

This man was a definite danger. He was a temptation.

Chase was still smiling, obviously proud of himself and confident that this had worked out and was already a done deal. "I'm going to figure out what we have to do next about the marriage, so I'll leave you two to get acquainted."

Alexis didn't want to be alone to Marcus. Not that she didn't trust him, but because he was making her feel things she hadn't felt in a long time and she didn't ever want to feel this way again. She was almost annoyed with herself for having had such a strong initial reaction to him.

"So…" she said once they were alone, her voice shaking ever so slightly.

Marcus shoved his hands in the pockets of his khaki-colored Bermuda shorts. "So, when are we going to get on with this sham?"

CHAPTER TWO

THE MOMENT HE said the words, he instantly regretted them.

He had been standing in the hall and listening to her and Chase. Marcus knew that Alexis wasn't really keen on this either, but she was doing this for Pepper and he could appreciate that. What he hadn't expected was how stunningly beautiful she was.

She was glowing.

Marcus couldn't remember the last time that he had actually had his breath taken away by a woman.

Actually he could. The last time was Dawna.

He shook that niggling thought away. Since Dawna, he'd been out on countless dates, but there had been very few second dates and definitely no long-term commitments.

It was one of the reasons he preferred to date tourists—because there was always an end date. Their time together was short, sweet and he didn't have to ever contemplate committing to just one woman.

Marcus didn't have to put his heart at risk.

It was so much better that way.

Is it?

He shoved that thought to the back of his mind.

It really didn't matter. He was here to marry Alexis so she could continue to take care of Pepper and all the other pregnant women in her care. He didn't need to get attached. The fact he was so attracted to her was a bit unnerving, but nothing he couldn't handle.

Her golden hair fell in soft waves around her heart-shaped face. Dark brown eyes, intense like a storm, met his gaze, and there was a slight peachy tinge to her creamy cheeks. He towered over her, but then that wasn't a surprise given he was over six feet.

The only woman who towered over him was Matthew's wife, Victoria, and that's because she insisted on wearing crazy tall heels.

Alexis might like those same kinds of heels, but she was wearing ballet flats at present, likely because of her pregnancy. His gazed roved over her body and settled on the swell of her abdomen. He'd guess she was about six months along, if this was her first, as it took longer to show in a first pregnancy.

A marriage of convenience meant it was going to be hard to keep his distance from her, but he would have to get control of himself because he currently couldn't tear his gaze from her. To try and shake himself out of his daze, he'd resorted to surliness.

And he regretted that.

This whole situation wasn't Alexis's fault.

It wasn't her idea.

"I'm sorry I sounded rude just now. I guess I'm still in shock."

She smiled, looking relieved. "I am too. Shocked, I mean."

"I mean, it's a ruse after all."

"Yes," she said in her plummy British accent. "I suppose it is a sham, isn't it?"

"Yes, but I told Chase that I would help. Pepper and the new baby are the priority now."

"You do realize this is possibly a two-year commitment? It says on every piece of information about this process that it can take eighteen to twenty-four months to be approved. It's a lot to ask… Sorry, I didn't quite catch your name."

"Marcus. Dr. Marcus Olesen."

Her brow furrowed, and she cocked her head to one side. "Wait, you're Dr. Olesen? Are you the surgeon that completed that domino surgery a few weeks ago?"

"No. That was my brother. I was involved though."

"So you're a surgeon?"

"No," he said quickly.

He never wanted to be mistaken for a surgeon. It was bad enough his brother had always pressured him to be a surgeon, and that his parents always kept going on about him being more like Matthew, but it was Dawna's leaving him for a surgeon that was the gut punch he couldn't handle and still couldn't quite move past.

Being a surgeon didn't always mean that you were better. He loved being a general practitioner. He did miss the fast pace of the emergency room from California, but he loved his practice here too. He formed relationships with his patients, he got to know them and he saw them for more than just a preoperative and postoperative visit.

It was more than cutting them open and patching them back up again.

You know that's not what Matthew does.

He felt bad for thinking it.

A pink tinge colored her cheeks. "I'm sorry, I assumed when you said that you were involved in the domino… Well, I thought you were a surgeon."

"I was involved because I was a donor. Chase and Pepper's son, Jonas, is my godson and I did it for him."

"So you donated your kidney to him?" she asked.

"No, not exactly. I donated my kidney to a patient who was a difficult match and her donor donated to Jonas. That's how the domino works. You have donors and recipients who are all mismatched but everyone ends up getting what they need. It was complicated, and I know there was a lot of paperwork and charts to keep it all straight. I was part of it, and even I don't feel like I can explain it well enough to people."

She quirked her eyebrow, her eyes widening. "That's a massive undertaking, but I understand the basics. Surgery is not my cup of tea. I could handle it, but just didn't like dealing with unconscious patients and surgeons all the time. Plus the smell and feel of an operating room has always bothered me."

He softened to her last remark because he felt the same way too. "It's the cautery and the cold I don't like."

"Quite." She smiled again, tucking a strand of blond hair behind her ear. "Still, a domino is quite fascinating all the same."

"It was, but I'm not here to talk about the domino. I'm here to talk to you about this marriage of convenience."

Alexis blushed again and sat down. She motioned for him to sit in the chair opposite, which he did gladly. He was thankful for the seat so he could rest. His side was bothering him and that was annoying. It frustrated him how long it was taking to heal.

"I want to thank you for doing this," she said quickly. "It seems to me that you've given so much to Chase and Pepper already."

"It's my pleasure."

He wasn't being entirely truthful. He was glad to be helping out his friends, but there was a part of him that was telling him that this wasn't the right thing to do. Especially now, having met Alexis. There was a part of him telling him that this was a bad idea and that he should run in the opposite direction, that his heart was in danger of being hurt.

Badly.

"We both know this is a long commitment and one between strangers," she said.

"Agreed."

"So, where do we even begin?"

"At the start." He smiled and she smiled back.

"Right. First things first. I think we'll have to start to get to know one another. Learn some basic information about each other, but I promise you that it will only be basic. I'm not completely comfortable with this situation or having a stranger know too much about my personal life."

Her honesty shocked him, but she wasn't wrong. They were strangers, and it would be prudent for him not to get too close to her. They would do what was necessary to convince the world their marriage was true and then, once Alexis got a green card, they would get a divorce. And if no one bothered with them in the meantime, they could live separate lives. He wouldn't have to get too involved in her life or the life of her child.

Her pregnancy was the major cause of his hesitation with this plan. There was a child involved, and he wouldn't do anything to hurt an innocent life.

As much as Marcus had always dreamed about having a wife and kids, when Dawna left him he had laid those dreams to rest. They weren't meant to be.

Matthew didn't think he would get married again, but he did.

Marcus ignored that voice and was annoyed that his conscience was becoming that little bit more vocal lately. It was unwelcome.

This marriage of convenience with Alexis was a business arrangement and nothing more.

And he had to keep reminding himself of that.

Alexis was having a hard time focusing. She had a vague idea of the basic information that Immigration would need, or ask, if they were questioned about their quickie marriage, but for some strange reason she just couldn't focus on it.

Not only was Marcus devilishly handsome, but he was also a kind soul. He was a bit of a hero stepping up and giving a kidney to a stranger in a complicated procedure just so his godson could get a kidney in return.

It was the gift of life, and it was priceless.

His lips were pursed in a thin line, and she couldn't help but wonder if he was in pain. She knew from Pepper that Jonas's surgery had been two months ago now, but he was obviously having some postoperative pain, and she felt bad that he had been dragged here, in the heat, to help her.

Alexis wasn't sure how or when she would ever be able to pay him back for the favor he was offering to do for her. She would be indebted to him.

"Maybe we should do this another day?" she said gently.

"What do you mean?" he asked stiffly.

"The getting-to-know-you questions. Maybe today is not the day."

"Today seems like a good enough time. Besides, knowing Chase, he'll pack us off to the courthouse in Charlotte Amalie to get married in an hour."

Alexis chuckled. "You're right. He's quite tenacious."

"Exactly. Why do you want to put it off?"

"You seem to be quite uncomfortable. And I mean pain wise. It's from the surgery, isn't it?"

"It is and I am, but I'm okay. The only way that I'm going to be able to return to my practice is if I push myself a bit more each day."

"I'm no surgeon, but I am a trained nurse practitioner in addition to being a midwife, and you have to rest," she said, as gently as she could.

Marcus had opened his mouth to say something further when one of the administrative staff who worked near the entrance of the clinic rushed into the room.

"Alexis!"

She jumped up, as fast as her pregnant belly allowed her to. "What's wrong, Margaret?"

The woman took a deep breath. "It's Mrs. Winston. She's on the floor of the waiting room, in labor. Her water broke and there's a lot of blood in it. We can't get her to Charlotte Amalie on a ferry, but an air ambulance has been called. Her husband is overseas and her mother is watching the other kids. She's alone."

Alexis swallowed the lump in her throat. "I'm coming."

"Can I help?" Marcus asked.

"Yes. Most of the midwife staff has left for the day. I'll need all the help I can get!"

Marcus nodded and followed Alexis out of her office. It was just a short distance to the waiting room. Alexis could tell that Mrs. Winston was in far more pain than she should be, and with the amount of brightly colored blood in the fluid on the floor, the first thing Alexis suspected was a placental abruption.

She'd seen this before.

Most of the time, it would mean the mother-to-be would need a Cesarean section, but that was beyond her abilities, and as they weren't set up for a surgery here, it wasn't an option.

"You said you called for the air ambulance from Charlotte Amalie?" Alexis said to Margaret.

"Yes, I already called Ziese Memorial and they're sending one."

Alexis grabbed one of the ready sterile birthing kits and carefully knelt beside Mrs. Winston.

"Marcie, tell me what happened. You were only four centimeters dilated when you had your appointment." Alexis spoke softly, trying not to alarm or panic her patient.

Marcie Winston panted. "I don't know. I was feeling fine—this is my fourth and I was planning on sticking around nearby so I'd be ready when the baby comes—but then it felt like I was hit in the stomach. It hurts so bad."

"I know. I'm so sorry." Alexis felt Marcie's belly. It was hard as a contraction moved through it, but there were strong kicks. "I'm going to do an exam. Is that okay?"

Marcie nodded Alexis draped her and then removed Marcie's undergarments.

She'd seen this before, when she had done training in Kenya, where hospitals were also few and far between.

Alexis would prefer to have her patient safely in hospital, but the baby was coming, and until the air ambulance came Alexis was all Marcie had.

"I'm just going to check to see how dilated you are." Alexis asked, gaining consent. She never took that it was implied. She wanted all her patients to be comfortable.

"Yes. Please. Just help," Marcie begged.

Alexis nodded and her did her exam. Marcie's four centimeters had turned into ten and she was now fully effaced. Alexis could see the baby making its way. This baby was coming fast and furious.

At this point there was no waiting for the helicopter.

"What can I do?" Marcus asked.

"Can you sit behind her, hold her? This baby is coming." Alexis readied what she needed. The rest of the staff in the clinic knew what to do as Marcus took his place behind Marcie, to help brace her as she pushed. Marcie was so weak Alexis was glad Marcus was here to help her.

"What's happening?" Mrs. Winston, asked.

"Marcie, your baby is coming. Fast. I think your placenta has detached, so we need to get the baby out as fast as we can. I know it hurts, but you're going to have to push," Alexis said encouragingly. She knew that it was going to be painful for Marcie, even though this wasn't her first baby. The placenta was tearing and the baby wasn't stopping.

"You can do this," Marcus said gently from behind Marcie, holding her shoulders as she bore down and pushed.

"You're doing so great," Alexis told her. She kept one hand on Marcie's abdomen as she kept her focus on the beautiful life that was being born into the world. This was why she loved her work so much.

Watching life begin.

The miracle of birth.

And soon it would be her, in another midwife's hands, as she brought forth her little miracle. She just wished that she had someone to share it with. She had thought Bruce was going to be that person.

Don't think about it now.

With a couple more pushes, Marcie's baby girl was born. Alexis cleared the baby's mouth and soon there was a lusty cry, angry at being ejected from a warm and safe place into a cold, bright world.

Marcie cried and held out her arms for the baby.

Usually Alexis liked to keep the baby attached to the cord until the placenta was delivered, but it wasn't possible in this instance, so she clamped and cut the cord. Margaret handed her a blanket and they wrapped the little girl before handing her over to her mother.

That's when the bleeding started, and Alexis knew for certain that it was an abruption.

"Do you have a Foley catheter?" Marcus asked.

"We do." Alexis stood and got one.

"Insert it and pack it. We don't want it to tear away from the uterine wall. I would suggest a massage on her abdomen, but if the placenta has abrupted she'll need surgery."

Alexis nodded as Marcus came to sit beside her,

pulling on gloves. He got sterile sponges and dressings, helping her as they packed Marcie to try and staunch the flow.

"Marcie, how are you doing?" Marcus asked.

"Not. Good. Tired," Marcie said, her words slurred.

Marcus took the baby. "Try and relax, the helicopter is nearly here."

"Okay," Marcie murmured.

In the background Alexis could hear the whir of the helicopter blades making an emergency landing out in the parking lot, and not a moment too soon.

There was so much blood.

Alexis watched Marcus hold the little girl so gently. He was so calm.

She was impressed that a general practitioner knew what to do in the case of a placental abruption. Usually only a midwife, nurse or obstetrician dealt with this situation enough to know what to do.

"What's her blood pressure?" Alexis grimly asked Margaret, who was monitoring it.

"It's eighty-nine over fifty-five," Margaret responded.

Alexis pursed her lips as the paramedics from Ziese Memorial Hospital came rushing into the clinic with a stretcher. Alexis stood up and took off her gloves as she started to fill them in on what had happened so far.

"This mother—gravida four, para four—has just delivered a female infant. There was quite a lot of blood and pain. I suspect a placental abruption. Her blood pressure is eight-nine systolic over fifty-five diastolic. She has not delivered the placenta yet. We placed a Foley catheter and packed her to try and staunch the bleeding."

The head paramedic nodded. "We'll take her to her OB/GYN surgeon who is ready and waiting."

"Please keep me posted on her progress."

The paramedic nodded, and Alexis stepped back as the paramedics got Mrs. Winston stable on the stretcher. There wasn't any room on the air ambulance for them, but Alexis was familiar with Dr. Baxter at Ziese Memorial Hospital and she was comfortable leaving Marcie in Dr. Baxter's capable hands.

Marcus made sure the baby was settled with her mother and was helping the paramedic hooking up the intravenous to get Marcie fluids.

She and Margaret sent Marcie's file electronically to the head of obstetrics at Ziese Memorial, and then there was nothing more Alexis could do.

"You did a great job," Marcus said.

"I'm not the only one," Alexis stated. "I was impressed by how you stepped in like that."

Marcus cocked an eyebrow. "Oh, really?"

"Yes. You knew right away to use a Foley catheter and about the massage."

"Well, I've had to deal with an unexpected birth or two in my time." He winced as he walked over to where she was standing, and she felt bad.

"Are you okay?" she asked.

"Just my incision site. It's taking me a bit longer to heal than I'd like and reminding me that I'm not as young as I once was." He half smiled, and there was a twinkle in his blue eyes.

Alexis couldn't help but smile back.

He was charming. She'd give him that.

They just stood there in awkward silence.

"Why don't we go talk in private?" Alexis finally offered.

Marcus nodded and they walked back to her office.

"So, like I was saying before, I suppose we need to get to know one another, make some appearances together to firm this whole thing up," Marcus said as he shut the door to her office.

"Yes. I suppose. I have to admit though that I'm apprehensive about this. I'm not quite sure it'll work."

"It apparently does, or people wouldn't even attempt it. I won't lie. I'm nervous about this, too, but we have to give it a try. How about we have dinner tonight? Say, around eight? We can go somewhere private and hash this thing all out. I'll cook."

"That sounds good," she replied.

It would be nice to get out of her little room at the dormitory.

She'd been here four months and hadn't really seen much of the island. She'd been too busy working and trying to get over her broken heart. Or rather, trying to get over her anger at being betrayed by the man who had promised to be by her side forever, in sickness and in health.

St. John was her fresh start and she wanted to stay.

This was going to be the start of her new life, and she'd do whatever it took to make it happen. Even fake a marriage to a charming man who was sacrificing his freedom—his life for the next two years—for her.

A stranger.

CHAPTER THREE

MARCUS KNEW THE moment the words came out of his mouth that it was a mistake to invite Alexis for dinner. Usually, when he asked a woman out on a dinner date, it was an opportunity to charm and seduce her.

Dates were casual.

Fun.

But the women he usually went out with were in and out of his life quickly. Anything they shared was always temporary.

Alexis would be in his life for a long while.

Yes, the marriage would just be on paper—they wouldn't really have a relationship—but he couldn't be caught dating around for the next couple of years, or the truth of their sham marriage would be exposed.

There was a part of him that wanted more with Alexis, maybe even a real relationship, but he quickly silenced that part and reminded himself that she was off-limits. This whole situation with Alexis was just a business arrangement. He wasn't here for romance. His heart wasn't open to that.

This was a marriage of convenience so that a talented midwife and nurse practitioner could stay in the country and take care of Pepper.

And there was no doubt in his mind that Alexis was talented. He'd seen her in action himself.

If the midwife clinic hadn't been there, if Mrs. Winston had gone into labor on her own at home, she would've bled out and died.

It was imperative that Alexis was able to stay and continue to provide this kind of service to the island of St. John. There was also part of him that acknowledged he could learn from her, so that he could better take care of his patients. As a general practitioner and with midwives on the islands, as well as a state-of-the-art hospital in Charlotte Amalie, there wasn't much call for him to attend births. But he found he wanted to learn—and he wanted Alexis to be the one to teach him.

He may not have always taken school as seriously as Matthew told him he should, but Marcus liked to learn and he liked to better himself...

"You could be a surgeon," Dawna said.

Marcus looked up from his charting. "Why? I like being a general practitioner. I get to develop real relationships with my patients."

Dawna rolled her eyes. "That's not where the money is though."

"I don't care about that. Money isn't everything."

"You're so hopeless," she said with a sigh.

Marcus shook that thought away. At the time he thought Dawna was teasing him, but now he realized they'd never quite seen eye to eye on the monetary issue. For Dawna, in the end, it was a big deal.

"So what are we having for dinner?" Alexis asked. "Is there anything you want me to bring?"

The question caught him off guard. He hadn't really thought much beyond inviting her. He would usually have dinner catered, but there wasn't much time to organize that at this point in the day.

"I don't know. You could bring dessert?"

Alexis nodded. "I can."

"Okay."

"You still didn't answer my question though. What're we having?"

"Are there foods that bother you?" he asked gently. "Or are you just picky?"

She grinned. "Not picky, but some things do inflame my morning sickness, and there are some things I just can't eat right now."

Marcus leaned back against her desk. "Like what?"

"Tomatoes," she stated. "Used to love them and I can't stand them now—not even sauces or ketchups or catsups or anything tomato adjacent."

"That's a shame. So no to tomatoes…"

"Or fish, or sushi or… I'm being a pest now, aren't I?"

"No." He smiled at her. "You're not. I think I can whip up something you'd like."

"I look forward to it."

Marcus got up. "Well, I'd better get ready. Shall I pick you up at the dorm?"

"That sounds wonderful."

Marcus left with an unexpected spring in his step. He was actually looking forward to dinner tonight. He always liked the dates he made, but this was something different and he couldn't quite put his finger on it.

Alexis was so different from the women he felt were a safe bet. Women he wouldn't get attached to.

He smiled to himself as he thought of how she had gone right to work when alerted to her patient's emergency and how focused she'd been throughout the surprise delivery. She didn't shy away from the challenge. Instead, she was gentle and kind, in total control as she took command.

And she was intelligent.

All qualities that he liked in a woman.

His pulse quickened as he thought of her, and all his old instincts kicked in. Matthew had always accused him of being a ladies' man, a notion that Marcus scoffed at, but maybe he was right. He'd always enjoyed the company of women but only when he had the safety net of his companions' firm departure date. It was different with Alexis though. He couldn't get her out of his mind.

He was thinking of her silken blond hair, her dark brown eyes and the peachy pink tinge to her cheeks that had appeared when he'd caused her to blush.

She's pregnant, you dolt.

And that was the kicker. She was six months pregnant with another man's child. Marcus didn't know what kind of relationship, if any, she currently had with the baby's father. Maybe once she got her green card she'd go back to him.

Alexis was not his.

And wouldn't be.

So he had to keep telling himself that this marriage of convenience was just that.

A contract.

A piece of paper.

Nothing more.

In a short amount of time he would be divorced. Or rather, *they* would be divorced and then he could get on with his life.

What life?

That was the crux of the matter. He didn't really have a life. At least not the one he'd always pictured. By now, according the original plans he'd made when he fell for Dawna, he should have a couple of kids of his own.

A house.

A wife.

Heck, he could even have a kid the same age as his godson, who was fifteen.

And then it struck him just how long ago he had made those plans for himself. What had he been doing with his life in the meantime?

Not living it, a little voice inside him whispered.

Marcus picked up supplies for salad, garlic bread and fettuccine Alfredo on the way home. He'd made it often before, usually for his late sister-in-law, Kirsten, because it was her favorite, but this was the first time he was cooking it for someone else, someone outside his family.

Having showered, changed and prepped everything for dinner, Marcus finally glanced at the clock and realized that he was late picking up Alexis. He cursed under his breath and disembarked his boat, the *Tryphine*, which was named for the patron saint of pregnant mothers, overdue mothers and sick children.

He ran down the gangplank and hopped into his small car, which was a beat-up thing that he drove around the island of St. John. Mostly, he preferred to get around by boat, but Marcus still hadn't been cleared for heavy lifting, so he couldn't exactly sail his boat on his own.

It was a short drive to the dormitories were the locum midwives were posted, and he found Alexis waiting outside for him. For the second time that day, she nearly took his breath away. She was wearing a long, flowery dress that was blowing in the breeze, and her blond hair fell in waves down over her bared shoulders.

She reminded him a bit of the painting of Venus in the clamshell, and his heart skipped a beat.

Marcus parked the car and got out to open the door for her. She blushed when he did that, tucking an errant strand of hair behind her ear, and he caught a whiff of green tea and honey as she moved. He wanted to lean forward and breathe that intoxicating scent in deeper, but knew he had to stop himself.

"Thank you," she said, her voice shaking slightly.

"You're welcome." He shut the door and ran back to the driver's side and climbed in.

"So where are we going?" she asked.

"You're full of questions."

"I ask questions when I'm nervous," she admitted.

"Are you nervous?" he asked.

"A bit. I don't know you."

"I don't bite. Much." He grinned and she laughed.

"Okay. Fine. So we're going to a mystery spot."

"No mystery. I told you I'd cook for you so we're going to my place. I live at the marina, in case you want to let someone know where you are."

She smiled appreciatively. "Thanks. I mean, we're technically strangers. I know you're Chase and Pepper's friend, but I still don't know *you*. I have to protect myself. And you told me you do bite, albeit not much."

Marcus laughed. "Fair enough. And you're right. We're strangers. If we're going to pull off this marriage, then we have to get to know one another better in case someone asks us questions about how we met or our 'relationship.'"

Alexis smiled and nodded. "Thank you. I'm glad you see it my way."

"You've been thanking me a lot, and I haven't even really laid on the charm." He grinned and winked. She laughed softly.

"Is that supposed to be some kind of pickup line?"

"No, just the truth."

"My, my…aren't we full of ourself?"

He glanced over at her and was relieved to see she was smiling. She was teasing him, and he couldn't help but laugh. He was glad she was someone who could take a joke, and that she was someone whom he could tease.

It would make their marriage seem more real, because it would appear to be so much more natural if they had a good rapport. As much as he wanted to stay a stranger to her, to keep away because he was so drawn to her, that wouldn't be good for their ruse.

"I'm sorry, I don't usually tease a stranger in such a familiar way," she apologized.

"No. I like it. I tease my brother something fierce now."

One of her finely arched brows quirked. "Now? That seems to imply that the relationship wasn't always so strong."

"It wasn't," Marcus admitted. Which was the truth.

There had been a point growing up when Matthew had taken it upon himself to almost parent him, and Marcus had resented his brother for it. He wanted a brother, not a warden, but Matthew was so serious, so worried.

The thing that frustrated Marcus the most was that there had been no reason for Matthew to have taken on that role. They had two parents—why couldn't they just have been brothers, there for one another?

"I'm sorry to hear that," she said.

"We're doing better now. Since my kidney donation, we've grown closer. It's a bit tenuous still, but it's a lot better than it was and I credit his wife, Vic, with a lot of my brother's softening."

Alexis smiled. "I hope I get to meet them."

"I'm sure you will." Marcus worried what Matthew would think about this whole situation. Would Matthew's parenting instinct kick in, setting them back? He could almost hear Matthew's voice now berating him for agreeing to such a foolish venture as a marriage of convenience. "Do you have any siblings?" he asked, trying to change the subject.

"No. I'm an only child."

She didn't elaborate. Just pressed her lips together in a firm line as if she was done talking about it. He'd seen patients do that before, unwilling to give up information, even if they knew that it would affect their health and that Marcus needed to know.

He wasn't going to press her about it right now, but he needed to know about her family eventually if he was going to pose as her husband. He parked his car in his parking space outside the marina and turned off the ignition, climbing out and opening her door again. She seemed confused as she looked around.

"You live down here?" she asked.

"Yes. On a boat."

"A boat?" she asked, surprised.

"Well, I did say I live at the marina. What did you expect?"

"I honestly don't know. I've never met a person who lived on a boat before."

"It's how I travel around the islands and visit my patients. When I'm practicing, that is. Right now, I haven't been cleared by my surgeon to go back to work just yet."

"I would've never pictured you as a boat type of person," she said.

He cocked his head to one side. "And what kind of person is a boat type of person?"

Alexis laughed nervously. "I don't know. I guess maybe someone with more stripes on their clothing—more navy and white. And they'd probably always wear deck shoes. Maybe even a nice white hat?"

"Well, at least you're picturing me as the skipper rather than a pirate," he teased.

She laughed. "Well, if your beard was a bit more scraggly, then maybe… Yeah, you'd look very pirate-like. Or maybe if you had a gold earring?"

"Thanks for the suggestions, but I think I'll just remain the inconspicuous boat person that you know me as."

The sun was setting, and all the lights strung on other masts made the marina look like a magical place, rather than just a bunch of boats moored together.

He stopped in front of the *Tryphine*.

"This is beautiful," she said in awe.

Marcus smiled.

Even with the sails down it *was* beautiful. Made of polished wood, the boat had a navy blue hull.

"Thanks. It was custom-built for my father in the late seventies, when it was super-chic to have a yacht like this. It was built by a naval architect who designed yachts that were meant for world travel and racing, though my father didn't do either."

"So why have a sailboat like this?"

Marcus grinned. "My father likes to have the best, but he doesn't have sea legs, or rather, doesn't have the sea legs to man a sailboat. There were a lot of un-expected swims in the sea and a mishap with a shark, so he gave me the sailboat. He has a motorized yacht now."

He instinctively held out his hand to help her aboard, and as she slipped her tiny, delicate hand into his he felt a jolt of electricity, a zing, pass through him.

It caught him by surprise.

As did the fact that he didn't want to let go.

"I hope there isn't retro seventies decor inside, like shag carpet and big gold and brown flowers," she said teasingly.

"And if there were?"

"Are there?" she asked, surprised.

"No, there was, but I retrofitted the inside myself to something more classic and sleek."

Marcus helped her down into his home. The *Try-phine* was his baby. His passion since he'd come back from California and his father gave it to him.

His brother got the luxury car and Marcus got the boat. It was in more disrepair than his brother's car, because it had sat dry-docked in Miami for some time, but Marcus hadn't cared. He'd wanted—needed—to do something to get his mind off what Dawna had done to his heart.

Kirsten, Matthew's late wife, had also encouraged him to pursue the renovations.

In fact, she was the one who had been responsible for picking out the colors, and he liked that there was a bit of his dearly beloved late sister-in-law here.

The name she'd given the boat was her real legacy though...

"What shall I call it? I really don't want a boat named after my mother," Marcus stated. *He planned to seduce women on this boat and having a boat named after your mom was not conducive to that...*

Matthew rolled his eyes. "There's nothing wrong with Freja."

Kirsten scolded him. "Don't be so mean to your brother. He's absolutely right that this is his vessel now, and he needs to choose a name he likes."

"Don't you like my mother?" Matthew teased.

Marcus couldn't help but be envious of them and the love they shared in that intimate, teasing moment.

"You know that I do," Kirsten said sweetly. "Still, a single man shouldn't have a boat named after this mother."

Marcus stuck his tongue out at Matthew and then laughed. He was glad that Kirsten was siding with him.

"Don't be childish, Marcus," Matthew groused, trying not to laugh as well.

"Don't be such a stick in the mud, Matthew," Marcus snapped back. "Kirsten, since you're always kind and sweet to me I want you to name her."

Kirsten smiled. "How about Tryphine?"

"What?" Matthew asked, confused.

"The patron saint of sick children, I believe," Marcus said.

"And of overdue mothers," Kirsten said sadly. "Mothers who never got to be mothers..."

The brothers shared a look. Marcus knew too how much Kirsten wanted a child. And with the cancer that just wasn't possible at the moment. If anyone deserved to be a mother, it was her and Marcus hurt for her more than ever in that moment.

"Tryphine it is, then!" Marcus announced. "She'll be the only one in the Caribbean, I'm sure."

He smiled at the memory.

"Are you okay?" Alexis asked, interrupting his thoughts.

"Yes. Fine, just thinking about something. Why don't you have a seat, and I'll get you a glass of lemonade?"

She smiled. "That would be great."

Marcus headed into the galley as Alexis made herself comfortable at the table that sat under the windows at stern. He closed the small pocket door that led into the galley, trying to collect his thoughts.

He was enjoying himself with her.

Too much.

This was going to be a long, trying night.

Alexis couldn't believe that Marcus had a sailboat and that he lived in it full time. One, he said, that was capable of going around the world. That had always been her dream. To sail off into the sunset and discover new places.

She'd wanted to travel so much more when she was younger, but her mother had dissuaded her, always telling her that she'd get murdered or taken advantage of by someone looking for a green card.

Alexis laughed at that thought, because now she was the one taking advantage of Marcus.

Either way, she'd been a little bit more timid back then and had listened to her mother. Then she'd met Bruce and her mother was happy for her. Alexis had thought she was happy too, so she'd let go of all those secret dreams of traveling. She was in love, and Bruce didn't want to live somewhere else. He wanted to stay in England and said she was foolish to want to move to somewhere exotic and start up a life with no family around.

When they'd tried and failed to get pregnant, Bruce had said it was meant to be, that they should just be happy with what they had, even though it broke Alexis's heart that she would never be a mother.

When she did finally become pregnant, and Bruce left her, her mother had actually questioned her about keeping her baby, suggesting that she would never be able to find another husband as a single mother because what man would want to raise another man's baby?

Knowing she was carrying a fragile life inside her, Alexis finally admitted to herself that her mother was controlling and her father was absent. That wasn't any kind of family to lean on or rely on.

It was all the impetus that Alexis needed to leave the toxic life she had been in for far too long. She didn't want to raise her baby in such an environment, so she took the first job she could, as far away as she could.

She wasn't sailing around the world and soon she'd

have a baby, but St. John, in the US Virgin Islands, was her paradise.

"One lemonade for the lady."

She looked up to see Marcus come out of the galley with two tall glasses of lemonade, and her heart literally skipped a beat. It had been a long time since someone had made her swoon like this, and she wasn't even completely sure that Bruce had ever made her feel exactly this way.

Marcus was not what she'd expected, and as she thought about it, she realized she wasn't exactly sure what she had been expecting. She was glad that he different though. It was nice to laugh with someone. It was nice to have a casual conversation again.

She'd been so focused on work, her patients and putting her past behind her that it had been a long time since she'd had a non-work-related conversation with someone. Of course, this meeting was work related in a way, about convincing Immigration that they were a real couple. The thought made her uncomfortable. Alexis was very much aware of what they were doing and that it was illegal, but what other choice did she have?

And if it wasn't for the situation she was in, she likely wouldn't have met Marcus at all, a thought that made her sad, she realized.

Marcus sat down across from her and stared out the aft windows at the marina. "If you squint hard, it could be Paris."

"Why would I want that? This is paradise. It's warm and sunny."

"Not right now. There's a wee chill tonight."

"Not the same chill I'm used to."

He grinned. "I suppose not."

"So," she said, setting the glass on the table. "What do we need to discuss?"

"Everything," Marcus said. "Which seems like a daunting task."

"I'm not sure that we need to know everything." And she didn't want him to know completely everything. After what Bruce did to her heart, she didn't want to be that open and vulnerable with someone. It wasn't safe. "This is a marriage on paper only."

"Right." Marcus nodded, and she got the sense that maybe there were things that he didn't want her to know either.

"So, you have one brother?"

He nodded. "Yes. Dr. Matthew Olesen, chief of surgery at Ziese Memorial Hospital in Charlotte Amalie, St. Thomas."

"Are you from Charlotte Amalie?" she asked.

"No, I was born in St. Croix. My parents are Dutch and American. My father is from the Netherlands and my mother is of Dutch descent, but born and raised in New York. Her family came over on one of the ships fleeing Europe in the 1600s. They were Huguenots, and they settled the area of New Paltz—Sleepy Hollow and all that."

"Doesn't the headless horseman come from there?" Alexis asked, intrigued.

"Yes. Washington Irving did write a story about that, didn't he? Yes, it was set there, and a lot of my mother's ancestors are buried there. You seem to have a fascination with the horseman. Your eyes lit up when you mentioned him."

Alexis felt her cheeks heat. "Well, when I was a

child and home alone, I would watch a lot of those cartoons from America and in the autumn they would have all these creepy stories about ghosts and witches. And the horseman. That story fascinated me. I don't know why. I couldn't help but wonder what happened to Ichabod."

Marcus smiled. "Well then, there is something unique I now know about you—you're fascinated with the macabre and Halloween."

She laughed. "I suppose."

"And you? You said you're an only child?"

Alexis nodded. "I am. I was born in London. My parents lived in the north end. They are quite well off, and I was sent to the finest schools but disappointed my father greatly when all I became was a midwife and a nurse practitioner."

"Only?" Marcus asked dryly. "That's something to be quite proud of I think."

"I think so, too," she said softly.

Marcus smiled again, his eyes sparkling in the shadows, and she could feel herself swoon again. They were strangers and yet…this moment with him felt so intimate. Like she'd known him for quite some time already.

"What about the father of your baby?" Marcus asked, breaking the spell and the silence.

Alexis swallowed the lump in her throat. She knew that he was going to ask that question, and she knew that he had to ask that question, but it was still a hard pill to swallow. She didn't like to talk about it because it brought up too many painful memories, too much hurt and betrayal, but then again, it also brought her a sense of unending happiness, because this baby was what she'd always wanted.

"The father is my ex-husband. He told me he always wanted children, and though we tried for a long time, it didn't happen. When we'd finally given up, I became pregnant. I thought he would be happy about it, but he'd changed his mind. It was then I discovered that he'd also changed his mind about me. He'd moved on and started an affair a year before."

"I'm sorry."

Alexis shrugged. "It's fine. It happens all the time."

"It does. Too often. My fiancée left me for another man, so trust me when I say I understand." Marcus reached across the table and took her hand in his. The simple touch sent a warming zing through her. She trembled and pulled her hand out of his, unbalanced by his touch.

He pulled his hand back. "Sorry, I didn't ask if you'd be comfortable with that."

"No," she said. "It just caught me off guard. I mean, we're still almost strangers."

"I'm hoping we'll become friends."

Her heart skipped a beat. "I would like that, too."

Marcus leaned back. "So, will I have to deal with your ex-husband during this?"

"No, Bruce signed away all parental rights. He's back in England and has moved on."

Marcus's eyes widened, as if he was shocked by that. "Okay. Well, I think we should have something to eat before we continue. This is getting a bit too heavy."

"Food would be divine." She was suddenly very hungry.

"I'll be back in a moment. I didn't make fish or anything like that. I know there are things you shouldn't eat being pregnant."

"I know. I miss sushi completely," Alexis complained.

Marcus grinned. "Just relax and I'll be back in a moment. I made fettuccine Alfredo."

"Oh, yum! I love Italian."

"Good, because this would be even more awkward if you didn't like Italian."

"No tomatoes though, right?" she asked.

"I swear. Relax." He disappeared into the galley.

Alexis leaned back against the chair and stared out at all the boats and lights in the marina, wondering what was in store for her.

And wondering what she had got herself into with a man like this.

They had a great, easygoing and relaxing dinner. Alexis couldn't remember the last time she'd felt so at ease with someone she'd just met. They talked a bit about their respective jobs and other nonsensical things, but it was the kind of stuff that would help convince anyone who would question them about their marriage, that they were in fact a legitimate couple.

The only problem was...they weren't.

She meant what she'd said before, that she would like to be his friend, even after all this was done. She was enjoying Marcus's company.

It had been a long time since she'd been on a first date.

It's not really a date.

After the dinner was over, they headed up on deck to

enjoy the evening breeze and listen to the faint noises of Pillsbury Sound.

"You know," he said, finally breaking the silence that had fallen between them. "You could just scoot over to the British Virgin Islands."

"I could, but then I wouldn't be able to return to the US Virgin Islands to work, and Pepper couldn't come to me. My patients are here in the United States. I have to be here with them."

Marcus nodded. "I understand that."

"No matter what way I do this, I'm putting myself in jeopardy, but it's worth it. I don't want to go back to England again."

"Because of your ex?"

"Not just him," she said softly.

She didn't want to talk about her loneliness there. And she didn't want to talk about her parents. There was nothing for her in the United Kingdom, but there was everything here for her, and this is where she wanted to stay.

St. John felt like home.

"Believe me, I understand. I don't want to return to mainland US and in particular not California. It holds too many bad memories. I went to the mainland because of schooling. I thought that I would like it there better, but I missed the islands. I missed the culture that I grew up with. This is home."

Alexis nodded, a lump forming in her throat. She was getting far too emotional, and she had to put some distance between the two of them. She didn't want to cry, which she seemed to do a lot lately, in front of Marcus.

Even though she was enjoying his company immensely, she wasn't going to be vulnerable to him. She wasn't going to be vulnerable to any man again.

"I think I need to call it a night. I'm exhausted."

"I can take you home."

"Thanks. So, what do we do now? Do you know our next steps?"

"Well, I think we have to go to the superior court on St. Thomas and apply for a marriage license. You'll have to bring your divorce decree. And dress nice—formal. They don't tolerate casual wear at the courthouse."

Alexis nodded. "Okay. I can do that."

"I'll take us over on the *Tryphine* tomorrow. I have a berth on St. Thomas."

Alexis nodded again, feeling extremely nervous. There was a knot in the pit of her stomach, and she began to wring her hands together. He reached out and took her hands in his.

"It'll be okay," he said, his voice reassuring.

"Are you sure?"

He smiled that half smile. "No, but I've agreed to help you and try. I choose to remain optimistic."

She smiled at him. "Okay. I'll be optimistic too."

Although she still wasn't sure this was the right idea, there was no denying that Marcus was a gem. He was so nice, but she worried she was ruining his life by allowing him to go ahead with this marriage.

And that was the last thing she wanted to do.

CHAPTER FOUR

MARCUS SHOULD HAVE gone and picked up Alexis himself, but he had to stay and ready the *Tryphine* for departure. She'd assured him last night, when he dropped her off, that he didn't need to come pick her up—she was perfectly capable of walking—but he still felt bad.

He felt like he needed to take care of her.

You're just worried about saying "I do."

Marcus tugged on his collar. It was a bit stifling. He hated wearing suits at the best of times, but today it felt like his tie and his collar were choking him like a noose.

He took another deep breath.

"You look dapper," Chase called out as he walked up the gangplank. He was dressed in a suit as well. They needed a witness to pull off this marriage, and since this was Chase and Pepper's brilliant idea, Chase had been volunteered.

"Thanks. I hate this, by the way," Marcus grumbled as he adjusted a knot on the rigging.

"I know, but you have no idea what this means to me, to Pepper…to our family."

Marcus smiled at Chase. "Thank goodness my boat is motorized so I can take her across without sailing.

I'm not supposed to be doing any 'jigging,' as Vic puts it."

"Isn't jigging dancing?"

"Yes, and I think you jig squid too, but I'd guess that none of that is allowed either."

Chase chuckled. "What're you going to tell Matthew and Vic?"

"About what?"

"Your marriage?" Chase asked.

Marcus frowned. He hadn't really thought about telling his brother. He had briefly let it pass through his mind, knowing that his brother would not approve of it, but that had been when he was just barely entertaining the idea. Now they were going across to St. Thomas to get a license and marry in front of a judge.

He couldn't hide this for the next two years. He would have to tell Matthew and Victoria about it, though he had no idea how or what he was going to tell them exactly.

Hey, this is my fake wife. I'm putting my medical license and freedom in jeopardy to commit fraud because Chase and Pepper asked me nicely.

It wasn't the most eloquent way of putting it.

Marcus didn't want to lie to Matthew. Since the domino surgery, they had been on a path to healing their relationship. They were trying to reconnect and if Marcus lied to his brother now, it could ruin the tenuous relationship they currently had, but on the flip side, Marcus didn't want a lot of people knowing that his marriage to Alexis was fake. If too many people knew that this was a marriage of convenience, then what they were doing here was a moot point.

Alexis would be deported.

Pepper would be in trouble, facing a risky birth without the one midwife she trusted to see her through it, and Marcus would most likely lose his medical license and face jail time.

What would his parents think about that?

It was bad enough that he mostly felt like he was the disappointment in the family. His parents and Matthew had told him time and time again that he wasn't, but there was still a part of him that felt like he could never live up to their expectations.

"I guess I'm going to have to tell Matthew," Marcus said, finally answering the question. The real question though was just how much he was going to tell his twin.

"No point in lying. You've got to rip the Band-Aid off sooner or later."

"You're full of bright ideas," Marcus groused.

"I am. So, when do we leave?"

"As soon as Alexis gets here."

"Here she comes now," Chase said, walking by as Marcus finished some of the more difficult tasks so that they could get underway.

Marcus glanced up and saw Alexis walk toward the mooring, and his breath caught in his throat at the sight of her. The world around him melted away as he just stared at the woman. Her honey hair was down in those soft waves that he loved. The flowy summer dress hit all the right curves, and he let his gaze wander over each and every one, even the swell of the life she carried under her heart.

She's not yours.

He climbed down and helped her on board, taking her tiny, delicate hand in his.

"Sorry, my hands are a bit rough."

"No doubt from all that pirating work," she quipped.

He chuckled. "Too right."

"Sorry I'm late," she apologized.

"You're not late. We'll get there in plenty of time."

"Oh, good."

"You look lovely," he said, and he hoped that his voice didn't shake as he said it.

That peachy pink he liked so much flooded her cheeks. "Thank you. You look very dashing yourself."

"I try," he teased, winking as he helped get her settled on deck. "We'll be leaving soon. It's a short trip to St. Thomas."

"How are you going to manage sailing when you're still recovering?" she asked.

"The *Tryphine* has a motor, so it isn't so much an all-hands-on-deck situation today."

"I was hoping to swashbuckle a bit this morning."

"Again with the pirate metaphor?" he asked.

She laughed. "I'm sorry. I promise it's the last one. I just can't help it."

He laughed. "I can see that."

Chase came back on deck and greeted Alexis before helping Marcus finish preparing the boat to leave. They slipped their moorings and headed out of the marina toward the open waters of the Caribbean Sea, leaving Cruz Bay behind them. The sun was bright, with big white clouds in the blue sky, and the water was calm, with only little whitecaps, as they sailed toward St. Thomas.

Marcus drank in the feel of the sun on his face. It felt good to get back out on the open water. This was what he loved to do. Just him and the *Tryphine*. Other than helping others by being a doctor, this was all he needed out of life.

And as much as he loved his home in the US Virgin Islands, there was a very small part of him that wanted to take the risk and set out on a world tour. Just him, his boat and the open sea.

Marcus had dreamed about it for some time, but he didn't know what was holding him back. The only thing he could think was that Dawna had always thought it was a silly idea to travel the world by boat, and her scorn had caused him to push the dream to the far corners of his mind.

She'd always favored vacations in five-star resorts, not that there was anything wrong with that, but it wasn't what Marcus really wanted. He wanted to take some time and really see the world. He wanted to get to know the people of faraway lands, and you couldn't really do that staying a five-star resort.

He glanced down at Alexis and smiled to himself as he watched her. She was glowing as she looked over the prow of the *Tryphine*. Marcus was in awe of her.

She'd come here after her marriage ended, pregnant and alone. Alexis had taken a huge chance and was taking another chance now doing whatever it took to stay here. Marcus admired her for that and couldn't help but wonder if he should take a leaf out of her book and go on his adventure for a year, once their marriage had ended.

Who would look after your patients then?

That thought sobered him.

He wouldn't let them down.

He couldn't let them down.

St. Thomas came into view just then, and as they

rounded the island they headed toward Charlotte
Amalie, the beautiful town filled with brightly roofed
houses clinging to the side of lush green hills. A horn
blared across the water as a cruise ship slowly made
its way into port.

"Oh, wow!" Alexis gasped.

Marcus smiled at her wonder as she took it all in.

"It's great, right?"

Alexis nodded. "I've always wanted to see the world
via ship or boat. This is just heaven."

His heart skipped a beat, because he understood
what she meant when she said it was heaven. He
agreed. Other than saving lives and helping his patients, this was a high he would never get tired of—
being at the mercy to the water, the wind, the tide.

It was the rhythm of life.

It was part of who he was.

Marcus guided the yacht to his mooring in French-
town in Charlotte Amalie. It was close to the restaurant
where Matthew and Victoria had had their supposed
work dinner when she'd first arrived and they'd been
reunited. Marcus knew now that Vic and Matthew had
been lovers years before Matthew married his late wife,
Kirsten. Vic had seen the *Tryphine* at its Charlotte
Amalie mooring, which annoyed his twin because Matthew had thought Marcus had returned to St. John.

It made him chuckle to himself.

The little bistro was beautiful, and maybe he could
get Matthew to pull some strings and he could take
Alexis there tonight for an intimate dinner after they
got married. They'd be alone as Chase was planning
to head back to St. John on the ferry.

Chase helped him tie the boat up and soon he was

helping Alexis down the gangplank, while Chase went out to hire a cab to take them to the superior court. Marcus would usually walk to it, but with him still recovering and Alexis six months pregnant, he didn't want to force either of them to walk in this heat.

It was a warm and sunny day, and he was already regretting his suit. He felt like he was melting in it.

They crammed into the back of the tiny cab, Chase leaning forward to speak with the driver and Marcus pressed up against Alexis. Instinctively he put his arm around her shoulders, and she didn't move away. It was nice having her pressed against him; it felt natural.

"It's busy today," she said, her voice shaking slightly.

"The tourists are coming in off the ships. I forgot about that. Tuesday is a particularly busy day at port."

The cab navigated the narrow streets from French-town to the superior court and Chase paid the driver, as Marcus and Alexis were in this predicament because of him. Marcus helped Alexis out of the cab, and they made their way into the courthouse.

Chase had a friend who worked there and had cleared everything for them so they had already arranged an appointment with the judge. And it didn't hurt that Marcus had given his kidney to Mrs. Van Luven, who had worked at the court as a clerk and was still well loved in the court office.

It made him feel all the more guilty for deceiving them, but he was here now to marry Alexis and there was no going back.

Alexis was nervous. She'd been so isolated in her little world at the midwife practice. She went to work and then went back to the dorm room near the clinic. Sometimes she'd go to the little market to get something to eat, but it had been four months since she'd been out in a big, bustling city with a lot of people around her.

She'd forgotten what a busy city was like, and it was a bit nerve racking to be in such a crush of people. Alexis never did like crowds. They made her feel as though she was suffocating.

Bruce had loved parties and people.

Often, she would spend her whole time at a party alone in a corner or glued to Bruce's side and bored out of her mind. He used to tease her about being such a wallflower or leaning on him, but Marcus didn't say anything.

As if he sensed her trepidation, he pulled her closer.

Although she should've shied away from him, she didn't. She was glad that she could lean on Marcus, and it felt good to have his arm around her. She felt safe, like she'd known him her whole life, which made her feel bad that he was part of this ruse. Maybe it would be easier if she didn't like him so much?

It would be easier on her to stay away from him, but she liked being with him.

He'd looked so handsome steering his boat across the channel to St. Thomas, like he belonged on the water, and it was amazing to have the wind in her face.

She could only imagine what it would be like to be out on open water and have the sails out. To see nothing but sea, sails and sky. The baby fluttered inside her and reminded her that she had to stay grounded.

It was her baby and the kind of life she wanted her baby to have that had brought her here to this moment, and she couldn't be greedy. Even if she wanted to be.

The courthouse was a bit calmer, but it was still

busy for a Tuesday morning. She let Chase and Marcus lead her to where she needed to go, barely able to pay attention to where they were going as she was so overwhelmed by sensations.

"Do you have your divorce decree?" Marcus asked, interrupting her thoughts.

"What? Yes." She reached into her purse and pulled out the documents. She wasn't sure when they had arrived at the counter to get their license.

The woman working there inputted the information and handed Marcus more paperwork with instructions to wait in the chairs until their names were called.

Alexis's heart was hammering, and she placed a hand on her chest as she took deep breaths, trying to calm her frayed nerves.

She swore, after what happened with Bruce, that she would never do this again. She would never get married and yet here she was, waiting to get married. Marcus filled out his information and Alexis filled out hers. A short time later they were called in to do a brief pre-ceremony interview to ensure they were both willingly entering into the union, and then they were told to wait once again to be called in for their wedding ceremony.

She still couldn't quite believe she was doing this. She was putting a lot at risk.

Marcus was too. Just to help her.

It weighed heavily on her, and she suddenly felt like she was going to have a panic attack.

"Olesen and Martin?" a clerk called.

"That's us." There was an edge to Marcus's voice as he took her hand and they headed to the chambers. Alexis's pulse thundered between her ears, and she felt like she was going to faint.

The judge entered the room.

He was an older man; his face was extremely red and he was sweating.

Profusely.

Alexis cocked her head, concerned. Besides the bloodred coloring in his cheeks and the sweat across his brow, his pallor was gray.

She'd seen this happen before, when she worked in an accident and emergency department in an inner-city hospital in London, and she couldn't tear her eyes from his face. All her mental alarms were going off that something was very wrong.

"This is a pretty standard procedure," the judge said through gasping breaths.

Marcus glanced at her, and she could tell by the way his brow was furrowed that he was concerned too.

The judge started to read the script, and in no time at all he reached the vows.

"Marcus Olesen, do you take Alexis Martin in matrimony?" the judge asked.

"I do," Marcus answered.

"And do you, Alexis Martin, take Marcus Olesen in matrimony?"

Alexis swallowed the lump in her throat. Her stomach was doing flip-flops. She felt like this was the biggest mistake.

What're you doing?

"I do."

"Then, by the powers vested in me by the United States Virgin Islands, I now pronounce you husband and wife." The judge's voice began to slur on the final word, and his face was drooping as he quickly signed the marriage certificate and then handed it over for each of them to sign. The paperwork all complete, he stamped it and moved to hand it over, but Alexis and Marcus watched in horror as the judge grabbed his arm holding the certificate, grimaced, cried out and then toppled over.

Marcus dove for the judge, and Alexis flung open the door as Chase helplessly watched on. "Someone call an ambulance. The judge has collapsed!"

"Alexis, are the paramedics on the way?" Marcus asked a few minutes later as he continued to administer CPR to the judge.

"Yes." Alexis was seeing if she could find what she needed in the first-aid kit.

"Blast," Marcus cursed. "His throat is closing. He's not getting oxygen."

"What do you need?" Alexis asked.

"Surgical kit," Marcus said grimly. "If they have one."

Alexis pressed her lips together and dug through the first-aid box. Thankfully, it was well stocked, in case of an emergency like a hurricane. At the very bottom of the box, she found a simple surgical kit. "How is this?" She handed him the kit.

"It's fine."

"What're you thinking?"

"Tracheotomy," Marcus stated. "He can't breathe. His throat is closed."

Alexis knelt beside Marcus, who slipped off his jacket and rolled up his sleeves.

"I'm going to need your help, Alexis," Marcus said. "It's been a while since I've done one."

"Same," Alexis said. "But tell me what to do."

Marcus nodded and she opened the kit, handing him

gloves and Betadine. Alexis put on gloves and watched as Marcus found the cricoid cartilage, just under the Adam's apple.

She handed Marcus the scalpel.

He made the incision, and Alexis prepared a straw she found in the judge's desk as a makeshift breathing tube.

"Here." She handed him the straw.

He smiled. "Good thinking."

Marcus inserted the straw and leaned over to breathe through it twice before continuing his chest compressions. The judge was still not breathing, so Marcus continued giving rescue breaths through the tube and performing CPR.

Finally the paramedics arrived, and Marcus helped them load the judge onto the gurney. He then continued with his compressions and breaths.

"Where should we take him, Dr. Olesen?" the paramedic asked.

"Ziese Memorial and be sure to page my brother, Dr. Olesen."

Alexis and Chase stood back as Marcus prepared to leave with the paramedics to go to the hospital.

"What should we do now?" Alexis asked.

"Well, we should probably go to Ziese Memorial. I think you and Marcus need to go to Immigration together, and that's kind of hard to do when your new husband is helping to save a life," Chase said.

Alexis chuckled. "Let's go then."

Chase hailed a cab, and it was a short ride across town to Ziese Memorial from the courthouse. Alexis could hear the wail of the siren as the cab followed closely behind.

The hospital was new and built, like all the other buildings in town, against the side of the hill, with a bright red roof and white plaster walls. It looked like one of those typical island hospitals, but Alexis knew that this was a state-of-the-art building.

It was the kind of hospital she would love to work at. And she knew from the domino that had recently been performed that they were the top of their game in the Caribbean.

Alexis stared around in wonder at it all.

"Can I help you?" a volunteer asked.

"I'm looking for Dr. Olesen." Alexis flashed her identification, showing that she was a nurse. It was an old habit to always carry it with her.

The volunteer smiled and nodded. "Follow me."

Alexis followed the volunteer who took her down through some halls that led out onto the surgical floor. She was worried about the judge, and the fact that they'd brought him straight to the surgical floor meant his condition was a lot more serious than she'd initially thought.

"He's right over there," the volunteer said, pointing across the room to where Marcus, in scrubs, was standing with his back to her talking with someone. She was surprised to see him in scrubs already, but not shocked as his brother was the chief of surgery and he'd just performed an emergency tracheotomy.

She'd been so impressed with his calm, collected head through the whole ordeal.

Marcus continued to impress and amaze her.

He was like no man she'd ever met before.

Marcus was one of a kind.

"Thank goodness I found you. I have the marriage certificate. How is the judge doing?" Alexis asked.

The man turned around and though the blue eyes—wide with shock—were the same, there was no beard and she could tell straightaway that this was Marcus's brother.

Apparently, Marcus hadn't thought it worth mentioning that his brother was his identical twin.

"I'm sorry?" he asked.

"You're not Marcus." She took a step back, mortified.

"No. I'm not. I'm his brother, Matthew," he said carefully as he assessed her. "And you are?"

"Alexis Martin. I'm a nurse practitioner and midwife."

"You said something about a marriage certificate… Are you telling me you're my brother's wife?"

Alexis worried her bottom lip. She had really stepped into it, and she only hoped that Marcus wasn't too annoyed with her that she'd let it slip.

"Yes. I am."

CHAPTER FIVE

MARCUS HAD TO continue to administer CPR in the ambulance and was up on the gurney with the patient as the paramedics wheeled him into the emergency room.

"Can someone please explain to me why my donor patient is straddling and treating a suspected stroke patient?"

Marcus cringed hearing his sister-in-law's voice boom across the emergency room.

When they finally had the judge in a pod, he was able to get off and hand over the compressions to the residents and the trauma team.

Marcus was still a bit shocked that minutes after the judge had pronounced him and Alexis as husband and wife he had been cutting open the man's throat to save his life.

Now he was in trouble with his surgeon.

"I didn't think that transplant surgeons graced the emergency room floor," Marcus teased after he signed over the judge to the ER team.

Vic crossed her arms and raised one eyebrow in question. "We do when one of her patients comes in. I just didn't expect to see *you* here."

"Is your patient okay?" Marcus asked.

"Fine. I'm wondering how you're doing." She took a step back. "You're in a suit. What were you doing at the superior court anyway?"

"How do you know I was at the courthouse?" Marcus asked.

Victoria pointed. "The judge?"

Marcus grinned. "Are you always this bossy with Matthew?"

She chuckled. "More, but seriously you're not even cleared to practice yet. What were you doing?"

"Saving a man's life?"

Victoria smiled. "Okay, but still, you have to be careful."

"Well…" Marcus trailed off and he glanced up to see his brother marching across the emergency room toward them, followed by Alexis, who looked worried.

Oh, no.

His stomach knotted and fell to the bottom of his feet. Actually, lower than that. It felt like he was walking around on it. Digging his heels into it. This was not how he wanted his brother to find out.

I'm sorry, Alexis mouthed behind Matthew, who stood in front of Marcus with his arms crossed.

"Hi, Matthew," Marcus said cheerfully.

Victoria was looking worried now. "What's going on?"

"Marcus is married," Matthew announced.

Victoria's eyes widened and she took a step back. "What?"

Marcus stepped forward and took Alexis's hand. "This is my wife, Alexis Martin. She's a nurse practitioner and a midwife on St. John, and we were married this afternoon. That's why I was at the superior court."

Alexis waved nervously.

"It's lovely to meet you!" Victoria stepped forward and hugged them both awkwardly. Then she stepped back and nudged Matthew.

"Welcome to the family," Matthew said, giving Alexis a hug and then shaking Marcus's hand. "I'm sorry for seeming a bit surprised. I didn't even know Marcus was dating anyone."

"Yeah, well, you've been a bit preoccupied, brother, with your new wife."

Matthew grinned and looked warmly at Victoria. "This is true."

Victoria sighed. "This isn't the best place to get to know one another."

Matthew nodded. "How about dinner tonight at our place?"

Marcus opened his mouth to decline, but Alexis nodded and said, "That sounds lovely. Thank you."

So much for his plan to have an intimate dinner alone. Though maybe dinner with this brother and Victoria would be better than tempting fate by spending more time alone with Alexis.

"Great," Victoria said. "How about six? Kind of early, but we're working until then."

"It's fine. We have some other business to attend to." Marcus took Alexis's hand. "We'll see you both tonight."

He escorted Alexis out of the emergency room of Ziese Memorial and didn't say anything to her until they were outside.

"I thought Chase was with you?" Marcus asked.

"He was, but then we got separated and someone

asked if they could help me. I figured it was the easiest way to find you."

Marcus ran a hand through his hair. "Well, I wanted to tell my brother. I just didn't expect you would be the one to actually do it."

"I thought he was you from behind," Alexis whispered. "You didn't tell me that your brother was an identical twin!"

He couldn't fault her on that as he hadn't told her that bit of information. He began to laugh thinking about what a shock it must've been for his brother.

"What's so funny?" Alexis asked.

"I was just picturing Matthew's face. What did you say to him exactly?"

Alexis smiled. "I said something about our marriage license. I can't remember exactly. He was a bit shocked, and when he turned around and I saw that it wasn't you, it furthered his shock. I don't think that he expected you were going to get married."

"Trust me, I understand his shock. It was never in my plans either."

It had been at one time, long ago when he'd been in love with a woman who he thought had loved him back. He'd been an absolute fool. So no, he didn't think marriage was for him, and he was only doing this out of the goodness of his heart.

This wasn't real.

Chase came running out of the hospital just then and came to an abrupt stop beside them. "Sorry, I went to look for intake and then I turned around and Alexis was gone. I'm glad you two found each other. How is the judge?"

Marcus frowned. "I don't know. He was handed off

to the trauma surgeons. Alexis and I have been invited to dinner at my brother's house later tonight. Maybe he'll tell us then."

Chase's eyes widened. "So he knows, then."

"He knows we're married," Alexis said quickly. "He doesn't know about the other part."

Chase nodded in understanding. "Gotcha. So what're you two going to do now?"

Marcus had no idea. It was several hours before he and Alexis were scheduled to have dinner with Victoria and Matthew, so the day was theirs. He wasn't sure what married couples did, beyond the obvious of what married couples tended to do… And he didn't want to think about that.

Not that he wouldn't like that to happen with Alexis, since he was highly attracted to her. It was just, it *couldn't* happen. Alexis was pregnant; she was off-limits. She had made it clear that she was just going to stay married to him so that she could stay in the country. This was not one of his holiday flings.

But suddenly the idea of having one of those kinds of flings again made him a bit queasy.

"Some sightseeing and lunch?" Marcus suggested. "What're you going to do?" he asked Chase.

"I'll catch the Cruz Bay ferry back to St. John. I don't like leaving Pepper alone for very long, and Jonas is still recovering. He's fine here, but I'm glad he'll be coming home soon!"

"That's great! Be safe," Marcus said, clapping his best friend on the back and pulling him into a hug.

"Thanks again, you two." Chase briefly hugged

Alexis and then hailed a cab to take him down to the ferry wharf.

It was just Marcus and Alexis now.

They were alone.

And he didn't want to stand outside a hospital killing time.

"What would you like to do?"

"I don't know. Since I got here I haven't had much time for sightseeing. I've just been working and dealing with morning sickness." She touched her belly gently, and Marcus fought the urge to reach out and touch her.

He didn't know what came over him in that moment that made him want to do that. It wasn't like he was going to be a part of the child's life.

"Well, most of the historic and touristy places will be teeming with tourists from the big cruise ships. Would you like to rent a car and go for a drive? Get away from the hustle and bustle of downtown Charlotte Amalie? I mean, the embassy is closed right now for lunch, so we have time to kill."

Alexis nodded. "Yes, I would like that very much, but do let me pay for it. You made me dinner the other night and brought me here."

"I'm the one that has a valid license for the Virgin Islands, and we drive on the right here."

She smiled and nodded. "Okay, but the next time I will take care of it."

"Next time?" He couldn't help but ask.

She blushed. "You know, in case we get a visit from Immigration or something. We'll have to present a united front for a while."

"How? It's a fake marriage."

"I know, but if anyone comes calling to check up on me, we'll have to…"

"Be in this together," he said, finishing off her sentence.

"Precisely."

"You're right." He cleared his throat.

"So what do we do?"

She worried her bottom lip. "I haven't quite thought it through."

"Well, we can start by some sightseeing. You stay here, and I'll go rent us a car. There's a car rental place not far from here."

Marcus had to put some distance between them. Even just for a moment. His pulse was racing, and he got so excited when she mentioned a next time. He was acting like he was a young man again, in that first flush of love and not the hardened, jaded playboy that he had become.

It wasn't long of a wait before Marcus pulled up in a small convertible, and Alexis couldn't contain her excitement when the little red car came to a stop beside her, with its top down. It was the kind of car that one should travel in when visiting an island paradise.

Or at least that was her opinion.

Marcus parked and got out of the car to open her door. She couldn't remember any man doing that for her, and just that simple gentlemanly act made her swoon just a bit. He really was the perfect package.

After he closed the door, he climbed into the driver's seat. "All buckled up?"

"Yep. I'm ready." She was more than ready to go

on an adventure. She didn't care where they went. It would just be nice to see more of one of the islands.

Marcus headed up a winding road in a northeastern direction, away from Ziese Memorial Hospital. There was a lot of traffic headed in the same direction, and she remembered reading that a lot of people chose to get married at the beaches that lined Magens Bay.

A beach wedding sounded nice.

Although the strange and surreal wedding that she and Marcus had had in the judge's office at the superior court before the judge collapsed was one they would be sure to talk about for some time.

Some time?

There would be no some time with Marcus.

Why was it so easy for her to forget that?

As the little red convertible wound its way up the hill, Marcus pulled into a turnout that had angled parking and a railing. She gasped when he parked the car and they could see Charlotte Amalie laid out below them, along with the sea, clouds and massive cruise ships in the harbor.

It was like something from a postcard. This was what she always pictured when she dreamed of the islands.

It was like stepping into that dream.

"Oh, wow! This is amazing."

"It's cool, right?"

Alexis undid her seat belt and got out of the car, not waiting for Marcus to open the door. She wandered to the edge of the railing and just drank in the sight of paradise from above. Marcus came and leaned against the railing next to her.

They didn't say anything. Just stared out at the city below them.

"You know, we didn't get to seal the deal."

"Seal the deal?" she asked, confused.

"The judge never got to the part where he says we can kiss, because he collapsed."

Her stomach did a flip. "He did sign the certificate though. We are still legally married."

"Yes, but the bride and groom always kiss after they're married and we didn't."

She'd been thinking about that too. When it was coming to that part, she got so nervous and she wasn't sure how she was going to handle the situation. It would look bad if she didn't kiss Marcus, but the idea of kissing him made her nervous.

And even thinking about it right now, as they stared out over Charlotte Amalie and the turquoise sea below them, her mouth went dry and her pulse raced. She had wanted to kiss him too, but Alexis felt it was too late. The moment to do it had passed.

She cleared her throat and stepped away from the railing.

And from him.

She needed to put distance between them.

"I really do hope the judge pulls through."

Not that she wanted to think about the judge in that moment, but it was a way to break the tension that she was feeling. It was a way to break the spell so she could step away.

"Me as well," Marcus said, standing up straight instead of leaning over the rail. "Well, we should carry on."

"Where to?" she asked, intrigued. "I thought this was it."

He gave her a look as if to say, come on. "A turnout at the side of the road is no way to kill a lot of time. It's a nice distraction, but do you think so little of me?"

It was a tease.

"Sorry." She laughed nervously. "I didn't mean to insult your honorable intentions for killing time before our awkward dinner with your twin and his wife."

Now it was Marcus's turn to laugh as he opened the car door for her. "Well, that's one way of putting it."

"I still feel extremely bad for spilling that news to your brother. You should have been the one to tell him. It wasn't my place," she said as he climbed back into the car.

"I was going to tell him. Honestly, I wish I had been there to see his face. That's the part I missed, the part I feel cheated out of." He grinned deviously.

"Well, he was certainly surprised."

"I can only imagine. And so I will keep trying to picture it. It'll bring me joy." He grinned and she laughed.

"That sounds mean."

"It's not. Not really. Not anymore. We spent so many years at odds that we, in a way, forgot to be brothers for a while. I guess it's a force of habit to be mean to one another."

"I wouldn't know. I don't have any siblings. My childhood was quite lonely, really." She found herself reaching down to touch her belly. Her child would never feel the loneliness that she had. Her lonely childhood had nothing to do with being an only child. It had more to do with her emotionally distant parents. It scared her, because there were times that Alexis wondered if she was actually genetically capable of emotion.

Of love.

She wasn't taught those things. It was one of Bruce's problems in their relationship, and she saw it now. He didn't think that she was loving enough. He was always annoyed that she didn't fawn over him, didn't cling to him.

Of course, what Bruce really wanted was a damsel in distress, which she was anything but. Still, she was scared that she wouldn't be able to be as demonstrative as she wanted to be and that her child would feel they lacked for love.

That's just fear talking. You know that.

Alexis had wanted this child so badly. She yearned to hold a piece of her heart and she was thrilled to be pregnant, even though it scared her to do this alone without support from anyone.

There had been so many times that she'd longed for a hug from her mother, but her mother was so self-absorbed and her father was always working. She couldn't count on anyone, but she was going to be here for her child. Even though it was just her, her child would never feel alone. Single parenthood might be difficult for her to navigate, but her child was going to know that it was loved. It might just be the two of them, but Alexis would make sure it was more than enough.

"I'm sorry to hear that," Marcus said, intruding on her thoughts.

Alexis shrugged. "I was lucky in other ways. I was educated, fed and safe."

"What about loved?" he asked softly.

"I'd like to think so, but my parents aren't very... They don't show it. They're a bit controlling. A bit cold."

And, of course, her mother thought that pleasing

one's husband was enough in life. It seemed so unhappy, so sad to live that way. To only live to please another person. But that was her mother's life, and her mother's choice.

Not hers.

"Well, I have a beautiful place we can walk through and enjoy. Somewhere to take our minds off all of it," he said brightly.

He slowed down near a gate on a dirt road, which had a sign advertising botanical gardens and a tea shop. Over the hedges Alexis could see the peak of greenhouses.

"Oh!" she exclaimed. "A garden sounds lovely."

"I thought you might like this. It's quiet, we can get some shade and they have a lovely tea shop in the center where we can get some lunch."

"Good choice."

"I'm glad you approve. My late sister-in-law loved this place."

Alexis noticed he said this with a hint of sadness in his voice. "Your late sister-in-law? Do you have another sibling?"

Marcus shook his head. "No, Matthew was married before, and his wife, Kirsten, died of cancer at quite a young age. When Matthew was working and she was feeling down, I would bring her here. She loved looking at the orchids and watching the birds."

"Sounds like you cared for her a great deal."

Marcus nodded. "Victoria is great too. She brought my brother back to life and she did save my life during the domino when I developed a blood clot in surgery, so I kind of owe her that."

Marcus winked and Alexis smiled.

He was such a kind soul. His kindness made her swoon, and she didn't understand why he was still single. How could any woman let a man like this get away?

Aren't you planning on doing that when this is done?

She shook that thought away as Marcus parked the car. This time Alexis paid the entrance fee, and they wound their way through the quiet gardens and straight to the conservatory that had the tearoom, which she was glad for. The gardens were beautiful, but she was tired and parched.

They found a table in the corner, next to a bubbly waterfall, and ordered simple tea with little sandwiches. Alexis leaned back in her chair and watched the water falling over the rocks and burbling at the bottom.

A parrot sat on a perch nearby, preening itself, and her stress began to melt away as she listened to the sounds of nature around her.

"So tomorrow we hit Immigration and the embassies?" Marcus asked.

Alexis nodded. "Yes. Hand in our paperwork, I suppose."

"Why is it so awkward between us again?" he asked.

"I don't know. I mean, we don't know much about each other and now we're married. And I'm pregnant. We haven't really talked about that either."

Marcus took a deep breath. "And we'll need to. Matthew and Victoria will want to know. It is sort of the elephant in the room and one of the reasons we got married, in a roundabout way."

"Exactly." She worried her bottom lip. "I don't know what to say."

"I can say it's mine. I mean, we'll be married for some time, so people will assume…"

Alexis's breath caught in her throat. Bruce didn't want his child, but here was a man she barely knew who was offering to claim her baby. Even though it secretly thrilled her, she couldn't let him do that.

"I can't let you. When we get divorced, what will you tell your brother and his wife when you have no custody rights?"

"I would tell them the truth. By then you'd be a US citizen."

A lump formed in her throat. "I hate that you have to be involved in this deception. I can't let you do this."

She was moved that Marcus saw the solution so black-and-white, but she didn't see it that way. There was a part of her that didn't trust him. Bruce had signed away his rights to their child, but she didn't want Marcus to try and claim rights down the road either.

Not that she expected he would, but she had to be careful.

She'd been burned and hurt one too many times, and Alexis didn't give her trust over so easily. There was a part of her that wanted to trust Marcus, but she couldn't.

"I have no problem. My brother would question me to the point of insanity if I told him the truth now. Me saying the baby is mine is less of a headache for me, but if I have to sign something or swear some kind of oath that I claim no rights, then I'll do that. We just need to present a united front on this so Immigration has no questions."

"Good point."

"So, on that point, I think it's prudent that we move in together."

Marcus couldn't believe the words when they came out of his mouth, until they were slipping past his lips.

What're you thinking?

That was the point. He wasn't thinking. It seemed that when he was around Alexis, he forgot himself. This was supposed to just be a marriage on paper.

Living together was more than just a business arrangement.

He had let himself get swept up with her, and that hadn't happened to him since Dawna. It scared him, but on the flip side, he found he'd missed this sort of connection with someone.

It was making him realize how lonely he had been for a really long time.

It still didn't register with him right away that he'd just asked Alexis to move in with him.

The *Tryphine* was a large sailboat, but it was still confined quarters with a woman who was off-limits and whom he was highly attracted to. On top of all that, she was pregnant with another man's baby. Although that fool had given up his child. What an idiot.

"Sorry, did I just hear you correctly? You want me to move in with you?" she asked, shocked.

"Well, we are married, and again, we need to keep up appearances."

Alexis's eyes were still wide, and she blinked a couple of times. "Yes, but…"

"But what? We're both putting a lot on the line to do this, so it only makes sense we live together."

"I suppose."

"And you live in a temporary residence, so I can't move in there with you."

"No, you can't. I just have a small room. It's tight quarters."

"There are two bedrooms on the *Tryphine*. I have room for you."

Alexis nodded. "Okay…yes, you're right, and it's only temporary."

The waitress brought their light lunch and tea just then, but as Marcus bit into a cucumber sandwich it tasted like sawdust in his mouth. Even his taste buds were rebelling against his bonkers idea to have her move in with him, but he knew it ultimately made perfect sense.

And even though she was worried about the deception of the baby being his and even though he told her it was no big deal, he did feel bad for lying to Matthew and Victoria. He was also envious of Matthew. Not many people knew yet, but Victoria was currently pregnant with their first child. Matthew had what Marcus had wanted years ago with Dawna—a family.

They finished their lunch and took a walk around the gardens. Marcus found it a bit boring, but it was a place to kill time before they had to head back to Charlotte Amalie for dinner at his brother's place.

Something he was dreading.

"I need to sit down for a moment," Alexis said. Her face was flushed, but not with heat. It immediately fired off his red flags that something was wrong.

Marcus guided her to a bench. Out of instinct, he

touched her face and checked her pulse, which was quite sluggish.

"How far along are you?" he asked.

"Twenty-six weeks."

"I know you're a midwife, but have you been tested for gestational diabetes? Do you track your ketones and protein?"

"I do. My protein has been a bit high, but I've been busy and stressed." She closed her eyes and took a deep breath.

He frowned. "We're going back to Ziese Memorial."

"I'm just overheated."

"So nurses are also bad patients too."

"How do mean?" she asked, confused.

"That old saying that doctors make the worst patients, well, the same goes for you. I've treated pregnant patients before they head off to their OB/GYN. I know what I'm talking about, and I know you know what you need to do. We're going to Charlotte Amalie, and we're going to get some tests done."

Marcus wasn't taking no for an answer. Alexis was stressed, but he was worried her stress had caught up with her and she'd missed the signs. She was awfully small too for how many weeks she was along. It was better to be safe than sorry in this situation.

"Okay, you're right. Let's go, Dr. Olesen. Thank you."

He shrugged and took her hand to make sure she didn't fall on the way back to the car. "It's what good husbands do."

CHAPTER SIX

MATTHEW HAD GIVEN Marcus hospital privileges so that his brother could order the tests, and then sent down one of his OB/GYN doctors to assist as Marcus couldn't act as Alexis's doctor since they were married.

It annoyed Marcus, both because Matthew was right and also because Marcus knew the truth. On paper he was Alexis's husband, but he wasn't actually. It also meant that Matthew had found out even more news about Alexis without Marcus being the one to tell him. He was already beginning to dread the conversation he had to have with his brother tonight…

The upcoming dinner was looming over him like some kind of great, big elephant ready to burst, which he knew wasn't the correct analogy, but he was feeling a bit stressed himself and couldn't seem to think of anything more bigger and awkward than an elephant.

Especially an exploding one.

"You're pacing," Alexis murmured from where she was lying down on an exam table.

"Am I?"

"What're you agitated about?"

"Elephants," he groused.

Alexis cocked an eyebrow and sat up. "What? That's an odd thing to be anxious about."

He grinned. "It isn't if it blows up."

"You're an interesting man, Marcus Olesen."

"Interesting is better than boring."

The OB/GYN, Dr. Baxter, came in after knocking. "I have your blood work. I'm going to send you to have a glucose tolerance test done, and you do have some high protein that worries me. Your blood pressure is slightly elevated as well."

Alexis worried her bottom lip, and Marcus instinctively took her hand in his. Alexis didn't pull away and almost seemed to lean into him, which was nice.

"When should I do the glucose test?" Alexis asked. "And can I do it at my clinic on St. John?"

Dr. Baxter nodded. "Yes, at your clinic is fine, but I need you to take it easy and I want to be your physician to monitor this. I would like you to take your blood pressure daily, because if you don't take it easy and it continues to elevate, I am going to put you on bed rest."

"I have to work to stay in the country," Alexis said quickly.

Dr. Baxter looked confused. "Didn't you two just get married? I think that makes your work visa a moot point now."

Alexis's cheeks flushed crimson. "Yes. It does."

And even Marcus held his breath in that moment. He had been worried about little slipups like this.

Thankfully, Dr. Baxter just smiled gently at them. "Besides, with a doctor's note, it wouldn't affect your visa. If you need bed rest, you need bed rest and you do need to take it easier. Now, how about an ultrasound? You're measuring quite small as well."

Alexis nodded, and Marcus helped her lie back down on the exam table. He knew she was worried, and even though he had no connection to the baby or her, he was concerned too.

Dr. Baxter spread the gel on her belly and Marcus watched the screen. It took a moment before he saw the little black-and-white fetus appear. Even though it wasn't his child and he'd seen ultrasounds before, he felt an instantaneous connection, right then and there, like a bolt of lightning. An awe overtook him that Alexis was carrying a life inside her.

Dr. Baxter smiled. "Everything looks good."

Alexis smiled. "I'm glad to hear that."

Dr. Baxter took some pictures and then wiped the gel off Alexis's belly with a towel. "I'll go book that test for you in Cruz Bay for the end of this week and get you a picture of your baby."

Dr. Baxter left and Alexis sat up.

"I feel like a fool," she muttered.

"Why?" Marcus asked.

"I'm a midwife and a nurse and I didn't see the signs. If I had been paying attention, I would've got the glucose test done earlier."

"Hey, as I said before, medical professionals are the worst patients and you've had a lot going on." He reached out and touched her chin, her skin so soft under his fingers. He felt like his hands were too tough, too clumsy, to touch her delicate skin, but he wanted to feel her.

It was surprising how much he wanted to take her in his arms and protect her.

She leaned forward and rested her forehead against his, her eyes closed.

"Thank you for being here for me," she murmured.

She opened her eyes and as their gazes locked, his pulse started thundering between his ears. She leaned down and kissed him then, a light fleeting kiss on the lips that seared his soul. And then he kissed her back the way he'd wanted to since the moment he met her.

Deeply.

Cupping her face in his hands and losing himself in the softness of her lips.

A knock on the door from Dr. Baxter made him break off the kiss and step back, even though his body was protesting because he wanted more.

So much more.

Alexis was flushed and wouldn't look at him.

Dr. Baxter was a bit oblivious to what had just happened, which was probably a good thing. Marcus wasn't sure what had come over him. He just got swept up in the moment. Which happened a lot when he was around her, now that he thought about it.

And now she was moving in. At his request. It was unsettling.

"The appointment is booked, and here's a picture of your baby. Congratulations again to you both." Dr. Baxter handed them the lab requisition and the picture before leaving.

Alexis didn't look at the picture, but slipped it in her purse.

"Well, I better get cleaned up," she stated.

"Right." Marcus rubbed the back of his neck, trying to calm his pulse. "I'll wait for you in the hall."

Alexis nodded and he slipped out of the room He couldn't seem to control himself when he was near her. He was confused. This was supposed to just be a business arrangement with Alexis. He shouldn't be feeling these emotions.

He shouldn't want her this much.

But he did.

They didn't say much as they left Ziese Memorial Hospital and headed over to Matthew and Victoria's home. Marcus was unusually quiet, and she could feel the tension between them again. And it was no surprise.

A lot had happened.

He'd suggested they move in together. Then he took care of her when she felt sick in the botanical gardens and was there when she saw her baby.

And then she had kissed him when she was at her most vulnerable.

Alexis was still reeling from that kiss.

She didn't know what possessed her to kiss him. She was just caught up in so many emotions, and seeing her baby for the first time had overwhelmed her completely. It was all she could do to keep from crying. Her mother taught her that tears were unladylike, so Alexis had swallowed them back.

Choked them back was more like it—just like she always did—but then she got angry at herself.

Marcus was right about that old saying, that medical professionals made the worst patients. If one of her patients had come into the clinic and presented with symptoms like that, she would've done the same as Dr. Baxter had done. And if she hadn't been so preoccupied with work and stressed about her visa situation, she would've noticed the symptoms sooner.

When she'd kissed Marcus, she'd been seeking comfort. What surprised her was that he'd kissed her back and kissed her with such intensity it scorched her blood. She had never felt that zing of electricity before.

The hunger for him had been intense.

Alexis was glad Dr. Baxter came back into the room and interrupted them, but she couldn't deny that there was a part of her that had wanted that kiss to continue. She wanted to see where it would lead to.

Alexis was not the one-night-stand type of girl. She was usually the type of woman who played it safe with men. She'd only ever been with Bruce, but the way Marcus had kissed her made her wish she was that type of brave, strong woman who went after what she wanted and who she wanted.

And right now her body still wanted Marcus.

"Here it is," Marcus said, breaking the silence that had fallen between them when they'd left the hospital.

Matthew and Victoria's house was a small little building built up against the hill, not far from the hospital. It had a brightly colored red roof, like so many of the other homes and buildings in Charlotte Amalie, and was nestled against the green of the trees.

"That's quaint," she said. And it wasn't meant disrespectfully; she loved quaint houses.

Marcus grinned. "Quaint? Just wait."

She cocked an eyebrow. "What do you mean by that?"

"You'll see."

"You're frustrating," she teased, relieved as the tension that had been lying heavy between them melted away.

"Sorry, but half the fun is watching people's faces when they see inside this place."

Now she was really curious.

Marcus opened the door and helped her out of the car. The simple touch when she slipped her hand into his sent a zip of heat through her, and she hoped she wasn't blushing. Marcus rang the doorbell and his brother answered it.

"Marcus," Matthew acknowledged.

"Matthew," Marcus said, nodding. "And you remember Alexis?"

Matthew smiled, those same but different eyes twinkling. "A pleasure to see you again, Alexis. Please come in."

Matthew stepped aside to let them in, and as Alexis stepped across the threshold, her mouth dropped open as she took in the beautiful, modern, spacious open concept home. It was a lot larger on the inside than it appeared to be on the outside.

Marcus chuckled and leaned over to whisper. "See?"

"Yes," Alexis murmured back. "I do. Your home is spectacular, Matthew."

He grinned. "Thank you. We are a work in progress. Some minor renovations to prep for when the baby comes."

"Oh! Congratulations," Alexis said. "Marcus didn't tell me."

Matthew snorted. "Not surprising. Of course he didn't really mention anything about you and your baby either."

Her cheeks flushed with warmth.

Marcus put his arm around her reassuringly. "Well, if you remember, dear brother, we haven't exactly been on overly friendly terms until very recently and you've been a wee bit preoccupied with your new job, Vic and the domino."

Matthew laughed. "Fine. You win. You're right."

"Are you two fighting again?" Victoria asked as she came in from the terrace.

"No!" Both Matthew and Marcus answered in unison, glaring at each other.

Victoria shook her head and then smiled warmly at Alexis. "Alexis, welcome."

"Thank you for having us," Alexis said nervously, still recalling the way Victoria had seemed to read right through her. A talent she found really good surgeons and physicians all had. She liked to think that she had that gift too, but having it turned on you was a bit unnerving.

"Our pleasure. I was so pleased when Matthew told me Marcus had gotten married, though it was bit shocking given his surgery was only eight weeks ago." Victoria's gaze was stern, friendly, but meant to strike fear into Marcus who seemed nonplussed about it.

Alexis hoped she wasn't blushing again, but she felt warm.

Victoria was apparently very perceptive, and they were being caught in a lie.

"I read about that surgery. It was impressive," Alexis said, trying to steer the conversation away from her marriage of convenience.

Victoria beamed. "Yes, you must've been worried about Marcus. Though I don't recall seeing you at the hospital."

"What is this?" Marcus asked. "An inquisition?"

"No, sorry. It's the surgeon in me. I don't mean to pry, Marcus," Victoria said. "I'm just curious to meet the woman who landed you."

"We were broken up at the time," Alexis said

quickly. "He didn't know I was pregnant and I didn't know he was having a kidney removed. Sort of like a secret baby kidney thing."

She was grasping at straws and thinking back to one of Pepper's favorite tropes or whatever she'd called it. It was from the book that had spawned Pepper's bright idea and led Alexis to Marcus, which had then led her here to lying to two amazing surgeons she really admired.

Victoria laughed. "Stranger things have happened. I thought we could have dinner out on the terrace. You two make yourself at home. Matthew, I need help in the kitchen."

Marcus placed his hand at the small of Alexis's back and guided her out to the private terrace. His touch was reassuring and it calmed her nerves.

Alexis took a seat at the table. This house was in the heart of Charlotte Amalie, but it was so quiet. It was peaceful.

"Good save," Marcus whispered, sitting next to her.

"I didn't know we'd get questioned so thoroughly."

"Neither did I. I mean, I knew there would be some questions, but not like that. I'm sorry."

"No, it's fine. They care for you. It's nice."

Alexis wished someone would care for her that much too. She was a bit envious.

"Still…"

"I know!" she exclaimed and they both laughed nervously.

Matthew appeared then with a tray of iced tea.

"It's sweetened," he said. "I've had iced tea that was just cold tea and it's not my favorite."

"Sweet tea is great. Thank you." Alexis took the

glass and took a sip. It cooled her down and her frayed nerves, which were on edge, relaxed a fraction.

"So if you don't mind me asking, how far along are you, Alexis?" Matthew asked.

"We do mind," Marcus said, firmly shooting his brother a look of daggers.

"No, it's quite all right," Alexis said gently. "I'm twenty-six weeks along."

"So you didn't know you were carrying Marcus's child when you broke up?"

"Correct." Alexis's cheeks heated again.

"The thing is," Marcus interrupted, "I thought she was a fling. She's British and I had no idea she was a midwife and working here."

"I told you all that womanizing would catch up with you," Matthew said, chastising him.

Marcus rolled his eyes. "Whatever, it's fine now. She's more than just a usual fling. She's my wife."

Alexis was shocked by Marcus's words. She had no idea he was a bit of a playboy. It surprised her, but it seemed everything about Marcus did. Then it made her wonder if his charm, his kiss, had all been a part of this seduction game that he clearly liked to play on women who weren't from here.

Was she just another conquest?

You're pregnant and he met you via Chase and Pepper. You're hardly a conquest.

Still, it reinforced how little she knew about Marcus.

"This was different," Marcus stated, and she realized she had tuned out part of their conversation. "I fell in love."

Marcus reached out and took her hand.

Her heart skipped a beat, and there was a part of her

that wished a man like Marcus did love her, but it was all a lie. And lying to Matthew and Victoria, dragging them into this made her queasy.

"Can I use your restroom?" Alexis asked, pulling her hand quickly away from Marcus.

Matthew stood, looking concerned. "Of course. Victoria will show you."

Alexis nodded and dashed inside.

Victoria saw her. "Alexis? Are you okay?"

"No. I feel a bit…"

Sick.

Off.

Guilty.

"Say no more. Third door on the left."

Alexis nodded and ran straight there. Once she'd closed the door she leaned against it, taking deep breaths. When had life become so complicated?

Probably when she'd told Bruce she was pregnant and he'd turned his back on her. That had led her here to the United States Virgin Islands. An escape to paradise. It had worked almost too well as now she didn't want to go back.

She had made friends here. She'd begun to truly live, free of the specter of the pain of what happened with Bruce looming over her…

"What do you mean you're pregnant?" Bruce asked.

"Isn't it wonderful?" she asked, excited.

"No. It's not. Alexis, we've been through so much because of the infertility issues."

"I know that was difficult, but I'm pregnant now. This is what we wanted."

"I've changed my mind."

She felt like she was going to be sick as the words sank in. "What?"

"I've never wanted children, and I've met someone else who feels the same."

"You've moved on? But how? When?"

Bruce sighed. "Does it matter? It's over, Alexis, and I don't want anything to do with the baby."

It had shaken her. She'd given her heart to Bruce and then he changed his mind and moved on so quickly, as if their marriage meant nothing. How could someone do that? She'd been so angry.

All she could think about was her baby and keeping it safe.

So she left Bruce and England behind.

How could she trust Marcus when he bounced from woman to woman?

She couldn't.

As soon as she had her green card and the marriage ended, she'd never have to see Marcus again.

"Alexis?" Victoria asked, knocking gently. "Are you okay?"

"I'm fine." Alexis opened the door and found Victoria was standing there with a cup of what smelled like warm ginger.

"It's tea. When I get nausea, it helps settle my stomach."

"Thank you." Alexis took the cup. "It's been a long day."

"Not exactly how you planned to spend your wedding night, huh?"

Alexis smiled. "It's unconventional for sure. How far along are you?"

"Only eight weeks," Victoria said. "Still worrying about everything. Babies were never part of my original plan and I don't know much about them, to be honest. I'm a transplant surgeon, and my rotation through obstetrical surgery was short-lived."

"I'm a midwife, so if you have any concerns, I'd be more than happy to help."

Victoria smiled, her dark eyes warm and friendly. "I hear you're a fantastic midwife."

"Who told you that?"

"Chase and Pepper. I was Jonas's surgeon. They tell me that you're familiar with sickle cell anemia?"

Alexis nodded. "When I was a student, I spent a month in Kenya where I learned from an amazing teacher who had not only studied it, but also fought it herself. I wanted to help in any way I could so learned as much as possible. Not so long ago that disease was a death sentence."

"Well, if you're twenty-six weeks, then you'll deliver way before me. I'll stick with Dr. Baxter for my prenatal care, but I will call you if I can't get through to her."

"Anytime. I'm glad to help."

"It'll be nice for my child to have a cousin so close in age though. I had no family growing up."

"None?" Alexis asked.

"I grew up in the foster system. My mother died when I was ten. Never knew my father. There was no one else. I was alone."

Alexis swallowed the lump in her throat. Now she felt even worse for dragging Matthew and Victoria into this deception. Alexis's baby wasn't related to Victoria's and so they wouldn't be cousins.

"Well, enough of this maudlin talk. Let's have a nice dinner," Victoria said, taking the empty cup from Alexis.

Alexis put on a brave face, but she still felt awful for lying to such nice people. This was not her; she wasn't a liar.

Victoria and Matthew were the type of couple she would like to have as friends. Even, perhaps, as family.

By the time dinner was over it was too late to sail the *Tryphine* home to St. John, so they decided to try out their soon-to-be living arrangements. Tonight would be a good test run. Marcus only hoped he could make Alexis feel comfortable.

He had been worried about her when she ran inside earlier. She looked so upset, but when she came back with Victoria she was calmer, and they had an enjoyable dinner all together. Marcus had given Matthew heck for grilling them, but Marcus also saw Matthew's point—a spur of the moment marriage was so unlike him. Especially when he'd spent years saying he was never going to settle down.

It's for Pepper and Chase.

Chase owed him big time.

Alexis had leaned her head against the window and was snoozing. She looked so peaceful. Almost like an angel.

Get ahold of yourself, man.

He parked the car at the marina lot and reluctantly woke Alexis up.

"Sorry," she murmured softly.

"No need. It's been a long day."

He helped her out of the car and down to the *Tryphine.* He always had his guest berth set up, just in case Jonas came out to stay, so that was a blessing. He wouldn't have to go digging for extra bedding and it was ready for her.

"This can be your room."

"It's lovely. Thank you." Alexis sat on the edge of the bed.

"Are you all right?" he asked.

"How do you mean?"

"I was worried when you ran inside."

"I was feeling ill. Victoria gave me some ginger tea and apologized for so many questions."

"My brother did go over the top," Marcus groused.

"It wasn't just that," she said softly.

"Oh?" he asked, squatting in front of her.

"You never told me you were such a ladies' man before."

"Does it matter?" he asked.

"I suppose not."

Only he could tell by the edge in her voice it did.

He sighed and ran his hand through his hair. "After my fiancée left, I really didn't ever want to settle down. Flings with tourists was the easiest option. They didn't stick around and I didn't get attached. It was perfect, but I haven't done that in a long time. When my godson, Jonas, got sick and needed a kidney I focused all my energy on that. Chase, Pepper and Jonas needed me. You're not cramping my style or anything. There hasn't been a fling like that for close to a year."

Alexis smiled. "I know I'm sort of invading your life."

Marcus leaned forward and smiled up at her. "I like the company."

And he did.

It wasn't just the fact that he had been busy helping out with Jonas. He was also just tired of the pursuit. He was tired of the casual dating, but he was terrified of trying for anything more. He didn't want his heart broken again.

It was too painful.

"Thanks again for all your help today," she said, tucking an errant strand of blond hair behind her ear.

"No problem. Get some rest now. Doctor's orders! We have to hit Immigration early tomorrow."

Alexis nodded. "Aye-aye."

Without thinking he stood, kissed the top of her head and then quickly left her berth. Why did he keep forgetting himself around her? What was this hold Alexis had on him? He noticed her purse had fallen over on the galley counter, and her baby's ultrasound picture had slipped out.

He picked it up so it wouldn't get ruined and saw the name typed on the image.

Baby Olesen.

His heart stopped for a moment as fear overcame him, followed by sadness, because the baby wasn't his. All he wanted in that moment, staring at that picture, was to be with her and be there for the baby whose real father had been a fool and thrown it all away.

CHAPTER SEVEN

ALEXIS STARED UP at the ceiling of her berth on the *Try-phine*. She was exhausted, but she couldn't sleep. She couldn't help but think about where she was and how this was certainly never part of the plan. After what had happened with Bruce, she never thought she would be married and living with a man again.

When she first agreed to this marriage of convenience, nothing in her life was supposed to change. But now everything was changing.

Throwing back the covers, she grabbed the robe that Marcus had lent her and left her berth. She just needed some air and the baby was kicking her, zooming around as if in response to her sleeplessness and everything that had happened in the last twenty-four hours.

A drink of water would help calm everything down. She made her way to the galley and flicked on the light, jumping when she saw Marcus sitting at the table, staring out of the windows.

"Alexis?" he asked. "Are you okay?"

"Just restless. I can't sleep. The baby is kicking me. Why are you up?"

"I can't sleep either. Of course, I don't have the excuse of being pregnant, so I don't really know why I'm still wide-awake."

"Do you mind if I join you?"

"Not at all."

Alexis took a seat across from him and sipped her water as she stared out the window. The city of Charlotte Amalie was lit up, and off in the distance she heard the sound of a horn of a much larger ship, out on the sea.

"It's always louder here off St. Thomas," he mused. "It's why I prefer St. John and my small marina outside of Cruz Bay. I have had offers to open a general practice here, but I don't care for the hustle and bustle."

"I like the quiet too. London was always so busy. I much prefer the country."

"I've never been to London," he said, leaning forward. "What is it like?"

"Rainy," she teased, and he smiled. "Seriously it's a wonderful place. So many old buildings and full of history, but also modern. It was just too…crowded for me."

It also reminded her of her years married to Bruce and how unhappy she'd been. Although the city wasn't to blame for her marriage failing.

"I worked in San Diego for some time. It was too crowded for me as well."

"How did you end up in California?"

"There was no medical school here when I was studying, so I had to go to the mainland. Matthew went to New York, but I preferred the West Coast vibe."

"And what is the West Coast vibe exactly?" she asked, her curiosity piqued.

"Surfing? Avocados?" he offered, teasing.

Alexis chuckled. "Really? That's how you sum up your life in California?"

"Surfing is fun. You should try it."

"Can't really do that in my condition."

He glanced down at her belly and smiled warmly. "No, I suppose you can't. When is the baby due?"

"I think my official date is October 30."

"Almost Halloween."

"I suppose it is. I never thought about it."

"You were the one that had an affinity to Sleepy Hollow. Please tell me you won't call the baby Ichabod."

Alexis started laughing uncontrollably. "No, I'm not that obsessed with the story."

"Good. I like the way you laugh," he said softly.

"It's easy to laugh with you."

Which was true.

She couldn't remember ever laughing this way with Bruce before. Why was it so easy with a man she barely knew? Probably because there was a part of her that felt she knew him better than she had ever known anyone before. It was a little unnerving to think about.

"Come on," he said, suddenly getting up.

"What?" she asked.

"We're going outside. Maybe some fresh air will help us sleep." He held out his hand.

She knew she should just head back to the privacy of her own berth, but she ignored that niggling little thought and took his hand, completely trusting him as she stood up and followed him out onto the top deck of the *Tryphine*.

The air was definitely cooler outside, and she took a deep breath of the salty air, blowing in off the open sea.

Just like the marina in Cruz Bay, the masts of the other boats in the marina were lit up with strings of light.

And the lights of the city of Charlotte Amalie illuminated the side of the hill that the city was built on. It was magical and they stood there, quietly looking up at the clear night sky where a few stars were starting to twinkle. Only, she found she wasn't interested in the stars tonight. She couldn't take her eyes off Matthew.

Her heart began to beat a bit faster, and her body heated at the thought of him being so close. Her husband.

He's not, though. Not really.

"It's a shame," he murmured.

"What is?" she asked.

"The city light drowns out the night sky. Sometimes I take a short sail to St. Croix and just watch the sky on a clear night like this. Once you're away from all the light pollution the stars are endless, like a sea of lights, and for moment I feel like one of those ancient mariners, navigating by the sky."

"I would like to see that," she murmured.

"Would you?" he asked.

His blue eyes were twinkling, and that half smile made her swoon.

She blushed, thankful that he couldn't see her heated cheeks in the darkness. "I would."

She was angry at herself. She shouldn't be considering making plans with a man who wasn't hers and wouldn't ever be hers. Alexis just couldn't bring about the notion or the idea to be with a man, to seriously and really be with a man, who would eventually leave her and her baby.

Maybe her heart could take another bout of heartbreak, but she wouldn't put her unborn baby's heart at risk.

She didn't want that for her child.

A tear slipped down her cheek as her thoughts overwhelmed her.

"Alexis?" Marcus whispered, turning her to look at him. "What's wrong?"

"Just thinking about…thinking about my baby and worrying."

"Worrying about what?" he asked softly.

"The future." She sighed. "I thought that I could do this on my own, but Victoria told me what happened to her and… I guess I'm letting my overactive imagination get away from me."

Marcus wiped the tear from her cheek, and she was embarrassed to be crying in front of him. Her mother told her to never cry in front of anyone because it showed weakness.

Alexis swallowed the hard lump in her throat, trying to swallow down the rocks of emotion that were welling up inside her so that she wouldn't appear weak in front of Marcus.

"I'm sorry," she said, trying to smile. "It's silly."

"It's not. Not at all." And he pulled her close, wrapping his arms around her, holding her. She leaned her head against his warm shoulder and let him hold her. She closed her eyes and felt all that worry and stress just dissipate.

She liked the way that she felt in his arms.

It felt right.

Even though it was so wrong. Even though her heart was at risk.

Even though it couldn't or wouldn't last.

* * *

Marcus couldn't sleep. He never particularly slept well when he was moored off Charlotte Amalie, but what added to this insomnia was that Alexis was on the *Tryphine* with him.

Usually when he had a woman on the *yacht* sleep wasn't involved.

His dalliances were just that.

Once it was over, the woman usually returned to her hotel or her cruise ship. They didn't sleep at his place. The only woman he'd ever shared a bed with and slept next to was Dawna. She'd been the only woman he trusted enough to do that with and look where that had got him.

He still wasn't sure what had possessed him to ask Alexis to live with him.

He'd thought that with her in the next berth, it would be fine.

Instead, he couldn't stop thinking about her.

Marcus didn't want to spend his night tossing and turning, so he got up to stare out the window and then she'd come out of her berth wearing his big blue terry-cloth robe. Her hair was a mess, and there were dark rings under her eyes as well.

The way she'd tied the robe accentuated her pregnant belly, and he found her completely enchanting.

And that was the problem.

When he was with her, it was so easy to get lost.

To get wrapped up in her.

And now, as he held her, he didn't want to let her go.

Except that he had to.

She wasn't his.

"Thanks," she murmured as she stepped out of his

embrace. The moment she left his arms, he felt lonely and he wanted to pull her back.

"No problem. That's what friends are for, or I guess friends slash husbands." He grinned and she smiled.

"I suppose so and yes, I guess we are friends, aren't we?"

"Exactly. No more of this stranger talk. We're new friends. Isn't there an old saying about making new friends and old ones are like leather or something?"

Alexis chuckled softly. "It's 'Make new friends, but keep the old. One is silver and the other is gold.' No leather involved."

"Leather sounds more daring I would think." He winked, which made her laugh again.

"I'm also worried about tomorrow," she said.

"The meeting with Immigration? Yeah, I am too. I hate standing in lines on the best of days, but it'll go well. We'll follow all the rules and fill out all the paperwork. It'll be fine. We don't make a fuss, we don't draw attention to ourselves and everything should go smoothly, right?"

He had a bad feeling that by uttering those words he was sealing his own doom by taunting the universe and karma in such a way.

"Right. Well, I should try and get some sleep. Good night, Marcus." She leaned over and kissed him quickly on the cheek. It sent a rush of heat through him and he caught her before she could leave, tipping up her chin to kiss her lightly on the lips.

Wanting more but resisting.

He could see the pink flush in her cheeks as she opened her eyes when he pulled away.

"Good night, Alexis."

She nodded once before hurrying away.

Marcus turned to look back out at the water, his blood racing and his heart in very serious danger of falling for a woman that he couldn't possibly have.

CHAPTER EIGHT

THEY WERE EARLY to Immigration, but still ended up stuck in a line to file their paperwork. Marcus was trying not to yawn too much, but he hadn't had the best sleep last night with Alexis being in the next room. So close, yet so far away.

All he could think about was Alexis and how much he wanted to have a real wedding night with her.

Last night had been wonderful. It was so great being with her and with Matthew and Victoria. It felt natural. Like they were meant to be a real family together.

He wanted more. Only he couldn't have more. What if the biological father of Alexis's baby came back? He didn't know how long they had been married, but they had been together by choice.

There was love.

He remembered when he'd been in love with Dawna. He had been so happy.

So clueless.

And he couldn't let himself fall for another woman who potentially might leave him for another man because it had hurt so much when Dawna left him.

He thought his heart had hardened since then, and

yet when he was with Alexis, he felt like his heart was softening.

It scared him.

The immigration process went as well as could be expected, and they didn't say much to each other as they headed outside and returned to the boat to sail back to St. John. There were a lot of things to do, like move Alexis onto the *Tryphine*.

Which meant, probably, many more sleepless nights.

As they were leaving, Marcus spied a heavily pregnant woman who seemed to be struggling up the steps to the government building. He glanced over at Alexis, who was watching the woman very closely.

"She looks like she's in pain," he said. "And her belly is quite low. I dare say that baby has dropped."

"I'll be right back," Alexis murmured. She veered right over to the struggling pregnant woman and asked, "Do you need assistance?"

The woman was sweating. It was hot out, but she was perspiring profusely. It looked like she was struggling to even take deep breaths as she gripped the handrails.

"I'm okay... I...no, I'm just having really bad heartburn, but I have some...paperwork," the woman panted.

Alexis motioned to Marcus to join her.

"Ma'am, I'm Dr. Olesen and this is Alexis, who is a midwife and nurse practitioner. I think we need to get you inside."

The woman nodded, not fighting. "I'm Jill."

"Jill, how far along are you?" Alexis asked as they helped her into the building.

"Forty-three weeks. A touch overdue," Jill panted.

Alexis and Marcus shared a look.

The woman was more than overdue, and he had a feeling that this baby was going to be born in the government building. As they brought Jill through the doors and approached the metal detectors, the security guard stood to meet them.

"We need a room, a first-aid kit and please call an ambulance," Alexis said firmly.

The guard nodded. "You can use the empty first-aid office at the end of the hall."

As soon as Marcus and Alexis had helped Jill into the room, her water broke.

"Oh, my God," Jill said, her voice shaking.

"I think your overdue baby is on its way," Alexis said.

Marcus helped Jill lie down on the nurse's couch and turned to Alexis. "What do you need?" he asked.

"First-aid kit, blankets, gloves."

Marcus made his way to the cupboards and was relieved to find everything Alexis had listed. Today was supposed to be simple. They were going to file their paperwork and then head back to St. John. Turned out nothing was ever easy for the two of them.

He grabbed the supplies he needed and headed back to where Alexis was examining Jill.

"How is it going?" Marcus asked, as he handed gloves to Alexis.

"She's ready to give birth. This one should go fairly smooth."

"What can I do?" Marcus asked.

"She's jaundiced," Alexis whispered. "Check her blood pressure."

Marcus nodded, pulled on some gloves and got out a blood pressure cuff and sphygmomanometer.

"Jill, is it okay if I check your blood pressure?"

"Sure," Jill said, wincing and breathing heavily.

Marcus took her blood pressure and it was higher than it should be, even considering the fact that Jill was stressed and in the middle of contractions. He checked her eyes and saw that they were yellowish. She was definitely jaundiced.

"Jill, have you been having pain in your upper abdomen?" he asked.

"Yes. I always thought it was labor, but every time I went to the general hospital in my small town I was sent home."

Marcus palpated, and she flinched when he touched where her gallbladder was.

"How's it going, Marcus?" Alexis asked.

"Tenderness under her right rib. I suspect cholestasis."

"What's that?" Jill asked, panicked.

"Your gallbladder. You might have a stone or an infection. It explains the pain."

"Oh, God," Jill moaned. She was sweaty and clammy.

"Your baby will be…" Alexis trailed off.

"What's wrong?" Marcus said quietly as he knelt beside her.

"The baby is breech. You need to help me when she pushes."

"Tell me what to do."

Alexis nodded. "I need you to press here when I say so."

Marcus put his hand on Jill's stomach where she'd indicated.

"What's happening?" Jill cried.

"Your baby is breech. We're going to try and help her out. It will be a bit uncomfortable but just for a moment."

"Okay." Jill whimpered.

Alexis was waiting for the next contraction, and Marcus waited for Alexis to tell him when to help.

"Now, Marcus," Alexis commanded.

Marcus helped push down on Jill's abdomen as the mother-to-be weakly pushed.

"Push hard, Jill!" Alexis shouted. "Come on, push. Push!"

Jill cried out and delivered her little girl, breech, as Marcus watched in awe. The little girl cried lustily, but Jill didn't respond and Marcus turned to find Jill was unconscious.

"Jill?" Marcus called.

Alexis dealt with the baby, cutting the cord. "I've got the baby."

Marcus checked Jill's pulse. It was choppy, and she was unresponsive. He was worried her gallbladder had ruptured.

He was angry at the emergency room doctors at the small hospital she went to for not checking other symptoms when she was having pains. They'd looked at her pregnant belly and dismissed her.

Now she was sick and would need surgery.

Thankfully, the paramedics arrived just then.

"Patient is Jill. Just delivered a female infant breech and had upper right quadrant pain, with jaundice. I suspect cholestasis. Her blood pressure is high, and her heart rate is dropping."

The paramedics started an intravenous line to get fluids and antibiotics into her, and Alexis handled the baby as the second ambulance crew arrived and brought in an incubator to transport the newborn safely.

"Make sure to take them to Ziese Memorial Hospital," Alexis said. "Let Dr. Miriam Baxter know the baby was born breech and at forty-three weeks."

The paramedics nodded and had it under control as Alexis and Marcus stood back to let them do their work.

As they escorted Jill and her newborn safely to the ambulance, Alexis let out a breath of relief.

"We make a pretty good team," she remarked. "She was so weak I was worried about losing them both. I don't know what would have happened if you hadn't been there to help."

"I'm annoyed her pain was passed off as labor. Though I have been told that gallstones are often worse than giving birth."

"Hopefully a woman told you that. If a man did, they don't have a comparison."

Marcus grinned. "It was a woman."

Alexis sighed as they cleaned up. "Why is it when we do something important to make our marriage of convenience official something like this happens? Are we tempting fate?"

"We're cursed," Marcus teased. "I forgot to tell you that."

A smile played on her pink, delectable lips that he was now very familiar with. "Perhaps."

They finished cleaning up the best they could—the rest would have to be done by the janitorial staff—and they left the government building.

"I say we head back to St. John," Marcus stated.

"Yes. I have to check on Pepper and get my glucose tolerance test done tomorrow."

"How are you feeling today?"

"Frazzled, but okay. I'll be glad when we're back home."

She had said the word "home" so casually, but it made his pulse race and his stomach twist. She was going to be living with him.

His home would also be hers and the baby's. He swallowed the lump that had formed in his throat. "And we should move your things onto the *Tryphine*."

Alexis paused. "Right. I forgot about that."

"It's safer, just in case someone comes calling."

He was worried about her moving into his space. Especially since he hadn't slept well last night. They left the building and headed back to the marina. Thankfully, it didn't take much for Marcus to release the *Tryphine* from its moorings. In fact, his incision site was feeling much better. He hoped he was finally on the mend after the domino surgery.

The only way to get his mind off Alexis was to return to his practice, and he was eager to get back to work.

Alexis sat on the deck near him as he headed out onto the open sea.

She was smiling, and as he watched her, he couldn't help but smile too. He had always loved sailing, but Dawna didn't like being out on the water. He should've seen it as a sign they weren't compatible, but he had been so blinded by love.

And honestly, now, being with Alexis, he was beginning to question what he had ever seen in Dawna.

It was a short ride to St. John, and as he pulled up to his mooring he found Chase was waiting at his berth.

Alexis frowned. "I hope nothing is wrong with Pepper."

"Doubtful. He probably just wanted to know how it all went. We were supposed to return last night."

Alexis chuckled. "I'm sure Pepper is dying to know what happened."

He laughed. "No doubt. She probably forced him to come here."

They both laughed at that, because they both knew Pepper so well.

As Marcus pulled up to his berth, he tossed a rope to Chase so his friend could help him dock the boat. Once the *Tryphine* was secured Chase helped Alexis then Marcus down onto the dock.

"So?" Chase asked. "How did it go?"

"It's all done and I'm moving in," Alexis said brightly. "How is Pepper?"

"Uncomfortable," Chase answered.

"I should go see her," Alexis said.

Marcus nodded. "Remember to take it easy yourself."

"I will. I'll see you later."

Marcus watched her go, and he let out a breath he didn't realize he had been holding in.

"So why didn't you come back last night?" Chase asked.

"My brother," Marcus responded.

Chase laughed. "Oh, I see."

"Alexis is moving in with me."

Chase raised his eyebrows. "So she said, and I have to say I'm kind of surprised."

Marcus shrugged. "Moving in makes sense. We're married. By the way, you owe me big."

"Is it really that bad?"

No.

"Yes." Marcus grinned.

Chase laughed. "You're a liar. I knew when I saw Alexis that you two would hit it off. She's your type."

"How? She's not the type of woman I usually go for."

"I know. You avoid women like Dawna."

"Alexis is nothing like Dawna."

"She's smart, intelligent and brave," Chase countered.

Chase wasn't wrong, but there was a huge difference between Alexis and Dawna. Alexis wasn't calculating or cold. He hadn't noticed it when he had been so in love with Dawna, but she was career and money driven to such a degree that it didn't matter who she hurt to get what she wanted. Alexis was the opposite. She was willing to do whatever it took to take care of her patients, even going as far as to marry a stranger.

There were similarities, of course, but Alexis was so much more than Dawna was.

Even in such a short amount of time, he could see it.

"You know I'm right," Chase told him.

Marcus rolled his eyes. "Don't let it go to your head."

Alexis changed her clothes and had something to eat before she headed back to the clinic to see Pepper. She was sure Pepper would have a lot of questions. In fact, she was sure that everyone at the clinic would probably have a lot of questions about her sudden marriage to Dr. Marcus Olesen.

Alexis cleaned out her purse and found the picture of the ultrasound. She hadn't looked at it since Dr. Baxter gave it to her as she had been so overwhelmed with everything that had followed yesterday. She smiled as she looked at her little baby. The one she had been longing for, for so long.

When she and Bruce went through all those treatments, they had taxed her emotions. Injections, painful procedures, heartache and loss. She had almost given up hope.

At least Bruce had given her this. Alexis touched the ultrasound, and then she noticed the name typed on the top in bold white letters.

Baby Olesen.

She took a deep breath, her hand shaking. It made sense that Dr. Baxter had assumed Marcus was the father. Still, it made her upset to see that name, and she didn't want Marcus to feel like he had to be a part of her baby's life.

What man would want to raise another man's baby? She shook her head, annoyed she'd let her mother's voice inside her head. Alexis knew plenty of men who would step up. Family wasn't just blood, after all, but there was no denying that Marcus didn't love her or her baby.

They didn't have a relationship. Their marriage wasn't real. The only reason Marcus was in her life, or on her baby's ultrasound picture, was because of Chase and Pepper.

There was a knock at the clinic door, and she tucked the picture away.

"Come in," Alexis called out, hoping her voice wasn't shaking.

The door opened and Pepper came in, her smile wide as she waddled into the room.

"You're back!" Pepper exclaimed.

"I am."

"Did everything go okay?" Pepper asked, closing the door.

"It went fine. I'm more concerned with how you're feeling."

"I'm okay. I've had some swelling."

"Swelling? Where?" Alexis asked.

"In my feet and ankles. Not sure if it's my sickle cell disease or pregnancy."

"Let me see," Alexis said gently. Pepper sat down on the exam table, and Alexis examined the swelling. Then she took Pepper's temperature and discovered that Pepper had a low-grade fever. "You have a fever."

Pepper sighed. "I know. I'm getting close to term, so I thought the pain might be that... I was hoping it was just pregnancy."

"Have you been drinking enough water?"

"I'm floating," Pepper replied sarcastically.

Alexis smiled. "You need to consider bone marrow transplant when this pregnancy is over. For your sickle cell disease."

Pepper nodded. "I know. It's so expensive though, and I have a rare blood type just like Jonas. It's hard to find a match. We're also still paying off Jonas's surgery."

"Well, from what I hear, there's a world-class transplant surgeon in Charlotte Amalie who would help if you asked."

Pepper blushed. "I know that. The domino saved Jonas's life, and I completely trust Victoria. She didn't even charge her fee for the surgery. The bill is just for the hospital stay."

"Well, we'll discuss it more after the baby is born. For now, let's measure you and I want to listen to the baby's heartbeat."

Pepper laid down and Alexis measured her. At eight months Pepper was measuring small, likely because one of the complications of sickle cell disease and pregnancy was preterm birth and low birth weight. The swelling and fever were concerning, though.

It was the kind of potential complication that had made Alexis so determined to stay here and watch over Pepper.

She helped Pepper sit back up.

"Everything is going well. Drink water, rest and that will help with the swelling. You should also take acetaminophen."

Pepper nodded. "I will. So tell me about the wedding."

Alexis chuckled. "What is there to tell? We dressed up, went to city hall and the judge had a stroke after he married us."

Pepper's eyes widened. "Is the judge all right?"

"Last I heard he was."

"Then what happened?"

"We went to the hospital with the judge, and I ran into Marcus's twin and accidentally broke the news of our marriage, not knowing that the man I thought was Marcus was actually Matthew."

Pepper laughed. "Oh, poor Matthew!"

"We ended up making plans for dinner, but I got a

little ill and I had to be checked up on by an OB/GYN at the hospital."

"Are you okay?" Pepper asked, concerned.

"I may have gestational diabetes. I have been so preoccupied I didn't get a glucose tolerance test when I was supposed to."

"You need to take care of yourself," Pepper said firmly in her best mom voice, which Jonas had once told Alexis scared him senseless.

"So Marcus said. Medical professionals are the worst patients."

"I can see that." Pepper stood up slowly. "You need to take care of yourself too. After all you've been through…"

Alexis hugged her. "Thank you for your help to keep me here."

"Anytime. I need you, I trust you and I feel safe with you," Pepper said earnestly.

Alexis's heart soared. This was why she did what she did. This was why she loved being a midwife and a nurse. "Try to get rest, Pepper."

"You as well."

"I have to pack up my belongings and move to Marcus's boat."

Pepper cocked an eyebrow. "You're moving in with Marcus?"

"We are married. I know it's one of convenience, but we do have a pretense to keep up."

Pepper grinned. "Of course, you're just 'keeping up appearances.' Sure. Well, I'll leave you to it."

There was something about the way she grinned. As if she knew how Alexis was struggling with her feelings, her attraction to Marcus.

Alexis wasn't worried about moving in with Marcus though. She had slept quite comfortably on the *Tryphine* last night. In fact, it had been some time since she had slept so soundly. It was probably because she felt safe with Marcus.

It unnerved her how comfortable she was with him.

CHAPTER NINE

"How much stuff do you have?" Marcus asked as he carried another box from her small temporary room that the clinic had provided, into her berth on the *Tryphine*.

She couldn't quite believe that she was moving in with him, but the place she had lived at the last four months had been temporary lodgings. If she wasn't planning to stay here because of Pepper and her pregnancy, she could actually be packing to head back to London.

And she was thankful that she could stay on because of Marcus.

The clinic was thankful too, but she still had to empty the room for another nurse or midwife.

Actually, after she delivered Pepper's child, she would have to form her own practice as the government-funded health clinic she'd been working at only offered temporary placements designed to entice new professionals to stay on in the islands.

It had certainly done the trick with her.

The point was, her contract at the clinic would soon be up, and she would have to figure out how she was going to fund and open her own clinic here.

You could ask your new husband to work with you? Or maybe see if there's an opening at his practice?

She shook that thought away. Even though she'd like to work with Marcus, she couldn't ask that from him. He'd already done more than enough to help her by marrying her.

"Hey, I had to move my whole life here as I sold my flat when I took this position."

Marcus set the box on the floor. "I'm glad there's no furniture, but I have to ask one thing."

"Oh?"

"Do you collect rocks?"

She gave him a light punch to his shoulder. "Very funny."

"This is the last box. You're all moved in."

Alexis sighed and sat down on the bed. "It feels weird."

"Hey, I haven't lived with anyone for a very long time. You're not the only one slightly freaked out about this joint venture."

"Did you live on a boat in California?"

"No. My ex-fiancée didn't like the seafaring life. I was definitely landlocked."

"Would you ever go back to being landlocked?" she asked.

He cocked an eyebrow. "Already complaining about my living arrangements, eh? Trying to get your husband to buy you a castle?"

"Hardly," she replied. "I was just curious. Just trying to get to know you better."

He smiled that half smile she loved so much, and there was a devious twinkle in the blue eyes. "Well, if

I ever planned on settling down for real, then I suppose that living here on the *Tryphine* would be tight quarters."

"Just a bit, but I get the appeal of it."

He cocked an eyebrow. "Do you?"

"Of course. You mentioned that you were able to stargaze when you traveled to St. Croix. I'm envious of your freedom to move around these islands."

"Well, the *Tryphine* can't go everywhere. There are some small cays, inlets that she can't get to, which is why I have a small dinghy. It gets me into some hidden places."

"Hidden places?"

He nodded. "Now that you're moved in, why don't we take the *Tryphine* on a short jaunt to other side of the island? I can show you a hidden waterfall that I found. It spills out into a pool and trickles out into a lagoon and into the ocean. Are you up for some gentle adventure?"

Her heart skipped a beat. "I am for sure!"

"Let's do it then! Secure your boxes and then meet me up on deck."

"Aye-aye, Captain."

He chuckled and disappeared back to the upper deck.

Alexis's heart was racing. She certainly wasn't expecting a trip, but she was excited all the same. It would get them away from Cruz Bay and all the lies they'd been having to tell.

And she would love to see a hidden tropical waterfall.

She secured her boxes and made sure everything was safe and sound before she headed up on deck. When she got there, Marcus was talking to someone on the pier. His arms were crossed and his brow was furrowed.

Alexis's heart sank.

Oh, no. It's Immigration.

That was her first irrational thought, but then she got ahold of her panic before it ran away from her and waited out of sight for Marcus to finish his conversation.

Marcus clapped the man on the back and nodded before heading back to the *Tryphine*.

"Is everything okay?" Alexis asked.

"Minor delay. I hope you'll be okay with it."

"Sure, what is it?"

"That was Jem. He's one of the owners of the marina, and one of his sons was working in the back room cleaning fish and sliced open his hand. They really don't want to take him to the hospital, and they were hoping that I could give the lad a quick suture."

"Do you need my help?" she asked.

"I thought you would never ask!" He grinned. "Let me grab a suturing kit and my bag, then we'll head over there."

"Sure."

Marcus was back in a few moments with his bag and what he needed to tend to Jem's son. He took her hand, almost like it was natural, and they walked down the gangplank to the small house where Jem lived.

He was waiting in the small fish-cleaning shack that was on the dock.

The moment Alexis got close, she got a whiff of the fish and her stomach turned.

"You okay?" Marcus asked. "You look a little bit green around the gills."

"It's the fish smell."

"Well, we'll bring the boy out here." Marcus set his bag out on the clean picnic table. "Jem, this is my wife, Alexis. She's a nurse."

Jem nodded. "Pleasure to meet you."

"Can you bring Henry out here? I think it's better we suture him up away from the scales and the fish parts."

Jem grinned. "Of course, Dr. Olesen."

Marcus laid out all the equipment and handed Alexis gloves. She took a seat on the opposite side of the table, because she knew that she would have to help keep the little boy calm.

Jem walked with Henry out of the fish hut and the poor boy had tears streaming down his cheeks. His hand was all wrapped up.

"Henry, lad, what happened?" Marcus asked.

"I cut myself cleaning a snapper." The boy sniffled, giving Alexis side-eye.

"Oh, that's my new wife. Her name is Alexis and she's a nurse, so she's going to help me today, okay?"

Henry nodded and sat down next to her. She rubbed his back.

"Can I see?" Marcus asked as he laid out a drop cloth.

Henry nodded and laid his hand across the sterile cloth. He was wincing.

"You're being awfully brave," Alexis said encouragingly.

"You are," Marcus agreed as he unwound the bandage. "Ouch. Nasty cut, but we'll take care of this. I promise."

Henry nodded and kept his eyes closed.

"I'm going to give you a quick, tiny shot to freeze everything," Marcus said. "Is that okay?"

"Yep," Henry said. As the little boy leaned against her and she continued to rub his back, her heart melted at his bravery. Stitches were never fun, but he was doing so well. And Marcus was so gentle and careful with him.

She watched Marcus in awe as he carefully irrigated the wound on the boy's palm. Marcus talked Henry through the whole thing, making jokes and telling stories as he stitched up the boy's hand. And when it was all done, Alexis bandaged the wound to keep it safe.

"There, that wasn't so bad, was it?" Marcus asked.

Henry opened his eyes and stared in disbelief at his hand. "No, it wasn't, Dr. Olesen."

Marcus grinned. "Why don't you go lay down for a bit? Get out of this heat and rest."

Henry nodded and ran back into his house.

"Thank you two so much," Jem said in relief. "I really appreciate it."

"Anytime." Marcus pulled out his prescription pad. "I'm going to write him a prescription for some antibiotics and painkillers, and I'd like to check on his stitches in a week, if you don't mind."

Jem nodded and took the paper. "Can I pay you, Dr. Olesen?"

Marcus shook his head. "Nope. I'm not supposed to be working right now and Henry does provide me with fresh fish, so we'll call it even."

Jem smiled. "Thanks, Dr. Olesen."

Marcus wrapped up the waste and disposed of it in

a garbage bin. The needle he dropped in his portable needle waste container.

"You were so gentle with that little boy," she said in awe.

"It's what I do. Henry is a good lad. Sorry we had to delay our little trip."

She took his free hand. "Don't be sorry. It was a pleasure to work with you again, even if I didn't do much."

"You bandaged that wound so nicely, and you were emotional support to Henry. That's worth a lot to me."

Her heart skipped a beat as they walked hand in hand back to the *Tryphine*. In that small moment she wished that she was really his wife and not just a fake one.

Even though he much preferred to have the sails unfurled, especially on a bright sunny day like today, Marcus still couldn't manage to get the sails out on his own. But the trip to the little island that was on the far side of the island of St. John, almost to the border of the British Virgin Islands, would be a short trip thanks to the engines on his boat.

Alexis was sitting close to him and drinking in the sun and the wind.

She seemed to enjoy the sea as much as he did.

Another thing to like about her.

Alexis was not making it easy for him to keep his distance from her.

It didn't take long for him to find the small cay. It was rare that anyone came up here because it was so close to the international border, but as long as they stayed on this leeside of the island, they would be fine.

"This is it?"

"It is. See all those other large islands in the distance?"

"I do."

"That's the British Virgin Islands."

"They're so close."

"They are, but if you end up on the wrong side of the border during this green card application, we're toast."

"Noted," she said.

He let down the anchor and then kicked the ladder down. The little dinghy that he used was waiting, and Marcus climbed down first to help Alexis.

For being more than halfway through her pregnancy, she was quite agile. And as he waited for her in the dinghy, he couldn't help but admire her bottom.

"Are you there?" she asked anxiously, dangling her foot down, searching for a foothold.

"I am." He reached for her, enjoying the feeling of holding her in his arms again. "Trust me. I have you."

Alexis let go and he helped her down into the dinghy, holding her so she wouldn't fall. She was laughing and a bit out of breath.

"I don't know how I'll manage to get back up there again," she panted.

"Oh, didn't I tell you I'm leaving you here?"

"Really?" she asked in disbelief.

"Yes. Much like Bluebeard locked his wives away in a castle, I'm confining you to this paradise."

"Yes, but didn't Bluebeard murder his wives because they peeped in his locked room?"

"The point is, it's about confining the wife," he teased, helping her sit down in the dinghy.

"Well, now that you've told me your plan, I can foil

it. I do know Krav Maga. I can render you helpless and confine *you* here to the island."

He laughed and untied the small boat, sitting beside the outboard motor. "Clearly I didn't think this all the way through."

He guided the boat from the small cay into the lagoon, past the small grove of mangrove trees and into the taller trees of kapok and turpentine. The sunlight filtered through the leaves, and the water turned from the aquamarine blue of saltwater to clear fresh water as they slowly wound their way through.

It wasn't long before they heard the roar and the rush of the small waterfall that trickled from farther up the side of the island. Marcus pulled the boat over and jumped out into the water. He pulled the dinghy on the shore and then helped Alexis out.

"This is amazing," she whispered.

"Take off your shoes and we can wade it in it. It's quite shallow."

Alexis kicked off her sneakers and he took her hand so she wouldn't fall on the slippery rocks. She clung to him as she navigated away from the shore into the knee-deep pool that flowed from the waterfall.

He should let her go, but he found that he couldn't.

"This is gorgeous. How did you find this place again?" she asked.

"Just on one of my jaunts. Being on my own, I had some time to explore. That was before my surgery."

"Well, I'm glad you found it." She tilted her head. "What kind of tree is that?"

He looked to where she was pointing and saw a tall tree that had yellow gray bark and spines. "Ah, that's is a sandbox tree, or a 'monkey no climb' tree. You would not want to touch that bark and get a spike in your skin."

She laughed nervously. "I'll take your word for it."

He wrapped his arms around her, just like he had done last night when they had stared out at the few stars over Charlotte Amalie. When she had been so tiny in his robe.

His pulse was racing.

It was just them, the trees and few birds that were squawking in the canopy above them.

"I'm glad you brought me here," she whispered. "This was a nice distraction from work and worry."

"I'm glad."

All he wanted to do was kiss her.

If she was anyone else, he would, but Alexis wasn't just anyone. She was a temptation and he wanted to indulge. It was then he felt a poke. His eyes flew open and he looked down.

"Your baby kicked me!"

Alexis chuckled. "Yes. I suppose so. You're the first person to feel the baby kick, besides me, that is."

"Can I?" he asked, gesturing toward her belly.

She nodded.

Marcus reached down and touched her gently. There was another little poke, much like a finger, and he couldn't help but smile in delight at that little life inside Alexis letting him know that it was there.

"It's amazing," he murmured.

"It is." She took a step back and looked a bit worried.

"What?" he asked.

"It's nothing. I'm glad you're involved but..."

"I know, Alexis. The baby isn't mine and I know there is a time limit to this whole arrangement, but after this is all said and done we can still be friends, can't we?"

She smiled weakly. "Sure. Of course."

Alexis walked away from him then, wading farther toward the waterfall, and Marcus took a deep breath. He was treading on dangerous ground.

He had to be more careful.

He was in danger of losing his heart not only to Alexis, but also to the possibility of being a father to a baby that wasn't his.

CHAPTER TEN

ALEXIS HADN'T SEEN much of Marcus since she'd moved in and they'd spent time at the secret waterfall. It had scared her when he held her in his arms and reveled in the feeling of the baby kicking. She had been longing for a moment like that to share with someone she loved, but she didn't have Marcus.

And even though she had loved every second of it, she had to protect her baby.

They had headed back to the *Tryphine* and Cruz Bay in silence, but as soon as they got back to the marina Marcus was his old self again. He was acting like nothing had happened, and it was probably for the best.

Really? It's for the best?

They'd tried to settle into some kind of existence together in tight quarters. Having been cleared by Victoria to return to work, he was now back to his practice and after her glucose tolerance test, she had been taking it fairly easy. A lot of the time that mean she went to bed early after a busy day at work.

They had been sort of living in tandem for the last two weeks, and she was finding herself missing him. That short time they had spent together after they were married had been one of the best times of her life, but she also liked this daily routine that she had fallen into with Marcus.

Bruce and she had worked so much, and she couldn't remember missing seeing him as much as she missed Marcus's company. It was nice to talk to someone, to share her day. Especially someone who was interested in her work.

She missed their long talks, missed working with him.

When they'd helped Jill give birth at the government building, Alexis had felt like they'd made a good team.

He was a good partner.

And also a playboy, remember?

From what Matthew had said, she knew Marcus was the type who bounced from woman to woman. Even though he said he hadn't done so in a year, she found it hard to believe that he wouldn't eventually go back to that lifestyle. Why was she falling for the wrong man again? Bruce had been the wrong man, she clearly saw that now, and Marcus, with his penchant for flings, was also obviously the wrong man, yet her mind and heart didn't want to believe that was true.

Alexis stared out of her office window. All she could see was the market. It was busy and the sun was shining. She smiled to herself despite her worried thoughts. She as so lucky to be in paradise.

Her phone rang.

"Alexis Martin speaking."

"Alexis? This is Dr. Baxter calling."

"Yes, Dr. Baxter. How can I help you?"

"I have the results of your glucose tolerance test."

"Oh?"

"It's negative. You don't have gestational diabetes, but you still need to take it easy."

"Thank you, Dr. Baxter."

"I'd like to see you in a couple of weeks for a follow-up ultrasound."

"Sure. Email me sometime and I'll fit it in."

"Very good. Take care, Alexis."

Alexis hung up and was absolutely ecstatic. She decided to go for a walk to clear her head, as she didn't have any more patients for the afternoon.

She made her way out of the clinic and toward the market, soaking in the sun and enjoying the breeze. This was a paradise and she didn't want to leave. For the first time in a long time she was happy with her life.

She couldn't remember being this happy before.

As she glanced across the market, she saw Marcus kneeling next to a little boy who was crying and clinging to his mother. She watched in wonder as Marcus tended to a wound on the little boy's leg. He was so gentle and kind as he cleaned and bandaged the wound.

Her heart melted watching him. The little boy smiled as Marcus finished and stood. Then Marcus rubbed the child's head before turning around to pick up his medical bag.

Maybe he wasn't the cad that she'd assumed he was. People could change, couldn't they?

Marcus looked up and when he saw her, he smiled warmly, like he had been expecting her. It made her heart skip a beat.

"Hi," Marcus said.

"Hi, yourself," she said brightly.

"What're you doing out here?" Marcus asked.

"No patients this afternoon. I thought I'd take a walk, maybe buy some fruit to celebrate."

"You got your green card?" he asked, with what sounded like hope in his voice.

He wants out of the marriage already.

"No, sorry. It's way too early for that."

"Then what was the good news?" Marcus asked, not picking up on her disappointment that he was obviously very eager to get out of their arrangement.

What do you expect?

"I don't have gestational diabetes, but I do have to have another ultrasound in a couple of weeks and Dr. Baxter still wants me to take it easy."

"Take it easy. That's simple enough."

"Is it?" she asked.

"My parents are still on their yearlong world cruise. Usually Matthew and Victoria go and check on my parents' home on St. Croix, but how about we go there for a visit? They have a pool and there's a private beach."

"That does sound relaxing." It really did. She could do with a day by the pool. When they had gone to that private little waterfall, she had desperately wanted to peel off her clothes and take a swim, but the water was so shallow and so she hadn't been able to.

A day of swimming was just what the doctor ordered.

"So let's go."

"Now?" she asked.

"Why not? The *Tryphine* is always ready to go out for a spin."

"Okay, but how far away is St. Croix?"

"Just over an hour. Usually people fly or take a ferry,

but we're not so locked in by schedules if we sail ourselves. How about you grab some things for dinner and I'll make arrangements? I'll meet you at home in a hour?"

"Home?" she asked, her heart skipping a beat.

"The *Tryphine*." He grinned.

"Yes. Of course." She nodded. "I'll go to the market and see you in an hour."

Marcus nodded and continued toward the marina, his bag swinging by his side. Even though she probably shouldn't go with him to St. Croix, she was looking forward to the outing. There may be no future for them, but why couldn't they be friends?

She had put her trust in him so that she could get her green card and stay in this place she loved so much. This place she wanted to make her home and raise her child in. And though she was beginning to care for Marcus, it was worth it if it meant she could stay here.

Alexis picked up some fruit and some sandwiches and carried it all back to the *Tryphine*.

Marcus was getting the boat ready. "Did you get something to eat?"

"I did. Did you tell Matthew we were headed there?"

"Yes. He's busy this week, so he's very grateful we're going to check on the house."

Alexis boarded and took the bags to the galley. She put the food away and then headed back up on deck where Marcus was getting some things ready.

"We're going to sail. There's a gorgeous wind today."

"Have you been cleared to sail?" she asked.

Marcus grinned, those blue eyes twinkling. "I have. Sort of. I'm fine."

She crossed her arms. "You're fine?"

"Perfectly."

"So, you're going to sail?"

"Yes, we are."

"We?" Alexis gasped.

"Yes. Nothing strenuous, but we can do this together."

"I don't know how to sail." She laughed nervously.

"I'll teach you."

"You really want me to help you with this?"

"I do," Marcus said happily.

"I don't think this is the wisest idea."

"You told me you wanted to learn how to sail, that you liked to be at sea, and the only way to learn is by doing."

"If you say so."

"What is with the apprehension?" Marcus asked as he released the moorings.

"I'm not the most graceful. My mother enrolled me in a dance class, and they asked me to leave after a couple of weeks because I kept taking out other dancers doing a simple pirouette."

"Well, there are no pirouettes or twirls here. I'll use the motor to get us out of the marina, and then we'll release the sails."

Alexis nodded nervously as Marcus started the engine and the *Tryphine* slipped away. It was a beautiful day, and there whitecaps out on the turquoise sea. There were other boats on the water, and she was excited for the trip and the chance to see St. Croix.

As they cleared the marina and headed out on the open water, Marcus stepped away from the wheel. "Alexis, take the wheel."

"Me?" She gasped.

"Yes. You."

Alexis stepped up to the wheel and her hands shook as she wrapped them around it.

"Keep her pointing west."

Alexis nodded as Marcus untied a knot and the *Tryphine's* white sail unfurled, flapping in the wind before catching and snapping taut, blinding white against clear blue sky.

She laughed. Joy was bubbling through her as the *Tryphine* conquered the waves and the wind whipped her in the face. Marcus tied off what he needed to and joined her back behind the wheel.

"You're headed north toward the mainland."

"I thought I was going west."

Marcus stood so close behind her she could feel the heat of his body on her back.

It caused her own blood to heat and she leaned closer. His arms came around her, resting his hands over top of hers. Her breath caught in her throat at his touch, and her pulse thundered in her ears as he guided her hands, gently urging her to turn the wheel.

"This way is west," he whispered against her ear, causing a zing to go down her spine and heat to pool between her legs. Her body was responding to him being so near, and she wanted to give into what she wanted.

And what she wanted was Marcus.

It's the hormones. You're twenty-eight weeks. This happens to a lot of women.

And now it was happening to her. Not surprising, given that her fake husband was one of the most handsome men she had ever seen. Lothario or not, she was completely attracted to him.

She wanted him.

And her body was telling her to indulge.

She cleared her throat and shrugged. Marcus stepped back and went to adjust the boom.

"You're doing great," he remarked. "Now that you're actually going in the right direction."

She laughed. "Thanks."

Marcus had missed her this last week, but he was so glad to be back at his practice and had been hopeful that his work would keep his mind off her.

It hadn't.

Instead, it had reminded him of her. She was such a talented midwife. So confident and knowledgeable. When he worked in his practice, he was all alone. He had a call service and no office. He traveled clinic to clinic and never usually had a reliable nurse.

Working with Alexis was like a breath of fresh air. He missed it, and for one brief moment, he wished they could form a practice so they could work together all the time. He wanted more than just a work relationship though. Even though they had only seen each other in passing these past two weeks, it had felt like home every time he was with her. Like they were supposed to be together.

He was glad they both had the afternoon off. It was chance to get back out on the water and spend time alone with her.

No other distractions.

Alexis had a bit of a struggle with steering. He went to help her, and instinctively he reached out to put his arms around her. If felt so right to be so close to her. Her hair smelled so good. Her body was so soft against him. He wanted to stay there with her pressed against him.

She was so soft.

So warm.

Then she'd tensed, and he realized he had taken it too far. She wasn't interested in him. Even though he was very interested in her. Attracted to her.

He wanted her.

It scared him how much he wanted her. It had been a long time since he'd wanted a woman like this. The flings were fun, but not completely overpowering. They ran their course, and then he moved on to the next conquest.

Alexis was different.

And for one fleeting moment, right here, right now, he didn't want their marriage to end. He wished it was real. He wished his heart wasn't so closed off.

Alexis did a good job and listened attentively as he pointed out various parts of the *Tryphine* and the sail.

Soon enough St. Croix loomed into view.

Marcus stepped to the wheel. "I'll take over. My parents have a private mooring near their beach."

"They have a private beach on St. Croix?"

"My parents are quite wealthy."

"Quite might be an understatement."

Marcus snorted. "Yes. Just wait until you see their castle."

"Castle?"

"That's what my father likes to think of his home. Bigger is always better to him."

"Bigger isn't always better though," Alexis said.

He smiled. "Agreed."

At the private mooring, his father's boat, the *Freja*, which was a replacement for the *Tryphine*, was in dry dock. As Marcus approached the pier, one of the local workers came out to help.

Alexis was staring at the *Freja* in awe.

"Why pay for a round-the-world cruise when you have that?"

Marcus chuckled. "That's my father. He doesn't want to do all the work for the whole year the cruise would take, and he always needs the best and biggest. I think he's compensating for a poor childhood."

"Was it tragic?" Alexis asked.

"No. Just cramped. He has a lot of siblings. Maybe that's why two was enough for my parents."

His father liked to show off, but he was also generous with his money.

"Colin," Marcus called out to the employee.

"Dr. Olesen, glad to see you again. I haven't seen you since your brother's wedding."

"I've been recovering. It's good to see you too, Colin."

Colin finished up and Marcus helped Alexis down. She was staring in awe at the cliff, which was topped by the house. Or the castle, as his parents like to call it.

"That's going to be quite the walk."

"My father keeps a couple of golf carts for just such an occasion. It's a steep climb, and he's not much of a climber."

Marcus found the golf car waiting, so they both got in. The cart lurched and Alexis cried out, screeching and then laughing. Then he managed to start it properly and tried to remember how to drive the blasted thing.

"Hold on," Marcus shouted over the engine as he took the winding back road up to the house.

Alexis gasped as they came closer. "It's beautiful!"

"It is. It's a great place to spend family time. Victoria and Matthew were married here shortly after the domino."

"I can see why they chose it."

Marcus parked the golf cart, and he opened the back gate that led to where the infinity pool clung to the edge of the cliff, next to the pool house.

"I figure this is a good enough place to have a relaxing afternoon."

"It's perfect."

"You can change in the pool house. I'm going to go for a swim."

"Excellent idea." Alexis made her way to the pool house as Marcus went inside and headed straight for his old bedroom. His parents insisted that Marcus and Matthew keep a stock of clothes there so they could come whenever they wanted, but Marcus suspected that his mother, who tended to baby him a bit, really didn't want an empty nest. Marcus didn't like to be coddled and had rebelled when he was a young man.

He wanted to forge his own path, which was why he went to California instead of New York like Matthew. Of course, he'd been in love, which was another reason why he didn't follow his twin. He loved California and he just wanted a simple life.

Only Dawna had a different idea. She'd wanted a different life, so he'd started to transform himself to fit that vision. Now he realized how unhappy that life had been. Being with Alexis had made him realize that he had been mourning a life that was never his design.

What he had to figure out now was what to do. What he wanted. Dawna had hurt him, and he never wanted to feel that again. He didn't want to transform his life for someone who was going to hurt him.

He finished getting dressed and headed back out to the pool.

Alexis was already there lying on a lounge chair. She wore a black one-piece, and he could see the swell of her abdomen clearly. The curves of her body. She was glowing and absolutely stunning.

Probably the most beautiful woman he had ever seen.

Alexis took his breath away, and he was in severe danger of falling for her.

A woman who didn't want him.

Marcus came out of the house, and Alexis tried not to stare at his broad, bronzed chest. There was a faint pink scar on his side from the domino surgery. She still couldn't believe he gave his kidney to a stranger. He was so unselfish.

There were so many things she admired about him. He made her weak in the knees and as she watched him swim, all she could think about was his arms around her. How safe he made her feel when she had been vulnerable.

How good he made her feel.

She thought of his lips on her and the kisses they'd shared. Her body heated and her stomach did a flip. Alexis couldn't remember the last time she'd wanted a man this much.

Why couldn't she indulge?

All her life she had always followed the rules and never her heart. Everything was thought through ad nauseam.

She trusted her gut, but never this instinct. Never pursued her desire.

Not in this way.

What would be the harm just this once?

"Are you coming in?" Marcus asked, treading water.

She nodded and slipped off her lounger to slowly walk into the saltwater infinity pool. The water was warm, and she didn't hesitate to sink into it. Marcus swam over to her. His blue eyes were twinkling as he wrapped his arms around her, pulling her tight against him.

"Is this relaxing enough?" he asked.

"Very," she murmured, her heart racing, and she wrapped her arms around his neck, leaning in closer. She couldn't help herself and kissed him lightly on the lips, as she had done before.

"I have missed you the last couple of weeks. I know we're strangers in a way, but I missed having talks with you. It's been nice sharing a home with you. I've been in the Virgin Islands for some months, and I didn't realize how lonely I was."

"I've missed you, too," Marcus whispered huskily. "I've gotten used to having you around."

She kissed him again. Deeper this time, letting him know just how much she wanted him. This marriage might be fake, but what she was feeling for Marcus was very real.

And for once in her life, she wanted to act on instinct. She wanted to feel.

Even though there was an end date to all of this, she

wanted to feel some kind of passion in her life before the baby came.

It had never happened to her this way before. She desired Marcus like no other man.

She craved him. She was treading on a dangerous path by kissing him, but she didn't care in this moment. All she wanted was Marcus. His hands skimmed over her, and a tingle of anticipation ran through her.

"You're so beautiful," Marcus murmured as he kissed her again, making her blood heat.

"I want you," she said, surprised at how uninhibited she was when she was around him.

Marcus kissed her again. "Are you sure?"

She nodded and kissed him again. "I'm very certain. I just want to be with you, Marcus."

Marcus lifted her up and carried her out of the pool. He carried her to the outdoor shower, and her body thrummed as he ran his hands over her and touched her intimately as they rinsed away the saltwater and peeled off their swimsuits. It was just them, nothing between them anymore, and he pulled her tight against him, kissing her neck.

Warmth spread through her veins as his lips moved down her body to her breasts. Alexis cried out at the sensation of his tongue on her nipple. It was pure pleasure. Her body was so sensitive to his touch, and he continued to run his hands over her before stroking her between her legs, bringing her to the edge before backing off, leaving her desperate for more. She wanted him. She needed him.

He picked her up again and carried her into the pool house, straight to the bedroom. He laid her down and kissed her again. She arched her back, silently begging him to take her.

She wanted more.

So much more.

Their gazes locked as he entered her and then paused.

Emotions overcame her and a tear slipped from her eye.

"I'm sorry," he whispered, brushing it away. "I'm hurting you."

"No. You're not. Don't stop," she murmured. "Keep going."

Marcus tenderly touched her cheek. "As long as I'm not hurting you."

"You aren't." She kissed him again.

If she was hurt, it wouldn't be his fault. It would be hers for letting herself fall for him.

Marcus nipped at her neck and began to move slowly, gently.

All she wanted was Marcus to take her.

Possess her.

She wanted him deeper and she wrapped her legs around his waist, begging him to stay close, but her belly was making it difficult to take him as deep as she wanted while she was lying on her back.

"Hold on," she murmured.

Marcus withdrew and she rolled on her side, her back to his chest. Marcus's hand slipped under her leg as if he knew exactly what to do. He draped her leg over his and moved his hand to her breast as he entered her again. Her body lit up as pleasure washed through her. She had never felt this way before.

She was falling in love with Marcus.

Alexis shook that thought away. There was no room in her life to love a man who didn't want her. She wasn't going to put her heart at risk again. So she was going to savor this moment, and she was going to hold on to this memory long after their marriage had ended.

Marcus quickened his pace and she came, crying out as heat washed through her.

Absolute pleasure.

Marcus soon followed and then gently eased her leg down.

"Alexis," he whispered, pulling her body closer to him.

"I know," she replied, trying to catch her breath, floating down from the high.

She wanted to tell him that she was falling in love with him, that she wished this marriage was real, that she wished she had met Marcus a long time ago and that she wished she hadn't been so hurt and he hadn't been so scarred.

Their timing sucked, but at least he had come into her life.

Even just briefly.

Marcus held Alexis close to him. He was spooning her, and her luscious bottom was snuggled up against him as she slept. He didn't want to disturb her, but he also couldn't stop touching her. He let his hand lightly touch her belly.

How he wished he could have her and the baby in his life. Try as he might, he just couldn't stay away from her. He was falling hard for her. If he wasn't so scared, he could reach out and just take it. He could have it all, but he wasn't sure if Alexis wanted it.

And that thought scared him.

How could he let her inside his heart only to have it shattered again when she chose someone else? The answer was simple, according to the logical part of his brain: he couldn't. Yet, his heart was begging him to take a chance.

It had taken him so long to mend himself after Dawna. Alexis understood that pain only too well. Her ex-husband had left her for another. But she had picked herself up and moved to a completely different country, starting over.

It made him angry that her ex-husband had thrown her away and that she'd felt she had no choice but to leave home.

Still, what if this Bruce guy wanted Alexis back?

The idea made Marcus angry. Bruce didn't deserve Alexis, but he wasn't going to stand in the way of the child's biological father either.

It made him anxious not knowing if Alexis wanted him, not knowing if her ex-husband might come back into her life. It made him feel powerless, and there was nothing he could do except wait it out. He wouldn't blame Alexis if she decided to go back to her ex-husband, because what did he have to offer her besides a green card?

CHAPTER ELEVEN

ALEXIS WOKE UP from a nap to find Marcus's arms around her. Their bodies were a naked tangle, the sheets damp, but the breezing wafting in through the open French doors was warm. The sun was low in the afternoon sky.

She rubbed her eyes, wondering what the buzzing sound was before realizing it was her phone. She fumbled through her purse and pulled it out.

"Alexis Martin," she said.

"Alexis! It's Chase!"

The panic in his voice woke her up. "Chase, what's wrong?"

"Pepper has gone into labor."

"How far apart are the contractions?"

As soon as she asked that, Marcus sprang up and left the pool house completely naked to go and get dressed.

"Fifteen minutes. You have time to get here."

"I'm on St. Croix."

"Oh… What…? Oh, no!"

"I'm going to get a flight. I'll be there as soon as I can."

"Okay. Hurry."

Alexis hung up the phone and grabbed her clothes,

pulling them on haphazardly. The last time she'd checked on Pepper this week she was stable with no signs of preterm labor, and her swelling from her sickle cell disease from a couple of weeks ago had dissipated. That was why Alexis had thought it would be safe to leave the island today.

Apparently, fate had other plans.

Marcus came back to the pool house looking concerned. "It's Pepper, right?"

Alexis nodded. "Yes. I need to get a flight back to St. John."

Marcus nodded. "I have a buddy with a private plane. I contacted him and he's going to take us. We have to drive to Christiansted and meet him at the airport."

"Let's go then."

Marcus led her to a garage and past some expensive and unique cars, choosing instead a beat-up truck that seemed out of place around all the luxury.

As if reading her thoughts, he said, "This is the truck I learned to drive in."

He started the engine, and then they were off on the short drive to the outskirts of Christiansted where Marcus's friend was waiting. The plane was tiny and made her a bit anxious as well as nauseous, but she held it together.

All she cared about was getting to Pepper. Until she met Marcus, Pepper was the first person she'd really connected to since her marriage ended. Her first real friend on the island when she'd arrived. Pepper was the reason Alexis was still here.

It was breaking her heart that she was so far away. She felt like she was letting Pepper down.

Contractions are fifteen minutes apart. There's time.

The flight took under half an hour. Marcus had called Matthew, and he was there waiting to pick them up at the airfield. Luckily, Matthew and Victoria had been visiting to check in on Jonas when Pepper had gone into labor.

When Marcus and Alexis got off the plane, Matthew's face relaxed, his relief evident.

"Thank goodness you're here," Matthew said.

"What's her status?" Alexis asked.

"There's swelling and she's jaundiced. I think it is a flare-up of her sickle cell disease, and I think that's what started her labor. We did start an intravenous line for fluids, but Pepper refuses to leave her home. She wants you."

Alexis's stomach knotted. "Are the paramedics on standby?"

Matthew nodded.

They all climbed into the car and raced over to Chase and Pepper's home. With Marcus following, Alexis made her way to the bedroom, passing Victoria and Jonas, who were sitting in the living room looking very worried.

Chase got up when Alexis entered. She had left a birth kit here for them, and she was glad to see that Chase had already pulled it out.

"Thank God," Chase said.

"I'm sorry I'm late." Alexis washed her hands and checked on Pepper. Her feet were red and swollen, as were her knuckles, and when Alexis took her temperature it was high.

"How far apart are the contractions now?" she asked.

"Five minutes," Chase said.

Alexis felt Pepper's belly. The head of the baby was not where it was supposed to be. Alexis did an internal exam and discovered that the baby was not engaged and was breech. Pepper was not quite fully dilated, so there was time to turn the baby.

If it didn't work, they would have to get Pepper to Ziese Memorial for an emergency C-section. Even then, it might be too late.

"Marcus, we need to give her a dose of antibiotics in her intravenous line. Then, we need to turn the baby. With the swelling she won't be able to deliver this baby breech, and we're running out of time to transfer her to Charlotte Amalie."

Marcus nodded and got what he needed from the paramedics, injecting the medicine into Pepper's intravenous line.

"Chase, keep her calm. We have to manually turn the baby. It will hurt her."

Chase paled, looking frightened.

He was terrified. She was too. Alexis had done this before and it was never pleasant. Now she was having to do it to her friend. A person she cared for deeply.

Pepper was crying from the pain and knowing it was about to get worse broke Alexis's heart. She was glad Marcus was here with her. She trusted his skill, and she needed him.

"Tell me what to do," Marcus said.

"Just follow me. We're going to try an external turn."

Marcus pressed his lips together, and they waited for the next contraction to pass before attempting to move the baby. Pepper cried out in agony as they did so, but Alexis could feel it work as the baby started to turn.

One more turn.

They waited until the next contraction passed.

"Now," Alexis said.

As soon as they turned the baby, Pepper's water broke and the baby descended. Alexis nodded at Marcus. "That will do."

Pepper had fully dilated, and Alexis could now see the baby's head. She took a cleansing breath, very relieved that the procedure had worked and that the premature baby was coming out in the right direction.

"What's happening?" Pepper asked groggily.

"Your baby is coming," Alexis responded.

"Alexis?" Pepper asked, confused.

"Yes. I'm here. Pepper, next contraction I'm going to need you to push."

"Okay," Pepper said with a whimper.

The contraction came and Pepper pushed, screaming as Alexis encouraged her. With each push the baby came closer until, with one last push, the tiny girl was born crying as she entered the world. Alexis felt tears sting her eyes as she held that beautiful baby. Though she had been taught not to cry, she couldn't help herself in these circumstances.

Chase and Pepper were ecstatic.

Alexis cut the cord and handed the baby over, waiting for the placenta to be delivered. There was some excessive bleeding, so Alexis spoke with the paramedics.

"We have to get you to Charlotte Amalie," Alexis said.

"Why?" Chase asked.

"She's bleeding heavily, and we need to treat her for her flare-up of sickle cell disease. Your baby is doing well, but she is early, so I want her checked out by the neonatal intensive care unit."

Chase nodded. "Will you come?"

"We all will," Marcus said.

Chase nodded again. Alexis stood back to let the paramedics load up Pepper and the baby. As she stepped out into the other room, Jonas sprang up from the couch.

"How's my mom?" he asked.

"She's fine. You have a new sister," Alexis said.

Jonas grinned. "Cool."

"We have to take them to the hospital to be checked out, but they're both going to be just fine."

Jonas nodded. "Okay."

"We'll bring him to our place," Victoria said. "You and Marcus can stay with us too. We have room."

"Yes," Matthew said. "I assume the *Tryphine* is still at St. Croix?"

"You assume right," Marcus replied. "Thank you both."

After Pepper and Chase were loaded into the ambulance, Victoria and Matthew drove Jonas to the ferry and Alexis and Marcus walked the short distance. Alexis needed some air.

"You were amazing in there, you know," Marcus said.

His compliment made her blush. "Just doing my job."

They shared a smile, her pulse racing.

"It's been quite a day," he said, staring up at the sky.

"And it's not over yet."

Marcus sat outside on Matthew's terrace. The sun had set. Pepper, Chase and Jonas were at the hospital with their new little girl, Charlotte. Victoria was also at the hospital with Matthew, working out how to convince the board to consider a pro bono bone marrow transplant surgery. If they were successful, they wanted to start the search right away to find a match for Pepper. Victoria had even mentioned grand plans of a database of rare blood types to be matched around the world.

As much as Alexis had wanted to stay with Pepper, she was exhausted and needed rest, so Chase had ordered Marcus to take her back to Matthew and Victoria's place for a shower and a nap.

He went to check on her then, and though he wanted to join her, he knew if he laid down next to her he would want her again. He couldn't quite believe they had made love this afternoon. It had been overwhelming.

He'd been completely lost to her. She had been so soft, so warm and so tight. His blood heated and he took a drink of his scotch, then set the glass down.

What was he doing?

It scared him how much he wanted her. How he wanted to bury himself inside her and claim her as his own. Except there was an expiration date to it all. He had always known it was going to end; he just hadn't considered the possibility of it ending early.

He had collected the mail before they left for St. Croix, and there was a letter for Alexis. It was from England, and Marcus suspected it was from her ex-husband. He knew it was only a matter of time before the other man would want to come back into her life. His fear seemed to be coming true.

She was talented.

Smart.

Beautiful.

What kind of man would want to give that up?

He certainly wouldn't.

He was falling for her.

Actually, he had already fallen for her. Which put his heart in jeopardy once again, because Alexis would definitely choose the father of her baby over the man she was fake married to.

Alexis came out onto the terrace, interrupting his spiraling thoughts. "I fell asleep again."

"It's okay. You had a busy day."

"Where is everyone?"

"Chase and Jonas are with Pepper and Charlotte. And Victoria and Matthew are working to get a bone marrow transplant for Pepper to alleviate her sickle cell disease."

"That's wonderful. That will help."

"It's just you and I here tonight."

"I should be with Pepper at the hospital."

"Why? Pepper and Charlotte are stable and in good hands. You need rest, Alexis."

"She's my patient. And my friend."

"Exactly and as your friend Pepper wants you to rest. She said so herself."

"Fine. You're right. I am tired."

Alexis took a seat next to Marcus.

"You were incredible," he said. "Did I already tell you that?"

She laughed nervously. "I've turned a baby before."

"That's not what I'm talking about."

Pink flushed her cheeks. He knelt in front of her and touched her. She trembled under his caress, and her breath caught in her throat. Though he shouldn't, he wanted her again. One time wasn't enough.

He wouldn't get her for a lifetime. So he just wanted this small fraction of time with her.

"I want to kiss you," Marcus whispered against her ear.

"Then kiss me," she said.

She pulled him close, and he sank into the deliciousness of her lips. He couldn't help himself when it came to her.

He was lost.

So lost.

He was also terrified of letting her go. He wanted this to last forever, but he didn't know how to make that happen. He could smell her scent, feel the warmth of her body. He wanted to drown himself in her.

"Marcus," she whispered, just as he felt her tears.

"You're crying?"

"I'm overwhelmed," she said. "My mother told me to never cry in front of other people. She said it was a weakness."

"Oh, no. It's not a weakness, Alexis. Far from it." Her skin was so soft as he traced her cheeks. "Never hide your tears from me."

Alexis laid her head against his shoulder and he drank in her scent, that luscious perfume of green tea and jasmine. She deserved more than him. She probably wanted someone better than him, just like Dawna had.

Dawna had found someone better, but he didn't want to think about her right now. He didn't want to think of her ever again.

"Marcus, thank you for being here with me."

"Anytime." He leaned in and kissed her again, just like he'd wanted to do since he woke up and watched her sleeping in the pool house, before the phone rang and all hell broke loose. He was glad that she was there for his best friends.

She fit into his world so naturally.

Before the phone rang he'd wanted her again, but he knew another brief stolen moment would never be enough. Not when it came to her.

"Marcus," she whispered against his lips.

"Alexis, I burn for you."

"I want you too." She kissed him again, hungrily. "I want you so much."

Marcus wanted to take his time with her. He didn't want to rush this moment. It was something he would hold on to for the rest of his life.

He scooped her up into his arms and carried her to their room. He set her gently on her feet, not wanting their connection to break. Not wanting their kiss to end. They made quick work of their clothing. He wanted nothing between them. Just skin to skin again as he made love to her.

She ran her hands over his body. He loved the feel of her touch; it made his skin break out in gooseflesh.

"I love the way you touch me," he said huskily.

"I love touching you."

He touched every part of her. Kissed every inch of her until she was wet with need.

They moved to the bed and settled onto it. He cradled her body from behind, just as before, so he wouldn't crush her. Her skin was soft as silk as he traced her curves. His blood was on fire as he slowly entered her. She was so tight and warm around him.

Alexis moaned.

"Please," she whispered, clinging to him. His hand

moved to her breast as he quickened his pace and she came around him, squeezing him. It wasn't long before he joined her.

Nothing had ever been like this with anyone else before. It was overwhelming.

Alexis fell asleep soon after and he stayed there, holding her, touching her skin. As his hand drifted across her belly, there was a push against him.

It was a kick.

He smiled, keeping his hand still so that he could feel it again.

Another kicked pushed at him.

He wanted to be in Alexis's life. He wanted to be a father to her baby, but he was worried he was not the one she wanted and that one day the man she truly wanted, the baby's father, would come back and his heart would be shattered again.

Marcus was gone when she woke up. He left her a note that he had flown back to St. Croix to retrieve the *Tryphine*.

She was a bit disappointed that he hadn't woken her. She wouldn't have minded sailing back from St. Croix to St. John with him. She cleaned up and got dressed before making her way to the kitchen to get something to eat.

Victoria and Matthew were in the kitchen.

"Good morning," Alexis said.

Victoria smiled. "Good morning."

"How is Pepper's transplant plan going?" Alexis asked.

"We've got it mostly figured out. Now we just need to take our plan to the board of directors and then find a donor once they approve it," Victoria answered, pouring a glass of orange juice.

"I doubt they'll say no to Victoria. She's quite bossy," Matthew teased, looking lovingly at his wife.

Alexis was envious of their love. She wished that Marcus looked at her like that. What Matthew and Victoria had was real. What she and Marcus had was lust and deception. The love she thought she'd had with Bruce wasn't deep like this. She wasn't sure if she'd ever known what true love really was until now.

"Maybe it has something to do with the fact that I performed an expert and successful domino surgery?" Victoria teased back, leaning over the counter to kiss Matthew.

Alexis wanted this, but she wasn't sure that she'd ever have that kind of connection. That kind of deep love.

"Well, I have to get to work." Matthew kissed Victoria again. "Try to take it easy."

Matthew left, and Victoria poured Alexis a glass of juice.

"Are you okay, Alexis?" Victoria asked.

"Just tired. Twenty-eight weeks and I seem to have hit a wall."

"You're a trooper," Vic said.

"As are you. As a surgeon you must be on your feet for hours."

"Not anymore. Dr. Baxter's orders." Victoria sighed. "Transplant surgeries are quite long, and Dr. Baxter doesn't want me on my feet as I'm an older mother-to-be."

"Transplant surgeons aren't the only victims to taking it easy. Dr. Baxter said the same to me."

Victoria smiled. "I'm glad I'm not alone."

"No, you're not."

"You seem a bit sad today though," Victoria said quietly.

Alexis forced a smile. "No. Not sad."

Which was a lie. Another lie. She hated lying to Victoria. She wanted to tell her the truth, but she was also ashamed that her marriage was fake. That her baby was not Marcus's. What seemed like a simple solution to stay in the country was becoming more and more complicated.

Especially when it came to her heart.

She was in love with Marcus, and though she should've said no to him last night, she couldn't help herself. She had to be with him again. Even if it was for one last time.

It had been so overwhelming. She couldn't help but cry. She was so overcome with the stress of Pepper's birth, her own pregnancy and falling for a stranger. She was annoyed with herself for being too vulnerable around him.

For letting him into her heart.

What was wrong with being vulnerable?

Alexis took a sip of her orange juice, but she found it was hard to swallow. It was like a rock going down and sat heavily in the pit of her stomach. She was done lying. She had to tell them all the truth, even if it meant that she would have to return to England.

Even if it meant that she would lose Marcus.

Victoria let out a little moan. Alexis glanced up to see Victoria's face had gone ghostly white, and she was gripping the counter as if her life depended upon it.

She was swaying back and forth, and there was a fine sheen of sweat on her brow.

"Victoria?" Alexis asked.

"I don't…" Victoria's eyes rolled into the back of her head and she went limp. Alexis had just enough time to leap up and blunt the woman's fall as Victoria fainted right in front of her.

CHAPTER TWELVE

ALEXIS WAS PACING outside Victoria's room. Dr. Baxter was in there with Victoria right now. After she had fainted and came to, Alexis drove her to the hospital and paged Dr. Baxter to come straightaway.

Matthew was in surgery and Marcus was still at sea. It was just Alexis as next of kin, though she wouldn't exactly call herself that.

So instead of being in the room with Victoria, she was pacing and waiting for the answer from Dr. Baxter. Alexis had her suspicions about what could've caused the episode of fainting, but she didn't know Victoria's medical history, and at this point all she could do was speculate.

And with the way she was already feeling—worried and anxious—her mind was racing to a bunch of horrible conclusions, which was not like her at all.

Dr. Baxter finally came out of the room and Alexis pounced.

"How is she?" Alexis asked.

"She's fine. I think given that pregnancy causes an increase in hormones, which in turn increases blood flow, it caused the blood vessels to dilate, which in this case led to the syncope."

Alexis let out a sigh of relief. "I'm glad it's nothing more than that."

Dr. Baxter nodded. "I'm going to keep her overnight for observation anyway. Not that she's too impressed."

Alexis smiled briefly. "I'm not surprised. I keep getting reminded that medical professionals make the worst patients."

"That they do. Speaking of which, how are you feeling? I hope you're taking it easy."

"I am. I'm tired, but I am doing the best I can to rest…"

"And relax. You seem stressed."

Alexis laughed nervously. "Well, it's been a hectic couple of days, what with Pepper Fredrick giving birth early."

"I was told you did an excellent job externally turning that baby, and that you studied the effects of sickle cell disease when you were a student."

Alexis nodded. "I did."

"I'm impressed, Alexis. Truly I am, but you need to take it easy. You're not a diabetic, but your blood pressure is still running higher than I'd like, and I'm concerned about preeclampsia."

That sobered Alexis. The only way to cure preeclampsia before it turned into the fatal eclampsia was to deliver the baby. She was only twenty-eight weeks along; it was too soon for her to deliver.

"I promise I'll take it easy."

"Please see that you do." Dr. Baxter left her then, and Alexis ran her hand over her face.

She knew that part of her stress was this fake marriage and all the lying, which meant she knew one very easy way to alleviate the stress. She could tell the truth.

She couldn't deceive these people anymore. It wasn't right. She liked Victoria and Matthew too much.

They were treating her like she was family, when she was anything but.

Alexis knocked softly and then entered Victoria's room.

Victoria was lying against the pillows and looked a little bit better than she did before, right when she'd first fainted.

"Your color is better," Alexis said brightly.

"I feel better." Victoria held up her arm to show an intravenous line. "I think the fluid is helping. I was also dehydrated."

"I'm glad to hear you're feeling more yourself." Alexis sat on the edge of the bed.

Victoria cocked an eyebrow. "There's something you want to tell me."

"Yes."

"And I think it's something you've wanted to tell me for some time."

Their gazes locked, and then she saw it in Victoria's eyes. That keen perception. There was no fooling a world-class surgeon.

"You know, don't you?"

Victoria smiled weakly. "I suspected. I know what kind of crazy ideas Pepper comes up with."

Alexis laughed softly. "Yes."

"So tell me. I promise I won't say anything outside of this room."

"I won't hold you to that, but I'll tell you because it's eating me alive and I don't like lying. I'm not that good at it. My work visa was expiring, but Pepper needed me. I understood her sickle cell disease better than any other midwife in the islands."

"Yes. Pepper really did need you."

"She came up with the idea that I should have a marriage of convenience. Straight out of one of her favorite books."

Victoria smiled, her eyes twinkling. "And Marcus, the ultimate playboy, agreed?"

"You've read the book?"

"I enjoy them." Victoria grinned. "So, Marcus agreed to the plot?"

"He did."

"And the baby?" Victoria asked gently.

"My ex-husband's. We tried for two years to have a baby, went through so many procedures. When I found out I was finally pregnant and told him, I thought he would be ecstatic. I was. It was everything I'd ever wanted, but he'd changed his mind."

"How dreadful," Victoria said softly. "I would've punched him. Did you?"

Alexis half smiled and then shrugged. "No. It is what it is. My mother wanted me to get rid of my baby. She felt it was a hindrance to me finding another husband. I don't have the most supportive parents."

Victoria shrugged. "You know my story. I can relate."

"I do. I'm sorry."

"It's okay."

"I always wanted a baby. Even though my parents were so emotionally distant. My ex signed away his parental rights. He didn't want my child and that was fine. I didn't expect Marcus to claim my baby when I met you, but he did and since then it's been eating away at me. You've all been so kind. I wasn't trying to take advantage of Marcus. I didn't want any of you to get hurt."

Victoria took her hand. "I know. I'm glad you told me the truth. I'm not mad at you. I understand why you did it, and I know things have changed."

"Changed?"

"You love him."

Alexis's breath caught in her throat, and there were tears stinging her eyes. Was she so transparent?

"Victoria?" Matthew stuck his head in the door. "Are you okay?"

"I fainted. Hormones, swollen blood vessels and a wee bit of dehydration," Victoria said. "I'm fine."

Matthew crossed the room and kissed his wife. "You're sure?"

"Ask Dr. Baxter yourself," Victoria said. "Thankfully, Alexis was with me when it happened."

Matthew turned and looked at her, gratitude etched on his face, one so like Marcus's and yet so different. "Thank you."

"My pleasure." Alexis snuck out of the room then, leaving the couple alone. It felt like a weight was off her shoulders, but now there was another issue.

She did love Marcus, but she wasn't sure of his feelings.

Just ask him.

Only, she was terrified to do that. She was so scared of Marcus turning her down like Bruce had. What man, who had made it quite clear that he was a playboy and had no interest in a real marriage, would be interested in a woman who was pregnant with another man's child?

Who would want to take on that kind of baggage?

She wasn't going to force that onto Marcus. She couldn't do that to him precisely because she loved him. She wished her marriage wasn't fake. She wished she didn't have to wait so long to hear about her green card, so that this whole charade could end.

Then Marcus would be free.

Even if the idea of being free of him tore at her very soul.

As she walked down the hall, she looked up to see Marcus coming toward her. Relief was evident on his face as he approached.

"I got your message. Is Victoria okay?" he asked.

"Yes, she is."

Marcus sighed with relief. "That's great."

Her stomach twisted in a knot, and he picked up on her tension.

"Marcus, there's something that I need to tell you."

"What?" he asked gently.

"I told her… I told Victoria."

"Told her what?"

"About our marriage of convenience and about how the baby isn't yours," she whispered.

"Why did you tell her that?" he asked, pulling her into an empty room and shutting the door so that they wouldn't be disturbed.

"I had to tell them. The guilt was too much."

"Yeah, but now you've implicated them. I didn't want them to know."

Alexis worried her bottom lip. "I'm sorry. They've been so kind, like family. They needed to know the truth about me and the baby."

"Yeah, but they're not your family. They're my

family, and you've put them in jeopardy by telling the truth."

It was like a slap to the face. It stung, and it hurt so much more than Bruce telling her that he didn't want their child. She had thought that Marcus was different.

Clearly he wasn't, and she was annoyed at herself for giving her heart to another man who didn't want her.

Clearly he saw her as just another conquest. How could she be so blind?

"That was not my intention."

"Yet, that's what you did. You weren't the only one taking a risk entering into this marriage. It was a business deal between the two of us."

"You brought your family into this when you didn't tell me you had an identical twin and claimed my child as yours!"

Alexis wasn't wrong. It was ultimately his fault that Matthew and Victoria were in danger.

She was only with him to get her green card, but there was a part of him that had hoped for so much more. Yet it was clear she didn't want him in her life, didn't want him claiming her child. If she did, wouldn't she want to continue the act?

He loved her, but he was so afraid of putting his heart on the line for someone who wouldn't stick around.

It was better that he remained single and live out that life that he'd originally wanted to pursue when he first headed to California, before life became complicated and before his heart was broken.

Even though this hurt, pushing her away was a lot

easier than having her stick around and hurt him in the end.

Marcus pulled out the envelope. "This came for you a couple of days ago."

Her eyes narrowed and she took the envelope. "It's from Bruce."

He nodded. "It is."

"Why did you hold on to this?"

He shrugged. "I forgot. Things got a bit hectic."

"You knew it was from my ex-husband, and you kept it from me?" she asked.

"I didn't realize a letter from your ex-husband was so important," he responded coldly.

"Well…it is. It is his child I carry."

"I'm sorry." And he was. For so many things. He hated hurting her, but it was better this way. Wasn't it?

Alexis opened the envelope, and her expression was unreadable. "He wants me back. Me and the baby."

"So our marriage is over."

She looked up at him. "No. I don't have my green card."

"So what? We stay married until you get your status?"

"We can't get divorced."

He nodded. "I get it. You were only with me so that you could get your green card. I suppose we both got swept up in the idea of having a marriage and family, but that's not what I want. Your ex does though."

"Why?" she asked quietly.

The question caught him off guard. "What do you mean why?"

"Why don't you want a family? What did this Dawna person do to you to harden your heart so much to the idea? You run from any kind of relationship. Isn't that why you only pursue women who have an expiration date? You know in advance when the end is coming so you won't be blindsided."

The truth hit him like a ton of bricks, but he didn't want to hear it. He couldn't hear it.

"I'm not the only one who ran away! You ran from England and took your child away from its biological father; a man you were married to. You said that he was not coming back, but here he is and he wants his child. Now who is the one who is clinging to a fake relationship that has an expiration date? You're just with me for citizenship, and then you'll run back into his arms. Well, I won't stand in the way. We'll be married on paper until you get your green card, but I don't want to be part of your life in the meantime."

Her eyes filled with tears, but she carefully folded her letter and put it back into the envelope. "You're absolutely right. This was a business arrangement, and you lived up to your end of the bargain. So, when the time comes, I'm going to give you your quickie divorce. I will move my things out of your place tonight. You'll hear from my lawyer."

Alexis pushed past him.

His heart was aching.

He couldn't believe he'd let himself be hurt like this again. When Dawna broke his heart, it had reminded him of all those lonely years in boarding school.

Everyone doted on Matthew and his academic excellence, but Marcus just wasn't as brilliant as his brother. He struggled, he acted out, he was the disappointment.

All he wanted to do was return home, but his parents wouldn't let him. They told him that he had to be independent, and he hated that. He was lonely, but he put on a brave face and sucked it up.

He was the only person who had never disappointed himself.

Liar.

Letting Alexis walk away was so hard, but this marriage wasn't real. No matter how much he wanted it to be. He didn't want to fail her. He didn't want to disappoint her, and he didn't want to hurt her child.

It was too much of a risk to everyone's heart.

It was easier to let her go, even though he was being torn up inside and it felt a lot like his heart was on the verge of breaking. He took a deep breath and sat down, dropping his head into his hands. All he wanted was her and her baby, but they were off-limits.

If he lost them, he couldn't go on living.

Except that he had already lost them, if he'd even ever truly had them.

He had pushed them away but it was for the best. Alexis had come here to take care of herself and her child. She didn't need to be shackled to a coward who wasn't sure that he could ever give his heart over completely, because he was too afraid about what the future might hold.

Because he was too afraid of losing any happiness that he might find.

CHAPTER THIRTEEN

IT HAD BEEN two weeks since Marcus had pushed Alexis away. Two horrible, lonely, awful weeks.

Was this really the better way?

He finished tying the knot he was working on and then realized it was completely wrong. His head wasn't in it at all. All he could think about was Alexis. He never stopped thinking about her. When he got back to the *Tryphine* at his Charlotte Amalie mooring, her berth had been emptied out. She was gone.

When he returned to St. John, he discovered she hadn't returned to her dormitory room either. It was like she had faded into nothing. She was gone, and he was worried about her. Worried that she wasn't taking care of herself, that she wasn't relaxing. That he'd broken her heart too deeply. And he couldn't help but wonder if her ex-husband had come back into her life. The thought of the man who threw her away touching her again was almost too much to bear.

Except he had thrown her away too.

Pushed her away, even.

Now he was the fool.

"You're an idiot, you know that, right?"

Marcus looked up to see Matthew standing on the dock of his St. John mooring.

"What?" Marcus asked.

"The knot is all wrong," Matthew said, pointing to it.

"What would do you know about sailing? You hated it," Marcus replied dryly.

"Okay," Matthew said, climbing up on the *Tryphine*. "Then you're still an idiot for another reason."

"Oh?"

"Alexis."

"What about her?" Marcus asked, grumpily tossing the rope down.

"Why did you let her go?" Matthew asked.

"Let her go? What do you mean I let her go?"

"You love her but you pushed her away."

Marcus frowned. "Our marriage wasn't real."

"It may have started that way, but you fell in love with her."

"What does it matter? Her ex-husband is the father of her baby, and he wants her back."

Matthew shrugged. "And what if he does? Is that what she wants?"

Marcus sighed. "It was her ex-husband. She loved him. I'm just the second choice. I'm the man she married so that she could stay in the country. I'm nobody."

"She's not Dawna," Matthew said gently.

"Why are you pestering me about this?" Marcus snapped. "I thought you said you weren't going to try and parent me again."

"This isn't parenting. I want to see you happy, you fool!"

Marcus snorted. "Sure."

Matthew leaned forward. "Look, buddy. I'm going to tell you what you told me when you were recovering from the domino. You told me that Victoria loved me and that I had always loved her. You also called me a chicken for not sticking it out in New York and running away all those years ago. You also accused me of trying to murder you by injecting morphine into your drip, but that's beside the point."

Marcus chuckled. "That's not fair, I was drugged up."

Matthew grinned. "You love her and I dare say she loves you, too."

"Did she tell you that?"

"No, but her actions made it clear that she cares for you. Why else would she tell Victoria the truth? The point is that Alexis cared enough about you and your family to tell the truth. She loves you, and you're too stubborn to see it."

Marcus's heart ached. Matthew was right. He had been too blind to see it.

Too stubborn.

He had fallen in love with her. He wanted to be a part of her life and her baby's life. He was still thinking about the way that little kick had felt against his palm. He was tired of being alone behind this wall that he'd built to keep his heart safe.

He groaned. "I am a fool."

Matthew grinned. "I've been saying it for years."

Marcus rolled his eyes. "Thank you for reminding me who I am, Matthew."

Matthew put his hand on his brother's shoulder. "And thank you for doing the same for me."

"Anytime, brother. There's just one problem."

"What's that?" Matthew asked.

"I don't know where she is."

It had been two weeks since Marcus had hurt her, but she still didn't think that he'd meant to hurt her.

What was he so afraid of? What was *she* so afraid of?

Her mother's voice was still rolling through her head as she mulled it all over while walking the halls of Ziese Memorial Hospital. She missed Marcus. She loved him and with how her heart ached, she realized her love for Bruce had never been the same.

It was so much more with Marcus.

He may have been a lothario in his past, but he was different now, and what they had shared was something deep. The moment she first met him—even though he may have been a stranger—her soul had felt like she had known him for a long time.

And though she wanted him back, she didn't want to put her heart back on the line again.

It was too hard.

And it wasn't just her heart that was in danger, but also her baby's. She placed her hand on her abdomen and felt her baby kick. All that mattered was protecting her child.

Alexis stopped in front of Pepper's door and knocked.

"Come in!"

Alexis entered the room to see Pepper cradling little Charlotte.

"How are you?" Alexis asked brightly.

"Feeling great and eager to go home."

"I'm sure."

"How are you?"

"I've been better." Alexis sat down on the bed to stare at the baby longingly.

"I heard you and Marcus called it off."

"Called it off? It was a marriage of convenience. As soon as I got my green card our deal was going to be over."

"Deal? I think it was more than that."

"What do mean?" Alexis asked, blushing.

"I saw the way he looked at you, and I saw the way you looked at him. You are in love with him and he's in love with you."

Alexis felt tears sting her eyes. "No. He's not in love with me. He pushed me away, and I don't blame him. He doesn't want me."

"Why? Why would you think he wouldn't want you?" Pepper asked gently.

"I'm pregnant with another man's baby."

Pepper shrugged. "So?"

"And my ex-husband wants me back."

"Do you want Bruce back?" Pepper asked.

"No, I don't."

"So what's the problem?"

"Marcus thinks I'll go back to him."

"Have you told Marcus you're not going to?"

Alexis sighed. "No."

"Then I don't see the problem."

"My mother said no other man would want to take on another man's child. I won't put my child at risk of Marcus leaving us one day."

"No offense, but your mother has very outdated views and didn't exactly care for you the way she should have."

Alexis chuckled softly. "She does have outdated

views, and you're right. I can see it. I don't think she ever really cared for me."

"They why did you let her into your head?"

It was a good point. She didn't know why she had let her mother's opinion control her actions. She'd worked hard her whole life to keep her mother out, but this one time, when it mattered the most, she'd let her in and ruined something precious as a result.

"You know how I know that your mother is wrong?" Pepper asked.

Alexis brushed away the tears. "How?"

"Jonas isn't Chase's biological son. I was pregnant with Jonas when I met Chase, but Chase didn't care. He became Jonas's father and we became a family. I've known Marcus for a long time. He's had flings, but he was never happy. With you, he was happy. With you, he found love."

Alexis began to cry and she leaned over to hug Pepper.

"Thank you," Alexis said.

"For what?"

"This crazy idea of a marriage of convenience."

Pepper grinned. "See, there's nothing wrong with a good happily-ever-after is there?"

"No. You're right, but that's if I *get* a happily-ever-after. What if I hurt Marcus too much? What if he doesn't want me back?"

"You've got to take the risk. It's worth it, Alexis. It's so worth it."

Alexis left Pepper's room and headed out into the hall. She had to find Marcus and make it right. She had to tell him how she felt about him. She was scared that he might turn her down, but she had to know for sure how he felt.

She walked down the hall, her pulse racing and turned the corner, stopping short when she saw Marcus at the end of the corridor.

He was dressed in a tuxedo, which was the strangest sight.

It made her heart skip a beat.

"Marcus?" she called out.

"You moved away," he said.

"Yes," she replied, her breath catching in her throat as she walked toward him. "I did."

"Where did you go?" he asked, closing the gap slowly.

"Pepper and Chase's. They gave me a room until I could find my own place."

"I went there. You weren't there," he said softly.

"I didn't want to see you."

"I know and that's my fault. I pushed you away. I was jealous your ex-husband had sent you that letter. I thought you would choose him, just like Dawna chose someone else over me."

"I didn't exactly stop you either. I pushed you away, too, because I was scared you would resent me, or resent being hitched with me and another man's child."

He smiled. "I know and I don't blame you. I hurt you, and I betrayed your trust keeping that letter from you."

"I hurt you too."

"Alexis, I love you."

Her heart skipped a beat, and she couldn't help but smile. "I love you, too."

He put his arms around her. "I don't care that the

baby is not biologically mine. The baby is a part of you, and I love you. I want you both in my life. I want us to be a family. Do you want that?"

Tears streamed down her face. "I do want that. More than anything."

"So what do we do about your ex and the baby?"

"I told him I wasn't coming back. He was angry, but he doesn't want the child or the responsibility of one without me. He can't be bothered with us, and we'll tell our child the truth about her genetics when the time is right, though I don't think blood matters."

"Our child?" he asked.

She smiled. "Yes. Our child."

"Did you say her?"

"I did. Sorry. Didn't mean to ruin the surprise. Are you angry?"

Marcus smiled and tipped her chin. "I'm going to kiss the bride now, properly, like I should've done when we were married a month ago."

Heat bloomed in her cheeks. "I would like that very much."

She didn't wait for anyone to pronounce them husband and wife, just wrapped her arms around him and let him kiss her.

When the kiss ended, she leaned her forehead against his, just like she had done when they had been in Dr. Baxter's office and seen their baby for the first time.

"You know, I was worried when I saw my ultrasound picture."

"Why is that?" he asked.

"It had your name on it, and I was worried that you would run then."

"I have a confession to make," he said. "I saw that photo. It fell out of your purse."

"How did you feel when you saw it?" she asked.

"Pride. I've always wanted a family, and I don't care what my family is comprised of. I learned a long time ago, when I met Chase, that family has nothing to do with blood and everything to do with love. And when the baby kicked me for the first time, the night we made love, I wanted to be your baby's father. I still want that more than anything."

"And you're the man I want. You're who we both want." She kissed him again.

"I'm glad," he said. "But we do have a minor problem."

"What's that?"

"As much as I hate to say it, the *Tryphine* is no place to raise a child."

"You're right. So what do we do? Where do we go? My contract at the clinic is up, and frankly I like working with you. I think we make a good team."

"I would love to have a nurse and a midwife as part of my practice. So you're okay staying on the island of St. John?"

"There's no place I'd rather be."

Marcus kissed her again, and they left the hospital hand in hand.

A family.

Finally.

Forever.

EPILOGUE

One year later, St. Croix, Halloween

"HOLD LUCY UP HIGHER, Marcus. I don't want to see your face. I just want to see my sweet granddaughter in her new birthday dress," his father demanded.

"Gee, thanks, Father." Marcus hoisted his daughter, Lucy, who was turning one today, up on his shoulders so that his father could take a photograph.

His parents had returned from their round-the-world cruise just in time for Alexis to give birth to their first grandchild. Four months later, Victoria had given birth to their second grandchild.

Another girl.

Lucy and Ava Olesen weren't exactly twins, but everyone liked to comment that they were as they both had dark hair and blue, blue eyes.

Marcus's parents didn't care that Lucy was not their biological grandchild. They loved her just the same.

The moment that Alexis had given birth to their daughter, which was the most nerve-racking moment of Marcus's life, he'd fallen in love with that beautiful girl who was placed in his arms. The baby that had kicked him for months.

Matthew had been sick with worry when he saw Marcus's haggard expression after the birth, because he had been worried about the same thing happening to him. And the same thing did happen to him.

When Victoria gave birth to their daughter, Ava, he had also been completely enraptured with his little girl.

Their father had seen it as a blessing, and he was the most doting grandfather to ever set foot on the island of St. Croix. He was constantly boasting about his grand-daughters, which was why Papa Olesen had insisted on throwing a lavish birthday party for Lucy at the family castle. Another lavish first birthday party was already planned for Ava in a couple of months' time.

"Give her to her papa."

Marcus handed over his daughter to his father, and the happy little girl laid kisses on her grandfather's face.

Freja, Marcus's mom, came out onto the lawn with the pink-and-white strawberry cake and Alexis followed behind, but she was a bit precarious on her feet. She was pregnant again, and this time it was twins. Three was enough though; Marcus was already drowning in diapers.

Matthew liked to tease him about how Marcus went from gadding about on the *Tryphine* to gadding about the superstore and stocking up on baby supplies.

Victoria was rocking Ava, who was napping, her little birthday hat crooked on the side of her head.

"He really is a great papa," Victoria murmured. "Our kids are so lucky to have them. To have this family."

Alexis sat down next to her. "I agree."

Marcus smiled at both of them and then shared a secret smile with his brother.

"I never thought in a million years that we would be here," Matthew whispered.

"Neither did I."

"I'm glad we are, though."

"Me, too."

And he was. For years he'd dreamed of having a life like this. He wanted big family gatherings, love and happiness. He and Matthew had spent too long competing and bickering; he was glad that they were so close again now. It was a closeness that he had missed sharing with his brother for too many years.

And they finally had it.

It only took the love of two good women to make it happen.

Marcus had moved his practice with Alexis to Ziese Memorial Hospital after Lucy was born as it was easier to go in on the costs of day care with his brother at the hospital and he liked working close to family.

They'd bought a small house not far from Matthew and Victoria in Charlotte Amalie, but they still kept the *Tryphine* for when they wanted to have a private getaway. And he loaned it out to his brother too.

This was what life was all about.

Family, and the love of a good woman.

Marcus sat down next to his wife. "How are you feeling?"

"Bloated," she murmured. "I think this might be my last trip to St. Croix for a while. Dr. Baxter doesn't want me leaving the city."

"I know. My parents will soon descend on the new condo they bought in Frenchtown."

"You can't keep Papa and Nana from the girls," Victoria said.

"Are you guys going to come and watch the birthday girl blow out her candles?" Freja asked.

"We'll be right there." Marcus stood and helped Alexis up.

Victoria slowly stood, trying not to wake Ava, who was letting out a sweet snore.

They all walked over to the table where Freja was lighting the candles. Lucy looked at him and held out her chubby little arms.

"Dada. Want Dada."

"Sorry, Dad. I outrank you."

His father grinned. "As you should."

Marcus took his little girl in his arms as the candles were lit. Even though she was only turning one, Nana had put several on there as a form of good luck.

Alexis wrapped her arm around his waist and laid her shoulder against him.

"Make a wish, Lucy," Marcus urged. "Then blow out the candles."

"No, Dada. You wish."

Alexis chuckled softly. "What're you going to wish for then, Dada?"

Marcus kissed the top of Alexis's head and then his daughter's. "I have everything I could ever wish for. Come on, Lucy, let's blow them out together."

He leaned over, and he and his little girl blew out the candles.

His heart was completely full.

He was whole.

His brother was whole.

His family was no longer broken.

And there was love in the castle on the hill.

* * * * *

COMING SOON!

We really hope you enjoyed reading this book. If you're looking for more romance, be sure to head to the shops when new books are available on

Thursday 28th April

To see which titles are coming soon, please visit

millsandboon.co.uk/nextmonth

MILLS & BOON®

Coming next month

SHOCK BABY FOR THE DOCTOR
Charlotte Hawkes

'First, however, we're going for a scan.'

Fear rose in Sienna's chest.

'We most certainly are not. I told you, I don't want the entire hospital gossiping about me, which will be inevitable if they know I'm pregnant. Let alone if you're the one accompanying me. I've had a scan. Everything was fine. I am definitely not going for another with you.'

He cast her a cool look.

'Are you quite finished with your rant?'

'I'm not being that conversion nurse who got pregnant with Bas Jensen's baby.'

'You will have that scan, Sienna. And I will be with you.' He folded his arms again, and this time she was struck by quite how authoritative the man was. How had she failed to appreciate quite what power looked like on a man? He didn't just bear the Jensen name, rather he epitomised everything it represented.

She glowered at him, but it seemed to bounce off his solid chest without making a dent.

'So you're…what? Taking charge now?' The idea of it should baulk more. So why didn't it? 'I told you, I don't need your help, I'm perfectly used to taking care of myself.'

'And I'm beginning to think you tell me a few too

many things whilst you aren't as keen to listen. But I suspect that part of the reason for telling me now is because this is beginning to overwhelm you.'

'You're deluded.'

'No, I'm not, but I think you are,' his voice dropped to a sudden, quiet hum. 'I suspect that whether you want to admit it or not, deep down, you don't want to be the one taking care of everything. You want someone to take the reins for once.'

And it was odd but it was still there, that lethal air, swirling beneath the surface like a rip-tide, just waiting to drag her under. But he was controlling it with a fierceness that struck an unexpected cord in her.

As though by controlling that, he could control some dark secret of his own. As if a man like him had dark secrets at all.

Continue reading
SHOCK BABY FOR THE DOCTOR
Charlotte Hawkes

Available next month
www.millsandboon.co.uk

MILLS & BOON

THE HEART OF ROMANCE

A ROMANCE FOR EVERY READER

MODERN

Prepare to be swept off your feet by sophisticated, sexy and seductive heroes, in some of the world's most glamourous and romantic locations, where power and passion collide.

HISTORICAL

Escape with historical heroes from time gone by. Whether your passion is for wicked Regency Rakes, muscled Vikings or rugged Highlanders, awaken the romance of the past.

MEDICAL

Set your pulse racing with dedicated, delectable doctors in the high-pressure world of medicine, where emotions run high and passion, comfort and love are the best medicine.

True Love

Celebrate true love with tender stories of heartfelt romance, from the rush of falling in love to the joy a new baby can bring, and a focus on the emotional heart of a relationship.

Desire

Indulge in secrets and scandal, intense drama and plenty of sizzling hot action with powerful and passionate heroes who have it all: wealth, status, good looks…everything but the right woman.

HEROES

Experience all the excitement of a gripping thriller, with an intense romance at its heart. Resourceful, true-to-life women and strong, fearless men face danger and desire - a killer combination!

To see which titles are coming soon, please visit

millsandboon.co.uk/nextmonth

JOIN US ON SOCIAL MEDIA!

Stay up to date with our latest releases, author news and gossip, special offers and discounts, and all the behind-the-scenes action from Mills & Boon...

 millsandboon

 millsandboonuk

 millsandboon

It might just be true love...